S0-BXI-779

THE BACK FORTY

THE BACK FORTY

The Hammersmiths of West Texas

WILLIAM W. JOHNSTONE

AND J.A. JOHNSTONE

PINNACLE BOOKS

Kensington Publishing Corp.

www.kensingtonbooks.com

PINNACLE BOOKS are published by

Kensington Publishing Corp.
900 Third Avenue
New York, NY 10022

All Kensington titles, imprints, and distributed lines are available at special quantity discounts for bulk purchases for sales promotion, premiums, fund-raising, and educational or institutional use.

Special book excerpts or customized printings can also be created to fit specific needs. For details, write or phone the office of the Kensington Sales Manager: Kensington Publishing Corp., 900 Third Avenue, New York, NY 10022. Attn. Sales Department. Phone: 1-800-221-2647.

PINNACLE BOOKS, the Pinnacle logo, and the WWJ steer head logo Reg. U.S. Pat. & TM Off.

First Printing: May 2024
ISBN-13: 978-0-7860-5050-5
ISBN-13: 978-0-7860-5051-2 (eBook)

10 9 8 7 6 5 4 3 2 1

Printed in the United States of America

CHAPTER 1

Marshal Hammersmith jerked upright in the saddle when he heard the shriek of pure agony. His hand moved to the Colt Peacemaker he wore in a cross-draw holster. His gnarled fingers tightened around the butt when a second cry echoed across the prairie. He had heard dying creatures make their final laments.

A man was close to dying, and it wasn't a peaceable death. Not if he made such hideous screeches.

Marsh glanced at the ground. He'd been tracking a stray. He hadn't spotted it, but he knew which one it was. More than once, this same contrary heifer had taken a foolish delight in leaving the safety of the herd in search of whatever passed for a bovine Eden. As drought-stricken as it had been the last year, the stray was more likely to die of thirst unless a coyote in even more dire need attacked it.

No tracks. He stood in the stirrups and pulled the brim of his black Stetson down to shield his eyes from the sun hanging low in the dusty West Texas sky. Nary a cloud to be seen. Every inch of the land in sight was his Twin M ranch. There should be cattle, a large herd of them, and grasslands . . . but not the sound of a man dying a terrible death.

The horrible shrieks rolled over him like a runaway freight train. There simply was no way to ignore such torment.

Marsh touched the stock of his sheathed Winchester and put his heels to his horse's flanks.

"Make like the wind, Derby." He bent forward until he hunkered down over the stallion's neck. The bay exploded under him, long legs devouring the land at a furious gallop.

Hot, dry air cut at his tanned cheeks. He pulled up his bandanna a little more. The West Texas wind had a way of aging a man before his years. The fifty-one he'd spent already didn't need to be rushed into adding even more.

A new sound joined the shrieks of pain. This was even more disturbing. Laughter. And more than one man laughing at another's misery.

"Come on, Derby. Race like the winner you are." Marsh bent even lower over the straining horse's neck as they topped a rise, giving a view of a shallow bowl.

Derby dug in all four hooves, sending up a dust cloud to rival any kicked up naturally in this arid land. Marsh grabbed for his rifle. Even with a full magazine, he might need more firepower. Scattered around the shallow depression on the down slope were a dozen Comanche braves. A sensible man would have turned tail and run.

Marshal Hammersmith considered himself possessed of brains enough to know how he faced death if he fired even a single shot. But his sense of decency and honor outweighed the personal threat.

Crucified in the middle of the depression hung another Indian. Even at this distance, Marsh saw why the usually stoic warrior had called out. His body was a mass of tiny cuts. Being hung up like he was in the setting sun only added to his torture. What he had endured—and that he was still counted among the living—was a tribute to his resolve to never give up.

Marsh admired that. And what the Comanche war party did was wrong. Kill a man or not. Don't torture him.

He yanked his rifle free and snugged it into his shoulder. He fired three times, then lifted the rifle high in the air and called at the top of his lungs, "I found 'em, men. Form your platoon and attack!"

He hoped it sounded like something a cavalry officer would shout as an order. Fort Davis wasn't far off. It was plausible for a patrol to be in this area, although Marsh hadn't caught sight of a single bluecoat soldier in ages.

"Attack! Charge!" He kept firing as he launched his one-man assault.

For a moment, he thought he'd played a losing card. The Comanches turned in his direction and reached for their rifles. Two loosed arrows, but he rode downhill too fast for easy targeting. His Stetson snapped away and flapped by the chin tie. His long blond hair flowed like a banner, whipping about in the setting sun until it turned to radiant gold. And the entire time, he shouted fake orders at the top of his lungs, as if he were a general commanding the entire Ninth Cavalry from Fort Davis.

Somehow, he achieved the impossible. One of his bullets struck the closest warrior. The Comanche recoiled and grabbed for his right side. A bloody streak appeared when he pulled his hand away. The brave held it up and stared at the blood as if he had never seen any before. Then he yelped something in the Comanche tongue. A few of the braves got off shots as Marsh continued his suicidal head-long attack.

After a quick exchange of frantic dialogue, they wheeled about and galloped away. In seconds, they vanished in a cloud of their own dust. Marsh fired as quickly as he could, screaming for his nonexistent command to halt and form a defensive perimeter. His Winchester came up empty. Fourteen rounds fired as quick as he could pull the trigger. He rested the blistering hot barrel across the saddle in front and reached for his six-shooter. There wasn't any call to draw. He was alone on the prairie.

Alone save for the crucified Indian.

Marsh twisted around and rummaged through his saddle-bags until he found a box of cartridges. The Comanches' victim was in sorry shape, but he moaned softly and stirred. The full effect of crucifixion wouldn't affect him for hours yet. The rancher carefully handled the cartridges to keep from dropping any. If the Comanches changed their minds or realized he wasn't at the head of a column of bluecoats, they'd return. This time, their crucified enemy would have a companion.

Methodically, he reloaded the rifle magazine until it carried the full thirteen .45 rounds. He finger-fed a fourteenth into the chamber. Still working slowly, he returned the half-empty box of cartridges to his gear and turned finally to see what could be done for the man now silently staring at him.

At first glance, Marsh thought it was the most humane thing to do if he put a bullet through the Indian's heart and ended his misery. Half a hundred tiny cuts oozed blood. Flies buzzed and drank of the red trickles. His arms looked as if they had been stretched an extra foot or two because of the way he sagged down from the crosspiece. His ankles had been lashed together and then fastened to the main upright post.

"What'd you do to get them so all fired mad at you?" Marsh asked but didn't expect an answer. The Comanches sometimes cut out the tongues of their captives.

A guttural string of words gushed forth. Marsh suspected

from the intensity and downright venom in the tone that they were pungent curses directed at the now departed war party.

"You're not Comanche," he said. "Apache?"

"Lépai-Ndé."

The words were muffled by thirst-starved tongue and lips, but there wasn't any venom added in. Not like the earlier outburst. Marsh nodded slowly and understood.

"Lipan," he said. "Lipan Apache."

He got a single nod in reply. The Comanches considered any Apache a mortal enemy, ones as hateful as the White Eyes with their settlements and railroads and ranches encroaching on tribal lands.

"I can't say this is your lucky day, but you're still alive." He released a gust of wind from his lungs and laughed ruefully. "And so am I. That makes it a really lucky day for me. I usually pay for being this stupid."

He rode closer and examined the problem of freeing the Apache. Rawhide thongs around the man's wrists supported his full weight. The thin strips had cut deeply into his flesh. Both hands were black from lack of circulation. His feet were in hardly better condition, although they no longer held his weight.

"I'll cut your ankles free first. If I started with your hands, you'd flop forward and bang your head against the post under your feet. Wouldn't want that happening. No, sir."

Dark eyes sharper and more alert than he expected watched him, taking in every word. Marsh drew his thick-bladed Bowie knife from the sheath fastened to his gun belt in the middle of his back. The setting sun flashed off the silver blade as he cut the ankle bonds with a single swift slash. Even though the Apache's weight was held on his wrists, his entire body slid lower on the cross.

"Whoa, let's get this done quick like." Marsh rode around the crucified man and returned to a spot directly in front. "Hang on for a second, if you can." He cut through the rawhide strip on the Apache's left hand. The man wasn't able to hold onto the crossbar. He flopped around and dangled from his right wrist.

Marsh wasted no time hopping down from Derby and severed that bond. The Lipan crashed to the ground and lay in a quivering pile.

"There, got you free." Marsh spoke more to buoy his own spirits as to reassure the Apache. He hopped down. Derby shied away, the smell of blood scaring him now that his rider was on foot.

He gentled his horse, took the canteen dangling behind the saddle, and popped the cork. He took a quick swig. More would slake his own thirst, but his rescued captive's need was greater. Marsh dropped to one knee and supported the man's head.

"Don't gulp the water. Your belly might explode if you take in too much right away."

Either the Lipan didn't understand or his need was too great. He tried to upend the canteen and drink all the water. Marsh wrestled it away. The man's strength was impressive, considering all he had been through. Their eyes locked. Marsh's Nordic blue dueled with the Athapascan's ebony. The battle of wills ended when Marsh allowed the Lipan to drink again. This time, the fierce need was gone. He drank more slowly and even pulled back while there was still water in the canteen.

He handed it back to Marsh. He had to use both hands clamped on either side of the canteen. His fingers were bloated and looked like blood sausages.

Marsh thanked him and took another pull. This seemed to surprise the Indian. He wondered if it was because of the sharing of the water or that his savior showed no reluctance to drink from the same canteen.

"Let's clear out of here. Your friends might return any time."

"Friends?" The Apache returned some of the water to the dry earth when he spat in contempt.

"Just a manner of speaking. They're not friends to either of us." Marsh touched his holstered six-shooter to emphasize his point.

He slid his arm around the Apache's shoulders and heaved him erect. The man was hardly five foot five, but his powerful shoulders and thick chest showed height mattered less than strength. He had been stripped down to a loincloth. No sign of a knife or any other weapon was in sight around the grassy bowl. Whatever horse he had ridden was long gone.

"I'd let you ride behind me but with those hands and all the cuts on your arms, you're likely to fall off. You'll ride in front of me." Marsh smiled just a little. The last person he'd taken for a ride like that was his younger daughter, Sarah, when she was hardly six years old. At sixteen, she was perfectly able to ride without her pa's arms holding her in the saddle.

If he was honest with himself, she had been capable of riding by herself a lot younger than six. It was as if she and whatever horse she rode shared a brain. She was about the best horsewoman he had ever seen, and that included some of the finest in all Texas.

The Apache hesitated, as if not understanding, but Marsh saw that he understood well. He might even speak English. If he didn't, he certainly followed about everything Marsh said.

"I'll mount and you can follow. I'll help."

The Apache put his flat palm against Marsh's chest and stopped him. He pulled back and held out his injured hand.

"Night Wolf," he said in his husky voice. "Of the Tall Grass People."

It took the rancher a second to reply. Indians weren't inclined to give out their names to White Eyes.

He took the outstretched hand and shook.

"Marshal Hammersmith, rancher. The Twin M's all mine now, since my twin brother lit out a few months back."

Night Wolf misunderstood. He grinned broadly and slapped Marsh on the back.

"Brothers!"

"Yeah, reckon we can be brothers. It'll be a first for my family. We came over from East Texas after living in New Braunfels a spell. And 'fore that, the grandparents came from Germany."

None of this caused Night Wolf to light up like being declared a brother to the man who had saved him.

"Brothers," Marsh agreed. "Now let's ride."

He swung up onto Derby. The stallion tried to buck as Marsh reached down and took Night Wolf's forearm to give him a boost up. This was unusual, and the horse had spent his entire existence avoiding raiders and horse thieves. Mostly, the still-oozing blood spooked him.

Derby's owner shared that fear. The Apache needed medical help or he'd bleed to death from the legion of cuts all over his upper torso, arms, and legs.

First things first, though. Getting away from this spot where the Comanche war party might return to see why the cavalry hadn't chased after them was his first concern. Rather than retrace his path, Marsh let Derby pick his own way around the broad hill. No sense tiring out the horse with needless climbing while carrying a double load.

Curiosity burned away at him, but Marsh held his tongue. How had Night Wolf come to get caught by the Comanches? What were any of them doing on his ranch? The answer to that was as obvious as the nose on his face. Both Apaches and Comanches hunted for strays to rustle. The heifer he'd chased earlier might have fallen victim to a band of hungry Indians. This part of the Twin M he laughingly called the back forty. It held fine grassland, when it rained, and even had a couple of stock ponds separate from the main ranchland.

The ponds out there were only about a quarter full. He increasingly relied on water from the Murphy brothers. That galled him, but there wasn't anything he could do about it. They had drilled a decent well and brought up an abundance of the precious water. He had hired the same crew and put down a half dozen dry wells until he wasn't able to afford further exploration. It proved cheaper to rely on purchase from the one good well on the Murphy's Double Cross ranch.

More than one night, he had lain awake worrying about that name, but so far Thomas and Daniel Murphy had played fair. They had developed some kind of unspoken arrangement because of him and Mason being twins and the Murphy brothers, while not twins, looking as if they should have been.

"Mase and Marsh, Tom and Dan," he muttered.

Night Wolf twisted around in his circling arms and tried to look at him.

"That's all right. I was just reminiscing out loud. What do you say to a little more water?"

"Water," Night Wolf repeated. He nodded once and turned to face forward.

"My stock pond's not far off. I'm thinking of digging an acequia from the main ranch if this drought keeps up. The pond usually fills from naturally falling rain, but it's been dry for quite a spell. But I don't have to tell you that, do I?"

Night Wolf grunted in reply.

Marsh would have paid plenty to learn about the Indian watering holes scattered across West Texas. They kept those a closely guarded secret and survived more than one Army expedition because they enjoyed water and the soldiers did not.

"There's my pond."

Derby jerked hard at the reins, anxious to drink some of the increasingly muddy water. He let the horse have its head.

"Drop on down. Have your fill. My horse is already ahead of us."

Night Wolf silently jumped to the ground. Marsh blinked and stared to be sure the Indian had dismounted. He'd heard nothing as the man's feet hit the hard-baked earth. He swung his leg around, noted how his hip protested just a little, then followed the Apache. His landing sounded like a sack of feed being dumped in comparison.

"I'll fill up the canteen while I'm at it." He took the canvas-covered canteen and filled it, then drank from it.

Derby guzzled water to his left and Night Wolf to his right.

"Go on and get some of that blood off. Dunk yourself in the pond," he urged the Lipan.

Night Wolf hesitated, then began splashing around, wiping away the dried blood from his body. Marsh watched. The way the Indian moved showed he was recovering, but he still needed some of the deeper cuts tended by a doctor. Stitches? Maybe a half dozen cuts required sewing. He shook his head. Going into Osborne to fetch the sawbones was the best solution. Showing up in town with a wounded Lipan in tow would only cause a ruckus he'd as soon avoid.

More than one person in town had lost relatives and friends to Indian raids. It hardly mattered most were killed in Comanche skirmishes and Night Wolf was a Lipan Apache.

For all he knew, the Lipan had added to that count of dead and wounded. The more he thought about it, the more certain he was. The Comanches were only the most recent predators sweeping across West Texas land.

Night Wolf came from the pond and shook off the water like an old hound dog. Water droplets flew everywhere. Marsh had to laugh.

"I've got some jerky in my saddlebags. What do you say to a quick meal before we get on back to my ranch house?"

Night Wolf pressed close, then backed away.

"Set yourself down on the edge of the pond. We can drink while we eat. This jerky's mighty dry without water to wash it down."

He found the oilcloth-wrapped jerky and turned. For a moment, he was a trifle confused. Night Wolf was nowhere to be seen.

He called out the Lipan's name. His only response was the soft whine of the evening wind. A quick look around failed to show where the man had gotten off to in the growing darkness.

"Well, now, Derby, it's just me and you." He settled on a rock beside the pond and reached for his knife to cut the tough beef.

His fingers found the empty sheath. No knife.

Marsh looked up and peered into the twilight as if he might find the thief lurking out there.

"Brothers share," he said, "but it was a fine knife and will be hard to replace." He bit down on a corner of the jerky and ripped it free. As he gnawed on it, he wondered what he would tell Leonore about being late for dinner. That he had lost his knife and hunted for it?

He shook his head. What he told her would be pared down so she wouldn't worry about an Indian running loose with a knife. Or a war party of Comanches riding through the back forty. Or his part in rescuing Night Wolf. But he would tell her some portion of the truth. That was always best.

CHAPTER 2

He had seen too many towns like this to be impressed with the banners and colored bunting and foofaraw. For Al Reed, the town of Osborne was yet another to suck dry before moving on. His life was laying track for the Union Pacific Railroad, and he was good at it. The best. Nobody kept the gangs working harder or put down more mileage in a day than he did.

Even now, having more Chinese workers than Irishmen was hardly a handicap for him. He had taken over construction in El Paso two months ago and was already there in the middle of West Texas. Before anyone knew it, he'd drive the last spike connecting the railroad tracks in San Antonio with the far distant terminus in California.

Then he'd move on to another project where the Union Pacific Railroad would pay him a king's ransom to work his magic with their steel and locomotives.

Until then, he had to dicker with local Osborne politicians and turn it into a jerkwater town. The engines needed water for their boilers. Osborne was perfectly situated to supply that water for trains coming south. It'd take some calculating, but he thought that Marfa provided another decent spot for watering, only that'd be for trains making their way north. All he needed to do was convince the local citizens they'd benefit and not be crushed under an iron heel.

He smiled crookedly as he walked along the main street, looking at the decorations welcoming the railroad—welcoming him. Al Reed, road superintendent and overseer extraordinary, was as far up the chain of command as anyone here would ever see. The real power behind the road seldom strayed from the West Coast and their fancy offices filled with mahogany desks, bustling assistants, and politicians coming to curry favor.

"Mister Reed, welcome." The red-faced man wore what was likely his best Sunday go-to-meeting clothes. He thrust out his hand. A stupid grin split his face and made him look like a fool. Only he didn't think so. And from what Reed saw all around, none of the townspeople watching thought so, either.

When Reed shook the proffered hand he felt thick calluses. This wasn't a politician. They had soft hands and a quick touch used to dipping into other men's pockets. Thomas Murphy worked for a living. A more careful look gave the man away. A rancher.

"Are you the mayor?" Reed tried not to sound too brusque. He had work to do. Real work. The first flatcar loaded with rail was scheduled to roll into camp ten miles north of town by sundown. The camp at the end of the road had to be secured and the men properly quartered and fed. With the Chinese workers fresh from the Southern Pacific construction far to the north, this wasn't a problem. They were a sober lot and kept to themselves.

Problems came from a different crew. The Irish always celebrated and got roaring drunk. Rowdy was one thing, but shooting up the camp in their enthusiasm for the work was something else. He had seen it too many times to be accepting of such horsing around. They had to be fit and working on track with the first light of a new dawn.

"Osborne doesn't have a real mayor, not exactly, the way I see it." Murphy said. His broad grin told the story. "The folks elected a fellow who likes to claim he's the mayor. There's a town council, too, but nobody pays them any mind. They all get together once a week to play poker. Me and my brother, well, let's say we keep things running smooth as silk."

"From your ranch?" Reed's question rocked Murphy back. His smile froze, then widened until he showed his canines.

"You're a clever man, finding out who you'll be dealing with. The Double Cross is my spread, mine and Daniel's. We keep the peace using our cowboys as an informal sheriff's department. If anything gets too out of hand, there's always the cavalry over at Fort Davis, though we prefer not to call on them."

"Because they're buffalo soldiers?" Reed probed to find how his Chinese workers would be received in Osborne. The way Murphy's smile turned sour told the tale. Let the Irish come to town, but keep the rest of his crew in camp. That'd maintain harmony until they moved on past the town. Luckily, that arrangement suited both the Chinese and the Irish.

"We prefer to put in a call to the Texas Rangers, should such an occasion present itself. The bluecoats at the fort spend a great deal of their time out in the desert chasing Indians that've come off the reservation up in Arizona and New Mexico."

"Comanches aren't a problem?"

"Not for townspeople," Murphy said, regaining his composure. "They rustle cattle, but that's a problem for the ranchers out east of town, not the fine community of Osborne." He made a sweeping gesture that encompassed the entirety of Main Street. "You can see how anxious we are to have you select Osborne as a major depot."

"A depot," Reed said, but he put enough of an inflection on it to show this wasn't a settled matter. "But more than that, we need water for the boilers. Our steam engines get mighty thirsty coming all the way from the West Coast."

"We can erect a water tower to your specifications inside a week. Anywhere you desire."

"And filled to overflowing?" Reed looked at the nearly empty watering troughs along the street. "You catch rainwater and put it out for the animals?"

"I know what's worrying you," Murphy said. "You've heard of our drought."

"Traveling down from El Paso across mighty barren land worried me about keeping our thirsty locomotives all full, I admit that."

"It shouldn't. You see, the Double Cross ranch has a fine well drilled and pumped using a windmill. We went down close to sixty feet to get the finest, sweetest water you ever did see." Thomas Murphy took Reed's elbow and steered him along a rickety boardwalk.

Reed would have preferred walking in the dusty street because of the way the poorly repaired planks twisted under his weight. Breaking an ankle before work began in earnest was nothing he wanted to experience. It had happened before. Being laid up for two weeks had put that section of track behind schedule, costing him a fat bonus. To this day, he growled like a feral dog when the name of Yuma was mentioned.

"How wet the water is matters more than if it's decent enough to drink. We can't use muddy water, mind you. That fouls the boilers. But nobody's going to be drinking what you put into the tank."

"Nobody except for the passengers waiting in the brand spanking new depot, eh?" Murphy nudged him in the ribs with his elbow.

Dealing with a politician would have been preferable.

But Reed had to negotiate with the ones best able to give him, to give the railroad, what it needed most. From what he'd seen of Osborne, the engine wouldn't take more than ten minutes to fill its boiler and *puff-puff-puff* along its iron ribbon all the way to San Antonio. Putting in a depot and staffing it wasn't in the cards.

"We need to lease the land where the tower will be built. I'll send out a survey team in a few days to find the proper spot."

"Me and my brother own the land you'll want to lease," Murphy said. He moved so that he partially blocked Reed. Quick as a rabbit, he guided the railroad overseer inside a saloon.

CHAPTER 3

Marshal Hammersmith wiped his hands on his jeans, then closed the corral gate. Derby frolicked about inside, as if he hadn't been ridden all day long, some of it with the added weight of the Apache bouncing along on his back. Marsh dipped his hands into a water trough and wiped his hands again until most of the dirt and blood was gone.

Explaining the blood was the worst part that he wanted to avoid. His wife, Leonore, had a sharp eye for such things. It was one of the many things he loved about her. She cared deeply about the entire family, but her sharp tongue had the ability to cut deeper than any knife blade.

Thinking about that, Marsh instinctively touched the empty sheath at the middle of his back. He grinned crookedly. Let Night Wolf use it to stay alive. That chore would tax an able-bodied man out on the arid grasslands. The Lipan had been severely tortured. How he had crept away without Marsh knowing was a mystery. Added to that was the ease with which he had slipped the Bowie knife from its sheath. Marsh had never felt a thing.

"He's a warrior," he said softly.

"What's that, dear?"

Marsh jerked up. He had been daydreaming about his

encounter with the Apache and hadn't noticed his wife on the back porch. She held a pan of biscuits in a thick towel.

"Cooling them off before dinner? I like them hot," he said.

"That's not all you like hot, Marshal Hammersmith," she said, laughing. "It's good that we share that."

"It keeps us married," he said, agreeing with her. A quick kiss and then he slipped around her into the kitchen. The heat hit him like a tornado, but no tornado ever carried so many savory odors, all mingled into a mouth-watering miasma.

Marsh looked into the big pot on the stove. His belly growled. He hadn't eaten much all day long save for the jerky. It was a good thing he didn't have to share that with Night Wolf. His hunger would have been even greater.

"Get yourself into the dining room," Leonore said, shooing him like he was a chicken. Before he ducked through the thin, bleached muslin curtains separating the two rooms, she grabbed his arm.

"What is it?"

"Your knife. It's not in the sheath. Did you lose it?"

A quick reach around pressed down on her long-fingered hand.

"I must have left it at the stock pond on the back forty. That's careless of me."

"It's not like you," she said, frowning. A quick toss of her head moved a stray lock of pure blond hair from her eyes. She fixed him with a polar stare. Her blue eyes were as hard as his when the need arose. "Caleb gave you that knife. He'll see that it's gone. You better have a good explanation of how you lost it." Her lips thinned. She had heard the untruth in his words. "How you really lost it. Now get on in there. Everyone's banging a spoon on their plate wanting food."

"I won't hold up the entire family. Getting between George and those biscuits is a good way to get a fork in the back of my hand." He tried to kiss her again, but she dodged with a sinuous move and returned to the kitchen.

His daughter, Sarah, wiggled past, distracted by juggling a platter loaded with baked potatoes. He watched as the sixteen-year-old girl moved to serve the others already seated around the large table. She was the spitting image of her ma. And she already showed a cussed streak that he admired—and which would make any man think twice about trying to spark her. Marsh wasn't sure how he felt about that. For the time being, that was a good thing. Let Sarah do a bit more growing up before choosing a beau.

"Where're George and Gustav?" he asked, looking around the table.

Leonore put the beef stew in front of him. He began ladling it out and passing the bowls around.

"George and Consuela took the baby into town. Poor little Joseph was running a fever."

"A fever," grumbled the old man seated at the far end of the table, down from Marsh. "In my day, nobody ran off to a quack because of a piddlin' little fever." Caleb muttered under his breath. "We was tougher."

"Baby Joseph has always been a mite sickly," Leonore said sharply. She was protective of her only grandchild. "Give him a chance to get over whatever bug's bitten him, Grandfather Caleb."

"We was tougher back in the day. And I still am."

"Pa," Marsh said, heaving a sigh. "He's only three months old."

"And I'm pushin' seventy. You don't catch me comin' down with all them germs or whatever they call 'em. Pass the gravy. I need somethin' to soften up these biscuits. They're hard as rocks."

Marsh reached out and laid his hand on his wife's forearm to calm her. She pulled away and turned her blazing eyes to the food on her plate. He knew how much effort it took to keep from snapping at the old man. Caleb got crankier by the day.

"When I was out on the trail, consortin' with bank robbers and traitors, there was none of this rushin' off to a sawbones every time one of us felt a bit under the weather. No, sir. We ignored the twinges. We was tough sons of—"

"Heidi, I wondered if you'd feel up to joining us," Marsh interrupted. His pa continued to mutter under his breath. The rest of the Hammersmith clan ignored him. Not even his son had any idea if a smidgeon of what Caleb claimed was true. He might have ridden with outlaws when he was younger—much younger—but his exploits always sounded farfetched. Marsh didn't put it past his pa to steal the stories of other men's lives or even spin a tall tale just to prove that he was still alive and kicking in a world that had passed him by.

"I was hunting for my son," Heidi said, pulling out a chair and sitting.

Her face was drawn, and her muddy brown eyes had sunk into deep pits. The dark circles and pale skin betrayed how little sleep she got. Since her husband, Mason, Marsh's twin, had disappeared, she had only picked at her food and spent more time than was healthy sitting in the barn loft, staring out across the grasslands as if Mase would ride back, as if nothing had happened.

Worse than her grieving over her husband's fate, their son, Gustav, had turned into a wild man. Marsh looked from Heidi to his pa. He wanted to ask if Caleb had filled the boy's head with his wild tales, but Gustav had the capacity of getting into trouble on his own. Even before his father had disappeared, Gustav had been a handful. If it wouldn't further grieve his sister-in-law, Marsh would have ordered Gustav off the Twin M ranch months ago.

Heidi was a fragile flower of a woman, and setting Gustav free to follow his own crooked trail would break her. Marsh owed it to her, to the memory of his brother, not to make life any worse for her until she was stronger. How long that might take was something he and Leonore had argued over for too many hours.

"I saw an Apache while I was hunting for the stray," he said to break a long, lingering silence that threatened to smother them all. No one dared to speak, save for Caleb, who continued muttering about the days when he had sowed his wild oats. And, if he was to be believed, wheat, corn, and barley as well.

"Did you chase him off?" Sarah sounded anxious for his safety.

"Reckon I did. He was off in the distance. Looked to be an Apache, though I found tracks from a Comanche war party. Maybe a dozen of them prowling about along the edge of the back graze."

"You shouldn't ride out alone, dear," Leonore said. "When you go out, have George or Gustav go with you."

"As if a Comanche *war party* wouldn't tangle with two riders instead of just one," Sarah said. "You should send a telegram to Fort Davis. It's their duty to keep the Indians off our land."

"They already patrol," Marsh said. "Even if they got a telegram, the Comanches would be long gone. It'd take days—longer—for a company of bluecoats to reach us."

"Vigilantes," Caleb said, looking up. "You need to whip up a posse. A bunch of armed men willing to chase 'em out of West Texas. Just like we done to Quanah Parker and his bunch. Me and Colonel Mackenzie chased that Injun all over 'fore we caught him. Shipped him off to Fort Sill for safe keepin'."

"Pa, that was only ten years back. You were here with Mase and me while we staked out the Twin M. You weren't with any Army colonel, and you didn't fight Indians."

"Did, too. I remember it as clear as the day you were born. You and that worthless brother of yours gave your ma a devil of a time. Difficult delivery. Worst I ever saw, and I seen a passel of them."

"Caleb, please. Not at the dinner table." Leonore picked up her plate. "Who's ready for some dessert? Peach cobbler."

"Sissies," Caleb said. "That's what you are."

"Pa, if you can't be polite, leave the table. Now apologize."

"To your wife? You're takin' her side and throwin' your old pappy to the wolves?" With a loud harrumph, he pushed away from the table and stood on unsteady legs. "I don't like peach cobbler." With that, the old man tottered off, leaving the dining room and disappearing into the depths of the rambling ranch house.

Marsh heaved a sigh of relief when his pa went away. Dealing with Caleb became more difficult every last day.

When Leonore returned with the cobbler, Marsh said, "He's getting worse. I apologize, dear."

She said nothing. That told him there'd be a longer discussion about letting his pa stay. Only it would be less a discussion and more of a lecture. And where was Caleb to go? They were his only surviving family after his two brothers and younger sister had all died years earlier.

"What are you smiling about, Papa?" asked Sarah. She looked from him to her mother and frowned.

He wasn't about to tell her or Leonore that his father had distracted everyone from asking more about the Apache he had found on their property. And the Comanches.

"Is that . . . ?" Heidi jumped to her feet and pushed aside

the curtains for a better look into the front yard. Her shoulders sagged, and she returned to the table. "It's only George and Consuela."

"They got back quick," Marsh said. "That probably means there's nothing much wrong with little Joseph."

"Come and sit down. There's plenty left over," Marsh called to his son and daughter-in-law as they came in the front way.

George and Consuela whispered for a few seconds, then she went up to the second story, where their bedroom looked toward the east. It was cooler in the summer, but both his son and daughter-in-law complained how chilly the room was in the winter. He considered adding another room on the second floor, one looking westward. That would be a furnace in the summer but much cozier in the cold winter months.

Marsh added that to the list of things to look into when he had time. Colder weather was still several months away.

George came in and sank into a chair. He looked as if he was the one who had fought off Indians.

"Well, son?"

"Nothing much to worry over. Doc Ferguson gave us some elixir to keep Joseph's temperature down."

"Consuela needs something to eat," Leonore said. "I'll take her a plate."

"I'll help. I want to see Joseph, too," Sarah said. They fixed a plate and went upstairs.

"It really wasn't anything serious?" Marsh asked.

George shook his head, then began shoveling food onto his plate. He swallowed a couple mouthfuls before answering.

"Just a touch of the ague. It could be serious, but with the medicine, he'll be right as rain in a few days."

Marsh studied his son. He had grown up to be a dependable man and one who knew the value of keeping his word.

"What?" George looked up. "You've got a strange look, Pa. Did something happen?"

"No, nothing to speak of."

"You can't fool me. You're gonna be like Grandpa and save up all those stories to bore Joseph with when he's old enough."

"Old enough," Marsh said, shaking his head. "Joseph'll be that old someday, but I hope I won't."

They sat in silence as George ate. When he polished off the last of the stew, he leaned back and tucked his thumbs under his suspenders, sated.

"That surely did hit the spot."

"You ma's a good cook." Marsh shifted his chair around. More aches and pains were starting to bother him now after his day in the saddle—and dealing with the Comanches. "You up for a quick ride around the ranch?"

"Reckon so. It's been a while since we counted that herd pastured to the north."

"We can do that. And I want your opinion on the big pond."

"I'll be ready right after breakfast. I'll want to be sure Joseph is resting easy."

"He will be. Consuela is a good mother."

George left his father alone in the dining room. So much had gone wrong during the day, but it all worked itself out. Night Wolf and the Comanche war party and his grandson running a fever. The Indians were long gone and Joseph was on the mend, even if Doctor Ferguson had whipped up one of his vile-tasting elixirs. If he had added a healthy dollop of alcohol, Marsh vowed that he'd sample it. He needed a drink, and Leonore was opposed to keeping liquor in the house.

Yes, he'd sample the snake oil the doctor had sent back with George. That'd do him more good than it would the baby.

Marsh Hammersmith heaved to his feet and stretched until he wanted to moan in pain at the way his joints betrayed him. Then he walked as softly as he could to the master bedroom at the far end of the house. It had been a long day, and he deserved a good night's rest.

CHAPTER 4

Marsh Hammersmith sat on his horse and stared into the dusty distance. He pulled down the wide brim of his Stetson to block a bit more of the sun. Bullet Butte poked up not three miles off, dun brown and imposing. It looked out of place on the flat grassland surrounding its base. The rock took on a color different from the land around it. It was obvious how it got its name from whatever pilgrim had passed by it a long time back.

The brown stone sides rose straight up and were capped by a lead-gray peak. The bottoms of the butte flared out like a cartridge. If the brown stone had been more coppery or even shiny like brass, the entire rocky edifice would have looked exactly like a cartridge dropped from some magnificently large gun onto the prairie.

"There's no rain coming, Pa," George Hammersmith said, drawing rein beside his father. He swiped at the sweat glistening on his forehead. It took a second pass of his bandanna to clear the perspiration. He retied the wet cloth around his neck, waiting for the tiny breeze to evaporate the moisture and cool him just a mite. "And you won't see him out there. You won't."

"Him?"

"Uncle Mason. He's not wandering around the ranch,

waiting to be found. And he certainly wouldn't be out here. He preferred the north pasture to about anywhere else."

"He's somewhere," Marsh said. His son's words irritated him. He hadn't been thinking of his missing brother, not until George mentioned it. Now all he could do was hunt for some small trace of the missing man.

His eyes narrowed, and he stared harder at the land. A bit of movement? No, only the restless wind moving through the ankle-high grass. Over at Bullet Butte? A shadow cast by a high cloud in the brilliant blue Texas sky. Nothing more. The cloud didn't even lie about the promise of rain. It never rained from such high-flying, quick-moving clouds that looked like a bleached white fish skeleton.

And Mason Hammersmith never came out there. George was right about that. Riding the range and letting the dark loneliness shroud him wasn't the way he preferred to live. His twin had been the rancher, keeping up with the herd and grazing and other details. Mason balanced accounts and worked tirelessly to expand the range and add acreage to the Twin M. They had argued long hours over how best to run the business, often yelling at each other.

Marsh missed him.

"Do you think Gustav ever hunts for him?" George looked over at him with a sour expression.

"I don't know why that boy's gone so much of the time. It's worrying his mother something fierce. First she loses her husband and then her son just kinda . . . leaves."

"He spends all his time in town drinking."

"Where's he get the money? He hasn't claimed his pay since Mason disappeared." Marsh scowled. He had suspected his nephew was in Osborne, but hearing it from his own son only made it worse. Everyone knew for a fact about Gustav's behavior, everyone save for him.

George coughed and looked sidelong at his pa. Marsh got the picture. His nephew wasn't working on the Twin M for money. That meant he took other jobs, ones that likely weren't—quite—legal. Or maybe Gustav had crossed the line and was an out-and-out road agent. Marsh hadn't heard of any robberies or other serious misdeeds. There hadn't been a bank robbery in Osborne since the day the cornerstone was laid at the courthouse years back.

But there were ways of getting petty cash. He wished Gustav would come back to the ranch house long enough for them to have a talk. It was hard for him, losing his father. Marsh knew that pain because he had lost a twin brother, but he had buckled down and picked up twice the load. It was what a man did.

"I don't like saying this about blood kin," George said, "but we've been losing a few head of cattle. I've hunted for their carcasses and haven't found them."

"Coyotes or wolves wouldn't eat the bones," Marsh mused.

"Even if buzzards picked the bones clean, there'd be a skeleton out there somewhere. I haven't found a trace."

"Don't jump to conclusions about Gustav. There're Comanches all around. I ran into a war party the other day. Maybe a dozen of them."

"I wondered about that. You did some fancy footwork to keep Ma from asking questions where you'd been. You had blood all over your shirt and pants."

"Wasn't mine."

"No, sir, it wasn't. I could tell that, but whose was it? Were you in a shootout with a war party? A *war* party?"

"We exchanged some lead, that I admit. I saved a man they were torturing."

"Why didn't you bring him back to the ranch? Ma'd fix him up and . . ." George's words trailed off. "It was another Comanche, wasn't it?"

Marsh had to fess up about Night Wolf.

"I declare, Pa, you're crazy. Why save an Apache who'll

steal our cattle? You think it's him and his people doing the thieving?"

"I don't know that. It's likely not the Comanches, either. That was a war party. They're not hanging around to dine off fine Twin M beef when they're looking to get into other mischief."

"Nobody may be dining off our meat," George said. "Come on. Ride with me and I'll show you." He whipped his horse into a gallop.

Marsh took a final look at Bullet Butte and saw no human movement. Even his herd wasn't grazing on the near pasture. He pulled his Stetson down onto his forehead and tightened the chin string, then tore out after his son. Derby showed what a winner he was. They overtook George and his mare halfway down the slope and blasted past into the flatlands.

"To the east, Pa. Race you to the acequia!"

Marsh felt the weight of responsibility slough off. Gone for the moment were the problems of running the ranch and finding his brother and worrying over his nephew. He raced the wind, chasing after his son the way they used to do when the boy was half the age he was now. Marsh had sometimes let George win those races, but not too often. He had to learn then about giving his utmost and how it might not be enough every time.

This race, in spite of Derby's long, powerful stride, went to George. Marsh was proud to say he hadn't let his boy win.

His grown-up son.

They drew to a halt along the deep irrigation ditch. The acequia needed cleaning. Weeds grew down to the water-line and below. Part of the problem, Marsh saw, was that the level had dropped a good foot.

"We're not getting the water we used to," George said.

"You can tell by the white marks along the sides of the acequia where the water used to reach."

"Murphy might not be pumping on the same schedule."

"I never liked it that the Murphy brothers supply so much of our stock's water," George said. "They can cheat us. There's no way to measure how fast the flow is or how much water we get. Even as hot and dry as it is, would we lose that much water to evaporation?"

"It hasn't been a problem before. Thomas opens the gate to the main water conduit and lets it flow all night long. That's been enough to fill our main ponds."

"One is almost dry. The other two are down about a foot."

"A foot? That's a whale of a lot of water missing from the big ponds," Marsh said. He grinned crookedly. George's expression showed that he had caught the pun, but the matter was too serious for even a chuckle.

"They're trying to steal our land. Daniel Murphy's offer for the back forty is downright insulting."

"How'd you hear about that?"

"Uncle Mason was steaming mad after he met with Murphy. I don't know he even saw me outside the house when he came storming out, yelling at Murphy not to come back."

"When was this?" Marsh tensed. He'd heard nothing about this or any recent offer the Murphys had made for part of the spread.

"Less than a week before Uncle Mason disappeared."

Marsh swallowed. His mouth had turned to cotton. Mechanically, he pulled up his canteen and popped the cork. He took a long drink of the tepid water. When he reached the bottom, he slid from the saddle and reached down into the sluggishly flowing water in the acequia. Then he shoved the cork stopper back into the full canteen and stood, looking up and down the length of the irrigation ditch.

"The water's muddier than usual. That means it's not flowing as fast. Maybe there's trouble pumping it up. I heard tell they had to drill down more'n sixty feet."

"I thought about that," George said. "It took me the better part of yesterday to see that the water running from their windmill pump's just as clear and sweet as ever."

"They're doing something different," Marsh said slowly. "And whatever they're doing is giving us short shrift."

"You want me to talk to them? I've never trusted either Daniel or Thomas."

"You spend more time in town than I do and hear stories," Marsh said. The rancher slung his canteen over Derby's rump. "But it's my place to dicker with them."

"You wouldn't catch me dead in that gin mill of theirs."

"Your ma'd kill you."

"She wouldn't be too pleased to find you'd been swilling that tarantula juice, either."

"It's still good to wet your whistle once in a while with a cool beer." Just the mention of a beer made his mouth water. Just a little, but not enough to make it worthwhile to ride all the way into Osborne.

"I prefer rye," George said. He looked sharply at his father.

Marsh didn't reply. His son was old enough to drink. Understanding the problems of too much liquor went with that. If only his nephew had as much horse sense.

"I'll corner one of the Murphy brothers and find out why we're not getting what we're paying for," Marsh said.

"I'll head on back to the house, Pa. You coming along?"

"I'd race you back and me and Derby would beat the socks off you, but I want to scout a bit more before dinner."

"See you at dinner, then." George hesitated, as if unsure

about leaving his pa alone. Then he turned his mare's face and trotted away.

Marsh watched him go. His son was sharp and had keen eyes, but he had missed the tracks in the muddy bank on the far side of the acequia. He backed away a few paces, then gave Derby his head. The stallion jumped clean over the flowing water and landed easily on the other side.

The tracks were too plentiful for a single rider. Marsh tried to count and decided it hardly mattered after finding six distinct sets of hoofprints. He saw that even though they were mounted, the horses were unshod. Indians had watered along the acequia. If Night Wolf had rejoined his people, those might be Apache horses.

Marsh trotted along the path leading away from the acequia, looking both left and right. He wasn't an expert tracker but thought at least a dozen braves rode in the band. Before he had gone much farther, a glint caught his eye. He circled the grassy hummock and then dismounted.

He picked up an arrow. From what he knew of the tribes, this flint arrowhead tipped an arrow built up for hunting birds. He ran his fingers along the smooth shaft until he touched the fletching. More than once, he had seen feathers attached to an arrow in the same fashion.

Only, the arrow shaft had been thicker and the flint arrowhead had been larger. The arrow had been stuck in the chest of a cowboy who'd ridden once for him.

And it had been a Comanche war arrow.

He snapped the shaft and threw down the pieces. The Twin M ranch was losing cattle, all right, and if he had been a gambling man, he'd be all in on the rustlers wearing Comanche war paint. This evidence made it seem he had been wrong about the Comanches clearing out on their way to do battle somewhere else.

CHAPTER 5

Marsh Hammersmith didn't care much for towns, but as it went Osborne wasn't too bad. He rode slowly down the middle of Main Street. As he passed by the saloon a fetid gust of wind blew from inside, carrying the nose-wrinkling odor of stale beer and staler cigarette smoke mingled with a hint of something more he couldn't recognize. He abided by Leonore's distaste for drinking, but a drop of beer right now would do a body a world of good. Riding anywhere these days meant crossing arid land in hot sun.

He looked around, not expecting to see either of the Murphy brothers. And he didn't. At this time in the afternoon, they'd be out at their ranch or working at one of the businesses they owned in town. The two men thought they owned the town, but their hold on Osborne was slippery at best. Several civic groups opposed them in about everything they tried. As much as the Murphy brothers refused to admit it, there were an elected mayor and a town council. As far as Marsh could tell, Mayor Galveston and his cronies did little to further the town's fortunes, preferring to get together once a week for a poker game in the back of Larson's Feed and Grain. That political neglect gave the Murphys free rein to do as they pleased because they owned so many of the important businesses.

The latest scheme they'd tried was to name the main street after themselves. Most all of the residents had risen up and opposed that. Marsh looked up. The two ranchers hadn't even named their own saloon. He'd heard Daniel and Thomas had argued over which of them got to name the gin mill. Another rumor had it they each wanted it named after them individually. Still another bit of gossip attributed the lack of name to even darker reasons. Marsh wished he'd heard what those might be, but no one would tell him. More likely, this was totally untrue.

If he asked Brown Jenks, the editor and owner of the town newspaper, he was sure to get the best story. Whether it was true hardly mattered. Jenks spun a wild and woolly tale at times, but it was always interesting. More than this, Brown Jenks opposed everything the Murphy boys tried. Where that animosity came from wasn't something Marsh wanted to know. Just hearing the name Murphy caused the newspaper editor to turn livid and start to sputter. Marsh imagined him as one of the railroad locomotives, building a powerful head of steam and ready to pop every rivet.

He pinched the brim of his hat in the direction of a pair of young ladies carrying brown-paper-wrapped parcels. They smiled and waved and one called out to him.

"Where's that handsome nephew of yours, Mister Hammersmith? Ain't he comin' to town with you anymore?"

"Miss Lisa, I've got Gustav working hard on the ranch. But I'm sure he'd be pleased as punch to see you."

"There's a barn dance at the Johnson place at the end of the month!" Lisa Gulliver and her friend giggled and hid their mouths behind their hands.

Marsh rode on. If Gustav took up with Miss Lisa, he'd have no objection. Heidi might, since she and the girl's mother often had words when they met. Still, Gustav could do worse than the girl. Only Gustav wasn't working the ranch and worked to sully his own reputation, instead.

Sadly, Marsh knew marrying his nephew off would only give woe to the woman and do nothing to settle down his wayward kin.

He dismounted in front of the livery and led Derby into the shade. The horse neighed loudly and tugged on the reins. He let the stallion drink from the rain barrel while he went to talk with the owner. Luther Wilkinson jumped to his feet when Marsh entered.

"What brings you to town, Marsh?"

From the hesitant way the livery stable owner spoke and the quaver to his words, Marsh guessed right away what the man thought.

"It's got nothing to do with Gustav. Has he been causing you trouble?"

"He owes me a few dollars." Luther spoke slowly, choosing his words so he wouldn't offend. "Are you good for his debt?" He licked his lips and rushed on. "He never claimed you was, but he's stabled his horse here and has been sleepin' in the back room most nights."

"That's good to know, Luther. I'm not backing his play, but if things get too . . . crowded, well, let me know. I'll see what I can do."

"He spends most all his money over at the Murphys' saloon. Ain't good to start drinkin' at sunup and still be at it past midnight. Word is he never pokes his snout outside . . . or anywhere but into a beer mug."

"That's no good if he owes you for tending his horse and giving him a place to sleep." Marsh fished around and found a silver dollar. He passed it over to the livery owner. "That'll take care of old Derby."

"I'll see that fine animal gets plenty of grain, Marsh. Thanks." Luther Wilkinson slid the coin into the watch pocket on his jeans.

Marsh turned back down the street and went directly to the saloon. If either Daniel or Thomas was anywhere to be found in town, it was there. He had already tapped one source of information at the livery. Finding out what he had about Gustav hadn't been pleasant, but at least his nephew wasn't in too much trouble. Not yet. The town girls didn't know he was in Osborne, so he wasn't making a nuisance of himself by bothering them. If he kept up the drinking, though, and Leonore found out, she'd throw him out of the house for good. Marsh felt an obligation to the young man, as much because of being kin as not wanting to give Heidi any more sorrow than she had already.

The stinky wind blowing from inside the bar caused him to stop dead in his tracks. There were enough scents mixed together to get him drunk and to fill his lungs with cigar smoke. The first deep breath made him woozy. The second brought a cough rumbling up from deep in his throat.

He pushed through the swinging doors and looked around. The bartender was a woman he'd never seen before, though from where he stood he saw plenty of her now. Her neckline plunged so low if it sank by another inch he'd see her navel. And too much else. Marsh turned away and tried to find either of the Murphys through the thick, smoky haze. He hardly expected to find them at this time of day, but he never knew. He might get lucky—if it could be called luck talking to either of the brothers.

Thomas spotted Marshal before he saw the man peddling him water for his herd.

"Marsh! Marshal Hammersmith! Come on back and get a drink. What'll it be?"

Marsh walked toward the voice. A half dozen steps into the choking fog brought Murphy into focus, no matter that Marsh's eyes watered. For two cents, he'd turn and head back onto the range where the air wasn't thicker than mud.

"Thomas," he said in greeting. He shook hands and took

the chair indicated. Sitting with his back to the room made him a mite nervous, but this was Murphy's saloon and he got to choose where he sat with his back pressed into a corner. Nobody snuck up on him this way. Nobody.

"Bring him a beer. That's your pleasure, right? I don't recollect you being a hard liquor fancier."

"A cold beer's just what the doctor ordered."

"Little Miss Molly's the nurse to cure what ails you."

Marsh shifted uncomfortably as the partially naked barkeep pressed close to him and put the beer mug on the table. She smiled. He tried not to shudder.

"You need anything, anything at all, you just whistle," she said. Her smile grew even wider and more feral. "After a beer, your whistle ought to be plenty wet." She sashayed off.

Marsh turned from her and gripped the beer mug with both hands. A shiver passed through him. The beer was especially cold.

"You can do worse in Osborne," Murphy said, laughing. "Trust me, I know."

"I can be a lot deader if my missus ever caught wind of me even being in a drinking emporium like this." He took a long pull on the beer. It was bitter but went down cold and ended the thirst built up on the dusty ride into town.

"She's got you on a short leash," Murphy said, more to himself than Marsh. "That figures."

"I was never one for small talk, Thomas." He took another drink and wiped the thin foam off his lip. "Water. We're not getting the allotment we're paying for."

"Do tell."

"The flow's half what it should be and makes the water muddy."

"That'll settle out once it reaches your stock pond," Murphy said. "Other than that advice, there's nothing I can do for you."

"Why are you cheating us out of water we paid for? When we get good rain, it doesn't matter so much, but you know how the weather's been lately. Even the mesquite trees are begging for a drop of rain."

"It might be that old pump's not bringing up as much as it used to." Murphy's eyes narrowed and a tiny smile curled his lips. Marsh wished they were playing poker. The man either couldn't control his emotions or, more likely, no longer cared what anyone thought. Openly taunting Marsh was a definite possibility.

"That's one explanation, but it's not the true one, is it, Thomas?"

"You're not the only one bidding for our water. The Double Cross needs more. That drought you're grousing about has hit us, too."

"You don't have half the herd I do," Marsh said. "There's something more you're not mentioning."

"Oh, you referring to the railroad? Now, that's something that'll improve the lives of everyone in town and not just a lone rancher out in the middle of nowhere."

Marsh slammed his fists onto the table. His beer mug jumped. Half standing, he glared at Murphy.

"We paid for that water. You can't give it to the railroaders."

"Can and will. Unless you want to pay double what you're paying now." Murphy looked smug. Then he said, "Forget that. The train's coming to Osborne because we can supply it water. No water for their boilers, no railroad."

"I'll sue you for this, Murphy. We signed a contract."

"Seems like we've been sending you the water you paid for. Prove we're not."

"There's no way to measure it." Marsh turned red in the face trying to hold back his anger. His fists clenched, and he slammed them down on the table again. "You're a double-dealing snake. You and that brother of yours."

"The Union Pacific Railroad is promising the folks of this fine town prosperity that'll never be theirs otherwise. What does the Twin M ranch give them? A few dollars for vet bills and feed and nothing else."

Marsh grabbed for Murphy across the table. His anger exploded like a volcano. Strangling Thomas Murphy would accomplish nothing but might make him feel better. His fingers closed on the man's lapels, and he slammed him face forward onto the table between them. Murphy let out a squawk like a stepped-on hen.

Then Marsh was lifted up and hurled through the air like a rag doll caught in a Texas tornado. He crashed to the floor. Sawdust flew all around like a tiny dust devil. Still seeing red, he grabbed for his Peacemaker. Only then did good sense return.

He stared into the barrels of four six-shooters.

"You want we should shoot him, boss?"

Marsh recognized the Double Cross foreman, Ben Wanamaker. The red-haired man dressed to the nines in spite of being in the saddle all day and tending the Murphy herd scattered across an arid prairie. His Schofield centered on Marsh's forehead. His trigger finger turned white from slowly increasing pressure. The slightest move would send hot lead drilling into his victim's brain. From the expression on his face, he'd enjoy watching Marsh die—or anyone. The green eyes were emerald hard and colder than the gemstone. Cruel anticipation of seeing another man die at his hand turned Wanamaker's expression into something demonic.

"Back off. He had too much to drink."

That infuriated Marsh anew. A single beer was hardly too much, but if this story got around town, gossip would turn him into a violent drunk.

"Yeah, I see that, but maybe I should wing him, just as a reminder not to cause a ruckus." Wanamaker shifted his aim to a spot under Marsh's belt. "Gelding him would be about right. He's already spawned enough times."

"Show him out, Ben. All the way out of town, and be sure he doesn't try to steal any Double Cross water."

Two of Murphy's ranch hands dragged Marsh to his feet and held his arms so he couldn't reach for his six-gun. They shoved him hard through the swinging doors. From behind the bar, Little Miss Molly shouted, "And don't come in here again, you worthless drunkard!"

The half dozen customers all laughed, then cheered when Thomas Murphy called for drinks on the house.

All that infuriated Marsh even more. He stumbled into the street and fell to one knee as he lost his balance. When a shadow blocked the sun, he looked up. In spite of being a short, stocky man, Wanamaker towered over him. The man's shock of red hair poked from under the flat-brimmed hat he wore, giving him a wild look.

"The boss said not to shoot you. He didn't say nuthin' 'bout roughin' you up."

Marsh ducked as the Double Cross foreman reared back and swung his pistol. The barrel clipped Marsh on the cheek and sent him flailing in the dirt. Blood oozed from the shallow cut opened by the Schofield's front sight. If his reactions hadn't been so good, the metal would have crushed his temple. He lay still and listened to Wanamaker boast to the others.

The foreman stepped closer. Through half-hooded eyes, Marsh saw the man's fancy Mexican boots shuffle into position to deliver a kick. The silver-tipped boot would break bones if the blow landed.

Wanamaker reared back. Marsh timed his attack just right. He flopped over and caught the man's leg with both arms. He drove his shoulder into Wanamaker's knee and toppled him backward. Without slowing, Marsh swarmed up and dropped. His knee crushed into the man's groin. Wanamaker made a sick sound and clutched the wounded part.

The sudden fall of their foreman stunned the other three cowboys. They gaped at the sudden turn of events, giving Marsh time to scoop up Wanamaker's six-gun. He planted his feet and whirled about. The Schofield's barrel crashed into the nearest wrangler's head. He dropped like a poleaxed steer. Continuing to spin around, Marsh thrust with the gun and used the muzzle as if it were the tip of a curiously shaped knife. The steel barrel half vanished into the second man's gut. He doubled over and flopped into the ground, retching noisily.

Marsh took scant pleasure seeing that the cowboy puked his guts out onto Wanamaker, ruining his foreman's fancy duds. He dropped the gun and turned to the remaining hand. The man stood and gawked. Marsh set his feet, judged distance, and proceeded to thrash him with a flurry of punches. Three to the midriff doubled him over. A quick shuffle set Marsh securely. He brought up his knee under the man's chin.

From the sound of bone snapping, he not only knocked him out but also broke his jaw.

Marsh stepped back and stared at the four men writhing about on the ground—the ones who hadn't been knocked out completely. He expected his anger to be drained after such a fight.

If anything, his fury mounted. He stared back at the saloon doors and considered defying Little Miss Molly by reentering. Then he scooped up his fallen Stetson, settled it on his head, and walked away slowly, still seething.

About everyone in town had witnessed the fight. Gossip now wasn't going to be about a drunk Marshal Hammersmith but about one capable of giving better than he got.

CHAPTER 6

Marsh Hammersmith ate breakfast slowly. His jaw popped every time he bit down. Sometime during the fight with Ben Wanamaker and his cutthroats, he had taken a punch to the jaw and hadn't known it at the time. After the ride home, Marsh found himself mumbling because of a swollen face. Explaining that to his wife had been a chore, doubly so since he could hardly tell Leonore he had been thrown out of a saloon for being drunk.

He counted on the fight having so many witnesses to erase that black lie. When Leonore went into town, all anyone would talk about was how her husband had taken on four ruffians in the middle of the main street in front of God and everyone and bested them. If his luck held, nothing would be said about the fight being the result of getting tossed out of the Murphys' saloon or Little Miss Molly's bogus allegations.

"You and George should go straightaway to the Murphy ranch and let them know you don't appreciate his drunk cowboys trying to beat you up," Leonore said. She lightly touched his swollen jaw. He refused to flinch. That only made her more protective. "The town needs a lawman."

"Won't be me," he grated out. With a convulsive gulp, he finished the rest of his biscuit soaked in gravy. Marsh followed it with a long draft of water. The simple act of eating had eased the swelling and let him talk better. He was in far better shape than any of the men who had attacked him.

He smiled as he thought about Ben Wanamaker. It'd be a cold day in hades before he faced Marshal Hammersmith again. Then the smile faded. A man like Wanamaker wouldn't face him. His style was more like shooting him in the back. Marsh pushed that fear out of his head. There wasn't any chance he and the Murphy brothers' foreman would cross paths any time soon. With any luck, the animosity would simmer for a spell, then fade away and be forgotten.

Marsh didn't believe that for an instant, but he could always wish for it.

"I wasn't saying you should ask the mayor to be the law." Leonore laughed unexpectedly. The sound was music to his ears. She had thought of something that amused her. And he was right when she said, "You'd be Marshal Marshal."

"Or maybe they'd call me Sheriff Marshal."

"Whichever, you'd bring some justice to Osborne. If it wasn't for the Murphy boys being such skinflints, there'd be law in town."

"They don't want a marshal breathing down their necks," he said. "That way they can do anything they like without worrying about being tossed into a cell."

"I worry about town now that those terrible railroaders are coming so close. You know how they are. Drunks, one and all. They blow into a place like Osborne to carouse and find ladies of the evening. The next thing you know, they'll be shooting up the place." Leonore gathered some of the dishes from the table and carried them into the kitchen. Marsh took the ones she'd left and joined her at the sink.

"All I've heard says the Union Pacific wants to lay track

and get to San Antone as quick as they can. That'll give them a link from the Pacific to a railhead with spur lines from Houston and Galveston."

"Thugs and ruffians," she said fiercely. "They're worse than cowboys coming to town on a Saturday night."

"How do you know? Have you been sneaking out and spying on them when I was asleep?"

"Oh, you. Of course they're rowdies. Why else would a man be laying track all day in the hot West Texas sun?"

Marsh looked up through the kitchen window when George galloped up outside.

"He's in a powerful hurry. Something must be wrong." He left the dishes unwashed and went to the back door, only to collide with his son.

"You're in a powerful hurry. What's wrong?"

"Pa, grab your gun. There's a pack of rustlers working to cut out twenty head from the main herd."

"Are you sure?"

"I found the tracks. Fresh. Not more than an hour old. I wasn't about to tangle with what must be a couple dozen rustlers."

"You shouldn't go after a gang that big. Not the two of you, all by yourselves." Leonore grabbed Marsh's arm to hold him back. He shrugged it off.

"If we can't stop them, we can run them off so they don't steal more beeves," he said. "If George is right, they just robbed us of two thousand dollars' worth of livestock."

He pushed past his wife and rushed into the house. He grabbed his gun belt with the heavy Colt in it and never broke stride when he pulled his Winchester from the wall rack. He fumbled a little getting a couple boxes of cartridges. If they spotted the rustlers, he didn't want to run out of ammo. Desperados like these, bold enough to steal in broad daylight, were treacherous men. Killing would be part and parcel of their existence.

Stepping out onto the porch, he was surprised to see Derby saddled and waiting for him. George was serious about them catching the rustlers. A quick vault onto horseback and he wheeled around. His son had already lit out.

"Fly like the wind," he told his stallion. Bent low, he wondered for a second if the horse hadn't grown wings. It overtook his son within a quarter mile.

"They cut out the cattle from the main stock pond," George yelled to him. "They're headed south with them. We can cut through that patch of trees near Jimson Weed Creek and catch them there."

For what seemed an eternity, they rode. Marsh's hard blue eyes turned bloodshot as tears streamed down his cheeks. The wind and dust cut at his flesh as much as it poked at his eyes. His face, already tanned, felt as if it cured into hard leather. Just when he began to wonder if the race was worth it, they spotted the stand of cottonwoods where the creek struggled to flow.

"They're watering the cattle. *Our* cattle!" George worked his rifle free.

"Hang back. We need to know what we're up against." Marsh pulled his own rifle from the saddle scabbard and cocked it, but he didn't bring it to his shoulder because of what he saw.

Two Comanche braves, decked out in war paint, sauntered from the wooded area.

"It's the war party that tortured Night Wolf," he called to his son.

"Who's that? Oh, the Apache. How'd you find out his name?"

"Never mind. There're more of those devils," Marsh said. "Maybe as many as a dozen."

Even as the words left his lips, four more came from the woods, laughing and joking.

"I saw tracks for more than that," George said. He drew

rein and came to a halt. "For once Ma was right. We can't fight them off."

"Through the trees by the stream. I see our cattle." Marsh's brain tumbled and turned with a fistful of ideas. None of them ended without two ranchers getting scalped by a hungry war party.

"They haven't spotted us. They're too busy enjoying how they put one over on us and stole our cattle." George's bitter appraisal of the problem gave Marsh the answer.

"They've corralled their horses in the woods. And the cattle are content to drink without being guarded."

He exchanged a look with his son. Their blue eyes locked and then glinted with determination.

"It might get us killed," George said.

"You stampede the cattle. I'll scatter the Comanches." Marsh took a deep breath and then gave Derby his head. Once again, he played out a dangerous bluff. The Indians were too battle hardened to fall for the same trick twice, but Marsh had few options. Either let them steal his valuable cattle in a drought year when every head meant the difference between survival and bankruptcy or risk it all.

He began firing as he rode. From the corner of his eye, he saw George riding hellbent for the creek. When his son splashed through the shallow stream, he began yelling and waving his rifle around in the air. Shots were all it took to frighten the cattle. They lit out amid loud sloshing in the water and blundered into one another. That added to their scare. They began running back in the direction of the herd where the Comanches had stolen them.

"Keep after the cattle!" Marsh wanted his son to keep the cattle running away. What he had to do was too dangerous to risk his son's life.

He fired at the cluster of four Indians and got the result he wanted. Although he missed hitting even one, they scattered. By the time he reached the creek, they had taken cover and were hunting for weapons. None carried anything more than a knife. Wherever they'd left their rifles, they were effectively out and responding to his attack.

Marsh plunged into the trees, dodging low-hanging branches and shooting at anything that moved. From a yelp of pain, he knew he'd hit one brave. He hadn't even gotten a good look at his target. Then he burst into a clearing where the Comanches had staked their horses. Bending low, he grabbed at reins and yanked.

The frightened horses reacted the way the cattle had. When he fired a couple times, they ran for their lives.

He had momentarily confused the Indians, and now had left them on foot until they ran down their mounts. Marsh swung about in a circle, shooting at any brave he spotted. Just when he decided it was time for him to retreat, a Comanche ran from the woods, knife in hand. With a prodigious leap, he launched himself at Marsh.

The blade missed cutting him, but the tip drove deep into his gun belt. The fierce stab unseated him. Marsh went flying through the air and fell heavily to the ground. The impact stunned him. His horse blocked his attacker from pursuing directly again, but when Marsh sat up, shaking his head, he faced not only the Comanche who had tried to gut him but also another who had burst from the woods.

He grabbed for his six-shooter as one brave came for him. Being seated made drawing awkward, even from his cross-draw holster, but Marsh was a good enough gun handler to draw and fire. He missed a killing shot, but his bullet tore into the warrior's leg, causing him to stumble.

Derby came to Marsh's aid. The stallion reared and lashed out with deadly front hooves. One crashed into the other brave's shoulder. Bones snapped with a belly-turning sound. The Comanche grabbed for his shoulder and spun away. His loud cries had to be curses directed at his White Eyes attacker.

Marsh crab-walked back to get away from the Indian he'd shot. The warrior refused to give up.

"Back off," Marsh shouted. "I'll let you live if you stop now."

Either the Comanche didn't understand or blood rage had turned him deaf. Lips pulled back in a feral snarl, he launched himself at the rancher. Marsh wasn't able to shoot with the Indian crashing down on him, but he managed to swing his Peacemaker in a short arc. He buffaloed the man. The blow to the side of his face knocked him off attack. Marsh kicked free and stood over the struggling man.

"I don't want to shoot," he said. The Comanche had been wounded, knocked in the head, and had dropped his knife. He was as close to helpless as he could get.

With a fierce cry, he lunged toward Marsh. The rancher fired. The bullet hit in the top of the brave's head. He dropped as if he were a marionette with its strings suddenly cut. Marsh stared for a moment, marveling at the lack of blood. His slug had blasted through the skull and gone down into the man's body without an exit wound. There was no telling what damage the bullet had done after passing through the brain and down the windpipe.

Marsh shook free of the shock of killing the Comanche and looked around. He was surrounded by the rest of the war party. Counting them was pointless. One or one hundred, he was in a pickle. Again, Derby came to his aid. The horse hadn't run away but had pawed and snorted at the ground where the Indian ponies had been staked. The stallion now trotted to him. Marsh swung into the saddle and drove his heels into the horse's flanks. The stallion shot off like a rocket, bursting through the ring of braves intent on killing him.

Marsh winced as one Indian slashed at him. This time, the blade found his calf. Then he galloped free of the trees and onto the prairie. He slowed to take a look at his cut. The blood ran down his leg and into his boot. That'd make walking a chore, but he was alive.

Movement at the edge of his vision spun him around. One determined Comanche ran like a fiend for him, waving a knife in the air. Marsh thought he saw blood on that blade. His blood? The single attack that had wounded him wasn't complete until the knife drove through his heart.

He lifted his six-shooter and took careful aim. The Comanche saw and kept running pell-mell. Marsh couldn't see the warrior's eyes but knew they were wild with fury. Nothing but death would sate that bloodlust. His first shot caused the Indian to jerk. The lead had come close but hadn't hit. And it didn't stop the brave from closing the distance between them.

Marsh could have ridden off faster than the Indian could run. But from the way the Comanche fought now, this battle wasn't over until one of them died. He took aim again and fired. And fired again. The third time his hammer fell on an empty chamber.

The fight was over. He had dropped the Comanche with his final shot.

Marsh saw several other Comanches on foot pounding relentlessly toward him. He considered reloading and finishing them off, too, until he saw that one brave had recovered his horse. It was only a matter of time before more were mounted. He had no desire to fight a half dozen mounted warriors who lived to fight astride their horses.

He turned Derby toward the north and galloped away. It had been a battle well fought—and won! Somehow, he felt as if he was the loser and not the victor.

CHAPTER 7

"That's not the way to drive a spike!" Al Reed yanked the hammer from the brawny man's grip. "Hold the spike." He swung the hammer around and poised it for the strike.

"You're gonna break my hand with that hammer if you miss. I ain't holdin' it!" The man backed off.

"If you don't, I'll smash in your worthless head." Reed twirled the nine-pound hammer as if it were nothing more than a stick.

"I quit!"

"Gerhardt, get him out of here. Whatever's on his back is all he leaves with. No other belongings and no pay. Not one red cent!"

Reed's right-hand man grabbed the balking worker by the collar and lifted. The man was strong from driving spikes with the hammer. Gerhardt was bigger, stronger, and from the look on his bulldog face, meaner. He carried the worker off like a terrier with a rat in its teeth.

"You," Reed bellowed. "Hold the spike." He gestured for the man who'd been placing spikes for the fired worker. The man was slight, and his eyes were glazed over in a way Reed saw too much on this crew. He had been chasing the dragon with the Chinese workers. The opium dulled his senses and left him looking like he'd just tumbled from his cot after failing to recover from a nightlong drunk.

He was dull in brain and senses, but he moved to obey. He placed the spike exactly. Reed swung and drove it into place with a single blow.

"Again. Faster." The railroad boss took a measured step to the side. The spike was already positioned. He drove it. "Again."

For five minutes, he drove spikes, getting into the rhythm he wanted his crew to follow. With sweat soaking his shirt and running in thick rivers from his forehead, he tossed aside the sledge and called, "Gather 'round. Listen up."

The crew shuffled into a half circle around him. The ones that weren't dulled by smoking opium shared an apprehensive look. They knew they'd be fired like the complaining worker a few minutes before. If Reed wasn't able to handle them if they protested, Gerhardt was. He glared at them, his colorless pig eyes buried at the bottom of pits rimmed with gristle and mean.

"That's how you drive spikes. That's what I want from you. What I demand. You're not gettin' fed today if you don't lay a mile of track before sundown."

"But, boss, them Chinese, they're slowin' us down."

Reed went to the man and faced him down.

"They're laying ties and dropping steel rails just fine. If you kept up with them, you'd have two miles done before sundown. Yeah, that's what I want. Two more miles or you don't get fed tonight or at breakfast." He shoved the man back into the crowd of workers. His glare caused a couple to wilt. Others looked at the ground, not daring to meet his ferocious gaze.

"What're you standin' 'round for?" Gerhardt stepped forward, dusting off his hands. "The boss told you what he wants from you. Do it. Do it, or by all that's holy I'll skin you alive and hang your worthless hide out to dry on the cowcatcher at the front of the locomotive."

Reed signaled his foreman to come with him to the Pullman car he used for an office. The locomotive pulling the car sat at the end of the line, puffing out a steady pillar of steam. Behind the Pullman were a half dozen tall cars outfitted with bunks for the workers. Four housed the Chinese workers, the other two were for the Irish. Beyond them were additional freight cars stuffed with supplies and a pair of almost empty flatcars used to bring steel rail and ties in from El Paso.

He sank into a padded chair behind a broad desk and closed his eyes. A quick swipe got rid of most of the sweat still running down his face. He took no pleasure dressing down his men like that. It drained him. It made him feel . . . diminished.

"What's up, boss? You sounded real angry out there."

"I should have cut the telegraph wires," he said tiredly. He sat up and reached across the desk. He slid a water tumbler toward his foreman and took another for himself. The whiskey he poured for them came almost to the brim of each glass. Reed closed his eyes for a moment, then knocked back half the fiery liquor. He choked, swallowed, and finished the glass. The sudden flood of alcohol into his belly dulled the world around him.

He considered another glass. Maybe that would make his troubles vanish entirely.

"We got to put up the telegraph lines," Gerhardt said. "That's part of the deal the railroad made with the government."

"Yeah, yeah, it makes sense. We're bringing steel rails and ties in. Why not telegraph poles and wire, too?"

"Does the railroad own the telegraph line?"

"It doesn't matter. The telegraph key at the end of the

line as we string it never stops chattering with orders from the main office."

Gerhardt stayed silent. Reed was glad for that. If his second-in-command had said a word, he might have shot him. No, he would have strangled him with his bare hands. That would have been more satisfying, even if he wasn't mad at Gerhardt.

He poured about half the whiskey he had downed the first time into his glass. Gerhardt still had most of his portion. And why not? He didn't carry the burden of laying tracks through the burning West Texas desert. The only parts worse were the mountains. All Gerhardt had to do was follow orders.

It was Reed's neck that was always on the chopping block. The railroad officers asked for the impossible and expected him to do it. He got paid well, but one day he'd mouth off and be fired. Or some vice president's son-in-law would need a job and Reed would find himself given the boot. Or—

He took another jolt of the whiskey. There were too many ways for him to lose his job through no fault of his own. When he'd started on this southern route, he had warned himself not to dwell on such things and only deal with problems confronting him. Like the one now giving him such a headache.

"The vice president is threatening to come out and personally cut off my sweetmeats if I don't speed up."

"We're doin' good, real good. Nobody in a fancy San Francisco office can do better."

"You know that. I know that. Every last damned soul out there laying down rails and driving spikes knows that. If he hadn't offered me that big bonus, I'd call his bluff." Reed took another stiff drink. Warmth spread throughout his body and calmed him. "Only it's not a bluff. He did that very thing to a supervisor on the line over the Sierras."

"I heard about that. I thought it was just a tall tale." Gerhardt finished his drink in a powerful gulp and looked uneasy. "I like workin' for you, boss. You quit, so will I."

"You'd be in line for my job and the thousand-dollar bonus. That's what they offered me to drive the line to San Antone by the end of the year."

"I heard tell they wanted a spur line off to Eagle Pass."

"That's something they decided on after I signed the contract." Reed looked at the two fingers of whiskey remaining in the bottle. Better save it for some other time. He wasn't sure he could even stand after drinking so much so fast.

"What are you gonna do?"

Reed looked at his foreman and thought on the matter. A crooked smile came to his lips.

"I can lash them all day long, but the Irish are so pigheaded they'll either stop working or revolt and come for my head. I need to find another way to make them work harder."

"I tried 'bout everything."

"No, Gerhardt, you haven't. I haven't. What would get them driving steel faster?"

"Booze. Ladies for rent."

"Not much of either since we're still ten miles outside Osborne. It'll be hell when we get close enough for them to sneak off at night."

"Too bad they're not like the Chinese. Give 'em a bowl of rice and a cup of water and they'll work forever. That and their opium."

"If they're all offered all the beef they can eat, do you think that'd spur them on?"

"I reckon so, but where are you gonna get even one cow?"

"That rancher in town runs a herd. He can spare a few head for a good cause."

"Where're you gettin' the money to pay him, boss? The money train's not due for another week."

Reed knew that. The payroll came every other week on a train from El Paso, along with new rails and ties. But the telegraph chattered endlessly, without stopping. The messages from the home office were almost more than he could tolerate.

"The Murphy brothers want more than money. And this is about the time to give it to them." Reed heaved to his feet. His step was surprisingly steady considering all the whiskey he had poured down his gullet.

"To what do I owe you coming into town during daylight hours?" Thomas Murphy asked, laughing.

"This is my foreman," Al Reed said, jerking his thumb over his shoulder at Gerhardt. "I decided he needed to look the place over since we're only a few days out from reaching the outskirts."

"Come on into the saloon. I'll stand you both a drink."

Reed licked his lips. The taste of liquor from back in his Pullman car lingered. Somehow its effects had left him like a fickle lady friend with a new beau.

"Only one drink. We need to get right-of-way matters straightened out."

"For the water tower," Murphy said. He ushered them to his table at the corner of the saloon and motioned for the bartender to bring a bottle.

Reed gave the floozy a quick look. He had seen others like her in too many towns where the railroad had built through. A quick elbow to Gerhardt's gut brought his attention back to business. He pointed to a chair beside Murphy for his foreman, while he took the one opposite.

He held his tongue until the bartender had poured their drinks and left.

"Bring in your survey crew whenever you want. If you need help, the county land agent's got equipment and a surveyor. He's only an apprentice but if you're shorthanded . . ."

"The county surveyor's name is Rendell. He's the one I told you 'bout, boss, the one who missed the property lines by close to a quarter mile." Gerhardt ran his finger around the rim of the shot glass. It squeaked. He jumped as if he had burned himself and fell silent.

"My foreman's right, isn't he? When you say 'apprentice,' you really mean he doesn't know what he's doing." Reed considered how far he could push Murphy before he made his real offer.

"It wasn't that much. Rendell was off a bit. A few yards, nothing like three hundred yards. And he is a state senator's son-in-law." From his defensive tone, Murphy might as well have confessed it all.

"We've got our own men for this. Have you figured out where you want the depot?"

Murphy perked up.

"Depot? So the Union Pacific has decided to make our fair town a permanent stopover?"

"Why not? If we take on water here, we might as well take on passengers and freight."

"And cows," Gerhardt added. "You got a whole danged prairie full of meat on the hoof. 'Less I miss my guess, it's all waitin' to be shipped to markets."

"A prairie full of beeves," mused Murphy. He shook his head, then grinned. "That's an exaggeration, but being able to load our herds would save us the drive all the way to Houston. Or northeast to Abilene."

"The line will connect to the transcontinental line that runs through New Mexico," Reed assured him. "Shipping your cattle will be far cheaper than driving them. You can sell them to slaughterhouses in Chicago as easy as to the West Coast or Houston."

Thomas Murphy rubbed his hands together and grinned ear to ear.

"The town government, such as it is, wants all kinds of concessions from the railroad. The depot alone will be perfect for our needs."

Reed tried not to laugh. Murphy had just negotiated away the town's position, wanting subsidies and land and preferential shipping rates in return for the water and tower. All he needed to do now was add one small item. Just a tiny one.

"Our lawyers have drawn up the papers. There won't be any problem getting your mayor to sign them?"

"The mayor," Murphy replied, scoffing. "He's a joke."

"He might be a joke, but the boys in the home office like to keep things official. Elected mayors have fancy gold seals to put on official documents."

"I can sign any papers . . ." Murphy's resolve faded just a bit. Reed looked grim. After a few seconds of silence, Murphy relented.

"He'll sign. Oh, yes, Mayor Galveston will sign whatever you want. Even if I have to stick the pen in his hand and move it around to scratch out his signature, you'll get the contracts signed."

"I'm glad that's settled. We need to know about where to put the depot right now and—"

"Boss, this is fine, coming to an agreement and all, but we should celebrate." Gerhardt looked pleased with himself. He had spoken up at precisely the right moment with words Reed had drilled into his head.

"My foreman is right, Mister Murphy. Your town can

celebrate, but it's not possible to bring my crew in to join them. Not yet."

"I can send a case of whiskey out to your construction," Murphy said.

"It's not such a good idea, boss. Not yet with that kind of celebration," Gerhardt said. Again, he played his part to perfection. Murphy looked concerned.

"Well, then, what can the town do to help with your crew's celebration of our mutual understanding?"

"A couple head of cattle would go a long way. We can have one of them Texas wing-dings I heard about all the way out in California." Gerhardt chewed at his lower lip, going over what he'd been told to say. He'd said his piece, and the boss picked up where he'd left off.

"Barbecue, you call it," Reed said. "But two head? That's not enough for my entire crew. No, make it five. That's even better."

"Five head of cattle?" Murphy licked his lips. "That's a considerable number of valuable beeves. You can't expect the Double Cross ranch to just give them to the railroad crew, now can you?"

"Of course not. And I can't expect the town of Osborne to do it," Reed said, choosing his words carefully. "Perhaps another town will. Marfa's not too far away, and I heard tell they have plenty of water to spare for our locomotives."

"But, but—" Thomas Murphy sputtered.

"The town of Murphyville." Reed whispered the words, but Murphy heard them plainly.

"Murphyville?" The rancher understood then what was being offered. Reed had denied the Murphy brothers the naming rights before. Now an officially sanctioned name change was on the table.

Reed shot to his feet and lifted his glass in toast.

"To Murphyville!"

Gerhardt echoed the toast.

Then Thomas Murphy and the handful of customers in the saloon joined in.

Reed kept from laughing out loud. For a worthless name change, he had bartered for enough cattle to feed his entire crew and a tower tank with water in it for thirsty Union Pacific Railroad steam engines. He wished all his problems were so easily and cheaply solved.

CHAPTER 8

"Where are you off to?" Daniel Murphy asked his brother.

Thomas looked around to be sure they were out of anyone else's earshot, then stepped closer and whispered, "I'm off to get what we deserve from this town."

"What's that mean? You're not up to something I should know about?"

"Brother, you'll thank me after I finish this little chore."

Daniel looked past his brother when Ben Wanamaker and four strangers rode up.

"You got the whole crew in town? You're not going to get them liquored up now, are you? Wanamaker is one mean drunk. Remember what he did last month to that new girl in the cribs. The cute one." He made a face as if he had bitten into a green persimmon. "The one what used to be cute, I mean. He's a mean one, drunk or sober. You should never have hired him to be foreman."

"You agreed. Now get yourself on into the saloon or go on back to the ranch. This doesn't concern you."

"I got the feeling it does. Let me ride along with you." Daniel started to push past, but Thomas pressed his palm hard into the middle of his chest.

"You got work to do to get us ready to welcome the

railroad when it comes through. They're about ready to find land for the depot."

"They've agreed to put a station here?" Daniel had to hand it to his brother. Thomas got things done, come hell or high water. "That's good news, but what've they got to do with it?" Again, he stared hard at Wanamaker. His foreman sneered back and made a big deal out of hocking out a gob. Wanamaker was dripping in contempt for his bosses—or one of them. Daniel wasn't much inclined to argue the point, even if he was the one calling the shots.

"They're putting in a depot but not in Osborne."

"No! They got to put one here. We worked for that. Even if they—"

"Don't get your dander up, Daniel. I've got it all worked out. You'll like it when they come to town, I guarantee it. Now skedaddle. Go on. Vamoose."

Thomas saw how his brother hesitated, then, as if against his better judgment, go to the saloon. He glanced back before disappearing through the swinging doors.

"How come you didn't invite him along for this nocturnal roundup?" Wanamaker spat again and laughed. "We can use another hand."

"He's got other work to do. Ranch work. This little excursion is for the sake of the town. My brother's got no call to know what we're doing." Thomas Murphy stepped up into the saddle and patted the lariat looped at his right knee. "Let's go find ourselves some prime beef."

"That's what I like to hear." Wanamaker signaled the four men with him.

"Who're they? I don't recognize any of them." Thomas's quick gaze shifted from one to the next. Strangers. All strangers.

"New hands. I hired them this afternoon."

"Is that smart? This isn't exactly a normal roundup."

"Call it for what it is, Mister Murphy. It's six gents goin' out to rustle cattle."

"We only need five head. We'll outnumber the beeves."

"How much experience do you have in a trail drive, Mister Murphy?" Wanamaker spat. The gob caught the early evening breeze and curved around, barely missing his boss.

"Not that much. Well, none, but I oversee the herd when it's grazing on our pastureland. It only takes a couple cowboys to go after strays. The cattle bunch up and don't go wandering off that much. They like to stay close to a watering hole."

"Shows what you know. I brung along the right number for this job."

"Lookouts? Scouts to make sure the Hammersmiths don't spot us?" Thomas swallowed hard. For the first time, what he'd agreed to settled down into his gut and tumbled around. "I don't care for any of them, but there's not going to be any gunplay. We take their cattle. If it looks like trouble, we hightail it. Do you understand?"

"I hear what you're sayin'," Wanamaker said. "Look, Mister Murphy, I been workin' for the Double Cross for the better part of six months. I know what you and your brother want to do in Osborne. That mayor's a thorn in your paw, all the time nay-sayin' you. This deal you worked with the railroad is bound to get you in good with the citizens." Wanamaker paused, then added, "How come you lied to your brother about the railroader agreein' to build a depot here?"

"He can't spill what he doesn't know. Let him be surprised when I announce the depot to everyone in town." Thomas made a dismissive gesture. "As to the mayor and those fools he calls a town council, I've never paid a whole lot of attention to them," he admitted. "They lack vision."

"Not like you, boss. Not at all like you." Wanamaker

switched his horse and raced ahead. Thomas Murphy hesitated, then his resolve hardened. He'd put Osborne—Murphyville!—on the map. They'd sit up and take notice down in Austin. After all, they had granted all the land in the XIT in exchange for construction.

Once Murphyville established itself as a prominent railroad depot, he knew a similar deal could be worked. All it took was getting noticed by the politicians. The Double Cross could double in size overnight once he and Daniel controlled the rail traffic into San Antonio. A few judicious slowdowns or sweetheart deals with southern politicians and the name of Murphy would be on every lip.

The XIT land deal would look like a piker after he dealt with the Union Pacific Railroad.

"That's all Hammersmith land," Thomas Murphy said. "Bullet Butte is smack dab in the middle of their pastureland."

"They got most of their cattle east of here since the land's turned so dry," Wanamaker said. "That works in our favor when we find part of their herd. They're not likely to have a night watch on a few hundred cattle."

"We only need five," Murphy said. He peered into the darkness. The stars that usually lit up the landscape were hidden behind high clouds. The half-moon wasn't due to rise for another hour or two. Blundering around wasn't going to get them anywhere. All he wanted was to take the five head and get the hell off the Twin M property.

"Pete's signalin'," Wanamaker said, pointing.

Murphy made out the silhouette of a man waving his hat back and forth.

"He found their cattle," Wanamaker said. He laughed

harshly and corrected himself. "Pete found *our* new cattle. We don't even have to run the brand."

"You know how to do that?"

"I'm a man of many skills, Mister Murphy." With a loud yee-haw, he galloped off.

Murphy followed more slowly, worrying about his horse stepping into a prairie dog hole and breaking a leg. When he fell far back, he threw caution to the winds and set out at a gallop. If Wanamaker wasn't afraid of losing his horse, there wasn't any reason for him to be, either. After all, he was the foreman's boss.

Cresting the rise, he drew rein beside Pete Peterson and Wanamaker. The two spoke rapidly, with much pointing and guffawing.

"What is it? What's he found?"

"We done hit the mother lode, Mister Murphy. Pete says there's a herd of fifty head grazing all peaceful-like as only a cow can."

"There ain't even a bull to be seen. A couple steers, maybe, but mostly heifers and their mamas. They all got polled horns, so we won't get gored if we get too close." Peterson stood in the stirrups and let out a loud shout.

"Quiet, man," Murphy cautioned. "You'll have the entire Hammersmith bunkhouse down on us."

"Not out here. They ain't got more'n three or four hands plus the family," Pete said. "Heard they'd loaned their punchers out for a week or two so's to save on salaries."

"And one of the family's in town getting hisself all drunk as a lord." Wanamaker spoke with some glee.

"Gustav Hammersmith has been a regular customer, but I haven't spoken with him," Murphy said. "He's all broken up over his pa vanishing the way he did."

"That's one less squarehead to deal with. Mason shoulda

vanished sooner." Wanamaker called to the rest of the hands as they arrived from different directions.

Murphy looked back over his shoulder. A chill went through him. They were ready to steal another ranchers' cattle. His resolve hardened when he thought of Hammersmith opposing him at every turn. The man deserved to help feed Murphy ambitions in town. His ranch would dry up and blow away without the water he bought from the Double Cross. When the railroad finished its railhead in Murphyville and the construction crew moved on, the Murphy brothers would see to driving out the Hammersmiths. That'd more than double the size of a better ranch, a ranch with plenty of water.

"You stayin' here or comin' with us to join in the fun, boss?" Wanamaker reached over and poked him. "If it offends your sensibilities, me and the boys can get the cattle back to the Double Cross without you."

"I'm coming," he said. He spurred his horse and galloped off in the direction the cowboy had indicated where the Twin M herd grazed.

As he rode, the wind cutting at his face and the partly starlit land flowing past, he felt invincible. What he did for the town was right. He'd show them all that the Murphy brothers weren't carpetbaggers coming into a town that would have vanished without them. A quick glance to either side showed Wanamaker on one flank keeping pace and Peterson on the other, gaining.

Murphy tried to get more speed from his horse, but it wasn't in the animal. Then they burst out of the ravine they rode through and onto a flat stretch where he slowed to let the horse catch its breath. Cattle lowed. He heard movement as they disturbed the beeves' sleep.

"Two that way, two get around to the far side," Wanamaker called. "We got ourselves a bonanza here."

"Must be fifty, at least," Pete called.

"That doesn't matter," Murphy pointed out. "We need five."

"Five, fifty, what's the difference? If we're caught with even one, they'll string us up as rustlers. We might as well run off as many as we can."

"But . . ." Murphy sputtered, but no argument came to his lips. Wanamaker was right. Why not hurt Hammersmith and take all the cattle? He deserved it, with his complaints. If he'd agreed to sell this parcel of land, the section with Bullet Butte smack in the middle, there wouldn't be any call to help him out. Hammersmith had caused his own problems.

Taking the cattle was a boon. They wouldn't die of thirst, not with the flood of pure, clean water pumped up from the Murphy well.

He watched as the four men with Wanamaker worked the herd expertly, yelling and snapping their lariats against bovine flanks to get the cattle moving. Amid the protests, Peterson shouted, "Forty-four. We got forty-four."

"A good night's work," Wanamaker said. He turned to look at his boss.

"You're right. A darned good night's work." Murphy turned his horse to lead the small herd off the MM ranchland. As he did, he felt a sting on his cheek. He reached up and rubbed the spot. His fingers came away wet with blood that looked like ink in the darkness.

"What?" He jerked around as another bullet whizzed past his head. It tore through the brim of his hat. Only the chin string kept it from flying into the night.

"Somebody's shootin' at us, boss!" Wanamaker turned in a complete circle. He had his six-gun out but failed to find a target. Then he yelled, "To the east. I saw a muzzle flash!"

His men began firing wildly. The night lit up with foot-long orange and yellow lances from his men's six-shooters. He reached for his own gun but thought the range was too great. Whoever shot at them used a rifle. The report was deeper, more powerful.

Another slug spooked his horse. Murphy fought to control the crow-hopping animal.

"Get what you can and let's ride!" Wanamaker emptied his pistol, reloaded, and kept firing.

"Can't take 'em all, Ben." Peterson rode to a spot between Murphy and the foreman.

"Drive off what you can," Murphy said. "There's no telling how many shooters we're facing."

"One. Just one," Wanamaker said. "We can—" He grunted as a slug caught him in the shoulder. He wobbled about and would have tumbled off his horse if Peterson hadn't reached out to support him. His weight carried both of them to the ground in a pile.

Wanamaker's horse reared and ran off. More rifle fire drove the animal's fright.

"Sling him over the saddle in front of me," Murphy said. "Then get out of here. All of you."

"We got a few head," reported another cowboy.

"Race the devil!" Murphy called. Peterson grunted as he heaved the foreman over the saddle in front of Murphy. His chore done, Peterson jumped up into the saddle and raced off.

Murphy clung to his feebly kicking foreman and put an arroyo's rim between him and the gunfire that was still making life dangerous. Taking his own advice, he followed the dry gully until he had a chance to scramble up the bank.

Peterson had cut out ten head and stampeded them. The others helped him, occasionally shooting back in the direction of what remained of the Hammersmith cattle they had failed to steal.

Thomas was never happier than when he got back onto his own property. And Ben Wanamaker was never angrier at having left behind so many cattle unrustled.

CHAPTER 9

Marsh Hammersmith gripped his rifle tighter as he tracked by the wan light from the rising half-moon. The spots on the ground were black, but even the thirsty ground hadn't had a chance to completely swallow the blotches. On one knee, he ran his finger through the largest puddle and sniffed. The coppery tang was as he feared.

Blood. And the only one who might have spilled it was his son.

He stood and began walking. He tracked the blood the best he could. Then the trail vanished entirely. He looked around, expecting to find George's corpse. Nothing. It was as if he had simply vanished. Marsh looked skyward, knowing he wouldn't see his son fluttering above on angel's wings as he ascended into heaven, but there was hardly any other explanation for how a wounded man just . . . disappeared.

He whistled. Derby trotted over. He stepped up and used the added height to scour the eerily lit land. In the distance rose Bullet Butte, looking even more like an upended cartridge at night than it did in the day. The lead "bullet" perched on the smooth, cylindrical upjut of rock caught the moonlight and turned it into an exact replica of a slug. Seeing it made him shudder.

The small herd of cattle milled about nervously. He circled them, soothed them, sang an off-key rendition of "Lorena," but the cattle didn't care that he couldn't carry a tune in a bucket. His presence was all that mattered. They quieted down and soon were asleep.

He envied them. They didn't worry about anything but eating, sleeping, and whatever momentarily frightened them.

His own fear rose higher. George had come out to watch over the cattle. The gunfire Marsh had heard on his way out to join his son in riding night herd had been fierce and prolonged. Most of the reports sounded like they had come from handguns, but one rifle had kept up a steady fusillade. That had to have been George.

As he rode, he spotted moonlight reflecting off metallic cartridges. He saw a spot where a dozen or more spent brasses were scattered around. George had used this as his post to fire toward the herd.

"Rustlers," he decided. "George took them all on."

He had no idea how many head should be in this small cluster of Twin M cattle. The rustlers might have made off with a hundred or none. Marsh would gladly have traded the entire herd for a glimpse of his son, unharmed and spitting fire because of the cattle thieves.

Finding the spots where the fresh blood trail had vanished and the sniper's nest, he laid a line between the two and started riding. Within a few minutes, it occurred to him that he was heading back to the ranch house. Marsh gave Derby his head and cantered along. He kept as sharp a lookout as possible, but he was still taken by surprise when a wordless cry echoed along an arroyo.

Derby reared. Marsh turned the horse into the ravine where a dark figure stood. A long shadow came toward Marsh because the moon was still low in the sky. He reached for his six-gun when he made out details of the hidden figure.

An Indian brave.

"He is wounded," came the low voice. "Take him to your medicine man."

"Night Wolf? Is that you?"

The figure faded into the shadows like the Lipan's namesake. By the time Marsh reached the spot where the Apache had stood, he was long gone. But a low moan caught his attention. He jumped to the sandy arroyo floor and ran to the steep bank where George sat propped up.

"Pa, he brought me here. An Indian. He wasn't a Comanche. Why?"

"Never mind that," Marsh said. "How badly hurt are you?" He quickly examined his son.

"How bad is it, Pa?"

"I've got some good news and some bad news. The bad news is you've got two bullet wounds, but the good news is that you get to ride Derby."

This brought a guarded chuckle to his son's lips. George had always liked riding and had asked repeatedly to ride the stallion when he was younger. It had always been denied him because a youngster would have trouble controlling such a spirited mount. Over the years, George had broken his own horses and settled on a strong mare. Riding Derby had never been considered after that.

Marsh hoisted his son into the saddle. George clung to the saddle horn and wobbled about but hung onto consciousness all the way back to the house. When Marsh helped George down, the ordeal finally proved too much. George passed out.

He caught his son up under the armpits and made his way up the steps to the front porch. There were only four steps, but each might as well have been as tall as Guadalupe Peak. Before he could worry open the door, Leonore yanked it open. She gasped, then cursed. Marsh wasn't sure the last time he'd ever heard her swear.

"Get him inside, Marshal. There's no way I can work on him out here." Leonore herded the two of them as if they were nothing more than balky calves.

George dropped onto the sofa with a gusty sigh. That small sound brought the other women in the house running. Consuela pushed her mother-in-law aside, but Heidi quickly came and proved herself the most practical, bringing bandages. Leonore barked out orders and got everything organized to fix her son's wounds, with Consuela doing most of the work on her husband. Heidi handed over bandages and needle and thread as needed, a silent, observant nurse.

"Looks like we're not needed, son." Caleb put his arm around Marsh and steered him back onto the porch. He silently pointed to a pair of chairs pulled together at the far end where they could look out over the expanse of the Twin M ranch.

Marsh sank down onto the hard, straight-backed chair. It felt as soft under him as if it had fluffy pillows. He hadn't realized how tense he had been bringing George home. Relaxing made his body conform to the chair as if it had been carved specially for him.

"Here. You look like you can use a nip."

Marsh's eyebrows rose. His father offered him a small silver flask.

"How'd you sneak that past Leonore? You know she doesn't cotton to liquor in the house."

"When you're as old as I am, son, you learn ways. Go on. Just don't take it all. I can use a drop to wet my whistle, too."

Marsh popped out the cork and sampled. It was surprisingly good whiskey. He had thought his pa would have swilled the cheapest rotgut he could find. He took another pull, then handed it back. Caleb wasn't as tentative about the way he drank. He smacked his lips, then tucked the flask back into the pocket of his coat.

"I suspect George tangled with rustlers. You, too?"

"I don't know how many head they drove off. George knows. He was the one who opened fire on them, so he saw 'bout every instant of the theft."

"He's a clever boy, your George. Sometimes, though, he don't think. He took on the whole gang, didn't he?"

"Gang? It might have been that Comanche war party coming after our stock again."

"Indians?" Caleb shook his head slowly. His bald pate caught the moonlight and made it look as if he wore a halo. Marsh knew that was about as far from the truth as possible. His pa was anything but angelic.

"You don't think so?"

"I heard the gunfire. A rifle. That was George openin' up on them varmints. The return fire was all teeny little pops. Handguns. At this distance, even with a still night, they was obviously not anything heavier."

"The Comanches didn't have any pistols. Just rifles and bows and arrows." He touched the spot at his waist and found a deep gash in his gun belt. "And knives. They all carried knives."

"'Course they did. They can sneak up on you in the dark and cut your throat 'fore you know it. They're sneaky like that. Or they shoot you from way off with a rifle or arrow. That's what they do. These rustlers had six-shooters."

"There must be a gang moving into the area, then. Just what I need. Osborne needs to hire a lawman. A sheriff would be nice to be able to go after rustlers."

"Or Texas Rangers," Caleb said. "Though it'd take more than stealin' a few head of cattle to get that lazy bunch motivated. They got it too soft in them barracks, if you ask me. It was never like that before."

Marsh closed his eyes and let the whiskey's warmth

spread from his belly through his body. His fingers had been tingling when he carried George into the house. Now they felt as if he had dipped them in warm water. He liked the sensation. Finding out how his pa snuck the whiskey past Leonore became more important. He could use some of this pain-killing, soul-soothing elixir more often.

"There's no rovin' gang come to prey on our cows," Caleb said after a long pause.

"So? Who is it? I don't see any reason for Daniel or Thomas to steal our cattle. They don't run that many head."

"They make all their money sellin' water that don't belong to them."

"They drilled for it on their own land and pump it up with a windmill they built."

"Water's God's gift to this parched land, not something those two Murphy scallywags should profit on by selling."

"My point is different, Pa. If they wanted our ranch, they'd cut off the water. We couldn't survive a season."

"Might be that's longer'n they want to wait. Daniel's always nosin' around, makin' insultin' offers to buy other ranches."

Marsh couldn't dispute that, but Daniel Murphy was inept and sometimes downright insulting, almost as if he wanted to be rejected.

"They're arrogant, that's what they are. Think they're better'n the rest of us and don't know their ways rankle." Caleb took out the flask again and ran his fingers up and down on the silvered side. A quick look over his shoulder assured him his daughter-in-law still busied herself patching up George. He took another sip, then upended the flask to show not a drop remained. He shrugged as Marsh watched.

The first two sips had done their work. Marsh wouldn't have turned down another drink but wasn't in need of more. Too much and a man became dependent on the feel. He had seen it happen too many times, sometimes to otherwise good, decent men he'd hired to ride for him. One man of the trio he'd kept on after the summer branding seemed to be in his cups all the time, but he had seen men act like that who were teetotalers. It was just their way.

"The two of them spend more time in town than on the Double Cross," Marsh said. "One of these days, a Murphy will be mayor. It won't be pretty watching what he does to the town."

"Gally is all puffed up with his own importance," Caleb said. "Yankin' the title of mayor from that man's gonna take a team of mules all pullin' together."

Marsh smiled. His pa and Frank Galveston were paper and match. Every time they saw each other, a blaze erupted. As far as he knew, they didn't have a single sore point to keep the feud going. They just took an intense dislike to one another.

"You should run against him, Pa. You'd make things real interesting in Osborne if you were the mayor."

"I can't stand a single one of them city councillors, they call theyselves. Councillors. Bah."

"So, if it's not Indians and there's no reason for the Murphys to steal our cattle, who's doing it?" Marsh worried that Night Wolf and his Apaches were responsible, but that didn't make a lick of sense. The same arguments about using six-guns applied to the Lipans as well as the Comanches.

And Marsh couldn't deny that Night Wolf had saved George's life. If the Lipans were the cattle rustlers and had shot it out with George, why would one of the braves do all he could to save his life? Marsh wasn't sure how much goodwill he had built saving Night Wolf, but he doubted it extended to not stealing cattle. Too much of Apache culture was wrapped up in heroic gestures.

If anything, Night Wolf would have taken George's

scalp since the boy was in such bad shape. A foe fallen in battle would never be saved unless it was for torture, like the Comanches had done to Night Wolf.

"It's them railroaders. They're the ones stealin' our cows," Caleb said forcefully. "Who else can it be?"

"Not Frank Galveston, that's for certain sure," Marsh said, laughing. The notion of Gally bestirring himself from behind his wide cherrywood desk to do anything more than go to Ella's Diner to beg a free meal was unthinkable. Since becoming mayor, Gally had put on fifty pounds. With his girth, it'd take two horses to even ride out onto the Twin M where the cattle had grazed.

"I'm not joshin', son. Think about it. You didn't have troubles like this until them railroaders come sniffing closer and closer to town. I've seen it a hundred times before. They're crooks, the lot of them. And this crew's got Irishmen *and* Chinese. That tells you everything you need to know."

"Feeding that lot has to be hard. I've heard folks in town complain that the railroad won't buy local supplies. Everything's brought in from El Paso every other week by the track they're laying."

"Mark my words, Marshal, them iron horse thieves are responsible."

"It makes sense, but there's no way you can be positive."

"I rode with enough gangs of rustlers in my day to know. What they done tonight's got all the earmarks of a rough and tumble bunch."

Marsh had argued with his father about making such claims before. Caleb insisted that he had ridden with every notorious outlaw band in Texas and a half dozen nearby states and territories. If it made the old man feel important, Marsh was willing to put up with it. As long as he didn't go spouting off in front of a real lawman, it was harmless enough, like spinning a tall tale around the campfire while on the trail.

Such boasting, though, didn't take away from the chance that he was right about the Union Pacific being responsible for the night's rustling. When George was able to talk, then was the time to find out what really had happened and think on what to do.

Caleb Hammersmith groaned as he stood and wobbled on his way to return inside. He paused at the door, balancing himself with a hand against the frame.

"Remember what I said, son. Railroaders. Them's the varmints you want. Ain't never been a railroader who wasn't as crooked as a dog's hind leg."

Marsh watched his pa go inside. He turned and looked out over the haunting silver-moonlit ranchland. West Texas was a cruel place, demanding, unforgiving. And this patch of it was all his.

"Railroaders," he said softly. Then he followed Caleb. He had earned himself a good night's sleep in a feather bed with Leonore beside him.

CHAPTER 10

Marshal Hammersmith sat in the chair at the end of the porch, staring across his property. He sipped at the drink in hand, wishing it were some of the firewater his pa had given him three nights before. All he got now was sarsaparilla his wife had bought in town. It quenched the thirst, at least in his mouth. It failed to give him the lift that the whiskey had.

And all the aches and pains remained. If a dose of tarantula juice wasn't available to chase them away, maybe some of the liniment he used on Derby's sore legs would do. Maybe.

Focusing on the distant, purpled horizon made him worry about everything happening on his property that lay just beyond his gaze. A noise behind him caused him to react. His hand went to the Peacemaker at his side. He relaxed when his son shuffled out of the house and collapsed into the chair next to him.

"You can't see 'em from here, Pa."

"Who's that?" he said, although he knew exactly who George meant. Rustlers.

"I'll be right as rain in a couple days. We can get back out and watch over the cattle as they graze." George moaned as he stretched out his long legs and leaned back in the chair. He sounded as if he felt every twinge like his father.

Marsh knew his son was too young to share those twinges, yet he did.

"I should send out the wranglers. Let them stand guard. They haven't got much to do around here now that the barn's been painted and the new corral's built." Marsh wasn't too confident any of the cowboys were up to such guard duty. They weren't gunfighters. They were shavers who had spent their short lives roping and branding and herding, not firing their six-shooters. A couple of them didn't even own six-guns and carried rifles he supplied.

"You know they've got their hands full doing real chores. The banks on the acequias need to be rebuilt. That fence out on the back forty doesn't mend itself and—"

"I know, I know," Marsh said, dejected. "At least you're sure it wasn't the Comanches we chased off before."

"That was a war party and we shamed them. They've put a hundred miles between us and them by now." George sounded sure of himself.

That made Marsh even more morose. Indians he understood. Where had the rustlers come from? And he doubted a single firefight drove them off.

"We showed them." He looked at George. His son seemed fine except for the way he sat a little too stiffly in the chair. One bullet had hit a rib. No bones broken but it left him sore. The second round that struck him had caused more damage. It had drilled into him while he was lying flat on the ground and had burrowed its way into the top of his shoulder. Again, no bones had been broken, but Consuela had fished around in the bullet track and pulled out two bits of white bone chipped from his collarbone. Moving his right arm had to be painful. He always winced as he moved it and more than once had blanched whiter than a muslin sheet.

It'd be longer than a day or two before George was even able to ride.

"The Indian that tried to bring me home. That was the one you saved from the war party, wasn't it?"

"His name's Night Wolf. I can't figure out his reason for saving you, but I owe him. So do you."

"Lipans, Comanches, they're all crisscrossing our property until I can't tell the difference."

"I haven't seen how many Apaches ride with Night Wolf, but they are likely a smaller band than the Comanche war party." Marsh grinned without humor. "At least the Comanches were more numerous until we whittled 'em down to size."

"Running, as I said. Like scalded dogs," George said. "But what about the Apaches?"

"I'm not going to track them down."

"What about the rustlers? I'm sure they were white men."

"Not Indians, not hungry soldiers from Fort Davis," Marsh said. "Who might they be?" He held back telling his son what Caleb had declared with such vehemence.

"Railroaders," Caleb had said. Marsh had thought hard and had to believe his pa knew what he was talking about. There was only one problem. He needed solid proof before he accused any of them.

"Excuse me, Pa. I'm feeling a mite tired." George climbed to his feet. He wobbled as he walked.

"You need help?"

"I can get Consuela to help me up the stairs to our bedroom. She likes to do what she can now that Joseph is feeling better. I swear, she ought to have been a nurse the way she enjoys taking care of the sick and wounded." Chuckling to himself, George went inside the house.

Marsh heard the steady click of his son's boots as he worked his way up the steps to the second floor bedrooms. He couldn't see his progress, but the sounds told him everything he needed to know. And that decided him.

"Proof. I don't have to see it, but the clues will be there in their camp." He got to his feet and went directly to the barn.

Derby was happy to see him since they hadn't been out for the last two days, but he wondered how excited the stallion would be when they sneaked into the railroad camp.

A few campfires with Chinese workers huddled around them to fend off the desert cold and lamps dangling along the side of the freight cars were the only lights Marsh saw. The majority of the workers had retired for the night. The triple-height sleeping cars would pour out a hundred or more men if he made too much noise.

Moving as quietly as he could, he skirted the campfires and walked the length of the train. A car behind the Pullman housed the cook and his supplies. Marsh took a deep whiff of the air.

"Beef," he said softly. That was a smell he recognized immediately. Long trail drives to Abilene, Kansas, had provided all the hands with more steak than they could eat. Many were sick of the single item in their diets, though Marsh never failed to dig in with a slab of meat on a platter in front of him.

He peered between ill-fitting slats and into the car but saw nothing. The aroma of beef proved nothing. There were a half dozen ranches in the area. The railroad might have bought a cow or two from any of them. Even though the Double Cross had only few cattle on its range, the Murphy brothers might have sold to the railroad. Or even given a head or two in exchange for some under-the-table deal.

Marsh crept to the end of the train. A locomotive huffed and puffed stoically, its boiler at minimum pressure. A turnaround had been built into the tracks there to reverse direction. The engine would steam away in a day or two, pulling empty freight and flat cars. In El Paso, new freight, ties, and steel rails would be loaded, and the train would return. With any luck, the engine had another few dozen miles to travel, though the end of the track was only a few miles from Osborne.

If gossip was right, the Union Pacific intended to build a depot there, alongside the water tower, and open the floodgates to prosperity such as West Texas had never seen.

He stopped and stayed quiet as a mouse when he heard movement in the locomotive cab. The fireman—Marsh thought of the youngster as a *Heizer*—tossed a few shovels of coal into the boiler. He kicked the door shut with his foot and settled back down. In no time, he snored as loudly as the hissing and popping in the furnace.

Marsh moved past, not sure what he hunted. He sought a pen with horses or other animals. Cows! But he came to the front of the locomotive and stared out into the cold night. Nothing he didn't expect to see in the desert met his eye. He stepped around the cowcatcher on the front of the train, then stumbled and went to one knee. His hand reached out for balance.

Breathing faster at what he felt, he moved until he got a good look at the cowhide stretched over the metal grating. He had spent much of his life curing animal hides. This was fresh. Someone had stretched out a hide on the cowcatcher to dry. He ran his hand over it until he found a part where the brand had been burned into the living animal.

A light touch sent his heart racing. He traced over the brand. To be sure, he took out a lucifer, struck it, and held it inches from the cowhide.

As plain as day, he saw the double M of the Twin M brand.

He yelped when the match burned his fingers. He got to his feet and held up the curing hide. This had been on one of the cows that were rustled a few nights back. And more than just being from a stolen cow, it was from one of *his* cows.

That angered him. He let out a roar of pure fury, knowing that someone in the railroad camp had stolen his cattle and, worse, had shot his son and almost killed him.

"If you move an inch, I'll blow you into the next county." The cold words made Marsh spin. "I got you covered with this here scattergun."

A man held a sawed-off shotgun in rock steady hands. At that range, he couldn't miss. The double-ought buck in that twelve-gauge would turn Marsh into bloody pulp.

"You stole my cattle," Marsh said, anger barely in check. "When you rustled the cattle, you almost killed my son."

"That's not your cow, mister. We was given it—the whole danged cow. Get your hands up!"

Marsh reached for his Peacemaker. Shotgun be damned! They had almost killed George!

"What's going on, Gerhardt? Who is this?"

"I don't know, sir. He was wavin' that cowhide around like a flag. When I told him to stop, he went for his six-shooter. I'm close to shootin' him right now if he doesn't stand down."

"He's just another sneak thief," Al Reed said. "Take his gun and boots and run him off. The same as we do all sneak thieves."

"You tried to kill my son. You stole my cattle. And you call *me* a sneak thief?" Marsh tossed the hide high into the air and dived to the side.

The shotgun blast ripped the hide to ribbons.

Marsh rolled twice and came to his knees. He grabbed for his six-gun and dragged it from the holster. One shot was all he got off before they swarmed him. Over and over they rolled. Marsh fired a couple more times, but both rounds dug their way into the sunbaked earth. When they stopped rolling, he was underneath the one who was the boss.

Reed held him down in a schoolboy pin. He bent low until his face was inches from Marsh's.

"You are making a big problem for me. There's no law in that godforsaken town to turn you over to."

"That's my brand on the hide. MM. I own the Twin M ranch. Come on. Let's go to town. I'll see that the townspeople string you up as a cattle thief!"

"Gerhardt, fetch O'Malley and Roarke. Now! Chop, chop!"

"Too much of them Chinese rubbed off on you, boss. You're speakin' their lingo."

"Get them."

Marsh tried to wiggle free, but as strong as he was, Reed was stronger and had the advantage of being on top. Marsh tried not to believe that the twenty years difference in their ages meant anything, but that was a disadvantage for him, too.

"You won't get away with rustling. We don't take kindly to that."

"I came by the five head honestly," Reed said.

"How? Are you saying you bought the cattle?"

"Nothing of the sort." Reed suddenly released Marsh by shifting his weight to one side.

The rancher surged up and found why the man had let him go. Hands strengthened by swinging a nine-pound sledge all day seized him. He didn't know which was Roarke and which was O'Malley. Each held one of his arms in a steely grip.

Then Gerhardt began working him over. Punch after punch landed in his breadbasket. Marsh tensed and robbed the first few blows of their full impact. Then he weakened.

By the time he wasn't able to put up any fight, Gerhardt was driving his fist into his gut all the way to the wrist.

Limp as a dishrag, Marsh hung between the two railroaders. In the far distance, over the roar in his ears, he heard their boss tell them to stop. But they didn't drop him. The two Irishmen dragged him, toes down and scraping through the dust, a ways along the track.

"Load him on, men."

Marsh crashed belly down onto a handcar. With one man on each side of the hand crank and the third holding him onto the car, they began to move slowly. The two men pumped the handle faster and faster until they sailed through the night. Steel wheels sparked against the rails. The smell of hot steel rose to choke him. Then he was flying through the air.

Marsh crashed into a cinder field along the tracks. His head hit a tie, causing him to recoil. As he did, he slid down an embankment. When he came to a halt at the bottom, he wondered what hurt more. His belly throbbed from the beating, but his head felt the size of a watermelon. The slide down the embankment had taken him through a patch of prickly pear cactus. Cinders had buried themselves under his skin.

He was a complete calamity. Marsh tried to sit up. Instead, he passed out.

CHAPTER 11

"If you don't want to ride, kin I sell your horse?"

Marshal Hammersmith stirred and instantly regretted it. His ears buzzed, and his body went beyond hurting. Along one side of his body, tiny pinpricks from dozens of prickly pear spines turned to venom. As he moved, he felt as if that part of his skin had swollen up and threatened to explode. He pushed himself to his hands and knees and shook all over like a dog. This didn't remove any of the cactus spines but did convince him nothing had been broken.

But his belly!

Even breathing shallowly was enough to push him around the bend.

"I'm not gonna get down and help you. These old bones ain't up to such punishment." A small chuckle. "Though it looks like the punishment you took's a ways beyond arthritis in the joints."

"Pa?" Marsh shook his head and regretted it. Things came loose inside. The buzzing sounded like a hive of bees. He turned his face up. All he saw was the silhouette of a man astride a horse. Reins dangled from his hand and went to another horse. "Derby?"

He received an answering whinny. This gave him strength

enough to come to his knees, then work his way to standing. When he coughed, he spat up blood.

"Terbaccy's better to spit. Stains the teeth, but it don't show how wrecked up inside you are. Can you ride, son?"

"What are you doing out here?" Marsh took a tentative step and fell forward. His fingers closed on his saddle horn. Using Derby to support himself, he finally stood erect.

"What do you think, you consarned fool? I knew you was gonna get yourself in a kettle of hot water."

"Feels like it came to a boil, with me still in the pot." Marsh stretched and began plucking spines from his left arm and side.

"Go on, strip off your coat and shirt. That's the quick way to pull out the thorns."

"Some of the tips have broke off in me."

"Getting rid of most is better than enduring the ride back. You know how cactus spines work their way in. They don't pop out, not unless you're in a bucket of ice."

Marsh slowly pulled off his coat and shirt. His pa was right. This careful disrobing yanked many of the spines free. He still knew where the tips that had broken off were. Each burned like the sun. With a quick snap, he waved his shirt and coat around.

"Don't think on putting them back on. Truth is, you should burn them."

"I'm cold."

"Put on your slicker. You got it in your saddlebags, don't you?"

"I don't remember," Marsh admitted. It had been so long since it'd rained, he might have decided to leave it and pack other gear. After poking around in his saddlebags for what seemed like an eternity due to the pain and the cold desert night air now causing him to shiver, he found the yellow slicker. He pulled it on. It effectively blocked the wind but rubbed every tender spot on his torso.

"Don't bother complainin', son. Just step on up and let's get out of here. Them railroaders ain't likely to check on you, not after leavin' you for dead, but stranger things have happened."

"You were right, Pa. I found a hide dangling on the front of the locomotive engine. Had the Twin M brand on it. They stole the cattle."

"Never knew a railroader I could trust. Steal your land, steal your cattle. Worse yet, they'll steal your woman. That happened to me over in Fort Worth."

Marsh wanted to use block and tackle to get into the saddle. He had to content himself with finally making it up on the third try. Wiggling about, he settled down. None of the prickly pear spines had found their way to his rear or inside his legs. That made riding easier—except that every bounce Derby made felt as if a railroad spike was being driven into his gut.

He lightly touched his stomach and winced. The bruise spread all over his belly and worked its way up to his sternum.

"Not that way, you fool. This way." Caleb Hammersmith trotted back and yanked the reins from his son's hands.

Marsh tried to hang on. His lack of strength betrayed him.

"I can ride."

"Stay in the saddle, maybe, but your wits are addled. Unless you want to ride on back into their bivouac, we need to circle wide around and let them dream their little dreams of beating a fine rancher nearly to death."

Caleb yanked hard on Derby's reins and brought the horse around to follow the mare he rode. Marsh mumbled that he understood and was able to guide his own horse. Caleb tossed him back the reins.

They rode in silence until the railroad camp was far

behind. Off to their right rose spirals of wood smoke from houses in Osborne. Soon enough those were left behind.

"That's Murphy's windmill," Caleb said. He spat toward it, then cursed a blue streak. "I'm gettin' so old I forget things, like never spit into the wind. That gob danged near curled back and hit me."

Marsh ignored his father's tirade. He stared at the windmill, limned against the starry night sky. The blades turned endlessly in the wind. He heard the distant gush of water coming up from twenty yards underground. There wasn't any hint that plenty of water wasn't being pumped.

"The Murphy brothers are selling the water to the railroad," Marsh said. "They're cutting back on what they give us and peddling it to the railroaders for the locomotive boiler and to keep their work crew from going thirsty."

"It's a long way to ship water if the Union Pacific has to ship it in. I've seen tank cars. Just like flat cars, only big metal tanks like the locomotive boilers with spouts."

"Buying the water from the Double Cross makes it cheaper to build the road."

"What makes you think they're payin' good money for the water?" Caleb asked. "Daniel and Thomas are such snakes they're likely tradin' the water for something they want more'n money."

"What's that?"

"Prestige. Fame. Admiration from the town. If they're the ones responsible for the depot gettin' itself built, then they can lay claim to bein' heroes. Who knows? The people are dumb enough to believe 'em."

"They've locked horns with Mayor Galveston more and more of late," Marsh said. "Getting him out of office would be easier if they claimed they brought prosperity to town because the railroad put in a stop."

"Getting him out of office would be easier if they used a

six-gun. I wouldn't put it past them Murphy boys to shoot a man in the back."

"I'm more interested in stopping the railroad from stealing my cattle."

"You ought to be more interested in not getting the snot knocked out of you. Another beating like you took'll put you six feet under. Your corpse'll be in such bad shape a coyote would puke dining on your brisket."

"Thanks for the show of confidence, Pa."

"There's the old homestead. You go on in and let me take care of them rustlers."

"What're you going to do?"

"What shoulda been done a month ago. We knew there was cows bein' stole from under our noses. Havin' you all whupped up on is the final straw."

"Pa . . ." That was all Marsh got out. He spat again. More blood. He felt all liquid inside. Every move seemed as if something went squish. Whatever his pa was up to, he was in no shape to stop him—or help him.

He slid from the saddle and used Derby as support again. He whipped the reins around a post and made his way up the steps. At the top, he had to rest. If he went in, Leonore would fuss over him like she had George. Only it'd be worse. He'd get a lecture about putting himself in a position to get beat up. Even when he had fought in a bare knuckles bout or two, he hadn't been in this bad a shape.

Marsh went to the end of the porch and settled into a chair. He found a position where nothing hurt. Not much. He closed his eyes and let the cold night surround him. That helped his bruises, and the soft sounds of the ranch soothed him.

Marsh snapped awake when he heard hoofbeats coming toward the ranch house. He reached out and caught at his Colt. The railroaders hadn't even bothered to pull his fangs.

Their contempt for him had to be enormous. If he'd had time he would have ended their days.

He slid the Peacemaker out and rested his thumb on the hammer. He'd get off the first shot, if it became necessary.

Four riders came into the yard. He rested his six-gun on the railing to steady his aim. There was no call to visit at this time of night. One called out, but the answer made him sit a little straighter.

"Smitty, that you?"

"Right here, Kingston. I see you brung the boys with you." This was definitely his pa's voice. Caleb Hammersmith knew the men who'd ridden up—and Marsh had no idea who they might be.

"I need all of them since you retired," Kingston said, laughing.

"Can't say you're wrong. I was the match for any three of you owlhoots."

The riders moved about, repositioning as Caleb greeted each of the other three by name. He shook hands and even had one complain that the old man's grip was too strong for his gun hand to endure.

"That's the trouble with you sissies these days," Caleb said. "You don't do any real work. I bet you ain't done nothing but ride the livelong day to get here."

"We came straightaway from Fort Worth," Kingston said.

"Livin' it up in Hell's Half Acre, were you? We got real trouble here on the Twin M, and you've been guzzlin' cheap whiskey and chasin' wild women."

"We've been chasing a band of renegade Comanches," Kingston said. "They slipped off the reservation and decided to cause trouble wherever they went."

"What's the bounty on an Indian these days?" Caleb spat. "That kinda work's beneath you boys."

"You want us to take over the rustling? We can do it. We got the skill, we got the guns. Who do you want us to hit?"

"Them railroaders got some of my stock. I don't much care how you get 'em back, but it might be as many as a dozen head."

"Depending on their appetites, a single railroader can eat a whole danged cow by his lonesome," another rider said. "There might not be much left but bones and horns."

"Have you been watchin' them varmints? The Union Pacific crew?" Caleb asked. "Of course you have. You don't like them any more'n I do."

"You're an old stick-in-the-mud, Smitty. Of course we like them putting tracks through West Texas. Think of all the gold they'll be shipping. The mail and passengers galore."

"You have to think about that, don't you, Kingston? Of course you do. That's what keeps you in business."

"How else could I afford the finer things in life? I got me a wife now."

"You mean church married and all?" Caleb asked. "I don't believe it. Where is she?"

"Fort Worth, maybe. Or Abilene. She moves around as much as I do. One step ahead of Ferd Larkins. That man's always annoying us."

"Larkins? He's a Ranger captain now?"

"The bane of our existence. Now tell us more about when the rustling happened." Kingston's voice trailed off as he, Caleb, and the rest walked their horses from the yard.

Marsh laid his six-shooter on the porch railing and rested his head beside it. He'd never believed the yarns his pa told about his wild younger days riding with outlaws and creating havoc throughout Texas and Indian Territory. Maybe he should have. These hard cases obviously knew him well.

And he knew them and how they dodged being caught by a Ranger captain.

He listened hard, trying to catch the slightest sounds, but the night had returned to normal. In the distance, a coyote howled and then fell silent. Not moving, having found a position where he wasn't in constant pain, Marsh closed his eyes and fell into a nightmare-filled sleep.

CHAPTER 12

"Stop wiggling around like a worm," Leonore Hammer-smith chided. "You need to rest."

"I need to get back to work. George is still healing up and the hands are probably out in some pasture, rolling smokes and not doing their work because there's nobody to supervise them." Marsh fumed. It had been four days since the beating, and he felt better. Moving gave him the twinges, but they were nothing he couldn't endure. It might be different if he tried riding, but he had to try.

"Doctor Ferguson says you need to stay in bed another week." Leonore fussed about, fluffing a pillow he didn't need and folding clean sheets to put back in the cedar chest.

"He fixed up baby Joseph with a potion. Why can't he give me something that'll get me on my feet right now?" Marsh tried not to show how stabs of pain almost made him gasp. The bruise on his belly had turned from black and violet to an unhealthy looking yellow. He had seen jaundice cases with better color.

"You don't have the croup. Why won't you tell me who beat you up so bad? I didn't smell liquor on your breath, so you didn't get into a barroom fight."

"It was a misunderstanding," he said. Accusing Al Reed and his crew of rustling would only open a different can of worms with his wife. She would demand that he contact the Texas Rangers. Without real proof, there wasn't much the Rangers could do. Getting them to write him off as a crank was the last thing he wanted. He had the feeling, deep down in his bruised and battered gut, that he'd need them soon enough.

"Those bruises show more than that. Whoever punched you meant it."

"Don't wanna be like the boy who cried wolf," he mumbled, eyelids drooping. He smiled just a little. That reminded him of Night Wolf. He should call on Night Wolf for help. Hadn't the Lipan Apache saved George?

His eyes closed entirely. Marsh forced himself to breathe slowly and evenly and not twitch when an errant pain jabbed into him. At least Leonore had pulled out all the prickly pear spines and used an ointment Consuela had whipped up to ease the swelling.

He listened as Leonore finished her housekeeping chores and softly walked across the room. Carefully lifting one eyelid, he looked out. The bedroom door was shut. Leonore had gone. He opened both eyes and pushed up to one elbow.

"So far, so good," he whispered. No pain—not much, compared with the way he'd felt the night Caleb had brought him back. He sat up and swung his bare feet around to the floor. A moment's dizziness passed. Stretching slowly, he mapped out the extent of his injuries.

He might still be healing inside, but his hide was in decent shape once more. Marsh got to his feet and padded to the wardrobe. He took longer dressing than usual, and pulling on his boots proved to be a chore, but he was ready for the range and ready to ride.

Making his way down the stairs, he kept a sharp lookout for any of his family. Caleb usually sat on the porch this time of day, smoking a quirrly, in spite of Leonore's antipathy to that vice. He wondered how she'd react if she knew her father-in-law also had a silver flask filled with decent whiskey

A drop of that tarantula juice would do him a world of good right now. But his pa wasn't anywhere to be seen.

That absence worried him. Caleb had been missing at dinner the night before and hadn't shown himself for breakfast. The former wasn't unusual, but Marsh wasn't sure his father had ever missed breakfast in his recollection. Something about eggs and bacon and biscuits, especially biscuits along with a dollop of gravy, pleased the old man more than about anything else.

Derby was glad to see Marsh, kicking at the side of the stall and rearing. He spent a few minutes calming the horse, then saddled and rode out slowly, careful to keep the barn between him and the house. It wouldn't do if Leonore spotted him. She'd be mad enough when she discovered he wasn't in bed sound asleep.

He wasn't sure where to start his hunt. Caleb was some-where on the expansive ranch, but Derby headed toward Bullet Butte, and Marsh wasn't going to deny the horse its head. The distinctive pile of rock appeared. Any herd there was small. He wondered if this was the part of his stock that Al Reed and his thieving railroaders had stolen. If it was, chances were good they'd try again. Riding halfway across the Twin M was risky. More than that, the rustlers had learned the lay of the land and knew how to use it to their advantage.

The sun dipped low behind Bullet Butte. It cast a long shadow as the wind kicked up. It was chilly, but some of the day's heat remained. Marsh rode closer to the butte and felt the heat pouring from it. The rock heated in the day and then slowly released it, at least for a few hours.

After another hour, the sun had set. Tonight the stars shined down so brightly it was almost like day. Clouds were few and far between. That suited Marsh now. He felt all tuckered out. In spite of riding all afternoon and never taking so much as a step on the arid land, he began nodding off in the saddle.

"Not up to full strength," he muttered to himself. "Should get a good night's sleep. Foolish to think I'd find rustlers. What'd I do if I did? What do you say, fella?" He patted Derby's neck.

For a moment he wondered at the stallion's reaction. The horse jerked away from his hand. Derby's ear pricked up and he turned his head. Then Marsh heard the thunder of hooves.

He caught his breath. Stampede! But none of the Twin M cattle were grazing in that direction.

He urged Derby to wheel around and walk in the direction of the distant noise. As he rounded the side of Bullet Butte, the sounds became clearer. Hooves, yes, but not cattle. Horses. Lots of them. He tapped Derby's flanks, and they galloped down into an arroyo. The hard-baked ravine bottom matched the main road into Osborne. He flew in the direction of the horses. Then he slowed.

Gunfire.

Lots of lead whined through the nighttime air. He looked up from the arroyo floor and saw the dark form of a rider cantering parallel to him. Marsh drew his pistol and cocked it, but his target vanished, going away from the gully.

He cursed under his breath and hunted for a break in the embankment. By the time he found it and he popped out, the rider had faded into the night. Marsh waited a moment, then saw the muzzle flashes off to his left. Rustlers might fire a round or two with the intent of stampeding a herd. But there weren't cattle there and an equal number of reports showed in the opposite direction. Who was out there? They were shooting it out and expending dozens of rounds.

Marsh heard a shot to his right, turned in the saddle, and took aim. His finger came back and then relaxed.

"Pa! What's going on? What are you doing out here?"

"I could ask you the same thing, Marshal." Caleb's stern voice carried more than a little disapproval.

Marsh swung a little more and fired. His father ducked and cursed a blue streak.

"What's got into you, boy? You're in terrible shape if you tried to kill your own flesh and blood."

"Behind you."

Caleb Hammersmith looked over his shoulder. On the ground, a man was sprawled on his back. His horse bolted and ran wildly into the darkness.

"You may be feelin' puny, son, but your eye's still good."

"What's going on?"

"Rustlers. We been waitin' for 'em for the past three nights. Finally found how they're ridin' onto our land."

"Who's 'we?'"

"Get yourself on back to the house 'fore you're laid up worse than you were. This ain't anywhere you ought to be."

"This is a gunfight!" Marsh wanted to scream at his father. "*You* don't have any call to be here."

"The ranch is mine as much as yours. You and Mason and me proved it. I've been lendin' a hand for all ten years of its existence. I've got every right to defend the land and the herd."

Marsh wanted to argue, but the middle of a gunfight wasn't the time or place.

"How do I recognize whoever's riding with you?"

"Stay behind me. Don't shoot at nobody. I can't take the time to educate you, boy." Caleb worked to reload his six-shooter.

Again, Marsh wanted to argue, but he saw his pa was right. He had come into this fight without knowing who was exchanging lead. From what he'd seen a few nights ago, anyone he might have shot then was likely to be a rustler. The difference was that his pa's friends were holding off the real rustlers. At least they were tonight. Tomorrow might be different.

"Smitty!" The clarion call came from some distance away. "We got 'em penned up. Get over here and help us."

"Is that Kingston?" asked Marsh. He wanted to show his father he wasn't entirely in the dark. Caleb never rose to the challenge.

"If he's askin' for help, he needs it. That man can take on an entire bunch of vigilantes and never blink an eye." Caleb slid his six-gun into its holster and set out at a dead gallop.

In the dark, such speed was dangerous. Besides prairie dog holes, the uneven plain provided more than enough chance for a horse to stumble. But Caleb showed no fear. Marsh patted Derby and whispered, "Go, old friend, go!"

The stallion exploded and raced after Caleb. Marsh over-took his pa within a minute. And ahead he saw four dark shapes spread out in a fan. They fired methodically, giving their partners a chance to advance while the other held off the rustlers.

"Reload." Kingston's sharp command sounded like a military man's. "Forward!"

Caleb joined the others and rode to the attack. They laid down a curtain of death, pushing the rustlers back. The men being herded so effectively were in complete disarray.

Marsh saw the sporadic return fire. Kingston and Caleb led the attack with the others trailing behind in a wedge for-mation. He was amazed at how they worked together so well—and how his pa fit in perfectly. It was as if they had drilled endlessly to develop such an effective assault.

"They'll get away down the acequia," Marsh warned. "Close on them now!"

Caleb's partners never twitched to obey. They listened

to Kingston and no one else. Marsh cut away and rode hard
to the irrigation ditch to cut off the rustlers' escape. He
crested the lip of the acequia as five riders passed below
him. Marsh hesitated. He didn't want to shoot at the men
riding with his father. Then he heard Kingston behind him.
A quick draw and the Peacemaker filled his grip. He fired,
but the shots went wild. All he succeeded in doing was
spurring on the riders.

They sloshed along the muddy bottom. Just when Marsh
steadied himself enough for an accurate shot, the hammer
fell on a spent cartridge. He shoved his pistol into its holster
and pulled out his rifle. Cocked and aimed . . . and no target.

The rustlers had vanished around a bend in the ditch. He
rode ahead a few yards, hunting for a good shot. The sound
of hoofbeats splashing in the shallow water slowly faded in
the distance. They had gotten away.

"You had a chance, son. You let 'em get clean away."
Caleb trotted up. His six-shooter still smoked from the rapid
firing.

"I got one back where we first crossed paths," Marsh said.
It sounded lame, but even one outlaw down redeemed him.

Kingston rode up and spoke quickly with Caleb. They
shook hands. Kingston rode away, leaving the Hammersmiths by themselves.

"You're not going to introduce me to your . . . friends?"

"How'd you know Kingston's name? Never mind. He
told me the one you shot wasn't dead. Not quite. He got to
his horse and hightailed it. We had the mangy cayuses, and
they all got away, thanks to you."

"All of them?" Marsh felt what elation he'd earned
drain. He was left dog-tired and ready to fall from the
saddle. Pushing so hard before he was fully healed had been
a mistake.

Worse, he had been responsible for letting the rustlers escape.

"Every last one skedaddled," Caleb said. "But they're a greedy lot, them railroaders. They'll try again. Next time, we'll catch 'em." He spat. "Naw, we won't catch 'em. We'll hang them from the highest tree. Every last spike-drivin', railroad-tie-layin' one of them."

Caleb shook his head and rode off slowly, mumbling to himself.

Marsh started to follow, then drew rein. Something bothered him. He turned and looked into the acequia where the riders had escaped. Less than two inches of water flowed sluggishly. During the night, this acequia ought to run almost full with water pumped from the Murphys' well.

Marsh remembered how George had told him the Murphys weren't living up to their agreement. He had confronted them, too, but it had been more a matter of pride, of finding something to argue over. But now?

Thomas and Daniel Murphy cheated him out of water already bought and paid for. Rustlers. Railroaders. Comanches. Now the owners of the Double Cross were living up to the name of their ranch. It all came crashing down on him.

CHAPTER 13

Marsh Hammersmith snapped awake. He reached for his six-gun and almost fell out of the chair. He had fallen asleep on the porch with some vague idea of keeping a lookout for rustlers. His belly ached, and that was an improvement over sharp, constant pain. Healing took a while, and worrying about his herd and everything else coming down on him like a torrential rain didn't help.

If it had rained like that, even if it flooded all the arroyos as it usually did, that would eliminate one problem. Water. Murphy selling them water, then stealing it to give away to the Union Pacific for their filthy locomotives. It had to be diverted to the railroad, though Marsh hadn't been able to find Murphy and demand an accounting.

"Yee haw!" The rider galloped to the barn and then fell from his horse.

Marsh picked himself up and, only for a moment shared some sympathy with the fallen horseman. A quick move stuffed his six-shooter back into its holster. Hardly moaning as he started the long walk to the barn, he tried to figure what he'd say.

Gustav Hammersmith called out to him, "If it ain't my

dear uncle. How's things, Unc? You come to tuck me in?"
The young man tried to stand. It was beyond his ability.

Even ten feet away, Marsh smelled the beer. If Gustav
had bathed in the foamy brew, the odor couldn't have been
stronger.

"I'd ask where you've been but it's obvious."

"That's you, ain't it? The smart one in the family.
Better'n the lot of us. You always thought you were better'n
my pa. You ain't!" Gustav Hammersmith clawed his way
to his feet and lurched forward. He clenched his hands into
meaty fists and reared back.

Marsh stepped up. The punch sailed harmlessly past his
head. All he had to do was put his hand flat on Gustav's
chest and shove. He knocked his nephew down.

"Drunk and stupid. You don't have to be, either. You're
Mason's boy. You've got Hammersmith blood flowing in
your veins. Act like it. Act like a man."

"You run him off. Pa couldn't take you always nagging
on him. He hated you. I hate you!"

Marsh stepped closer and grabbed Gustav's flailing arm.
With a powerful tug, he got him to his feet. The effort
caused him to strain belly muscles, but showing any weakness to Gustav was out of the question. If he wanted to save
his nephew from his despair and downright bad attitude, it
had to be now.

"You've been swilling the Murphys' brew. That's about
the only saloon in these parts. Did they throw you out?"

"I . . . I got tired of them. And there was . . ." Gustav's
voice trailed off and he stared at the ground. Marsh had
seen guilty children.

"What'd you do to get thrown out?"

"Nothin'! I just left because of her."

"You got into trouble over a woman?" Marsh sighed.

It was the next logical step from spending all his time and money getting drunk. "Who was it?"

"Lil." Gustav's reply came out small, tiny like a mouse creeping around a mean barn cat.

For a moment, Marsh was puzzled. He frowned, trying to imagine who his nephew meant. A shudder passed through him, and things fell into place.

"Lilith Murphy," he said. "You fooled around with Thomas Murphy's wife? Did he catch you two together?"

"Wanamaker did. He was powerful mad. I think the two of them fooled around before I went to town. She wants me, not Murphy's foreman."

"Who she wants doesn't matter. Being with her is adultery. That's a sin." Marsh was no prude but marriage vows were sacred. There were always circumstances and situations where temptation loomed bigger than morality, and it was always wrong.

"So it's all right for her and Wanamaker to sneak around behind Murphy's back?" Gustav was sobering up. Anger did that to a man. His words came out crisper and not as slurred, but he still needed to support himself by a hand on the barn wall.

"What they do's their damned business," Marsh snapped. "What you do is my business, it's the business of the entire family. What would your ma say?"

"Lil's too old for me," Gustav said. He snickered, then sobered a bit more. "She's older, but she's real good because she's so experienced. She can—"

"Gustav!" Marsh barked. "Don't go telling your mother one little detail. I swear, I ought to thrash you, but you're a grown man. A grown man without a lick of sense."

"You're just scared I'm more of a man than you, Unc. I've seen the way you look at Lilith. All the men in town do, but she picked me."

"After her husband and Wanamaker and who knows how many others. You're nothing to her. She used you, Gustav. You're only something to get back at Thomas."

Marsh closed his eyes for a moment. Maybe selling the water to the railroad wasn't all wrapped in the Murphy brothers being greedy and out to ruin him. It might be a blow against the entire Hammersmith family because Thomas found out what his wife and Gustav had been up to.

"He's a miserable moneygrubbing . . ." Gustav trailed off when he wasn't able to think of more names to call Thomas Murphy.

"He's all of that, and he's legally married to her. And she's hitched to him. Do you understand?"

"She's special," Gustav got out. "Get out of my way. I can see why my pa left. He couldn't put up with you anymore." The stocky youth yanked at his horse's reins and clumsily mounted.

Marsh moved to pull him down, but Gustav kicked out and shoved his uncle back. Rather than fight, Marsh let him ride off.

"Good riddance," he said. He stewed for a minute and then realized what Gustav's departure would mean to his mother. Heidi was holding up well after Mason's mysterious disappearance, but if she lost her son in such a sinful way, she might break. Marsh saw her as a strong lady and had been pleased to invite her into the family when Mason married her, but everyone had a limit. Gustav pushed Marsh close to his.

Never seeing her son again or, worse, hearing gossip of his wild exploits in Osborne would push anyone to the point of no return.

He snorted in disgust, saddled Derby, and lit out after Gustav. If he couldn't talk sense into him, he'd lasso him and drag him back to the house. If Gustav sobered up enough, talking sense to him might do the trick. If not, Marsh was willing to leave him hog-tied until he came around and settled down.

Marsh owed it to the memory of his twin. Gustav was nothing like George, and for that he was grateful. But Gustav was family. Marshal Hammersmith was the head of the family.

As he galloped toward town, he wondered what Caleb would do. The old man had solutions for every problem. As far as Marsh was concerned, his own pa was as big a problem as his nephew. Who were the riders who called his pa Smitty? They knew one another, but he found it hard to believe even one of the tall tales Caleb spun was true. He made himself out to be a real desperado, riding with the worst outlaws in Texas, being at every important massacre and gunfight and robbery that had ever occurred.

His nephew was a philandering drunkard and his father had turned senile, unable to sort out reality from his wild imaginings.

One good thing came from his frantic ride into town. He worried so much about everyone else in the family that he ignored his own aches and pains. Only it felt like he'd been beat up all over again when he slowed Derby to a walk and rode down the middle of the main street, hunting for Gustav.

He stopped in front of the saloon. At the side, tied to an iron ring mounted on the wall, stood Gustav's horse. The animal snorted and tugged at the reins, trying to get away. Marsh almost untied the horse. It'd take off at a dead run for the Twin M. If Gustav wanted the horse back, he'd have to come beg for it. After all, it carried a MM brand on its haunch. It belonged to the ranch and not the rider.

Marsh knew he'd never do such a thing. By now, Gustav must have sobered up. He dropped to the ground and hesitated a moment to let the pain from the landing fade. A quick turn of the reins lashed Derby next to Gustav's horse.

He made sure his six-gun rode easy in the holster and then went around to the front of the building. The swinging doors moved fitfully, like a bird with broken wings trying to take flight. The smoke-laden air current flowing from inside made his eyes water. He hitched up his gun belt and went in, determined to have it out with Gustav.

The interior was darker than he expected. Of ten lanterns spaced around the walls, only three were lit. Either the bartender hadn't filled them or the Murphys were trying to save money.

He expected to see Little Miss Molly behind the bar, but a burly brute half a head taller than Marsh paced the length of the bar like a tiger in a cage. Two customers leaned against the bar, nursing beers. Marsh peered through the thick smoke haze and saw Gustav seated at a table in the back corner of the saloon. A man sat across from him.

Knowing that was the Murphys' table told him where his nephew had run. He pushed through the batwing doors and marched straight for the rear.

"Wait, mister. You can't disturb Mister Murphy. He's doin' business."

"It's my business he has to deal with," Marsh said, ignoring the giant barkeep's order.

The bartender hurried around and planted himself in front of Marsh. He so completely blocked the way Marsh wasn't able to see which Murphy brother Gustav talked to so earnestly.

"Out of my way."

"This here saloon's only for customers. You gotta order somethin' to drink. And you can't bother Mister—"

That was as far as he got. Marsh's patience had run out. He turned halfway around, then swung using the full strength of his body to deliver the blow. His fist crashed into the barkeep's solar plexus. For an instant, Marsh thought he'd punched a rock wall. Then he felt his knuckles sink a little bit down. The impact had sent shock waves through the huge man. He made a funny sound and simply sat down.

The expression on his face showed he was surprised and stunned at being unable to move. Marsh stepped around him and planted himself next to the table. He ignored Gustav and addressed Thomas Murphy directly.

"I don't ever want Gustav to come into this establishment again. Understand?"

"Marsh, how good to see you," Thomas Murphy said with fake cheerfulness. "I'd offer you a drink, but the barkeep looks a mite inconvenienced at the moment."

The giant made gurgling noises and kicked his heels feebly against the floor. Marsh had taken him out by poking him where all the nerves came together. He'd recover in a short while. Marsh would either be done with Murphy by then or have to shoot the bartender. It was just as well Little Miss Molly wasn't working the bar tonight. He wasn't up to shooting women, for any reason.

"Come with me, Gustav. We're leaving."

"Leave me be! You got no call to tell me what to do."

"Your ma needs you."

Gustav said something vile. The idea flashed through Marsh's head to tell Thomas Murphy what had been going on between Gustav and his wife. He stopped before he threw that kerosene onto a smoldering fire. Everyone would be shooting at everyone else.

"It doesn't sound as if the boy wants to return to your ranch. There's not anything there for him since his pappy lit a shuck. You have any idea where your brother went, Marsh?"

"If you don't leave now, Gustav, don't bother coming back."

"Won't that make my ma bawl her eyes out?" Gustav spat the words. "Maybe you can comfort her. You're real good at that, aren't you? You always liked her more'n you should have."

Marsh backhanded his nephew. Gustav fell from the chair and landed on the floor. He scrambled to his feet and reached for the six-shooter holstered at his side.

He saw his uncle's polar blue eyes and knew he would be a loser in any fight. He might be thirty years younger, but right then, Marshal Hammersmith had the look of a gunfighter. Worse, he had the look of a man who had been pushed to the brink of killing rage.

"Gentlemen, please," Murphy said. "There's no need to bring a family squabble into the saloon."

"You've made your bed," Marsh said, glaring at his nephew. His words quavered. "Now lie in it."

"It's good you came by when you did. You're the first to know, Marsh, that I hired Gustav to work for me."

Marsh jerked around. His hand twitched at his side, but he held back from drawing on Murphy.

"What're you going to have him do?"

"This and that," Murphy said lightly. He leaned out to look around Marsh. The barkeep only now was beginning to recover. "It looks as if I need a new bartender." He grinned wickedly.

"I don't know how to do that," Gustav said.

"Little Miss Molly will be happy to show you . . . everything." Murphy said it to get Marsh's goat. It took all his willpower not to shoot back how Lilith Murphy had already shown Gustav everything. There was no point now.

"You might want to say goodbye to your ma," Marsh said. "Don't do it while I'm there." He whirled around and stalked out. He was fuming the whole way. When he passed the downed bartender, he kicked out and knocked the man flat on his back.

Laughter from the customers, groans from the barkeep, and curses from Gustav Hammersmith followed him from the saloon. That pointless act of revenge didn't make him feel one whit better.

CHAPTER 14

Every clop of Derby's hooves was a new punch to his gut.
Marsh Hammersmith tried to shake the feeling he had done
everything wrong in dealing with Gustav. He should never
have lost his temper. Hitting him will drive the boy further
away.

"Boy?" Marsh snorted and shook his head. Gustav was
no boy. He was a grown man and ought to act like one.

Marsh held out his hand. The pale moonlight caught it
and turned the flesh into silver like some ancient knight's
armored fist. Too much wore on him to keep his temper
when confronted with such arrogance on Gustav's part.

"Let him be Thomas Murphy's toady. He'll only find
himself on the wrong end of a barrel when Murphy finds
out his wife's been fooling around with the new hired
hand."

He knew nothing about Lilith Murphy. Gossip never
interested him, and he was sure that he'd never said more
than "Good day" to her. She had seemed aloof and content
enough with her husband. That, as much as anything else,
would have kept him from striking up a conversation. Neither of the Murphy brothers ranked high on his list of men
to have as friends.

Marsh tried to push his nephew and all the worry about

him from his mind. He tried and failed. The longer he rode, the more emotional mountains he climbed and cliffs he fell from. Telling his sister-in-law what her son had done was nothing he looked forward to. Not mentioning Lilith Murphy would help, but not much. Heidi had lost a husband, and now her son was slipping away.

Or was Gustav gone for good?

Derby stopped suddenly and reared. Marsh reached for his six-gun. Snakes out in the cold night were unusual but not unheard of. If a rattler found a large rock to warm it, that might cause the horse to shy.

"Whoa, settle down, whoa." He turned the horse's head with the reins and looked at the shadowy ground. If a snake lurked, it was hidden from his sight. Listening hard for rattling got him nowhere. The light breeze moved through the grass with a gentle sighing.

Then he heard something completely out of place. Marsh drew and fired blindly at a low bush along the trail. The gunshot was immediately followed by the snap of a bowstring and the whine of an arrow that seared past his ear. Instinctively ducking, he bent low and fired again. A second arrow came his way but went wide of its target.

The Indian fell to one knee, showing himself. He tried to stand but got tangled in the creosote bush. This time Marsh had time to aim. His target was revealed and not moving fast. The round caught the Indian in the upper arm. A guttural cry escaped his lips. The brave lifted his arm and looked, not at the arm but at a hole in his side. Marsh had shot through the biceps and drilled deep into the man's chest.

The Indian keeled over, kicked feebly, and then died.

Marsh got control of his horse and slowly advanced. If one Indian had ambushed him, there must be others nearby. The gunshots would alert them that something had gone wrong with their deadly trap. He looked down at the dead brave. Only a bow and arrow. No firearm and no war paint. While not an expert on Indian trappings, he didn't think this was a Comanche.

"An Apache," he sighed. One of Night Wolf's tribe had tried to kill him.

He reloaded the spent chambers and looked around with more attention paid to the bushes and clumps of cactus where someone could lie in wait for him.

Marsh knew he'd be safer cutting across country and avoiding the trail he'd taken from town. But the trail was quicker, and Derby wasn't going to step into an animal's burrow on the sun-baked track.

He put his heels to the stallion's flanks and shot ahead. Marsh looked left and right as he rode. The Indian hadn't been out on his own, not lying in wait along the trail as he had been. The brave had been hunting—and it wasn't for rabbits.

Before he had ridden a half mile, Marsh saw silhouettes briefly appear on a nearby ridge. They popped up and sank back down rapidly. Marsh thought as many as five were after him now. He sank lower and urged Derby to greater speed. Then he saw the futility of this attempted escape.

On either side of the trail ahead of him were more dimly seen figures. When one turned and moonlight caught his face to show wavy lines and bright dabs of war paint, Marsh savagely yanked at the reins to turn his horse. The Indian swung a bow around and drew back until it looked as though either the bowstring or the wooden bow should have snapped under the strain. Then an arrow passed through the air where he had been a split second before.

Marshal hadn't wanted to cut across the rangeland. There wasn't any choice now. Looking over his shoulder, he spotted no fewer than ten riders coming after him. He wondered at this, if these were Apaches. He'd always heard they refused to go out at night for fear of snakes. The warriors closing the gap showed no fear of fighting at night. If anyone ought to have been scared of the dark, it was Marshal Hammersmith.

After another minute of hard riding, he slowed to get his bearings. This was his land. As far as the eye could see, this was Twin M range. He knew it better than any Apache war party. Or did he?

Ahead were two riders sitting their horses, waiting patiently for him. He was being herded.

The looming, dark Bullet Butte rose off to his left. Ahead were at least two warriors. Standing and fighting meant his death. Marsh slued right. A deep arroyo would provide cover for him. Fighting off so many Apaches wasn't likely to end well, but he'd take as many with him as he could. Derby changed gait and jumped over a low rise. Marsh caught his breath as he plunged downward. The ravine had appeared much sooner than he expected. The landing jolted him and sent pain knifing into his gut from the still healing bruises and internal damage. His body reacted better than it should have. He recovered his balance as he tried to ignore the pain chewing at his gut like a hungry rat.

His weight shifted and stayed in the saddle. Derby turned and galloped along the far arroyo embankment. Roots sticking out and protruding rocks cut at Marsh's arm. He steered away from the side and found a better path down the middle of the dried runoff channel. For a moment, hope sprouted. He might get around the Indians and escape at the bottom of the ravine.

Two riders pacing him on higher ground ended that fever dream.

He drew and fired across his body. One rider vanished. Then he let out a whoop of triumph when he hit the other Apache. The warrior tumbled from horseback, teetered on the edge of the arroyo, and fell in. From a quick look back,

Marsh saw his target wasn't moving. He had reduced the attackers by one.

By one. He still faced certain death. He was tiring quickly, and his hands shook from strain. The beating given by the railroaders was going to be the death of him, even if they hadn't been the ones beating him to death right now.

A break in the arroyo wall let him scramble to the far rim. He was turned around. After he found Bullet Butte and got his bearings, he started back to town. Osborne didn't have a sheriff or marshal, but the Apaches weren't likely to follow him where every citizen had a gun and was willing to use it on invaders.

Before he had ridden as long as ten seconds, he spotted another Apache on a small rise.

"Come with me. You will lose your scalp if you don't."

Night Wolf called out to him. He lifted his rifle and started to fire. The Lipans fought the Comanches, but did Night Wolf also fight his own people? Marsh had no idea about the internal struggles, but it hardly seemed likely Night Wolf intended to help him this time. However, Marsh didn't empty his six-gun in the Lipan's direction. He had no chance at all fighting the rest of the Indian band.

"What have I got to lose?" he asked Derby. The horse lowered his head and gave a fresh burst of speed in Night Wolf's direction. That settled the matter for Marsh. In some peculiar way, if he had to die at an Indian's hand, he preferred it to be Night Wolf wielding the knife.

Marsh laughed grimly. The Lipan had stolen *his* knife. If he was going to get his hair lifted, it'd be with his own knife.

"This way. Hurry." Night Wolf wheeled his pony about and cut off across the prairie.

Marsh wanted to protest. Night Wolf rode straight for Bullet Butte. There wasn't much in the way of protection afforded by sheer, rising rock walls. If he tried to hide by wedging himself into one of the niches slicing into the stone, that would end up as his tomb.

"Where are we going?" He shouted at Night Wolf, who either couldn't hear over the thunder of his horse's hooves or chose not to answer. Marsh tried once more but saw he was wasting his breath. Worse, if the other Apaches heard him, they'd swarm all over him before he found out Night Wolf's intentions.

Just when he thought they had evaded the war party, Marsh saw movement ahead in an unlikely spot. Three Apaches were scaling the side of Bullet Butte. At first he thought they were climbing higher to get a better view of the prairie to direct the warriors to him. Then he saw they were clambering down. All three had heavy packs slung on their backs.

In spite of his predicament, he had to admire how agile they were. The packs were obviously heavy, yet none of the three faltered. They clung to the rock face with fingers and toes dug into the side. As he rode past, he saw two of them jump the final few feet to the ground. They landed heavily. Whatever they carried pushed them to the limits of their strength. The trio staggered away under their load, never noticing Marsh or Night Wolf. They made their way to a crude cart and put their packs in it. A mule hitched to the front began pulling. In a few seconds, they faded into the night.

He caught up with his guide. Night Wolf waited impatiently in front of a dark crevice in the side of the rocky prominence.

"What were they carrying? It looked like it was gold the way they strained. Do you have a gold mine up there?" Marsh looked up at the sheer rock face rising to block out the moon. Vagrant moonbeams crept around the top, turning the gray cap to silver. "Is it silver? Are your people mining silver up higher?"

"In there. Don't come out. I will lead them far away."

"Night Wolf, wait!"

Marsh spoke to empty air. The Apache brave rode like the wind, circling the base of the rocky spire. He began whooping and hollering. Marsh tried to make out the words, but Night Wolf shouted in Apache. Again, for just a moment, he feared the Lipan had betrayed him.

And again, what choice did he have? He knew riding away from Bullet Butte was suicide. The Apaches would spot him in a flash. He tried to make out details of the hidey-hole Night Wolf had picked for him. He saw only darkness so intense it was as if all light in the entire world had been banished forever and ever.

"In we go. Don't try to rear. Come on, good, good, Derby. Keep moving."

The crevice was so tight he scraped both arms against the rock. Derby fit—barely. The horse tried to bolt, but there wasn't nowhere to go except ahead. Backing from the narrow rocky chute was impossible.

Deeper and deeper into the side of the butte they rode. Just when Marsh thought he'd be stuck forever, the passage opened into a sandy arena. It wasn't very roomy, but after the journey in, it was the wide-open spaces. Marsh let Derby prance around a little and then dismounted. The horse had earned a rest.

So had he.

He regained his strength and explored the stony, walled den. The way in was the only exit. Knowing the danger, on foot he retraced his path to the outside world. The moon had risen further and cast its eerie light on the entrance to the rocky arena. He whipped out his six-shooter and aimed. His line of fire was limited, but with a single shot he could take out any of three Apaches.

They rode aimlessly back and forth, coming and going from his field of vision. He lowered his pistol. Any shot now sealed his death warrant. The three were joined by a half dozen more. Then Night Wolf galloped up. He yelled and spat and gestured wildly until he had all their attention.

Marsh wished he spoke Apache, but the gist of Night Wolf's harangue became obvious after the warrior stabbed his finger in the direction around the base of Bullet Butte several times. The others muttered among themselves as Night Wolf continued to shout. Then he wheeled about and raced off. The others followed at top speed.

In seconds, only the still night remained. All traces of the war party were gone, except in Marsh's memory. He twisted and turned around, bouncing from wall to wall as he made his way in the dark back to where Derby awaited him. Once more, Night Wolf had rescued him. Before, he had been mad the Indian had stolen his knife. Now Marsh would gladly give him a hundred blades. Or a thousand. Whatever his life was worth, he'd give Night Wolf that many knives and more.

CHAPTER 15

Marsh Hammersmith edged his way back into the rocky arena and stopped to stare. His horse licked at the far wall. Derby wasn't prone to eating odd things. The loud lapping sound stopped as he came around to the side and grabbed the reins to pull the stallion back.

"What are you getting yourself into, old boy?" He patted the horse's neck and bent closer to the wall.

The wet spot was obvious. Moonlight came down almost from overhead now, but too many shadows hid details of the rock wall. Marsh pressed his hand against the stone and then rubbed. His palm came away damp. The horse had been nuzzling the rock like it was a salt lick. Feeling foolish but with curiosity running wild, he bent over and gave the spot a lick, too.

He spat. The dust he expected wasn't there, but why should it be? Derby had licked away any dust or rocky debris. Then he pressed his cheek against the wall. A distant roaring noise made him pull back. It wasn't the rush of a steam engine or anything he had ever heard before. Leaning close, he pressed his hand into the stone.

It felt colder than rock should be, but this spot wasn't in direct sunlight much of the day. The sandy pit lay at the bottom of a chimney that opened upward. The bulk of

Bullet Butte lay above the wall. He rested his hand again. Cool. Even cold. And a distinct vibration made his fingers tingle.

He pushed back his Stetson and scratched his head. There was a chance that the Apaches used some kind of mining equipment high up on the far side of the butte. He'd never heard of a gold or silver strike anywhere near. That didn't mean the precious metals weren't hidden there. West Texas was wide open and unexplored for the most part. Its vast plains and deserts swallowed up men and left behind their bleached bones. Their discoveries were hidden until they learned to talk from beyond the grave.

He leaned against the wall. The distant vibration soothed his aching shoulder. He swung about and pressed his back into the cold stone. A shiver passed through him, but the experience wasn't uncomfortable. He moved back several paces and looked up this wall.

"The Apaches climb the outer wall of the butte. There's no reason I can't scale this part." He took his lariat from the saddle and played out a loop. A few quick spins and a cast sent the rope uncurling in the air. It took two tries before he secured the rope around a stony spire twenty feet up. A tug assured him it was secure.

Marsh began climbing. At first, the going was easy. Then his strength started to fade. Because he felt fine while not exerting himself didn't mean he was back to his usual robust good health. Fifteen feet up, his hands began to slip. He leaned into the wall, rested for a moment, then made a final effort to reach the needle of rock he had lassoed.

With a two-armed grab, he circled the stone and hugged it close. Moving carefully, he eased around and sat on a ledge until he regained his strength. Looking down made him dizzy. He saw movement—Derby protesting his absence. But the inky blackness made it look as if he stared into a bottomless hole.

Craning around, he looked up. Unfastening his rope, he repeated his lassoing and gained another fifteen feet. Bit by bit, he worked up the chimney until he reached a flatter area. The bulk of Bullet Butte still lay above him. He had never thought about it, but the solitary pile of stone had to be more than two hundred feet tall. He had come barely a third of the way to the top.

He explored this new section and found a passageway around to the face where the Apaches had scaled the peak. Marsh scraped his way through a tight opening and stood on a large stone platform. From the moccasins prints in the dust, a passel of Apaches had come this way. They had a harder climb, having to find handholds and footholds. They probably reached this point and rested on their way even higher.

He went to the edge of the cliff and looked up. The Indians had dug out holes to use as a crude stone ladder. This made it easier for them to climb than finding natural crevices and handholds, but he wondered why they didn't build ladders if getting to the top was so important to them. He had heard stories of how the cliff dweller Indians in New Mexico Territory used ladders. They'd scale the ladders and pull them up after themselves to avoid enemies.

Marsh examined the wall. Stepping into a set of footholds and swinging out to continue the climb to the top was tricky but something he could do. He looked up. The side of the butte was lighted by stars and a bit of the moon that sneaked through the rocks. An urge to climb to see what they mined made him judge the distances and think about how his pointed toe boots would fit. They wore moccasins and could feel the stone to get a better step up.

A noise behind him made him spin around. An Apache poked his head up over the edge. He had been scaling the butte, and Marsh had missed him in the dark. The brave heaved himself up and rolled over to come to his feet.

For a heart-stopping instant, the two stood frozen. Their eyes locked. Dark Apache and polar blue German-American.

The Indian came out of the shock at seeing an adversary first. He let out a war cry and pounced like an eagle swooping on its prey. His weight bowled over Marsh. The rancher stumbled back and slipped in the dust, crashing to the rocky floor.

He fought the weight of the Indian pinning him down. He held both wrists in his hands, but he weakened quickly. The climb from the sandy pit had exhausted him. His grip faded, and the Apache yanked one hand free. Marsh saw the Indian lift a wickedly sharp knife high above his head, then bring it plunging down.

If the tip had landed, it would have impaled Marsh's throat. He gripped the brawny wrist with both hands. With the downward pressure increasing, Marsh thrashed about to escape the pin. His grip strength wasn't as vital now as the power in his arms. He held the knife at bay, but the Apache used both his strength and his weight to shove it down a little bit at a time.

When the cold steel tip pinked Marsh's throat, he let out a bull-throated cry and heaved. He weighed more than the Apache and desperation drove him. If he failed now, he died. That knowledge gave him the strength he needed to heave the Indian off him.

The Apache rolled and came to his feet, as supple and sleek as a mountain lion. He spun the knife around from a position of using it to stab down to hold it in front like a sword. He lunged, intending to gut Marsh. The knife slid past—barely.

The tip cut into Marsh's shirt but didn't draw blood. The Indian danced around, evaluating his opponent. Marsh was quick on the draw but saw how impossible drawing and firing was before the Apache could attack. Having a gun in his hand was pointless if he also had a knife thrust into his belly.

"Come on, come on. You're a yellowbelly coward," Marsh taunted. He doubted the Apache understood him, but he certainly caught the mocking tone.

With a roar, the Apache charged like an infuriated bull. Marsh sidestepped at the last instant, kicked out, and tripped his would-be killer. The Apache skidded along the dirty stone floor on his belly and popped to his feet, facing away from his opponent. If they had been fighting on the plains, Marsh would have faced certain death. All he did now was shove. Just a little. The Apache flailed about, trying to recover his balance.

One foot slipped over the edge. A second push sent the man flying through the air. When he hit the ground, he screamed what could only be his final cry, his death song. He had fallen close to a hundred feet. There was no surviving that.

Marsh pulled back. Several of the man's war party had rushed to his body. He didn't want them looking up and seeing his head poking over the edge. Any chance of climbing higher using the way chipped out of the stone face was long gone, in spite of the darkness shrouding him. Marsh brushed away what he could of his footprints in the dust. If the Apaches came to investigate, they might miss in the dark any spots Marsh failed to obliterate.

He squeezed back through the narrow passageway that had brought him there. Sounds from below warned that some of the braves were climbing up to see what had happened. Marsh cried out when, in his haste, he pressed too hard against the wall. A sharp stone cut into his belly. He bit his lip to keep from making more noise.

He pulled free and pressed his hand into the wound. It bled sluggishly, but he left a trail even a child could follow—if they saw it. The Apaches tracked and hunted expertly. Could they follow a fresh blood trail by scent alone? He had heard so many stories that he wasn't sure if they were superhuman or not.

If they were, he was a goner.

He pushed deeper into the passage as the first Apache appeared at the edge of the ledge. Then Marsh froze. If he made any sound, however slight, the warrior would hear him. He held his breath as the man prowled about, looking this way and that, then dropped to hands and knees and sniffed like a dog.

Marsh was sure he'd scent the blood and come for him. But the Apache hopped to his feet and leaned over the ledge. He called down. Any reply was lost, not that Marsh would have understood the discussion. He finally gasped, the pent-up air blasting from his lungs when the warrior swung over the side and climbed back down on their hollowed out stairway.

It had taken him minutes to find the tight passage and examine the ledge. Returning dragged into hours, or so it seemed. His knees barely worked, and his legs had turned to dough.

"But I'm alive. Alive and the Apaches aren't after me." He took no pleasure in possibly reducing their number by one more. He had killed two or three, but four times that many remained. If this was an entire clan, there might be even more prowling around on his property. The only reason for them to be there was to steal his cattle.

Right now, he'd give half his herd just to be home in bed, Leonore beside him, his family scattered throughout the sprawling ranch house.

He reached the top stone needle where his lasso still circled the rock. A few tugs moved the loop to the very tip. He slid down to the lower ledge. It took some doing, but he worked the rope off the upper spire and refastened it to the one just above where his horse pawed at the ground, snorted, and made an unholy amount of noise. He had to get down there to quiet Derby or the horse would alert the Indians.

Marsh tugged a few times on the rope to be sure it was secure, then swung out. He started down but knew something was wrong right away. The rope jerked in his hand, and he fell backward. The sharp stone had cut through the loop he had secured.

He landed with enough force to knock the wind from his lungs. Seconds later, he felt a wet tongue on his face. Derby nuzzled and licked him like a dog, but it worked to bring him back to consciousness. His chest hurt, and moving proved so painful he worried he had busted up something inside. However, he had landed on sand. Unlike the Apache who'd taken the tumble off the higher ledge, his landing had been relatively soft.

That was little comfort when he tried to sit up. Nothing worked right. His belly hurt, and breathing felt as if he was sucking fire into his lungs. He focused on Derby. The horse danced about, as if it wanted to frolic. Again, Marsh tried to sit up, and this time he knew he'd never make it. The pain would make him pass out.

Rolling onto his belly, he started crawling for the crevice leading out of the arena. Bit by bit, he pulled himself along. His fingers turned bloody from grasping sharp-edged stones. If Derby followed him, he'd have to find a way to mount and ride. If the horse remained in the tiny rock corral, he'd have to think of something else.

It took the better part of an hour to pull himself through the crevice. The moon was setting and cast only a wan, parting glow on the land. Derby had not come after him.

Marsh doubted he'd make it much longer without help. He lips were dried and cracked, he needed water, and the last of his strength flowed from him like a waterfall. All he could think to do was pull his six-gun and fire it.

The report made him flinch. The sound could be heard for miles. He needed someone other than the war party to come see what the ruckus was all about. If only Night Wolf heard and once more pulled his fat from the fire. All he needed to see was a single rider.

A tight knot of five men on horseback approached. He had gambled and lost. Marsh passed out.

CHAPTER 16

"Think we ought to bury him here? He ain't gonna make it."

"Naw, he's tougher than that. He'll pull through," another voice said, but there wasn't any conviction to the words.

Marsh Hammersmith strained to look up at the riders. He didn't recognize the voices.

"Rustlers," he gasped out. These had to be the rustlers preying on his herd, and now they'd found him when he was unable to stop them. It didn't seem fair. Nothing seemed fair. He had survived the night, battling Apaches and climbing mountains, and it had come to this.

They wanted to bury him alive!

"Not as tough as Smitty."

"Who is?"

The two laughed. Marsh tried to make sense of what they said. He flopped around and got both hands on the butt of his Peacemaker. He hadn't drawn the attention of the Apaches, but these two riders weren't any improvement. Rustlers! That thought sent a surge of strength into his arm, his hand, his finger. His trigger finger curled back. His six-shooter fired and then he collapsed, drained again.

"You think he meant to shoot us, King?"

"No way of telling. He fired into the ground. You look

like a dust cloud, Clay. I'll give you that. You never bother to brush off the trail that accumulates on your clothes. He mighta confused the two of you, you and a dust devil."

"He was shootin' at you 'cuz he can't tell an ass from a hole in the ground."

"Hush up. I'll have you up on charges for insulting me, Clay. You got a mouth on you."

"It's true, King, it's true. I freely 'fess up to that. That don't answer what we do with him. As beat up as he is, he'd bleed all over my saddle if I flopped him across it."

"Don't want blood on your saddle," the one called King said.

Marsh coughed and brought himself up to his elbows. It stretched his stomach muscles and bent his back to the point he cried out in pain. He focused on the two shadow-cloaked riders.

"Kingston," he gasped out. "You're the one called Kingston."

"See, Clay? I'm danged famous. Here's a dyin' man who knows me."

"Infamous. You ought to have your ugly puss splashed all over a wanted poster."

"If I did, the reward'd be a thousand dollars. A hundred thousand. That's what it means to be really famous."

"What about him?" Clay asked.

Marsh tried to lift his six-shooter once more, but his head spun and his muscles turned to water. He rested his forehead on the ground and waited for the inevitable. If they intended to bury him at the base of Bullet Butte, he hoped they'd have the decency to shoot him first. It was a particular fear of his to be buried alive.

After a long silence, Marsh forced himself to look up again. For a moment, he thought he was blind. He saw nothing but darkness. He blinked hard and got dirt from his watering eyes. The stars had seemed to dim. Then he figured out why. The rising sun was blotting out the night and bringing a new day. A new day. He wasn't dead. Not yet!

Marsh brought up his knees and pushed hard. He came to hands and knees. With some effort, he rocked back and looked around. Blotting out the rising sun were the outlines of several more riders coming in his direction. Even using both hands, he wasn't able to lift the three pounds of iron and take a shot. He sagged in defeat. He had fought so hard and lost.

"There he is. Get him!"

The lead rider shouted, then galloped toward him. Five more followed. One of the lagging riders passed the leader.

"Pa. You're alive."

"What are you doing out here, George? You're supposed to be resting up." He wobbled and fell. Strong arms caught him and then eased him lower until he stretched out on his back. Marsh blinked and saw his son cradling him.

"You had us worried. Where'd you get off to? Aunt Heidi said Gustav was missing, too. We all thought whatever happened to him happened to you, too."

He shook his head. Words failed to form until one of the riders dribbled water from a canteen across his lips. When his mouth stopped feeling like the inside of a cotton bale, he drank more and choked. He knew better and tried to explain.

"Easy now, Pa. Just a little water."

George let him drink more when he showed he wasn't going to suck it all down in one long gulp. For once, he felt some sympathy with a thirsty horse drinking until it bloated.

"How'd you find me?"

"You can thank Gramps. He was out for an early morning ride and told us he saw you come this way. We heard a couple shots. From your gun, it looks." George plucked the pistol from his nerveless fingers and tucked it back into Marsh's holster.

"Caleb?"

"Come on, let's see if you can stand. You'll have to ride double with me."

"Derby," he said, pointing into the crevice. "He's back there. In a rocky space."

"Go fetch his horse," George ordered. One of the riders grumbled but dismounted and slithered away in the narrow passage. Derby's neighs echoed out.

The sound bolstered Marsh's spirit. He got to his feet under his own power.

"Don't circle around like a buzzard," Marsh told his son. "You're learning bad habits from your mother."

"It's good that me and the boys were out hunting for rustlers."

Marsh looked over the men arrayed in a fan around him. He didn't recognize any of them.

"New hires? Where'd you get them?"

"Gramps talked to a friend of his. I hired them cheap, for a month or two. They were passing through from Fort Worth on their way down to Eagle Pass."

"Fort Worth?" Marsh took a shaky step closer to the nearest man. His face was leathery from riding the range. Thin to the point of emaciation, he was made of oak and steel. The six-gun riding low on his hip showed hard use. Marsh had seen a few cowboys with this look. He had seen more stone cold killers with the identical look.

He needed both right now.

"You know Kingston?" he asked.

The man he'd singled out reared back in the saddle and rubbed his eyes. After a long pause, he bent forward resting on his pommel and said, "I know plenty of gents with that moniker. You have anyone in particular in mind?"

"Come on, Pa. It's sunrise. Time to get up and do the

chores," George said. "And time for you to rest up. You look like buzzard bait."

"The way I feel, no self-respecting buzzard would touch me."

George laughed and, arm around Marsh's shoulder, led him to where Derby pawed the ground and tried to pull free of the cowboy holding his reins.

"I wouldn't have made it without you," Marsh said.

"You'd have done just fine," George said, mistaking the sentiment as being directed at him rather than the stallion.

The horse knew who was being complimented and responded with a nicker. Marsh patted Derby and pulled himself into the saddle. He had meant the stallion, not his son. But everyone was content with figuring out his intentions by themselves. They all rode slowly back toward the ranch house, but about halfway, the cowboys split off and scattered across the Twin M.

"It's a good idea getting more hands to help out right now. Their salaries are small compared to the loss of even one steer right now," he told George.

"That's what Gramps said. Every now and then he comes up with a good idea, even if most of what he spews is pure bunkum."

"I wonder," Marsh said, thinking about Caleb's tall tales. After seeing him with Kingston and the wild bunch, Marsh wondered what was the truth and what was exaggeration. Or even outright lies.

"You feeling up to a little detour?"

"I reckon so," Marsh said.

"I'd come this way to see how much water is flowing through the acequia from the Murphy pumps."

Marsh topped the rim and looked down at the irrigation channel. The water purchased from the Murphys flowed into the largest stock pond on the Twin M. From there, in the morning sun, he wasn't able to judge much about the water or how much of it there was.

"Watch, Pa." George heaved a dried prickly pear pad into the water. "Now watch."

Marsh started to ask what he was supposed to see. Then he understood. The dried cactus hunk whirled this way and that as it moved along with the sluggish current. He counted how long it took for the cactus pad to travel from one rock marker to another.

He rode closer to the acequia and walked Derby between the rocks he had used to estimate the flow rate. Quick calculations in his head made him angry.

"The water's barely flowing. And it's low."

"I did some ciphering—Consuela checked my numbers— and we're getting less than ten percent of what we're paying for."

"Ten percent?" Marsh chewed on his lower lip. One part in ten was being delivered. That meant one cow instead of ten got the proper amount of water added into the stock pond. With the drought the way it was and rain showers few and far between, the ranch would begin losing cattle at an increasing rate soon.

"This kind of cheating has started range wars, Pa. We might think on hiring more cowboys like Rod."

"Rod?"

"Rodriguez. The hand you talked to back at Bullet Butte. He's handy with that six-gun of his, and after talking to him a few minutes, I don't think he's the type to turn tail and run if the going gets tough."

"Rodriguez," he repeated. A man Caleb had recommended. And he had met with Kingston and several others. Marsh hadn't been in great shape, but his hearing wasn't diminished. He felt control of the ranch slipping away as his pa brought in strangers with gunfighting skills and the hard look of desperados.

"Rod knows his job. I saw him working with a stray. He's as good as any hand we ever hired. And then there's . . ."

George began telling about the others he'd hired. Marsh found himself staring at the acequia and imagining it going completely dry. If the herd died off, that'd take away worry about rustlers.

He fell into the rhythm of Derby's gait. By the time they reached the house, Marsh was dozing in the saddle. He hardly remembered George helping him down or his wife and daughter half dragging him into the house. It had been a long day. A very long day and worse was to come.

CHAPTER 17

"He's slept around the clock." George Hammersmith came to the sofa and stood over his father. "Is he ever going to recover?"

"He's been through so much, George. You saw all the new cuts and scrapes. Thank heavens you found him when you did. If he'd lain out in the desert for the entire night, well, it would have done him in for sure." Leonore Hammersmith came over and put a filled water pitcher and a drinking cup on a table beside the sofa. "That's for when he wakes up." She turned to her son and asked, "How'd you happen to find him? There wasn't any call for you and the riders to go to Bullet Butte, was there?"

"Gramps told us to go over. I don't know how he knew," George said. He frowned. "Sometimes, I think he's got second sight. He seems to know things he shouldn't."

"He's annoying, what with all those stories of his, but this time he came through for us. For Marshal."

They stood silently for a few seconds, each lost in their own thoughts.

George finally spoke.

"Ma, I really need him. I'm in over my head."

"You should take care of yourself, too," Leonore said. "It's not that you haven't been shot and run ragged these past weeks. That's a burden running the entire ranch when you're fit as a fiddle. All banged up . . ." Leonore shook her head. She took George by the arm and pulled him from the sitting room. "It's time to fix dinner. You must have things to do, too, before we eat."

"The new men," George said, distracted. He stared at his father stretched out, a thin blanket tossed over him. "I need to be sure they know what I want from them."

"Especially the ones carrying iron," Leonore said. "Don't argue with me, George, about them. I saw those men. They're killers. Some of them. That's what we need with rustlers and Indians and who knows what all prowling around on our property." She wiped her hands on her apron and got a distant look in her eyes.

"The railroaders are stealing our cattle," George said. His voice faded as he went into the kitchen with his mother. "Gramps was right about that, as well. Imagine him figuring out who was stealing our cattle before Pa."

Marsh opened one eye halfway and looked around. They'd left. He had heard every word they'd said. He should have jumped up and agreed with George about how they needed every hand on the range now. And he was the boss. He owned the Twin M, and everyone depended on him.

That simple thought tuckered him out all over again. He wasn't as young as he used to be, and these things brought that home too hard for comfort. Any man who'd taken the beating he had and then traipsed around in the desert, climbing Bullet Butte and fighting the Apaches and almost dying, any man who survived was one tough hombre. He knew that. He also knew he'd be recovered by now if his bones didn't ache and his joints hadn't turned to glue from old age.

Right now, he wanted to sleep some more.

His eyes popped open when the cuckoo clock began its

chirping. He counted five, but it was daylight. He sank back down onto the hard cushions when he got it all straight. Five in the afternoon. Dinner. Slept around the clock. He pushed back the blanket and sat up. The water on the table looked mighty attractive, though he wanted a nip of whiskey. That was the medicine that'd cure what ailed him.

He drank down an entire cup, then hesitated to take more. The water formed a cold lump in his belly, reminding him of the damage done inside.

"Marshal, you're awake. I need to talk." Heidi came down the stairs, taking each step slowly and carefully.

She was a lovely woman. He had liked her from the minute Mason had brought her around. Hardy, with short brunette hair, square face, and deep-set, honest brown eyes, she looked capable of meeting any challenge. That appraisal changed just a mite now when he saw the tracks of tears down her round, rosy cheeks. Those chocolate-colored eyes showed bloodshot, and her lower lip quivered.

"I've got news of Gustav," he said. "That's what's upsetting you, isn't it?"

She sat, knees pressed together, hands folded in her lap. Her head bobbed up and down. She wasn't able to stare at him directly. She looked much younger than her forty-three years. More than anything else now, she reminded him of a schoolgirl facing a wrathful teacher. Unable to put more than a few words together without sniffling, she dabbed at her eyes with an embroidered hanky.

Marsh caught his breath. He saw the initials on it. MH. It was a handkerchief she had made specially for Mason. He wondered if she had trouble facing him because he and Mason were twins. Did he remind her that her husband was gone these past few months?

"He's gone, too, isn't he, Marshal? Gustav. He snuck in during the night and took all his belongings. His room is . . .

It looks like a tornado blew through it. And his clothes and gear are all gone."

"He's moved away, Heidi," he told her. Another cup of water eased the desert-parched feeling in his mouth. "Gone into town."

"Wh-what's he going to do there?"

"You know what he's been up to since his pa disappeared. If there'd been any lawman in Osborne, he'd have been thrown into the calaboose for being drunk and disorderly."

"Is he stealing?"

Marsh hesitated. He had no good idea how Gustav had been supporting himself. He knew now where the money would come from.

"He's got a job."

"A job? Really?" She perked up and looked at him for the first time. "You're not just saying that, are you, Marshal?"

"It's not the greatest job in the world, but it's honest work." He had to bite his tongue to keep from reflecting on the Murphy brothers' honesty or the kind of trouble Gustav could find working in a saloon. He doubted Thomas Murphy had hired Gustav as a barkeep. He'd use him as a bouncer.

That was as much to get back at the entire Hammersmith clan as it was in appreciation of Gustav's dependability.

"I'm glad to hear he hasn't moved on. I don't think I could bear not knowing where he was. He's my only son." Heidi sniffled some more. "He's the only family I have left."

"That's not true. You're a Hammersmith. You've got the lot of us, me and Leonore, George and Sarah and Consuela and there's little Joseph. He needs an aunt's good loving."

"I don't have a place here, Marshal. I don't. Not with both Mase and Gustav gone. If Leonore wants me to go, I will."

"Where'd you go?" He sounded a bit sharper than he intended. Even this short conversation was taxing him. Heidi had to listen to reason, and she wanted him to argue with her into staying. His strength drained away like grains of sand in an hourglass.

"I still have family in New Braunfels. Not close family, but—"

"We're close family, Heidi Hammersmith. Don't let me hear any more of this nonsense. Now, Leonore is in the kitchen. She needs some help, I suspect. Some of that strudel you make would be a fine dessert."

"It takes so long to fix —"

"Then you'd best get to it. Or the two of you put your lovely heads together and figure out something else." He drained a third cup of water. Potent rotgut couldn't have had more effect on him. He lay back down and fumbled for the blanket.

Heidi covered him and lightly kissed his cheek. She whispered, "You're like your brother. You're both good men."

He started to protest such flattery, but he lacked the willpower. Marsh slipped off into a light sleep that was again disturbed by nearby voices. At first, he thought it was his wife and Heidi in the kitchen, but their voices were higher pitched. He stirred, then heaved himself off the sofa. Getting sleep wasn't possible.

The window behind the sofa was half open, and the sounds came from outside. At least four men talked all at once. Marsh made his way to the window to see what the commotion was. He sank down and rested his cheek against the frame when he saw Kingston and Rodriguez standing nose to nose, arguing.

"It's them Injuns we're after," Kingston insisted.

"Smitty was right. It's railroaders. Comanches don't ride shod horses."

"They do if they stole them from ranches around here," came a third voice. A man stepped up. "We need to find out who we're after."

"Railroaders," Rodriguez said.

"Comanches," Kingston said. "The Apaches are still in the area. The Comanches haven't run them off yet."

"They won't go. They have a secret watering hole somewhere out there," the third man said. "I'd give my left arm to know where it is."

"So would the buffalo soldiers from over at Fort Davis," Kingston said. "But we're losing sight of our mission."

Marsh frowned. Kingston spoke like a military man. The others fell silent rather than continue to argue. That hardly fit with most cowboys he'd encountered. It certainly seemed odd with a bunch of outlaws. Even more curious was how Kingston wanted to find who the rustlers were. Why would one outlaw need to identify his competition? There were plenty of cattle to go around, not only on the Twin M but also from surrounding ranches.

Marsh started to pull himself up and get a better look at the men outside the window, but he sank back when another horse trotted up.

"You're s'pposed to be out huntin' the bad guys." Caleb Hammersmith swung down and complained about being in the saddle so long. "You gents can't rely on me doin' all your work."

"Smitty, you're the reason we're here. You asked us to patrol around your ranch. We're doing our best, but to do it the way you want we need a dozen more men."

"So get 'em," Caleb said. "This whole part of Texas is lawless."

"Get the mayor to hire a marshal over in Osborne. You need a sheriff in Brewster County. Depending on the soldiers to keep the law is gonna fail. They chase Indians, not out-laws, unless them varmints do something especially bad."

"There's the Texas Rangers," Caleb said. "That's the law we have to depend on, ain't it?"

The three men with his father all laughed. Marsh chanced a quick look out. Kingston slapped Caleb on the back in a friendly manner.

"You always did have a fine sense of humor, Smitty. Of course there's the Texas Rangers. Now where should we hunt for rustlers?"

"Rod there thinks the land around Bullet Butte is where they hide out. You know anywhere else? Your boy was poking around there for some reason." Kingston drew a map in the dirt with his toe, then crushed down with his boot heel over Bullet Butte.

"It danged near got him killed," Caleb said. "I think he's learned his lesson. He'll be healin' up for a good, long time and not meddlin' in matters that don't concern him."

"He's the owner, Smitty. He's not giving up," said Kingston. He laughed. It sounded more like a snort of disgust. "He's got more of you in 'im than you care to admit. He's persistent. And from the look of that scar on his forehead, he'd been kicked in the head by a mule, too."

"So ride around him. You're good at avoidin' people doin' that," Caleb said.

"You think we are? Boys, did I ever tell you about the time that me and Smitty were down in Corpus Christi and . . ."

Kingston's voice faded away. Marsh chanced another look. The men, along with his father, walked toward the barn. With their backs toward him, their voices were increasingly faint. He sank down and rested his cheek against the cool wall. His eyelids drooped, and he fell into an exhausted sleep, dreaming of rustlers and Texas Rangers and

Thomas Murphy telling him he wasn't allowed any more water.

He slept like that until his wife shook him awake for supper, complaining that he had left the sofa and had fallen asleep against the wall.

CHAPTER 18

"Wake up. I'm not paying you to sleep on the job."

Gustav Hammersmith grunted when a sharp kick to the ribs sent a jolt throughout his body. He surged to his feet, hand going for his six-shooter. Only good reflexes stopped him from drawing and shooting. Nobody treated him like that. Especially when he was enjoying the warmth and inner glow from having downed a few shots of whiskey.

He and Little Miss Molly had hit it off just fine. She slipped him a drink or two when nobody was looking. That was a good thing since he was flat broke and couldn't pay, and she enjoyed stealing from the boss. He wasn't sure about that, but the petite woman got all hot and bothered at the notion she snuck one past Thomas Murphy. Gustav had no idea what the man had done to her to spark such a reaction, but he wasn't going to gripe about it. She even gave him the prime stuff kept under the bar for Thomas himself.

The whiskey went down smooth and warm, and he enjoyed thinking of all the ways Murphy might have gotten on her bad side. Some of them were downright naughty.

"Sorry, boss," Gustav said.

Thomas Murphy glared at him, then pointed to the iron holstered at his side—the one he'd almost drawn to kill whoever had roused him from his daydreaming.

"You know how to use that?"

"This?" Gustav drew as quick as he could. The gun pointed away from Murphy, though he had, for just an instant, thought about pointing the muzzle straight at the rancher's gut. Little Miss Molly watched closely. He thought he'd impress her if it looked as if he could plug their boss.

"Well, I suppose it'll do. You're a tad on the slow side, aren't you?"

"What? I'm not—"

"Your draw, you fool, your draw. On your own time, practice and get quicker. I don't suppose you're much of a marksman, either."

Gustav fumed but said nothing. He slid his six-gun back into the holster. Showing the arrogant man how good a shot he was right now would only get him in trouble. Murphy might even fire him if he shot out a lamp or hit a bottle of whiskey on the back bar.

"Come with me while I make my rounds. If there's any trouble, use that piece." Murphy pointed at Gustav's six-shooter.

Murphy hefted a large leather bag and held it close to himself, cradling it like he would a newborn. He left the saloon, never giving Gustav a second glance.

Gustav paused at the swinging doors and looked back. Little Miss Molly blew him a kiss. He gave her a broad grin and then hurried out when Murphy barked at him not to dawdle. He stepped into the bright sunlight and looked around. Murphy hadn't said, but Gustav figured he was supposed to guard the man and keep him from being robbed. The way his boss clutched the satchel hinted at the money inside.

Visions of robbing Murphy flashed through his mind. However much was in the bag would be more than enough for him and Little Miss Molly to settle down somewhere else. He'd heard El Paso was a decent enough place, for a border town. And if that wasn't far enough to run, the Union Pacific Railroad went all the way out to the California coast. Buy a ticket to Yuma, then sneak on board for the rest of the trip. That'd make sure Murphy or his cutthroats led by Wanamaker would never track him down. No ticket, no trail.

Nobody would be able to follow them. And he'd be rich.

"Hammersmith, are you coming along? Should I send word out to the ranch and have Wanamaker come in?"

"I'm bein' careful, boss. Lookin' around for trouble. I don't see anything suspicious."

Murphy harrumphed, but Gustav saw how he grew a little uneasier. He wiped sweat from his forehead with a white linen handkerchief and then touched a spot under his left arm. Gustav hadn't noticed before, but the butt of a small caliber pistol poked out from under Murphy's coat. The rancher carried his piece in a shoulder rig.

Gustav looked at Murphy with contempt. Even the slickest tinhorn gambler had trouble unlimbering a gun from a shoulder rig. Gustav could draw and fire until his six-gun came up empty before Murphy ever cleared his holster.

The notion that he really was a guard doing a needed job puffed him up.

"I'm meeting with some important men. Stay four or five steps behind me and don't make yourself too conspicuous."

"I won't," Gustav said, not quite sure what his new boss meant. Whatever Murphy meant, it was better than riding herd with his uncle. Marsh Hammersmith was a harsh taskmaster and yelled at him all the time. Most of what happened wasn't his fault. Stopping the corralled horses from banging into the rails and knocking them down hadn't been his fault. And they were fast horses. Rounding up all that had escaped from the remuda was more than any single rider could do. He knew. He'd asked the couple of cowboys who rode for the Twin M. They gave it to him straight about how they'd be hard-pressed to catch such fast horses.

They had laughed as they said that, but Gustav knew what they meant. They were only showing how they wanted to be friends with the boss's kid.

But that had been before his pa upped and left. Gustav had half a mind to go after him and drag him back, wherever he had gotten off to.

"Interfere with me and Little Miss Molly's plans," he said to himself on a raspy whisper. "Interfere and be damned." He jerked around when Murphy stopped and glared at him. The man held the satchel with the money even closer, as if he was a mind reader and knew all about El Paso. Or California and Little Miss Molly.

Thomas Murphy waved him around back of the building the town used as a city hall. Gustav strutted around to the rear, then after Murphy went inside, he backtracked a few paces to position himself under an open window. He heard Murphy greet someone.

Standing on tiptoe, he peered in. Seated behind a desk, Mayor Galveston shuffled papers around. Gustav caught sight of the top sheet. Frank Galveston held it upside down. He only wanted to look busy for his visitor.

"Pull up a chair, Thomas. And set that bag down on the desk. No need for you to keep clinging to it like it's a wild mustang."

Murphy kicked over a chair and sat, but he kept the bag on his lap.

"You have the votes rounded up?"

"You don't mince words, do you, Thomas? Get right down to business. Would you like a drink? I had a courier bring in a bottle of Billy Taylor's finest bourbon for special events."

"I won't be staying that long."

"You might think the swill you serve in that saloon of yours is better. Try a nip. You'll be a convert to the finer things in life." Galveston pointed to the bag. "That there is going to help me buy this by the case." The mayor lifted his glass in salute.

"Buy all the bourbon you want. Just deliver what you promised." Murphy placed the satchel on the edge of the desk. He made Galveston stand and reach to pull it all the way across.

Gustav dropped back for a moment. His legs were cramping from standing on his toes. Pressing his ear against the wall let him hear almost as good as spying by peeking into the office.

"This is a fine amount of money, yes, sir," the mayor said. He smacked his lips in appreciation.

"A thousand dollars. You're sure you can buy the town council's votes to build?"

"I'm sure," Galveston said. "What I'm not so sure about is why you want me to oppose it. My vote's as good as any of those slackers."

"We don't want to be too obvious. They vote for the depot, you vote against. Who's to say any money changed hands? It looks as if you're standing on principle."

"I have opposed the notion of the railroad even coming through. It'll mean the end of Osborne as we know it."

"It'll mean you lose control. The ranchers won't listen to you anymore. The people in town will see how prosperous we've become with the railroad bringing in new passengers and freight."

"The ranchers will appreciate loading their stock on cars. Cattle drives in West Texas will be a thing of the past," Galveston said. He paused and sipped at his whiskey, then asked, "Why can't I change my mind and declare for the depot?"

"You'll look like a hypocrite, that's why. Stand up for your beliefs."

"My vote can mean the difference between passing and failing," Galveston said carefully.

"You just don't want to spend any of that money when you can keep it by changing your own vote. Do as I say or I'll see you strung up. There's no one in this town who wouldn't volunteer to build the gallows if it looks like you're taking a bribe."

"You're the one giving the bribe," Galveston said, a trifle uneasy. "You can't tar me and not have the same brush used on you."

The laugh Murphy gave was bone-chilling.

"Don't cross me, Mister Mayor. You won't like it, and you'll find that I'm untouchable. Get the vote done tonight at the council meeting." Murphy stood. "And you *will* be the only one voting against the measure. That's important."

"I certainly have plenty of reasons to do as you suggest, Thomas." Galveston clutched the money-filled satchel to his chest the way Murphy had on the way over to make the bribe.

"That's so you'll do as I tell you."

Gustav slid along under the window and rushed to the rear of the building. He rounded the corner just as Murphy exited the back door.

"Have you seen anyone prowling around?"

"Nary a soul, boss. You worried about somebody seeing you?"

"Come along. Stay back a few paces."

"Where's the bag you were carrying?" Gustav felt a twinge of devilishness. He knew where the satchel had ended up—and the thousand dollars in it. Poking Murphy just a little made him feel superior.

"Mind your tongue." Murphy stalked away.

Gustav wasn't sure what to do. He trailed Murphy, but

his new employer never even glanced back. Gustav slowed and finally stopped. Murphy had wanted protection while he carried the bag of bribe money to the mayor. With the money turned over, Gustav's job was done. Or so it seemed to him.

He started to go to the saloon, then saw that Thomas Murphy had already entered. He found himself at loose ends and wandered aimlessly through the streets, not sure what to do with himself. It wouldn't be long before Little Miss Molly was off work. He started for the boardinghouse where she lived. Then he slowed, stopped, and stared. His ire rose when he saw the Double Cross foreman grab Lilith Murphy and swing her around.

They were on the porch of the Hanson House Hotel. Gustav turned and cocked his head in their direction, trying to eavesdrop on their conversation. Both were upset, but he wasn't able to read their expressions too well.

He felt a hollowness in his gut when he realized Lilith had been in the hotel with Ben Wanamaker. Gustav and Mrs. Murphy had enjoyed a little fling, but she had told him not to come by again. Going onto the Double Cross ranch-land for a brief assignation had been exciting at first, but he realized the danger scared him. If either of the Murphy brothers had caught him, his body'd never be found.

From the way Wanamaker and Lilith faced each other now, Gustav counted himself as doubly lucky. Daniel Murphy would be angry. Lilith Murphy's husband, Thomas, would be furious if he caught her fooling around. And Ben Wanamaker? He was worst of all. He'd be cold, calculating, and cruel.

Gustav jumped when a sound like a gunshot echoed down the street. Lilith had slapped Wanamaker so hard it caused the man to stumble back a step. He rubbed his cheek and said something more to the woman that made her rear back to slap him again. This time, Wanamaker caught her wrist before her hand reached his face.

He stepped forward and twisted, threatening to break her bones. She let out a squeal of pain. Gustav touched the six-shooter at his side, then knew he'd never match Wanamaker. The man carried himself more like a gunfighter than a cowboy.

The two continued to struggle. Rather than intervene, Gustav ran for the saloon. Panting, he burst through the doors. They swung out and back, whacking him in the rear as he looked around, frantically searching for Thomas Murphy.

The man sat at his usual table in the corner, nursing a drink. Little Miss Molly waved to him from behind the bar to shoo him off, but he ignored her and went directly to Murphy. His boss looked up, irritated.

"What do you want? I don't need you guarding me anymore. Not right now."

"It's your wife. Lilith. Mrs. Murphy," Gustav gasped out. He was as winded from the run as he was seized by fright. "Her and Wanamaker."

"What are you saying? Ben's out at the ranch and my wife's shopping."

"Don't know what she's shopping for, but she bought herself a heap of trouble. I think Wanamaker tried to kiss her, and she slapped him."

Gustav doubted a single kiss was all that had gone on in the hotel, but he wasn't going to tell Murphy of his suspicions. He wasn't even sure why he ratted out Wanamaker and Lilith. Their affair was . . . their affair. He and Mrs. Murphy were history.

He looked quickly toward the bar. Little Miss Molly worked to sell a drunk another beer, but he was tapped out. That didn't stop her from trying to squeeze just one more nickel from him. Gustav and the barkeep were together right now, and Lilith and he were in the past. But Lilith was an attractive woman and Little Miss Molly was . . . homely.

He wasn't sure what made him tell Thomas Murphy, but it got the rancher powerful angry.

With a bull-throated roar, Murphy pushed past Gustav and ran from the saloon. Hesitant but not wanting to miss a moment of what might happen, Gustav trailed his boss.

He saw Murphy storm over to where Wanamaker and Lilith still stood toe-to-toe. Gustav wasn't able to hear what was said, but the words were hot. Murphy shoved his foreman back and made like he was fixing to throw down. Gustav tensed. Murphy could never get his gun out before Wanamaker cleared leather and opened fire at point blank range.

Lilith stepped between the two men and talked rapidly to Murphy. Wanamaker rested his hand on his pistol's butt, then took it away. He spun and left while husband and wife argued.

Gustav wished he could see Ben Wanamaker's face. That would tell the story of what was likely to happen. But he couldn't.

He had to be content watching Lilith and Thomas Murphy enter the hotel. A few minutes later Wanamaker rode past on his way out of town. Gustav slowly grinned. He knew where everyone would be for a spell. He went back into the saloon to cadge a drink from Little Miss Molly. And maybe just a bit more. He had the time.

CHAPTER 19

Marsh Hammersmith mended his tack, sitting in the warm sun and feeling a world better than he had even a few days earlier. He shifted on the hay bale and called to Derby, "You ready to go for a ride? It's been a while."

The horse neighed in answer and kicked at the stall. Marsh took that as a sign the stallion was as tired of doing nothing but eating and sleeping as he was. They were of a type, he and Derby. They had to be set free to run.

"All sewed up. Now to get you saddled." He patted the horse, then threw a blanket over the horse's back and started to lift the saddle.

"Pa, you shouldn't do that. Lifting too big a weight will put you in bed for another week."

Marshal looked over his horse to where George stood, hands on his hips. He sounded just like his ma when it came to mother-henning him.

"You can ride with me."

"You shouldn't go riding alone," George said. He entered and stood at the rear of the stall, wary of being kicked by the feisty stallion.

"I heard gunshots."

"That's not the reason, Pa. You're . . ."

"What? What are you going to say? Fragile? I heard

Sarah call me that last night when she was talking to your ma. They didn't know I heard."

"They thought you were asleep. You need to—"

"Who was swapping lead? The gunshots went on for the better part of ten minutes. It wasn't fireworks, either. Rustlers?"

"The men riding with Gramps mixed it up with a half dozen riders."

"And when you asked your grandpa, he didn't have any idea who was shooting at him. He was with those owlhoots, wasn't he?"

"His gang, as he calls 'em? Yeah, he was in the middle of it. I watched when he cleaned his six-shooter. He was the one doing most of the shooting."

"But they chased off rustlers?" Marsh frowned. He wished his pa would be straight with him. Were his friends outlaws, too? Or bounty hunters looking for easy pickings on the Twin M? Most times there wasn't much difference between an outlaw and a man who hunted down owlhoots for the reward money.

"They chased them halfway to Bullet Butte before losing them. It was mighty dark then, which is why the rustlers thought they'd be able to make off with twenty or thirty head."

"Does he still think the railroad crew's responsible? They're knocking on the town's front door right now. From what I've heard, they've been killing themselves to get track down."

"Mayor Gally fought the town council but lost," George said. "The railroad's able to buy land for a full-fledged depot now. That was something of a surprise to the folks at the meeting. Before they'd only wanted a water tower."

"Osborne, a jerkwater town," Marsh said, shaking his head. He led Derby from the barn. Without being too obvious about it, he'd made sure that his Winchester rode in the saddle scabbard and that he had a couple spare boxes of cartridges in his saddlebags.

"A major stopover now, and the Murphy brothers are making a pretty penny off it, too."

"Let me guess. The land for the new depot is on land they own, and they'll be leasing it to the railroad for a tidy sum."

"That and the water they're selling," George said, his voice turning cold. "Selling our water's a dirty trick. I should do something about it."

"We've got a contract. The circuit judge'll swing back through Osborne in a few weeks. We'll force them to honor the contract."

"Especially since we paid in advance."

"I don't want a refund," Marsh said. "We need the water more every day it doesn't rain."

They rode side by side from the yard. Marsh wasn't sure where to head. He watched for a twitch and a tic to beset his son. That would be the direction he wasn't supposed to ride. When George kept glancing toward the main acequia feeding the big stock pond, Marsh turned Derby in that direction. George started to protest, then fell silent. This made Marsh even more certain they rode in the direction that would give him the most information about what was going on.

This was *his* ranch, dammit.

"It's getting low," George said when they reached the bank of the stock pond.

"It used to be as big as any lake in West Texas. Not now." Instinctively, he looked at the sky. The bright blue sky was almost empty of clouds. Even the high one that looked like wispy white threads showed no promise of moisture.

"We need to get one of the Indians to do us a rain dance. That's supposed to work."

Marsh snorted and shook his head. They needed more than someone shaking a handful of feathers at the sky and dancing around in a circle to bring the downpour they hadn't seen in nigh on a year.

"We need to get all our allotment of water from the Murphys," he said. "Rain dances are not enough."

"Hard to tell if it does, but you're right, Pa. Even a teeny cloud giving shade would be a boon. I—" Before George said another word, gunshots echoed from the direction of Bullet Butte.

They both lit out, galloping hard. The gunfire increased. Marsh bent low and let Derby jump the almost dry acequia. He landed hard. The jolt shocked him into a groan, but he doubted George heard. His son was outpacing him. He called for George to hold back, but he kept riding hard.

By the time Marsh drew alongside, his son had pulled his rifle from the saddle sheath and was studying the rolling prairie. Ankle-high grass swayed to a feeble breeze.

"There," George said, pointing. "Three men took cover behind a low rise."

"And it's Caleb's doing, whatever they are attacking. They're hiding in the grass. I make out four of them. All are on their bellies, creeping forward." Marsh shielded his eyes from the sun. He made out Kingston and his right-hand man, Clay. The only other one he had heard named was Rodriguez. He didn't see him anywhere.

"Yonder," George said. "That's Gramps and another of that gang."

Marsh knew then where Rodriguez had gone. He and his father flanked the three men pinned down. Words were shouted, muffled by distance. A few more reports rang out, and then the three men threw down their guns and came out, hands up.

Marsh held his breath. He expected the bounty hunters to cut down the trio. Worse, he worried that his father would fire the first shot.

Nothing like that happened. Caleb and Rodriguez marched the men through the grass toward Kingston and the rest, all of whom kept their rifles trained on their prisoners.

Marsh rode down, his rifle resting across the saddle in front of him. He didn't want to pose a threat to Kingston's men. They were as likely to shoot him as they were the rustlers.

He sagged when he saw the three men captured. When he reached a spot a few yards away, he ordered Kingston to lower his rifle. "I know them. That's Daniel Murphy and the one with him is his foreman, Ben Wanamaker. I don't know the other one."

Daniel Murphy stalked over and glared up at Marsh.

"You got a lot of nerve having your filthy riders shoot at us. We didn't do anything to deserve getting ventilated!"

"They're back to steal your cattle," Kingston said. "Clay here's mighty sure they've been raiding during the night."

"Danged bold of them to come steal away your cows in broad daylight," Clay piped up. "We can take care of 'em right now." The man lifted the rifle to his shoulder and sighted in on Daniel Murphy.

Marsh's admiration for Daniel went up a notch. The man never flinched. Thomas would have been wheedling or even outright pleading for mercy.

"Hold your horses, Clay, my boy," Caleb said. "It'll be better if they stand trial before we hang 'em. That'll serve as a warning. That one's got a brother ten times as nasty."

"You old goat," Daniel Murphy raged. "You've got no

call to talk about Thomas that way!" He started toward Caleb. George rode to place himself and his horse between the two men.

"Nobody's going to hang," Marsh said. He had commanded cowboys on a trail drive and knew how to use his voice. The snap and steel to it made everyone look toward him. "Nobody's going to hang, that is, if you can give a good reason for being on my pastureland."

"We don't need a reason," Wanamaker said. He growled like an animal. Marsh almost told Kingston he could do with the men what he pleased, but that would start a range war.

He had to live with the Double Cross adjoining his land. Worse, he depended more and more on the Murphy water pumped up from their well. Nothing else would fill his main stock pond. Just to be sure, he glanced at the dome of the sky arching above. A single tiny cloud formed to the southeast. That was a good direction. Those storms came off the Gulf of Mexico, but even as he watched the cloud turned to wisps and disappeared.

"Pa? Pa." George leaned over and tugged on his sleeve. "What do you want to do with them?"

Marsh realized he had been drifting. Or maybe he had reached a point where making just one more decision was too much for him. He looked at the faces all turned to him. He was the judge, jury, and executioner for the three. And all they had done was ride on his land.

"There's not been much water flowing onto my property of late," he said, pinning Daniel Murphy with his gaze. "If you were trespassing to find out why that is, the matter might be resolved."

"You don't deserve a drop of water." Ben Wanamaker snarled, showing his teeth like a feral dog. "This entire spread's gonna dry up and blow away."

"We paid for the water, my brother and I. We're not getting our due."

Daniel Murphy looked at his foreman, as if needing Wanamaker's approval. More likely he wanted to be sure he had someone backing his play.

"Someone's been stealing our water. I wanted to be sure it wasn't you," Murphy said.

Marsh heard the lie. So did everyone else in the circle. Rodriguez outright laughed and Caleb snorted derisively. He tried to silence his father, but Caleb turned red in the face, then exploded in righteous anger.

"You're sellin' it to them railroaders. And they're the ones stealin' our cattle!" Caleb spat to emphasize his disdain.

His father was getting mad, but Marsh saw something else. Whatever the Murphy brothers did to shut off their water was on their heads. But stealing Twin M cattle? Reed and his railroad crew weren't the rustlers.

If a man could be strung up because of the guilt smeared all over his face, Ben Wanamaker would be doing a midair two-step for all eternity. Marsh started to tell Kingston, then knew better. Wanamaker was guilty as sin, but there wasn't proof. Hang him for his crime and there'd be a range war.

With the drought, the water all flowing out of a Murphy well, and everything else boiling around him, Marsh wasn't up to causing such a feud. No matter how much justice needed to be served, watching his back, having night riders burning him out, random gunshots in the direction of his wife and family—that was just the beginning of what a range war with Daniel and Thomas Murphy would be like.

Everyone in Osborne would take sides. He had a dislike for the Murphy brothers that nudged near hatred, but some in town would back them for no reason other than they didn't cotton much to Marsh or Mason Hammersmith.

His brother had been a prickly sort and hadn't gone out of his way to make friends. If he was downright honest with himself, Marsh had to confess to being like his twin.

It was Leonore and Consuela who knew people in town and who had friends. Even among the other ranchers, Marsh couldn't say any were his friends.

A range war might spread. The citizens of Osborne would choose sides. So would the other ranchers. Marsh had no idea how the lines would be drawn.

But he was sure that Ben Wanamaker was stealing his cattle. Without proof, he wasn't about to light the fuse to hostilities that would make the Indian wars and Comanche raids seem insignificant.

"Clear out. Get off my land," he said. "And see that the water we've bought and paid for fills up the acequias."

"We'll cut off all your water!" Wanamaker strained forward. His boss held him back.

"You've made some serious accusations, Hammersmith. Ones you can't prove. You're going to regret insulting me and my foreman and—"

The gunshot caused everyone to jump. Daniel Murphy moaned and dropped to one knee. He clutched the toe of his boot where a bullet had drilled through.

"My boy told you to vamoose. Now git!" Caleb pointed his pistol at Murphy. "Clear out 'fore I decide to blow off some part of your anatomy that you think's real important."

Wanamaker helped his boss hobble along. The other cowboy backed away, expecting to get shot in the back. He turned and ran.

Marsh wished his father hadn't blown off the other rancher's toe. Then he smiled ruefully. He should have been the one doing the shooting. He would have enjoyed that more'n anything else that he'd done in ages.

"What now?" he asked.

Kingston shrugged, gathered his men, and rode away. Caleb started to say something to his son and grandson, then galloped off with Kingston, Clay, Rodriguez and the others.

When he and George were left alone, his son turned and said, "That's a real good question. What now?"

Marsh wished he had an answer that wasn't drenched in blood.

CHAPTER 20

The cowboy emptied his six-shooter into the ceiling. Plaster came falling down, and thick white dust mingled with the gun smoke.

Gustav Hammersmith choked on it. He rubbed his eyes to get the irritating dust from his vision. Then he heaved to his feet, hitched up his gun belt, and stalked over to the drunk. A heavy hand on the man's shoulder caused him to spin around. His wild, bloodshot eyes showed more than drunkenness. He had gone plumb loco.

"Outside," Gustav said. "You can't go around shootin' up the ceiling like that. When it rains, there's gonna be puddles everywhere."

"Rain?" The cowboy threw his head back and laughed uproariously. "It ain't rained in a month of Sundays. Lemme reload so I can put more holes in the sky. I wanna see stars just by lookin' up."

He kicked out one spent brass after another as he struggled to focus hard enough to actually reload.

"You want stars, you'll get stars." Gustav planted his feet, cocked his fist back, and unloaded a punch with all his weight behind it. The impact lifted the cowboy off his feet. For an instant, he hung suspended in air. Then he crashed to the saloon floor. The entire building shook with the impact of his heavy body.

Gustav shook his fist. It hurt so bad it brought more tears to his eyes. He knew better than to punch a man on the chin. That was a good way to bust every bone in his hand. So he had aimed for the cowboy's cheek and had connected just a tad higher. There'd be a black eye for the man to brag on. From the feel, Gustav was sure a bone had broken. The only problem was figuring out if it was one of his or his drunken victim's.

"You better get him outta here fast," Little Miss Molly called from behind the bar. "Mister Murphy's fixin' to come in any second now."

Gustav rubbed his skinned knuckles. Nothing felt broken. He smiled broadly at the girl and said, "For you, little darlin', anything."

She blew him a kiss that kept him going. He grabbed the cowboy by the heels and began pulling him along the floor. At the swinging doors, he collided with a customer coming in.

Only it wasn't a customer.

"What do you want?" Gustav snapped.

"I need to talk to you," Marsh Hammersmith said. He looked down at the unconscious cowboy. "You the bouncer here, too?"

"I get paid to do a lot of chores. Now get outta my way." He shouldered his uncle aside and pulled his victim onto the boardwalk. Gustav sank low, grabbed, and heaved. The cowboy stood straight for an instant, then toppled over the hitching rail and flopped into the water trough.

"Are you going to let him drown? He's not even blowing bubbles now."

Gustav glared at his uncle, went into the street, and grabbed a handful of wet collar. Again, he heaved and dropped the cowboy to the ground, where he sputtered and coughed.

Gustav stepped back and launched a kick that ended in the man's gut. He spewed out what water he had swallowed.

"You'll never have the parson approve of such behavior, not while the man's knocked out," Marsh said.

Gustav started to kick the drunk a second time, but his uncle pulled him away. Gustav jerked free, turned, and braced to throw down on his kin. He'd had enough and was sick of getting pushed around.

"What do you want? I'm workin'."

"Yeah, if you call this working," Marsh said derisively. "The town needs law, not vigilantes."

"Vigilantes?" Gustav snorted in contempt. "If Mister Murphy wants to get a vigilante group together to keep the peace, I'll volunteer. That's more'n you'd do." He thrust out his chin, as if daring Marsh to punch him. "The first thing I'd want to do is find what happened to my pa. You don't care about that, though, do you? You've got the whole Twin M now, no partner, nobody to take half the profits."

"If we can prove Mase is dead, you're half owner of the ranch," Marsh said. "You're his heir."

"Keep it. I don't want your filthy cattle or anything to do with the ranch. It never brought me anything but trouble." Gustav tried to pull away, but Marsh held him too firmly. He lifted his arm to break the grip, but his uncle was like a bulldog. He'd clamped onto him and wasn't going to let loose.

"You don't mean that," Marsh said.

"I've got my own life now, and it isn't none of your concern. I'm doin' just fine."

"Being a bouncer in Murphy's saloon?"

"I do other work for him." Gustav hesitated as he remembered being the guard when Murphy took a bag of money to the mayor. He sneered as he said, "I'm his confidant. That's the word, ain't it? I know about his business dealings. The railroad's fixin' to start on the depot any day now, and I'll be dealt into that hand. I'm gonna make a mint of money, wait and see. And it's all because I earned it."

"Things between the Murphys and Hammersmiths are turning sour," Marsh said. "I don't want you getting caught in the cross fire. Come on home."

"Home? I don't have a home, old man." Gustav finally jerked free and stepped back. He squared off. He was boiling inside, and if his uncle pushed him much more, he'd throw down on him.

"Careful, boy. You might think you're good with that hogleg, but I'm faster. A lot faster." Marsh flexed his fingers and rested his hand on his cross-draw holster.

"I don't believe you. You're getting too much like Gramps, with all his tall tales. He spins a good yarn about ridin' with outlaws and bein' a desperado, but they're lies. Or not lies, maybe, but ravings of a senile old man."

Gustav wasn't sure why he pushed his own uncle into a fight, but he did. It felt good to be in charge. If that old, wrinkled hand so much as twitched, he was going for his own six-shooter.

Marsh slowly moved his hand away from his holster.

"I'm not fighting you, Gustav. You're my blood, my brother's son. I'd never be able to explain what happened to your ma."

"My ma," Gustav spat. "You and her are against me, aren't you? Are you enjoying her between the sheets?"

Gustav saw his uncle turn red in the face. His lips thinned to a razor's slash, and his eyes turned colder than any glacier.

"Things are going to get worse between the Murphys and me," Marsh said. His face turned just a little more florid as he fought to control his temper. "If you stay in town, you're likely to end up dog meat."

"Dog meat," Gustav said. "Better that than your lap

dog." He glanced toward the saloon's swinging doors. Little Miss Molly peered out over the tops.

"Run along now. Drink your water—while you've still got some." Gustav felt bigger than life making the threat, but some part of him held back saying more. His uncle was mad enough.

"Don't bother coming back to the ranch," Marsh said. He stepped away, glanced at Little Miss Molly, then gave Gustav one final long, hard look. "And your ma and me are family. But not like you said. Ever."

Marsh whirled around and took two steps before he halted. Gustav stepped to one side and saw why his uncle had stopped. Thomas Murphy walked down the street, his coat pulled back to free up the six-gun in his shoulder rig. The set to his face showed he meant business. Gustav shuddered, knowing what that business was.

"Get out of my town, Hammersmith," Thomas Murphy called. "Leave on your horse or leave draped over it. I don't care which."

"Open the valves on the water, Murphy. We paid for it, and we're entitled to it."

"I heard what you and that bunch of renegades did to Daniel. If Wanamaker hadn't been with him, you'd have shot him dead. It'll serve you right if we cut off all your water and make you go thirsty. You and your scrawny cows."

"Don't try it, Murphy. We got a legal contract."

"Sue me." Murphy stopped and widened his stance. His hand rested at his left hip just inches from the polished hard leather shoulder holster. His fingers drummed away nervously. He was a mousetrap ready to snap shut.

"Is that what you want me to do? You must've bought the judge. Maybe I'll see about taking the water you're giving away to the railroad. We ought to rank above them when it comes to who gets the water."

"Leave them alone. You mess with that crowd and you'll

regret it. They can handle you and any problem you throw their way."

"Reed and his thugs tried once. I'm still standing. I don't care that you're all against me and everyone on the Twin M. You're not getting away with it."

"The town backs me."

"From what I heard, Mayor Galveston doesn't."

Gustav burst out laughing. Both of the other men looked at him. He bit his lip. He wasn't supposed to know how Galveston had bribed the town council and then voted against them, knowing his vote wasn't going to count. Gustav wasn't sure why Murphy had demanded that, but it was a secret he and Murphy shared. That made him feel big, knowing something hardly anyone else in town did.

"Since he opposed the railroad building the depot, not too many in town support him. I'm going to be the next mayor, Hammersmith. Me. I'm the one who has the best interests of Murphyville at heart."

"Murphyville?" Marsh shook his head. He glanced back over his shoulder at Gustav. "Last chance, boy. This is what you're throwing in with. Murphyville." He spat out the name as if it burned his tongue.

"Who do you stand with, Gustav? Me or this loser?" Murphy began sliding his hand up and down against the slick leather holster.

"You, Mister Murphy. You."

Gustav saw the starch go out of his uncle. His shoulders sagged, then he forced himself erect. Without another word, he turned, mounted his horse, and rode out of Osborne.

Out of Murphyville.

Gustav was sure he'd picked the right side, even when Thomas Murphy snapped, "Get to work, you lazy lout." Murphy pushed past him and entered the saloon.

Gustav started to call out such arrogance on Murphy's

part, then he stifled his anger. He had taken the job of his own free will.

But . . .

He spun around and stared down the main street. All that remained to show his uncle had been in town was a slowly settling dust cloud.

CHAPTER 21

The mesquite tree provided some shade. Not much but enough for Marsh to crawl up near the roots and lie back. He put his laced fingers under his head and stared through the greasy, green-gray leaves at the eye-dazzling blue sky. No rain. Nowhere in sight.

He stirred a little when Derby came over and began nipping at the mesquite seed pods. Somehow, the horse avoided getting the sharp spines stuck in his nose.

Marsh envied his horse at that moment. The stallion was still going strong after a long morning of riding the range. Marsh was tuckered out and ready for a long nap. He was mostly recovered from all his physical injuries, but the emotional ones cut deep and kept him from drifting off for a short midday nap.

Mason's disappearance was as big a thorn in his side as any from the mesquite above him. He had conjured up a dozen reasons for his twin to simply vanish, and none of them were good enough. Mase wasn't a flighty man, even if he had his dark moods. He always seemed a bit stand-offish, but simply riding away wasn't like him.

Heidi was finally beginning to accept her husband's absence, but Gustav? Marsh went over and over his last encounter with his nephew. None of it had been pleasant.

Knocking him down and hog-tying him to drag back to the house was the one thing he hadn't considered when he faced him. But a lariat and a few quick turns around the boy's ankles would have solved a lot of problems.

Even if he had to keep him tied up in the barn. The idea of the increasing unpleasantness with the Murphy brothers rankled, but it was worse that his own kin had chosen the other side. Marsh tried to find an excuse so he could move on. He always circled back to blaming Gustav and never thinking of the right words to persuade his muleheaded nephew. Sometimes there wasn't a good solution to a problem.

He took a drink of tepid water from his canteen and leaned back again. A bit of scooting around scooped out hollows in the sand for his hips and shoulders. His eyelids began to droop as he let the afternoon warmth blanket him.

Marsh came awake with a start when Derby reared. The stallion pawed at the air and then landed hard enough to send a tiny earthquake into Marsh's shoulders.

"What's wrong, boy? Something spook you?"

It was the middle of the day. Too hot for snakes. The predators were all hidden away in their burrows waiting for the cool twilight when their prey emerged to nibble at grass and leaves. He pushed to his feet and brushed off the dirt. He slung his canteen behind the saddle and mounted.

The instant he gained horseback, he heard what Derby already had. Cattle nearby stirred. More. Something caused them to begin moving away from their pasture. The restless sound of cattle hooves had aroused Derby.

Marsh rode to the top of a low hill and looked over the herd grazing on the acreage stretching all the way to the eastern horizon. He spotted the fifty head beginning to cut themselves off from the main herd. Marsh pulled out his field glasses and slowly scanned the area. Whatever caused the cattle to decide to leave the safety of the larger herd was a mystery.

"If I live to be a hundred, I'll never understand what goes on in a cow's head," he said. He patted Derby on the neck and added, "Or what a horse thinks, either. You're quite a mystery, Derby, you and . . ."

Marsh jerked back and focused the field glasses to give a little sharper view. Then he put the instrument back into his saddlebags and looked behind him. George was around somewhere. So were three hands he had hired. But they were nowhere to be seen.

And the four riders he had seen bobbing up and down in an arroyo near the beeves weren't his men.

Rustlers.

Since he had argued with Gustav in town and almost lost his temper, he had tried very hard to keep his hair-trigger anger in check. He snapped now. He couldn't get rid of the rustlers. They kept coming back. Now it was up to him to stop them once and for all. Otherwise, the thieves would make off with several thousand dollars' worth of stock.

He touched the rifle in its saddle sheath. Shooting it out with the outlaws wouldn't get him anywhere but in a shallow grave—if he was lucky. More likely they'd shoot him and leave him for the coyotes and buzzards.

"Come on, Derby. We don't have much time." He trotted the horse toward the main herd, away from the segment being rustled.

He wanted to hurry, but what he intended required that he make his way through the main herd with its thousand head. He left the rise and reached the plains. The knee-high grass was turning brown from lack of rain. It wouldn't be long until the only pastureland fit for grazing was that irrigated by the main stock pond.

And even that was rapidly drying up, both from thirsty

cattle and from not being replenished as it should have been.

He reached the edge of the herd and worked his way in. The cattle protested but reluctantly gave way as he began using his lariat to lash out at them. With typical bovine resistance, they tried to crowd him when he had reached a spot a quarter of the way into the grazing beasts. They were spaced out there as they hunted fresher grass.

Marsh secured his lariat and drew his rifle. He took a deep breath and then fired it in the air repeatedly. The first shot caused the cattle around him to jerk alert. As he continued to fire, he let out a hoarse shout and heeled Derby to a gallop in the direction of the rustlers.

The mass of beef stirred, slowly at first and then with more determination. By the time panic settled on the cattle, he had several hundred stampeding in the direction he wanted. As he galloped along, the cattle pacing him, he stopped firing and kept shouting. Saving his ammunition became important now.

The cattle thieves were flushed out of their arroyo. They had stolen several dozen head, but those cattle joined in the stampede as the first frightened beeves raced by. Marsh saw two rustlers cut away from the stampede and head for higher ground. By the time he reached the spot where they had turned tail and run, he had most of the herd between him and them.

But ahead he saw the remaining two rustlers bent low over their horses trying to outrun the cattle. Marsh lifted the rifle to his shoulder and fired. He missed the rustlers, but the slug came close enough to the lead rider that he jerked violently.

He twisted so much he lost his balance and fell to the ground.

Marsh figured the man was a goner. The cattle would tromp him into the ground. But his partner wheeled about and raced back. He bent low and extended his arm. The man on the ground reached up and grabbed the hand. Marsh winced. The jerk as the rustler was yanked up behind his rescuer had to pull his shoulder out of joint.

Then he stopped feeling sorry for the man. He swung his rifle around and fired. The thief who had been afoot jerked. Marsh had the range. He fired until the magazine came up empty. Furious all over again at not bringing down at least one of the rustlers, he drew his six-gun and carefully fired.

Shooting at two men on horseback while on a galloping horse made accurate aiming impossible. But Marsh refused to let them go without them paying some price.

He cut away from the back of the stampede. In typical bovine fashion, in spite of the gunfire and settling into a hard run, the cattle simply stopped. The stampede was over, but it had served its purpose.

Marsh had run off two of the cattle thieves and was hot in pursuit of the other two. He had a better chance of catching the latter pair and bringing them to justice. Two men on one tiring horse made for an easy capture.

Again, Marsh was fooling himself.

The pair rode to a small stand of cottonwoods and dismounted, ready to shoot it out. As he galloped toward them, he calculated his odds. He had reduced it from four against one to only being outnumbered two to one. As he charged their position among the trees, he caught sight of one and fired.

The man's hat flew from his head. He grabbed but failed to catch it. Rather than go after the errant hat, he fled deeper into the small grove.

Marsh slowed and then halted. To ride blindly into the trees was sure death. By now, both of the rustlers had staked out a position and laid an ambush for him.

He wheeled about and rode down into a ravine where a thin ribbon of water made its way toward the grassland.

Kicking his leg out, he slid from the saddle and landed in mud. When he stepped into the water, it barely came up over his soles. He took out his rifle again, fished around in the saddlebags, found his spare box of ammo, and took the time to reload the magazine. He was glad he had remembered to stash the extra ammo before riding out.

Loaded for bear, Marsh hiked along the stream. He knew this section well. The trees poked up from the prairie and made a convenient way station to rest. He and Leonore had come there on occasion for a picnic.

Now he was going to turn it into a graveyard.

Marsh found a notch in the ravine that led up to level ground. He moved slowly, not wanting to betray his approach. When he reached the notch, he saw one of the rustlers crouched behind a tree, pistol in hand. He took careful aim and fired. The man half stood, then keeled over. Marsh wanted to rush forward, but his anger had faded and common sense prevailed. One more rustler and then he could celebrate.

Working toward the trees, he decided the other man had to be at the edge of the grove. Several rocks there afforded shelter, but they gave protection only from an attack coming off the plains. He advanced from the flank.

He eased around a tree and saw he had figured right. The rustler crouched exactly where he had anticipated. Marsh took aim and squeezed back on the trigger, only to lurch forward and fire into the dirt when he was struck from behind. Falling to his knees, he twisted around and pointed the rifle behind him at his unseen assailant.

The man he had thought he'd finished off towered above him. Blood smeared the man's shirt, and his coat was ripped and torn. He held his six-gun like a club. He reared up and crashed down atop Marsh, hammering away with the butt of his gun.

Marsh got his rifle between them. When the other man's

weight crushed down, he fired. The rustler grunted and jerked away. He dropped his gun. Marsh saw why the man tried to bludgeon him with it rather than shoot him in the back. A bullet had smashed into the cylinder and left it severely damaged.

"Here," Marsh said, flipping the gun up toward the rustler. The man's reflexes worked against him. He grabbed for the gun.

Marsh shot him again. He took a step back, then sat down. The look of surprise on his face told that he hadn't expected to die, not like that, not so fast. The outlaw pressed both hands into his chest. Blood oozed between his clenched fingers. He looked up at Marsh. His lips moved but no sound came out. He slipped over onto his side, dead.

Marsh had finally taken out the one desperado. But he knew the other one, the unwounded one, had plenty of time to find a new spot for an ambush. Moving quickly, he put a tree between himself and the rocky fort where he had sighted the other rustler. A quick peek confirmed his fear.

In disgust, he scanned the whole area for a target. The outlaw was gone.

Marsh moved fast, darting from tree to tree and then moving out behind a low wall of rocks. When he saw movement, he fired. Then he realized what was happening. The rustler wasn't afoot any longer. He had retrieved his horse and galloped off. Marsh climbed on the rocks and fired in vain at the escaping outlaw.

He vented his wrath by emptying his rifle's magazine into a cottonwood trunk, then cooled down a mite.

"Lost one," he grumbled, "but got another. And ran off two more. The cattle are safe and sound."

He prowled around the area and found the fleeing rustler's hat. There were three bullet holes in the broad brim. Marsh smiled crookedly and shook his head. If his aim had been a few inches lower and to one side, he would have had a second rustler's scalp to claim.

The chin string was broken, so Marsh tucked the hat under his arm and returned to where he had killed the other man. He hated to do it in a spot where he and his wife had come to picnic and could have again, but he had no desire to drag off the body. It took him an hour to dig a shallow grave for the outlaw.

"Good riddance," he said, rolling the man in. The dirt wasn't deep enough to keep away coyotes, so he stacked stones on the mound of dirt. That might not deter hungry scavengers, but it was more than the owlhoot deserved.

With the other rustler's hat tucked under his arm, he mounted Derby and rode back toward the herd. He had quite a story to tell George. And unlike Caleb's yarns, he had proof. The bullet-holed hat even had a smear of blood inside on the sweat band.

He'd tell a good story and have proof, too. It had been a decent day.

If only he had buried the other three rustlers alongside the one he had shot . . .

CHAPTER 22

Marsh Hammersmith drew his six-shooter and checked to be sure it was fully loaded. When he rode herd, he only kept five rounds in the chamber, the hammer riding on an empty to prevent accidental discharge.

If he fired the gun now, it would be deliberate, and he'd know the target. He wanted a full cylinder to give him that much more of an edge in a gunfight.

He drew rein under the wrought iron arch above the entry to the Double Cross ranch. From there, it was almost a quarter mile to the Murphy house. He had ridden this way more than a few times over the years. Those trips had been more businesslike and if not amiable, then not hostile.

"Come on, Derby. We've got a busy few minutes ahead of us."

The horse shook its head and tried to turn away. Marsh insisted. The horse relented. They walked toward the house. He felt eyes on him, although he saw no one. The ranch house looked deserted. No one sat outside the bunkhouse where cowboys usually took a break, smoking or just telling one another lies. The barnyard farther downhill behind the house was similarly empty.

He stopped in front of the house and waited. A curtain on a second floor window stirred. Sounds of movement from inside came to him, faint and ominous. Marsh strained to hear the metallic click of a cocking six-gun. All he heard was a soft wind causing the weather vane atop the house to move slightly with a rusty, squeaking noise.

When the front door opened, he about went for his Peacemaker. It took a second to realize there was no need. Daniel Murphy wasn't toting a rifle or shotgun. No six-shooter hung at his hip.

"What do you want, Hammersmith?"

"You're mad about it, aren't you?"

"What's that you got struck in your craw, man? Spit it out, then get the hell off my land."

"I came to return this." Marsh held out the hat with the bullet holes in the brim. "It's a mite damaged, but I don't think Wanamaker will care. It must have cost him a pretty penny. He's a gaudy dresser. A hat like this would set him back twenty dollars."

He sent the hat flying, to land at the other rancher's feet. Murphy kicked it away.

"I don't know what you mean."

"I buried one of your men out at the junction of the two acequias. You know the one near Bullet Butte?"

"You murdered one of my men. Is that what you're confessing to?" Murphy put his fingers into his mouth and whistled.

Marsh wasn't surprised this time. A sniper in the upstairs window showed himself, and Ben Wanamaker came from inside the house. He wore his iron riding low on his hip, the holster tied down to his leg like a gunfighter.

"You want me to run him off the ranch, boss?" Wanamaker sneered.

"That's your hat," Marsh told him. "Better put it on. We wouldn't want you getting sunstroke, would we? The sun pounding down on that bare pate of yours can be downright dangerous." Marsh watched the foreman start to pick up the fallen hat. Instead, he caught himself and kicked it back toward Marsh.

"I don't know what you're goin' on about, Hammer-smith." Wanamaker widened his stance and rested his hand on his holster.

Marsh could draw and fire fast, but doing so from horse-back was a count against him.

"You know, but I'm not so sure your employer does. Your wrangler's been out on my land stealing my cattle. Do you bother using a running iron, or do you just sell them to the railroad?" Marsh saw he had hit the target by the way Wanamaker reacted.

Daniel Murphy's reaction was different, unreadable. Marsh wasn't sure if the Double Cross owner had any idea what his foreman was doing. Wanamaker worked for him, so Murphy was responsible whether he ordered the rustling or not. Besides, Marsh had another bone to pick.

"He took the words out of my mouth. Ride on out and there won't be any trouble." Murphy hooked his thumbs under his suspenders and thrust out his chest.

"You've cut off my water," Marsh said.

"It ain't your water," Wanamaker said.

"It's not yours, either. It's his. And him and me, we have a contract. You're not delivering what I've paid for," Marsh added, directing his words to Murphy.

"The deal was with your brother. Send him around," Wanamaker said. "Oh, wait, he's taken a powder. You ain't got a deal no more." He ran his fingers up and down the outside of his holster. From the set to his jaw, he was going to throw down on Marsh at any instant.

"Is he your mouthpiece now, Murphy? Are you letting him do all your talking?"

"He's right. It's Double Cross water, not yours. And where's Mason? Rumor has it you done him in so you could steal the entire ranch for yourself."

Daniel Murphy was only trying to rile him. Without a gun, he showed he was the peaceable one. His foreman did all the dirty work.

"That's why I have a signed contract. You and your brother both put your names on the bottom, across from mine and Mase's. *I want my water.*"

"Now aren't you the bold one?" Wanamaker said, stepping forward. "Comin' here and makin' wild claims"— he glanced toward his hat laying in the dust—"and demandin' things you ain't allowed to have."

Marsh's thoughts tumbled all around like two wolves fighting. The circuit judge was likely bought and paid for by the Murphys. Calling in the Texas Rangers was futile. He had no proof that Wanamaker was rustling his cattle. If anything, the foreman and both Murphys had a decent claim that he had murdered one of their riders. He hadn't bothered to bury that body too deep. It'd be his word against Wanamaker's about what had happened.

If only there was a law dog in Osborne. But he'd likely be bought off, too.

"It's about time for some justice to come to our fair county," Murphy said. "Mayor Galveston's not providing it. So I've decided it's up to me to change that."

"What do you mean?" Marsh turned wary. He glanced up to the second story. The rifleman there drew a bead on him.

"Thomas is going to run against Galveston for mayor. And until he gets in office and hires a full-time sheriff, some of my boys will patrol the town to keep the peace."

"Not only in town but outside, too," Wanamaker said.

"A vigilante gang?"

"Don't think of it that way, Hammersmith. I'll be fair," the foreman said.

"You're riding at the head of a bunch of vigilantes? Not any men from town? All taken from your wranglers?" Marsh saw how the Murphys were wrapping up the entire county in a tight ribbon—and the ribbon had their name all over it.

"I know how to recruit dependable men," Murphy said. "They'll enforce the law and keep away rustlers, no matter where they find them."

"And trespassers. I'll be certain they don't allow trespassin' like you're doin' now." Wanamaker stepped forward and moved his hand to rest on the butt of his iron.

"The folks in Osborne won't vote for you," Marsh said. "Gally's been mayor since before my family moved here."

"Osborne? Osborne? Where's this Osborne?" Wanamaker looked around as if hunting for a snipe. "I kinda remember a town bein' called that . . . once upon a time."

"What are you talking about?" Marsh's fuse was burning short. He snapped out the question. It made him even madder when he saw this was exactly what Murphy had wanted him to ask.

"He means the town's now called Murphyville, all done up legal by the town council and approved by the railroad as their next major depot in West Texas. In fact, it was their overseer that suggested we change the name," Murphy said.

"Get the water flowing to the Twin M. And there'll be hell to pay if I catch any more rustlers on my property, whether you call them vigilantes or not." Marsh tugged on the reins and let Derby step on Wanamaker's battered hat.

As he trotted off, he cast a look over his shoulder. The sniper in the window was gone. Wanamaker had ducked back into the house, leaving Daniel Murphy alone to watch his unwanted guest depart.

Icy claws scratched up and down his spine as he rode. Marsh kept a sharp lookout, but this section of land was flat enough to see for a ways. The windmill pumping up water from sixty feet below spun endlessly. Even from some distance away he heard the gurgle and splash of pumped well water spilling into a holding tank before being sent along its way.

Only that way wasn't to his ranch where it belonged.

The windmill mocked him, but he rode under the wrought iron arch and onto the main road going into Osborne.

"Murphyville," he said contemptuously. Only he realized how the Murphys had worked so hard and long to become the power in Brewster County. They had the railroad over a barrel—a water barrel.

That control was enough to get the Union Pacific to build a major junction in the middle of nowhere. The railroad had no reason other than water to put a depot in Osborne. Another hold over the railroad was supplying them stolen beef. They got food for their crew and didn't have to freight it down from El Paso on the newly laid line. Every car could be loaded with ties and rails, saving the need to buy and transport food.

The railroad crew would move on soon, leaving behind Murphyville with the Double Cross owners in charge.

"Vigilantes," Marsh grumbled. "They have everything sewn up tighter'n a shroud."

He paused at the road. He owed it to Heidi to make one last try to convince Gustav to return to the ranch. More than that, more than ever, he needed his nephew to watch over the herd. But the railroad and the town weren't the only things Thomas and Daniel Murphy had bought lock, stock, and barrel.

Marsh turned from town and trotted back, intending to reach his spread before sundown. He had plenty to talk over with everyone else in the family. Even Caleb. Those "friends" of his only added to the worry.

He looked to his left and saw a crew digging a ditch on the far side of the road. This was still Double Cross land, but his curiosity got the better of him. Cutting across the plains, he reached the men, all stripped to the waist and sweating buckets as they dug.

One man looked up, then rested on his shovel until Marsh stopped a few feet away.

"What're you doing?"

"You one of them?"

Marsh wasn't sure how to take the question. The men were all Mexicans and didn't have the look of vaqueros come to work on the Murphy herd.

"Reckon I might be," Marsh said. "How's the work coming along?"

The man pointed to the shallow ditch. He barked out orders in Spanish that kept the others working. They all silently went back to shoveling hard earth from the track laid out by strings pulled tight between stakes driven into the ground.

"You can see for yourself."

The ditch was already three feet deep. If the intent was to build an irrigation acequia, they had several more feet to dig through the rock-hard caliche.

"You new to this part of the country?" Marsh asked.

The man nodded. "We wanted to work for you, but they said you already had enough Chinese and Irish. Do not know what Irish are, but they got hired and we did not. Except for this."

"Murphy hired you?"

The man nodded. He wiped sweat from his forehead.

"When will the acequia reach town?"

"Your depot?" The man shrugged. "We work hard, but the sun is hot and tires us. You will get your water when we finish. No sooner."

"Why not take a break? Find some shade and rest? There's no hurry," Marsh said.

"You of the railroad do not want it yesterday, like the big man said?" The worker looked surprised.

"You mean Reed? He's always like that. Don't worry about him or either of the Murphys. Go on. Take a break until it's not the hottest part of the day."

"*Muchas gracias,*" the man said. "You are not like the other, the one who works for Murphy."

"His foreman? No, I'm nothing like him. *Buenos días.*"

Marsh touched the brim of his hat and rode back to the road. Slowing down the theft of his water and its transfer to the railroad was a small victory, but it was still a win. The ride back to the Twin M seemed a little shorter, a little brighter.

Even if a range war was brewing.

CHAPTER 23

The ride to the main stock pond depressed him. The grass had turned brown, making it less useful for grazing cattle than to catch fire and burn down the entirety of West Texas. A dropped match or a spark off a horseshoe, and the blaze would stretch for a hundred miles. He had seen one too many range fires. Once they gnawed away at the grassland, they had to be left alone to burn themselves out. The best any rancher could do was move his herd and possibly dig a fire break around the house.

Prairie fires were unstoppable.

Marsh Hammersmith looked up at the sky. Clouds formed. Some had leaden bellies and showed signs of carrying water. He hoped that was all that came with the clouds. A lightning bolt striking would set off the fire he feared most. There would never be enough rain following the lightning to put out a real blaze.

He followed the dirt track to the pond and looked across what had once been the size of a real lake. White streaks along the banks marked the steady retreat of the water. With no rain to help fill it and the Murphys' contribution gone, the level sank daily. Marsh forced himself not to believe his eyes. The water wasn't going down as he watched. That was his imagination.

Riding slowly around the pond, he tried to estimate how much water remained and what that meant for his large herd. For the first time, he considered selling cattle to the railroad for pennies on the dollar. Some money was better than having to watch buzzards peck at the bony carcasses of hundreds of dead cows.

"A week," he said to himself. "Two at the most before the water's all gone."

He continued his circuit of the large pond. Survival now meant that he had to force Daniel Murphy to open the floodgates and fill the acequias that flowed into this pond and other, smaller ones scattered around the Twin M. Without that water, the ranch would dry up and blow away.

Knowing his predicament, the Murphy brothers had to be plotting to offer him a pittance for the ranch—land and stock. They already controlled Osborne—he choked on his own bile at calling it Murphyville. Within a year, there wouldn't be anything for a hundred miles that wasn't owned or controlled by them.

When he, Mase, and their young families had come to this land a decade earlier, it had been hard. The arid land was at the best of times resistant to farming or ranching. Together, they had fought the first three years, then the drenching rains had filled ponds—lakes!—and caused the prairie to sprout waist-high grass. Running a herd then had been as easy as chasing the cattle from one pasture to the next. When one was grazed down, a new one offered even better fodder for the uncaring beeves.

Those had been the halcyon days when nothing went wrong.

He eyed the clouds again. They formed to the far west over the Davis Mountains. The raging Rio Grande fed those

clouds, he guessed. If only there were a way of lassoing a
rain cloud and dragging it over the Twin M. But those
clouds never drifted that way in the summer. The mountains
caught and held them. The best rain came from the direction
of the Gulf of Mexico. And in winter, the fierce blue
northers that whipped down from the Panhandle laid heavy
blankets of snow across the land that, when melted in the
spring, sent the grass exploding upward.

Not much in the prior winter except cold and no wind
blowing off the Gulf coming from the southeast made it
more likely that he'd go bankrupt. It was good that Mase
wasn't there to see such abject failure.

"Water," he said forcefully. Then he shouted it as if the
act loosened the valves on the irrigation system running to
his pond from the Double Cross ranch.

He stopped and glared at the remaining water. Tiny
ripples danced on the surface, caused by a light, hot wind.
Every ripple created a mirror that reflected the cloudless
sky. Except for . . .

Marsh dismounted and waded into the pond to scoop up
something floating there. He held it high and shook it dry.

A buzzard feather. He looked at the sky, but none of
the carrion birds circled above. The feather hadn't been in the
water long, though. Turning it over and over, something
about it bothered him. Then he saw what it was.

Notches had been carved the length of the quill, all
equally spaced and of the same depth. Holding it up to blot
out the sun, he saw how the barb had been carefully shaped.
This hadn't come from a living bird. It had been dropped
from an Indian's headdress.

"They're stealing my water," he grumbled. Retreating to
the bank, he looked around the soft ground.

His guess about the feather proved accurate. In the soft
earth, he found moccasin tracks where the Indians had

come to the pond. They had walked far enough into the water not to leave deeper tracks, but in his mind's eye, he pictured them laughing and splashing about and one of them losing a feather from his headband. Then they filled their canteens or skin bladders with water and left.

"Filled with *my* water," he said. He doubted even an entire band of warriors could take enough water to matter, but they lived off the land. And they lived off his cattle.

He touched his rifle, then mounted. The faint tracks led east. He rode slowly until he found a spot a hundred yards distant where the dried grass and earth had been chopped up by several horses. Without giving a thought to what he was getting himself into, his temper getting the better of him, he galloped along the path taken by the Indians.

A mile later, Derby began to tire. Marsh's anger still boiled and kept him hot under the collar, but he respected the stallion too much to push on. He slowed Derby to a walk, then drew back on the reins to come to a halt to rest his mount.

When the soft *thud-thud* of Derby's hooves ceased, he heard distant yells. Faint, far off. Then he jerked around, his hand flashing to his Peacemaker, when a gunshot rang out.

The single report hung in the air. Then came a volley. A battle was being fought. Derby responded when he urged the horse to a gallop. They didn't have to go far. Following a depression brought them out onto a rolling plain dotted with trees.

It was as if one stand of trees had declared war on another, nearby one. Bullets tore through the groves and shredded leaves. He paused to figure out who was engaged in such a vicious exchange of lead. From the stand closest to him, he saw a battered Stetson poke up from behind a fallen tree trunk. The man wearing it waved him off.

He took out his field glasses and got a better look at the

farther clump of cottonwoods. A Comanche brave showed himself immediately.

Sides determined, Marsh made his way to where the cowboys fought with military precision. As he got closer, Kingston popped up and shouted, "Get out of here, you danged fool. You'll get yourself killed dead."

Marsh put his head down low and let Derby jump a ring of rocks into the trees. Hardly more than a dozen grew there, hinting at water deep underground. He slid from the saddle, grabbed his rifle, and joined the men sheltering behind the sturdy cottonwood trunks.

"What are you doin' here? I told you to clear out," Kingston said. He duckwalked to Marsh and shoved him. "You git!"

Marsh avoided tumbling off balance and dropped to his knees.

"This is my ranch. Those thieves stole my water." He pulled the feather from his belt and held it up.

"Comanche, no doubt about that," Kingston said. "They've been doin' more than sippin' your precious water. They're rustling cattle, not only from your ranch but two others adjoinin' yours."

"We pared 'em down by a couple," one of Kingston's men called. "Lefty got one right in the breadbasket, doubled him over good and proper. Clay winged another but not too serious. You know how Clay is. He couldn't hit the broad side of as barn if he was locked inside."

This brought angry curses from a few yards away. Then Clay's reply was drowned out by a new volley fired by the Indians. They all ducked down to keep from having their heads blown off.

"How many are left?" Marsh jerked free when Kingston tried to pull him back.

The look he got was one of pure disgust. Marsh knew he

was the odd man out, no matter what. But he wanted to defend his property.

"How many?" Kingston asked. This got an immediate response from Marsh.

"Maybe eight others. It won't be long 'til they either mount up and skedaddle or figure out they got us outnumbered two to one."

"They'll try to outflank you," Marsh said. "There's a ravine they can take that'll protect them until they pop up right around that rock." He pointed it out to Kingston.

"That's from one direction. Can they get to us from the other flank?"

Marsh nodded. He tried to remember the terrain. He wasn't as inclined to ride across this stretch of the Twin M as he was in the other direction, out toward Bullet Butte.

"The mesquite? See it? They'll use it for cover if they sneak down that other arroyo."

"Clay, watch left. You want to stare at the mesquite and take a potshot if they come at us that way, Hammersmith?"

"You'll keep up the fight where they are hidden in the trees?"

Kingston nodded, then moved to a protected spot to add his rifle to the fusillade.

"How'd you come across them?" Marsh asked.

"We found their camp. Or the one they used last night north of here on Circle Y land. They came due south to raid you again. This is where we caught them."

"They took my water first." Marsh held down his temper. He was getting angry all over again at the idea of the Comanches drinking his precious water.

"Might have," Kingston said. He fired methodically. Marsh wasn't sure if the man had a target or if he fired to keep the Comanches pinned down. After emptying a magazine, he stopped shooting.

"Clay? You see anything?"

"Nothing."

"What're they up to, King?" asked another man. "They ain't run dry on their ammo."

Kingston poked Clay to pay attention to the right and he glanced at Marsh, then toward the mesquite.

Marsh understood. If the Indians drew out their attackers by duping them into believing they'd run out of bullets, fine. Otherwise, the lull gave them the chance to try the flanking action Marsh predicted.

He caught his breath when the thorny bush shook more than the fitful breeze could explain. He started to warn Kingston, but the man was aware.

"Don't miss," King whispered.

Marsh jerked the trigger on his first shot. A Comanche had appeared suddenly and ran on silent feet toward them. The bullet went high. His second one took the Indian's leg out from under him. Then he had a second and a third target. His steady fire drove them back. He winged a second one who tried to rescue his wounded companion.

Marsh glanced over his shoulder. Clay had dropped two Comanches attacking from the other direction. Kingston cried in triumph when he drilled one in the distant grove.

"That'll make 'em think twice about takin' us on," Clay said.

"Get the horses. We'll have a race to run them down, but they won't stick around here," Kingston said.

"Are you sure? Marsh asked. "They might leave their wounded to ambush you."

"The band's too small. Chances are good we wounded the leader of the war party and maybe one or two of his sons. We've seen this before. They're on the run." Kingston caught up the reins of his horse as Clay rode up and handed them over. Kingston was no spring chicken, but he mounted with an easy grace.

"I'll come with you," Marsh said.

"You'll get on back to your ranch. Let us do our work."

"What is that exactly, Mister Kingston?" Marsh stood and stared up the weathered rider.

"Ask Smitty. He might tell you," Kingston said.

"Naw, he'll lie through his rotted teeth, the way he always did," piped up another of the riders.

"You'll end up with a war arrow in your heart or a few ounces of Comanche lead in your belly. Now git!" With that, Kingston wheeled his horse around and led the small band on the trail of the fleeing marauders.

Marsh wondered what that band was. Rustlers driving off competition? Bounty hunters? Or a band of outlaws out to even the score with the Indians?

Whatever they were, he knew he'd never get a straight answer out of his pa. Caleb Hammersmith would sooner take the truth to his grave than ease his son's worry about the gang running roughshod over Twin M land.

CHAPTER 24

"Mud. Nothing but mud. In the sun, that'll all be dried up in a day or two." George Hammersmith picked up a rock and threw it into the acequia. The stone made a *sploosh* sound and sank into the mud—more like damp dirt now.

"We've got enough water in the stock ponds for a while yet," Marsh said. He looked into the West Texas sky and let out a long breath of resignation. The weather wasn't cooperating with him at all. The few clouds in the sky were all wrong to bring rain. Right now, he'd even welcome the heavy-bellied clouds filled with lightning if they also dropped enough rain to fill his ponds.

"A week. Two at the outside? That's going to ruin us in a month, Pa." George tossed another stone into the irrigation ditch. This one skipped off the sunbaked surface as if mocking him.

"There's got to be something we can do. Finding the circuit judge and asking for an injunction isn't going to work."

"The Murphys have him in their hip pocket. Bet on it. The most any judge would do is make them give back the money we paid on the contract. That'd be worse for us than this." George kicked a dirt clod into the acequia.

Marsh had to agree. Having a legal decision forcing the Murphys to give back the money took away any reason for them to deliver water. They'd have an argument that they and the Hammersmith family were all square.

And then it would get really thirsty on the Twin M ranch.

"Do we take the water, Pa? We'll need to hire on some wranglers."

"Wranglers? You mean gunmen. Do you want to start a range war? Nobody wins."

"Those men Gramps is friends with," George went on, ignoring his father. "They've got the look of hard cases."

"We don't know why they're here. They're chasing the Comanches, but who posts a reward for Indians?"

"From what you said, they're at the point of chasing off all the Comanches. That leaves the band of Apaches lurking around. I think I saw one the other night."

"What? When?"

"It was after midnight," George said. "He was skulking around the house. I grabbed my gun, but he was gone by the time I got outside."

"What was he doing?"

"Looking in the windows. Probably hunting for something to steal. Can you imagine what Ma would do if she thought some savage was poking around outside at night?" George shook his head.

This was the first Marsh had heard of any prowler. His son hadn't mentioned it for a reason, and he thought he knew why. He'd recognized the Apache as Night Wolf and remembered what Marsh had said about him. Risking his life a couple times to save Marsh failed to fit the tale of a marauding Indian.

"Are you sure it wasn't somebody Daniel Murphy sent over? He was furious with me after I faced him down over the way his foreman tried rustling our cattle." Marsh smiled just a little. Did Murphy find out how Marsh had meddled with his work crew? Telling the crew to take the day off until it cooled down only slowed the progress of the acequia being dug to furnish the railroad with water, but every minute mattered.

He stared at the mud flat in the bottom of the acequia. It mocked him.

"Why would Murphy scratch a picture on the side of the house?"

Marsh stared at his son. Too much went on that he knew nothing about. If he didn't get a better grip on everything happening around him, they were all going to be in a wagon driving to another future. After spending a decade pioneering the ranch and a life he enjoyed, pulling up stakes wasn't an attractive alternative. He was getting too old to keep moving on to the next risky venture.

Besides, as he stared out across the prairie, he liked the land. In spite of all the problems, it was *his* land.

He turned back to George and asked, "What did it look like? The picture?"

"Just scratches on the wall. I've already covered it up."

"Sketch it out for me in the dirt. Can you remember?"

"I'm not Gramps," George said in disgust. "Of course I can remember. It was maybe a warning." George used his boot toe to draw a long loop and then closed it with a flat line. "There was something else at the round end."

"Like the bullet in a brass cartridge?"

"Yeah, like that." George looked up. "You think the Indian was giving us a warning that he'd shoot us?"

"Why not do it that night? How long was he prowling around before you saw him?"

"I don't think it was that long." George scowled. "Just long enough to draw that."

"Was it cut into the wall with a knife point or painted?"

"He used his finger in dirt. Why's that matter?"

Marsh thought that if Night Wolf meant them harm, he'd have used the knife he stole so long ago. He stared at the crude drawing, then looked up and stared into the distance.

"You ride on and check the herd. I'll do some exploring along this acequia."

"It runs back to the Murphy ranch. You don't want to tangle with Murphy or that foreman of his without someone watching your back, Pa."

"I'm not going that far."

They mounted, and George rode along the acequia to the main stock pond. Marsh urged Derby through the ditch's muddy bottom and turned west toward Bullet Butte. He rode in silence, turning over in his head everything his son had told him.

More than once, Night Wolf had steered him toward Bullet Butte. The pile of stone meant something to the Apaches. Watching them climb the side with heavy packs was proof of that. The Lipans, like other tribes, cared little for gold. The Yaquis and Navajos used silver in their ceremonial jewelry, but he had never seen that to be true with the Apaches.

They might be taking ore down from Bullet Butte to trade. Or maybe that gray cap on the cylindrical spire actually was lead. Making their own bullets might save them from dealing with unscrupulous traders.

He shook his head. That made no sense. Melting lead took a forge. The Apaches were nomads, always on the move. That was especially true now that the Comanches had driven them from their traditional land and the U.S. Cavalry sent out patrols to round them up and take them to reservations in New Mexico and Arizona.

The rocky tower poked up steep and dark when he got closer. Marsh stopped and stared at it. Maybe all Night Wolf wanted was to share a sacred shrine. Marsh felt no religious experience as he studied the side of Bullet Butte using his field glasses. On this side, he saw a spot where the Apaches had scaled the peak.

He judged Bullet Butte to be three or four hundred feet

tall. For a mountain, it was more of a hill, but rising from the prairie, it stood out as a landmark. Turning it into some sacred spot where the sky spirits came to earth was possible.

"What do I need with sky spirits? Unless they can summon storm clouds all filled up to overflowing with rain?" He laughed at the idea of him dressed in a deerskin breechcloth and doing a rain dance in front of the butte. If that was what it took to save his ranch, he'd start whooping and hollering and shaking a rattle. But he'd feel silly doing it.

Walking Derby slowly around the base, he found the narrow crevice where he had hidden and then scaled the interior chimney. A shudder passed through him. He wasn't up to enduring the tight passage again. Not right now. Marsh kept riding. When he got to the spot where the Apache had fallen to his death, he dismounted.

At first, he couldn't find where the man had crashed into the ground. Marsh began searching in earnest. Nowhere did he find so much as a trace until he turned and caught a silvery glint in the sand. Digging, he unearthed a small knife. Whether it had fallen from the dead brave's belt or had been dropped some other time was a mystery.

The edge had been sharpened to a razor thinness.

"No rust," he said. If the blade had been in the ground very long, some rust should have dulled it. As dry as it had been meant it might have survived without corrosion a bit longer, but he didn't think so.

Marsh looked around for signs that the body had been dragged off by coyotes. The ground showed no sign of being any different from any patch ten feet or a hundred away. Craning his neck, he looked up. This was the spot where the Apache had fallen.

The only explanation was that the others in the Lipan band had carefully erased any signs that their brother had died there. Marsh made his way to the base of the sheer stone face and looked at the rock. The footholds and handholds had been disguised, too.

The Apaches wanted this spot kept secret from any casual passerby. A great deal of care had been expended to hide that anyone had ever been there. Marsh remembered the climbers and their packs. All traces of their passage were gone.

"They intend to keep this place secret, but Night Wolf keeps pointing me in this direction."

He took his canteen from his saddle, then slung it and the strap on his field glasses over his shoulder. Marsh took a final look up, sucked in a breath, and went to the rock face. He had to jump to catch the first handhold. Straining, he lifted his foot to a depression. It took him a few seconds to settle down, then he sought the next depressions for his feet. They weren't as far apart as he thought. Neither were the rock nubs giving hand grips. Marsh began climbing with little effort.

Before he realized he had gone so far, he flopped over the edge of the spot where he and the Apache had fought. Even there, evidence of anyone walking around was gone. The Apaches had done the same fine job of hiding all traces of their presence.

Marsh swung around and brought his field glasses to his eyes. From this altitude, he had a good view of most of his ranch, or at least the part he called the back forty. The herd was too far for him to count the number grazing on the sere grass. He swung the field glasses around to the acequias.

From this high up, they looked even drier than from the ground. The bottoms weren't damp. They were solid, dry earth. Tracing one after another, he slowly worked toward the large stock pond. Then he found the junction of two acequias, one not far from the bottom of Bullet Butte. He couldn't help himself. He imagined new irrigation channels cut through to join all his irrigation into one giant system.

One day, given the water, those channels would carry water across the entire prairie. The Twin M would grow waist-high grass again. With enough water, alfalfa fields could flourish. The King Ranch would have nothing on the Twin M. Nothing.

He took a long pull on the canteen, replaced the cork, and stood. The mystery of why the Lipans guarded this place was still to be solved. Marsh walked around the small cave until the ceiling narrowed, forcing him to walk bent over.

This made his still-healing belly muscles ache. His back began to twinge, and even his knees hurt after scuttling around like some kind of lizard. There wasn't anything in this part of the cave to interest him. As he turned, he caught the canteen strap on a rock. It jerked him around and cut the strap.

He cursed when the canteen hit the rocky floor and split open. The water inside splashed out and began running down a narrow channel in the floor he hadn't seen. Marsh grabbed the canteen, but it was already empty. He turned it over and over in his hand. The metal needed to be patched before he could use it again. It took a few seconds to tie the torn ends of the strap together and tug on the knot to be sure it was secure.

With a deliberate motion, he slung it back over his shoulder.

In disgust, he looked at the damp spot on the floor. He was already getting a cottony mouth, and a drink would go down just fine now.

"What's going on?" he wondered. Marsh got on his hands and knees and followed the channel in the floor— hardly more than a crevice—to the wall. The water hadn't soaked into solid rock. It ran off. Through the wall.

He ran his fingers along the floor and found a space. Digging as far as he could, he jerked back when something cold and wet ran over his fingertips. His hands were soaked.

Probing further, he discovered that most of the wall was put together like a mosaic tile. Bit by bit, he pulled pieces free until he found the keystone. The sudden tumble of rock left a hole more than large enough to crawl through. He immediately noticed something else. His nostrils flared. The scent of water made his heart hammer away in his chest.

Marsh edged forward over smooth, damp stone. The slick stone grew moss. It took a steady dampness in a cave for moss this thick to carpet bare rock. Marsh crawled faster, and the tunnel suddenly expanded into a cavern.

He licked his lips as he stared across the dimly lit chamber. Light slid down from several crevices in the high, vaulted roof. But where the light touched the floor, the ripples told him a small sea of water was dammed there. He carefully edged forward, dropped to his knees, and plunged his arm down into the water.

When it sloshed over his shoulder, he touched the bottom. The small reservoir held hundreds of gallons of water. More!

This was what Night Wolf had so insistently directed him to find.

He sat back and began stripping off his clothes until he got down to his long johns. Marsh sucked in his breath and slid into the pool. He went down and down until his lungs threatened to explode. Only then did he paddle to the surface. He broke above the water and let out a cry of glee.

Water!

He swam around, hunting for the way the water came to the pool. It didn't make any sense that it came from above. If a huge water catch on top of the butte filled whenever it rained and then drained there, it should have been exhausted months ago. There had to be an ocean to keep this much water after the prolonged drought. He couldn't imagine such a large catch existed.

Marsh paddled to the center of the water, then dived again. He felt a sluggish current rising from the bottom. Still holding his breath, he went to the edges of the basin and found any number of places where the water flowed out.

He kicked to the surface, then rolled onto his back and idly paddled about. The water bubbled up from an artesian well and then was drained back down through lava tubes. Since he had never spotted any wet spots around the base of Bullet Butte, the channels had to direct the flow deep underground. The water had to return to the water table the Murphys tapped with their well.

With a deft roll, he splashed around onto his belly and dog paddled to the path leading to the pool from outside. He shook off the water, pressed his long johns as dry as he could, and dressed.

When he reached the narrow ledge overlooking his ranch, he let out a long, loud cry of triumph.

"Thank you, Night Wolf, thank you!"

CHAPTER 25

The screech of tearing metal brought Daniel Murphy upright in bed. He rubbed his eyes to get the sleep from them. Then came a crash that shook the entire house. Stretching across the bed, he grabbed for his six-shooter on the bedside table.

He had it cocked and was waving it about when yet another crash sounded.

Murphy cursed all the way to the front door. He burst out onto the porch and looked around for whatever had caused the commotion. The screech and crash didn't repeat themselves, but a steady hissing sound filled the night.

Barefoot, wearing only his BVDs, he shivered as the cold night air engulfed him. Murphy swung around, pistol ready, when a horseman trotted up.

"What's going on?" he demanded.

"That you, boss?" Ben Wanamaker leaned over to get a better look. When Murphy stepped from shadow into the bright starlight, the foreman drew back. "You ain't takin' to sleepwalkin', now are you?"

"You didn't hear it?"

"I hear that hissin' sound." Wanamaker slowly turned in the saddle, homing in on the noise. "It's comin' from the direction of the well."

"The damned valve busted. The water's all leaking out!"

In spite of his mostly unclothed state, Daniel Murphy lit out in the direction of the well. Halfway there, he slowed, stopped, and stared.

"You see it, Ben? You see it?"

"I don't know what you mean, boss." Wanamaker stopped beside his employer. "There's nuthin' to make out in this dim light."

"It's what's not there."

"I—" Then Wanamaker twigged to what the rancher meant. "The windmill's gone!" He galloped ahead, letting the bootless Murphy trail behind.

By the time Murphy got to the wellhead, he knew what had happened. The tower supporting the windmill blades had collapsed. That had been the screeching sound, when one leg gave way. The crash came when the wheel with the blades had smashed to the ground. He saw pieces scattered all over the area. The bright metal blades reflected the starlight in a crazy, eerie pattern that made him dizzy.

Adding to the confusion was the three-foot-high geyser spurting from the well. Even as he watched, the column of water shrank and finally bubbled away.

"The water's done gone!" Wanamaker cried out. "There ain't no more water!"

"It's still down in the ground. It's not an artesian well. There's no pressure to bring it up. That's why it has to be pumped up, you fool." Murphy stalked forward and stared at the ruptured pipes. He stood in ankle-deep mud. The cold water rippled sluggishly over his feet and sent shivers up his legs.

He took a step forward and began dancing around as sharp metal from the tower and the windmill blades cut into his bare feet. Black blood from the cuts mingled with the water. It all drained away and disappeared into the thirsty soil.

"What happened?" Murphy asked over and over, circling

the base of the tower, examining the broken metal struts and whatever else remained. "There wasn't any wind strong enough to do this. It'd take a tornado to bring down the tower. The driller promised that."

"Lookee here, boss." Wanamaker held up part of the tower leg. "It's got a rope tied around it. Somebody yanked this leg out and brought the whole shebang down."

"You mean they hitched the rope to a horse and pulled the windmill over?" Murphy tried to understand. Sleep and confusion addled him. Then anger burned it all away. "I've been sabotaged!"

"Now who might be the one to do that?" Wanamaker asked.

Murphy deciphered the man's sarcastic tone easily enough.

"It's got to be Hammersmith's doing. If he can't get the water legally, he'll destroy the well it comes from."

"Mister Murphy, sir, I think you're right about that. I think the only one who'd do such a terrible thing is Marshal Hammersmith." Wanamaker hid a smile behind his hand.

Murphy saw it and wondered what amused his foreman.

"Where have you been? If you hadn't been coming in from the main road, I'd wonder if you did this."

"You got no call accusin' me of doin' this, boss," Wanamaker said. "I was in town lookin' after affairs."

"Too bad you didn't fetch Thomas back with you. Since he and Lilith moved into town, they never spend any time out here. This might not have happened if both of us were here."

"Running Osborne, excuse me, Murphyville, is a full-time job. It's best for him to stay in the hotel to be closer to the town and all your other businesses there."

"He should have been here." Daniel Murphy fired his six-shooter into the air in frustration. "He should have been here!"

"Well, sir, me and you agree on that. Thomas should have been out here. What are you going to do about this?" Wanamaker kicked at a twisted metal leg. "You can't let Hammersmith get away with this."

"Don't go setting your vigilantes on him. I'll take care of this. By damn, I will take care of it! This is personal now."

Daniel Murphy stormed back to the house to dress. It was a long ride to the Twin M ranch house. If he rode fast enough, he might catch Hammersmith returning from this wanton destruction. Then there'd be hell to pay.

Furious beyond words, he emptied his six-gun into the sky, went inside, and before putting on his clothing, made sure he had shells for a sawed-off shotgun.

"Let me handle it, boss," Ben Wanamaker said. "He may be an old geezer, but he's tougher than he looks."

"I can do this," Daniel Murphy said, grinding his teeth together until his jaw ached.

"If he's half as mean as his brother, you don't want to face him down."

"I want him to confess to destroying my windmill."

"A bullet to the back of his head would be better," the foreman said.

Murphy ignored him. They paused at the juncture of the Twin M ranch entrance and the main road into Murphyville. He opened his shotgun for the tenth time and made sure two shells rested in the chambers. He snapped it shut and heeled his horse to a gallop all the way to Hammersmith's front door. He reined in so hard that his horse dug in all four hooves and created a huge dust cloud. It rolled forward over the Hammersmith house.

"Get your ass out here," Murphy shouted. "If you dare, that is, you yellow-bellied no-account!"

The sun barely poked up over the far horizon. Long

shadows stretched along the Hammersmith porch, now covered in a thick blanket of dust. When Marsh stepped from the house, the darkness pooled around his feet, leaving his shoulders and face in the dawn light.

"What's got you so riled, Murphy? You've already cut off my water. What more devilment are you up to this early?"

"You know why I'm here. I'm calling you out!"

"Let me get this right. You violated our contract, you shut off my water thinking you'll force me off my family spread, then you come here all hot and bothered and want to shoot me? What part of that's wrong, Murphy?"

"You know what you've done." Murphy kicked his leg over his saddle horn and dropped to the ground. He carried the shotgun down by his side. A mere twitch would bring it to bear. At this range, Marshal Hammersmith would be a bloody smear across his own front door. And that's what Murphy intended. He'd taken enough from this upstart.

"I know you've got a barn blaster hanging at your side." Marsh moved his hands out on either side of his body. "I'm not armed. Is that going to stop you, Murphy?"

"Boss, let me. I'd enjoy addin' him to the list of sidewinders I've killed." Wanamaker fought to keep his horse under control.

"What's that supposed to mean, Wanamaker? Who've you killed? Or are you only spewing hot air to puff yourself up?" Marsh stood his ground.

Murphy swore that if his foe moved so much as a muscle, he'd use both barrels on him. At this range there wasn't any way to miss.

He jerked away when Wanamaker rode between him and Hammersmith. For an instant, he thought he should shoot anyway. He could get another foreman. Then Wanamaker's horse reared and the ruckus began.

Whether Wanamaker was thrown off the horse or jumped

didn't matter. Murphy ducked and tried to see around the prancing horse. All he saw was his foreman and Marsh Hammersmith locked together, trying to hit each other and flailing around on the ground. The two rolled over and over, kicking up a dust cloud matching the one caused by his horse when they'd stopped so suddenly.

Murphy grabbed the horse's reins and yanked it away. He avoided the front hooves that lashed out as he got into position. He cocked the rabbit-ear hammers and snugged the shotgun stock between his side and his upper arm.

"Get out of the way, Wanamaker. I need to take a shot."

Marsh saw the danger and clung to Wanamaker with an even more tenacious grip. He forced the cowboy in line with his boss. If Murphy fired, he'd kill his own man and Hammersmith might get away.

Murphy stepped to one side and still wasn't able to target Hammersmith. He kicked out and caught the rancher in the side. Marsh screeched in pain and heaved Wanamaker straight up into the air, only to let him crash down beside him. Somewhere in the commotion, Marsh grabbed Wanamaker's pistol.

"Drop it," Marsh ordered. He thrust the cocked six-shooter at Murphy,

Murphy was crazy with rage. He'd take an ounce of lead in exchange for emptying both barrels into the supine rancher.

"You're a dead man if you don't back off."

Murphy looked up and saw Hammersmith's son on the porch. He had a rifle trained on him. Murphy glanced back at Marsh, then up at George as he calculated his chances. They weren't good. He wanted to see Marshal Hammersmith dead. If George killed him, he'd be robbed of that pleasure.

"He deserves to die," Murphy snarled. He turned back, determined to shoot. Only things had changed again.

Hammersmith's left arm curled around Wanamaker's neck, holding him as a shield. With the foreman's own pistol pointed at him, Murphy would take fire from two directions. Marsh was close enough not to miss. George Hammersmith was a good enough shot to hit his target from twenty feet away.

"Don't let him kill me, boss." Wanamaker struggled in Hammersmith's grip. He used both hands to claw at the muscular arm circling his throat.

"Where do you want to be buried?" Marsh asked. "You an Elk? They've got nice plots in the Osborne cemetery."

"I'm neither," Murphy said. He lowered his shotgun. Either of the two had a chance to murder him. It was possible that they would go ahead even if he gave up, but his fury had died down. "Stop sniveling," he said to his foreman. "They're not going to shoot."

The flash in Marshal Hammersmith's eyes hinted that might not be true, but Murphy was drained.

Marsh got to his feet, then shoved Wanamaker forward. He opened the gate on the six-shooter and knocked out one bullet after another before tossing the empty weapon back to the foreman.

"That's so you won't accidentally shoot yourself in the foot," Hammersmith said.

"Here," Murphy said, pulling his wallet from his coat pocket. He pulled out a handful of greenbacks and flung them at the other rancher. "That buys out your contract. You're never, *ever* going to taste another drop of Murphy brothers' water."

He spun and stormed off to retrieve his horse. The back of his neck itched as he waited for one of them to shoot him. That was all he expected from men like the Hammersmiths.

The ride back to the Double Cross was made in utter silence. Once or twice, Wanamaker started to say something but saw that wasn't the smart thing to do. When they reached the house, Daniel Murphy went in and Wanamaker rode off at a dead gallop.

Murphy started to call out to his foreman, then fell silent. When the windmill had been destroyed, Wanamaker had ridden in from town. It was mighty late at night, and the man hadn't smelled of liquor. What had he been up to in Osborne?

In Murphyville?

He shrugged it off and went into the house, muttering to himself that he should have pulled both triggers on his shotgun and devil take the hindmost. That would have rid him of the Hammersmiths, even if he'd have taken a slug or two.

It would have been worth it, and now his chance had passed. He had to find some other way to get back at them.

CHAPTER 26

"We can be ten miles farther south if we don't stop to build that worthless depot," Gerhardt said. He picked his teeth with an iron sliver from a broken railroad spike. When he had rooted around enough to free the trapped bit of food, he spat, then ran the iron sliver in and out of his coat lapel like a pin.

Al Reed had to agree with his foreman. Osborne wasn't the sort of place the Union Pacific Railroad sought for a stop. Or a stop other than to take on water. The population was small, and the wild country around it overflowed with desperados and Indians. What commerce there was to flow through this jerkwater town was seasonal. The ranchers would have the chance to freight their herds to either El Paso or San Antonio rather than forming a trail drive.

That would save them money. And it would cost the railroad about as much as the profit it'd make transporting the herds. Other than that, there wasn't any commerce to be generated in the town.

"They haven't even built the water tank they promised," Gerhardt complained. "Give me a few days and the crew and I'll put it up outside town where we intended."

Reed shook his head sadly. Part of the deal with the

Murphy brothers moved the water tower to a location inside the Osborne town limits.

Murphyville, he corrected himself. He smiled wanly. Renaming the town to please the two ranchers hadn't cost the railroad a dime. His boss appreciated that, but less favorable were the telegrams sent from Yuma and the main office out in California about deadlines and miles of track still to be laid.

He'd fallen behind schedule. That was a worse crime than if they'd caught him stealing railroad funds.

"The Chinese are working their queues off," Reed said. "I want to get all the Irish to building the station house, but they're taking their sweet time with simple framing."

"When they were a few miles outside town, it was hard for them to go to that saloon and get knee-walking drunk. Working a hundred yards from that gin mill is going to cost us a life or two when they start getting really soused. The longer they take with the carpentry, the more often they can whoop it up. They're a rowdy bunch."

"Fights," Reed said. He had seen this happen too often. "And they start developing grudges against others in the crew for beating up friends."

"One slip of a sledgehammer means somebody loses a hand when they're driving spikes," Gerhardt said.

"Or their head. I saw that when I worked on the northern spur. I never saw such an ungodly mess in all my born days."

Reed began walking toward the construction site where the railroad depot was taking shape. The platform had gone up fast. That made loading and unloading the Pullman cars easy, but the freight cars and flat cars carried most of the supplies from El Paso. Those were unloaded yards away from the depot.

"A waste of wood," Gerhardt said. He kicked at a stack of studs intended for the ticket agent's office and waiting room. "We could burn it and be another mile down the line."

"Results," Reed said. "We need to report success to the home office. If giving in to the locals is what it takes, fine."

He stopped to yell at a carpenter putting up a framework of studs.

"Don't drive the nails so far apart. The wall's going to blow away in the first strong wind."

The Irishman gave him a dull look, spat, and went back to work. He still spaced the nails a couple yards apart. The wall would hold and even look good when the town mayor cut the ribbon and made fine speeches, but the entire depot would collapse before the end of the year.

"I'll take care of it, boss," Gerhardt promised. "Sean there's not too bright."

"Like hell," Reed snapped. "He's stealing nails. It looks as if he's using them all, but when you check the supplies, he'll be a couple kegs shy. He's selling them in town."

"You know that for a fact? I never did an inventory."

"Do it. We're getting skinned alive by the locals. I want to escape with our own men only robbing us blind. Letting the town do it to us is an insult." He hitched up his trousers. "I have to explain everything to the vice president in charge of getting explanations."

Gerhardt laughed, then sobered when Reed glared at him.

"And aren't we the blessed ones today?" Reed ran his sleeve over his cracked lips. A drop or two of whiskey would go a long way toward improving his mood. If he played his cards right, he might cadge a drink off Ben Wanamaker. The cowboy's boss owed him. The entire damned town owed him that much.

The Double Cross foreman strutted over. He planted himself in front of Reed, demanding immediate attention as if he owned Reed and everything in his sight.

"Go on, Gerhardt, get to work. I'll check later."

"We need to begin construction on the water tower real soon, boss." Gerhardt looked as if he wanted to spit on Wanamaker. Reed understood. He felt the same way. Still, he motioned for his foreman to go.

Gerhardt pushed past Wanamaker and began yelling at the crew putting up the depot framework.

"Keep 'em workin', that's what I always say." Wanamaker was too smug for his own good, but Reed had to put up with him. For a while longer.

"You just come by for some chin music or do you have a message from Murphy?"

"I've got a business proposition." Wanamaker took Reed by the arm and steered him away from Gerhardt and the workmen. Reed tried not to flinch. This was almost as bad as having a snake slithering around, touching his flesh, turning him slimy. "I'll stand you a drink if Murphy's not there."

"You violating some rule about drinking during the day?"

"It's not that. It's just that this business is betwixt me and you." Wanamaker winked broadly.

Reed paced the Double Cross foreman as they walked down the street. He hardly listened to the small talk and became distracted when a lovely woman came out on the hotel's upper balcony.

"That's one purty filly," Wanamaker said, grinning from ear to ear. "Her and me, well, we've got an agreement, if you know what I mean."

"That's Thomas Murphy's wife," Reed said, looking at Wanamaker in surprise. "You mean you're catting around with your boss's wife?"

"Me and Lilith don't pay much attention to Murphy. And he don't pay any attention to his wife. Right now, he's at the edge of town overseeing some men he hired to build himself a fancy new house."

"He's coming into town to live?"

"He's leaving his brother out on the ranch. That suits both of them. Daniel doesn't cotton much to city life, and Thomas never enjoyed chasing cattle around."

"How's that work for you? You can't be in town and out on the range at the same time."

Wanamaker laughed and waved to Lilith Murphy. She saw him and pointedly spun about and went back into the hotel.

"She don't want anybody to know about us," he said with some pride. "I can come to town whenever I want, but I'll spend most of my time at the ranch. And more than herding cattle and damn fool cowboys who don't have good sense, I'm in charge of the water."

"I heard rumors that somebody tore down the windmill and you can't pump water. Any truth to that?"

"Well, now, I can guarantee all the water you want. But here's a deal I thought up. You agree to pay double what's already been agreed to."

"What!" Reed was outraged. "The board of directors would never agree to that!"

"They would," Wanamaker said confidently. "You've done laid the track. What are they gonna do? Abandon all that track? Add a tank car just for the engine boiler? It's a mighty long and mighty dry trip between El Paso and San Antone."

"They . . ." Reed's words trailed off. The Double Cross foreman was living up to the ranch moniker.

"You're beginnin' to catch my meanin', ain't you? You get the Union Pacific to pay double, I give half to Murphy accordin' to the deal you already made and then me and you split the other half."

"Fifty-fifty?" Reed doubted that was the deal Wanamaker had in mind.

"I'm the one doin' all the work. Sixty-forty. That's still a fair amount more than gettin' nuthin' out of the current deal, the way you are. Them railroad robber barons are cheatin' you, I know it. Get some of the money you deserve."

Reed chewed on his lower lip as he worked over the deal. It never occurred to Wanamaker that he was making the under-the-table deal with a man who would keep on laying track. In a week, he'd be halfway to the Eagle Pass spur, and in a month he'd be living it up in San Antonio.

"Going back on a contract is a mite illegal," Reed said, fishing for some idea how far the foreman was willing to go.

"The other brother gave me a stack of money to recruit a vigilante committee. He wants me to chase after rustlers."

"Rustlers," Reed said. "Like the ones who steal the Twin M cattle so you can sell them to the railroad?"

"You noticed the different brands. Well, now, you ain't got a reason to complain. I'm sellin' those cows to the railroad at a fraction what you should be payin'. I'm doin' that to show my good faith."

Cattle stolen from the adjoining ranch. Water theft from his own employer. Fooling around with his other boss's wife. And leading a vigilante band that kept anyone in town or off the nearby ranches from doing anything about his thievery. Ben Wanamaker was setting himself up as king in Murphyville.

"Are you looking to change the name of the town again?"

For a moment, Wanamaker stared, slack-jawed. Then he laughed.

"You're a real funny fellow, Al. You see what's goin' on when nobody else does."

Reed almost blurted that everything he knew had been confessed to him. Wanamaker had to brag on everything he did to someone. He thought the railroad overseer was as crooked as he was.

"You get my water tower built and fill 'er to overflowing," Reed said. "I want to start service to Murphyville as quick as possible."

"Then we've got a deal." Wanamaker thrust out his hand. Reed shook it, wondering how to renege on the deal. He was an honest man, or as honest as the railroad permitted him to be. Cheating the Union Pacific simply wasn't done. He had seen how the railroad officers handled such larceny. The railroad dicks did more than keep scavengers from riding for free. They were an army beholden only to the home office.

"You buying me that drink?"

"Step right into the saloon. Don't you think it's kinda stupid not to name a watering hole like this? Neither of the Murphy boys ever came up with a decent name so they never bothered callin' it anything at all."

Wanamaker snapped his fingers. The pale, thin woman working behind the bar gave up on her intimate talk with a man who waved to Wanamaker and came over.

"Al, my good man, this is Little Miss Molly. She'll fix you right up. Anything your heart desires. Anything." He nudged Reed in the ribs.

"A cold beer will get me started," Reed said.

"Coming up," the woman said.

"Coming up, sir," Wanamaker said coldly.

"Yeah, that," she said.

Reed saw there wasn't any love lost between these two. He figured it had to do with the power struggle going on behind the scenes. Wanamaker wanted more, but this was Thomas Murphy's domain.

"You make yourself at home, Al. I need to tend to some business."

Wanamaker went to the man Little Miss Molly had

been talking to. They exchanged words. The man seemed reluctant to do whatever the Double Cross foreman asked, then brightened. He knocked back a shot of whiskey and almost ran from the saloon.

Rather than come back to the table, Wanamaker slipped out the back way. Reed sampled the beer the pasty-faced waif set down on front of him. She started to return to the bar, but he caught her by the wrist. Little Miss Molly looked at him with resignation.

"What's your pleasure?" she asked in a dead voice.

"Who was that who lit a shuck? The one Wanamaker had words with."

"Him. That's Gustav." Her face took on some animation. Reed guessed there was more between her and Gustav than just working together in a saloon with no name.

"He looks familiar. Where might I have seen him before?"

"He's Marsh Hammersmith's nephew."

"The owner of the Twin M." Reed sucked in his breath. The problem with small towns was how everyone was related. His crew dined on Twin M beef bought for a few dollars a head, and there he was drinking in the saloon where one of the family worked.

"He's had it rough the past few months," she said. "His pa—"

Gunshots interrupted her. She looked at the swinging doors. The sound came from outside, so it wasn't any of her business. But Reed was curious. He took another gulp of his beer and went to the door. The furor in the street caused him to look toward the hotel.

Two men wrestled with Gustav Hammersmith. He heard him crying, "It wasn't me. I didn't do it!"

Reed felt someone behind him. He glanced over his shoulder at Ben Wanamaker. If ever he had seen an expression on a man's face showing how the cat ate the canary, it was right there. Wanamaker might as well have had feathers around his mouth.

"A shame," he said. "Thomas Murphy killed like that and by Gustav Hammersmith."

Reed started to speak, then clamped his mouth shut. It wasn't his place to butt in.

"This is definitely a job for the vigilance committee. Yes, sir, it is." Wanamaker pushed past Reed, hitched up his gun belt, and walked briskly to where the two men held their prisoner.

CHAPTER 27

He didn't like being bossed around, especially by the likes of Ben Wanamaker. The man thought he was the high and mighty saloon owner and ran things. Gustav wanted to complain to Thomas Murphy, but knew he'd lose his job, such as it was, if he sounded like he was whining. Even though some of the assignments Murphy gave him seemed a tad on the illegal side—dropping off that bag of money to the mayor still bothered him—but he could endure about anything when he considered the alternative. The thought of crawling back to his uncle and begging to work again on the Twin M made him sick to stomach.

Gustav hurried across the street to the hotel as Lilith came out from the lobby onto the porch. She looked at him, her smile a trifle sad.

"I'm supposed to find Mister Murphy. Is he inside?" Gustav pointed to the hotel.

"He's with the workers building that cursed house."

Her rough language startled him. She looked like a fine lady, all elegant and delicate and sweet.

"Don't look so shocked," she said. She came over and locked her arm through his. "You always run off like a rabbit whenever I talk to you. Are you afraid of . . . girls?"

"No, ma'am," he said. "I'm a bit shy, though." He didn't

understand her change of attitude. She had shown nothing but indifference—coldness—toward him when they'd been together out on the Double Cross ranch. He felt a stirring deep down at what they had done then. Afterward, she had turned distant. And now she was changed again. He almost believed she wanted him again . . . in that way.

"It must be a living hell riding out there on the range for months on end with the only females you see have horns and moo if you goose them." She laughed at him again. He tried to pull his arm free, but she had a death's grip on him. Lilith pulled strongly.

Their hips bumped. Gustav blushed. A little. Being this intimate with a married woman in public wasn't right. His pa had always cut a swathe with the ladies. Gustav remembered a barn dance where he had romanced every woman there and how it had embarrassed his ma. The row they had after they got home stuck with him over the years.

He wished he was more like that now. Sparking Little Miss Molly was one thing. She'd fall for any man who spoke to her in a civil tone. But Lilith Murphy was married and she was downright beautiful. She dressed like a fine lady and—

"Where's your head right now?" she asked. "You're thinking mighty hard about something. I hope it's me." She lowered her voice and whispered, "I really hope it's me that's made you so quiet while you remember the two of us and what we did before . . ."

"Yes, ma'am," he said. "I mean, no, that's not right."

"Call me Lil. When we're alone, you can call me a lot of other things. Your pa always did." She squeezed even more on his arm. "Come along, walk with me. I need an escort." Lilith Murphy looked around. "I'm not sure if I need a bodyguard, too. The townspeople are turning more hostile every day." She snuggled closer. "Will you guard my body? You're certainly strong enough."

Gustav's head spun. Confused, he nodded. The only women who said such things to him were soiled doves. The wife of his employer couldn't possibly be one. Lilith was too pretty. She dressed better than any other woman in town, and she was married to the richest man in all of West Texas.

He swallowed hard. She was married, and there they were sauntering along the street for God and everyone to see. It slowly penetrated that she was using him for her own purposes and knew the precise bait to put on the hook. She was showing him off to get a reaction—from someone else. If it was her husband, getting fired was the least of his worries.

"You want me to escort you to the house?"

"House?"

"The one Mister Murphy is building. That'll be your home once it's done, won't it?"

"Yes, of course it will. I never liked being stranded out in the middle of nowhere at the ranch house. It's lonely there, with only Daniel around most of the time. And he ignores me, fussing about with his windmill and cows and I don't know what else." She looked around and wrinkled her nose. "Not that Osborne is any better."

"Murphyville," Gustav corrected. "Your husband got the railroad man to agree to a name change. And he paid off the mayor to see that the town council voted that way, too."

"Did he now? You're certainly the man with his finger on the pulse." She pressed her fingers into his wrist. Her wicked smile set his emotions racing. "Yes, that's quite a pulse you have. Can it be something causing it to race?" Lilith looked around as if hunting for someone. She turned back when she failed to find whoever it was.

"I don't know why, but he insisted that Mayor Galveston vote against it."

"Thomas paid for that?" Lilith stopped abruptly and

stamped her foot. "Damnation, he's going to run for mayor. He wanted Gally to look like he wasn't doing the right thing for Osb— For Murphyville."

"Why are you mad about that?"

"He never told me."

"Might be he wanted to surprise you. The town's name change and all, then him being elected mayor."

"He's got something else up his sleeve."

"Ask him," Gustav said. He winced as she dug her fingernails into his arm when she saw her husband hurrying toward them.

Gustav tried to pull free, but Lilith clung to him like a rattler with its fangs stuck into its victim's leg.

"Lilith, what are you doing on the street? I thought I told you to stay in the room."

"It was so dreary there, Thomas. Taking a stroll with this young man brightened my day." She looked at Gustav. He blushed even more. He knew how that looked to the woman's husband. This was what she had been angling for, causing Thomas Murphy to react.

"Mister Murphy, we haven't done anything. Not like that. I mean her and me, we—"

Gustav jerked back when blood spattered his face. Lilith screamed, and her husband stood upright with a shocked look. A huge hole gaped in his forehead.

"What . . . ?" That was all Gustav could get out before Thomas Murphy fell bonelessly to the street.

"Someone shot him from behind," Lilith said in a voice that came out more hopeful than frightened or shocked.

"Mister Murphy?" Gustav knelt and rolled the dead man over. Sightless eyes stared up at the vivid blue sky. For the barest instant, a cloud passed across the sun and laid a shadow on Murphy's face. Then bright sunlight returned.

Gustav turned to Lilith, but before he croaked out a

word, strong hands grabbed his arms and yanked him around.

"He shot Murphy. We caught him red-handed."

Whoever lifted the cry brought a crowd. Gustav tried to object. He hadn't done anything but watch his employer get shot.

"Wait, no, that's wrong. See? My gun's not been fired." He lifted it from his holster, only to have a strong hand grip his wrist. He dropped his gun.

"Don't let him kill Mrs. Murphy, too. The man's a cold-blooded killer!"

Gustav jerked around and thought he saw Ben Wanamaker, but that had to be wrong. The Double Cross foreman had sent him out there. He was still in the saloon. Before he could be sure of that, the gathering crowd pressed against him and blocked his view.

"String him up. We got the right. We're with the Murphyville Vigilance Committee."

"Wait, no, I never shot him. My gun's not been fired." Gustav struggled in vain against the hands holding him.

Nobody listened to him. The noise from the crowd increased. All Gustav heard were the demands that he be strung up.

"I've got a rope right here. Let's drop him from the church steeple. That's tall enough for this murderin' varmint."

A small argument passed through the crowd about the propriety of using the church bell tower for a hanging. It didn't last long enough for Gustav to get his wits back. Hands shoved him this way and that. It took him a few seconds to realize they were herding him toward the church.

All he saw was the tall steeple. A small brass bell that Reverend Dalton rang to notify people of his Sunday sermon swung back and forth, catching the sun and shining in his eyes. Gustav tried to block the blinding light, but someone caught his arm and twisted it around. Rope quickly fastened his hands behind his back. Every second that passed brought him closer to doing a midair two-step.

"I didn't do. I can prove it in court. I want a trial!"

"He says he's innocent. Tell that to Thomas Murphy, layin' face down in the dirt back at the hotel."

"He's not face down. I rolled him over."

"Look at the blood all over him. He's a bloody-handed murderer!"

"Wait, he's right."

This brought a new round of argument, but the man who prevailed had some kind of authority.

"What are you sayin', Petey? You think he's innocent?"

"I think he deserves a trial. As the senior member of the vigilance committee, I'll be the judge. You, you, all of you, you're the jury."

"I'll persecute," yelled a man at the back of the crowd.

"Who'll defend this guilty sidewinder?" Pete Peterson asked. When no one stepped forward, he said, "He can defend himself. We ain't got the time to find Wayne Cummins."

"That shyster? He's likely drunk by now."

Gustav knew Cummins. He was a drunk who had to be thrown out of the saloon once or twice a week and not much of a lawyer, but in Murphyville there wasn't much call for legal pleadings. What wasn't settled in a good fistfight ended with lead being swapped until one side either gave up or was killed.

"Let's get this trial movin' along," Petey called. "Drinks are on the house, in memory of poor dead Thomas Murphy, when we've convicted his killer."

"You're supposed to be impartial," Gustav protested.

"The defendant will shut his pie hole, or I'll order it shut with your own sweaty bandanna. Now, whichever one of you said he'd tell us why we need to hang him, say your piece."

The man lumbered forward. Gustav recognized him as one of the Double Cross riders.

"It's real simple. He done it. He killed Murphy and deserves to have his neck stretched for it."

"I'll decide the sentence. That's what a judge does," Petey chided. "All right, jury, what's your verdict?"

"I didn't have a chance to defend myself." Gustav panicked now. He thrashed around but couldn't free his hands. Two men he recognized as working in the town's lumber yard held him so tight his arms began to tingle from lack of circulation.

Peterson sneered at him.

"You say you didn't do it. The prosecutor there says you did. Them's the facts." He turned again. "Jurors? What's the verdict?"

All of them shouted "Guilty!" at the same time. Their decision echoed through the streets of Murphyville.

"It's unanimous," Petey said.

"No, it ain't," protested one juror. "We all agreed on it."

The others shushed him. Peterson left the jurors to educate their protesting member and turned to Gustav. "You've been found guilty by a jury of your peers. By the power vested in me by the Murphyville Vigilance Committee, I sentence you to get strung up." He turned and pointed dramatically at the steeple. "From up there. Right now."

A great cheer rose from the crowd. Gustav was shoved forward and stumbled into Reverend Dalton's arms. The man supported him and looked around, horrified.

"What are you people doing? You can't string him up from the church steeple. It's against God's will to—"

The reverend was bowled over as the crowd pushed forward. Gustav fought, but he might as well have been a leaf in a strong river current. Carried along, he finally reached the narrow staircase leading up. One man with the rope rushed ahead. Every step he took on the wood steps rang like a new death sentence.

"I'll see that he meets his destiny," the man behind him said. Gustav cringed as a muzzle was shoved hard into his spine. "I'd just as soon shoot you as watch you fall, but the folks want a show. You're gonna give it to them, dead or alive."

"You'd kill me and then hang me?"

"Can't be too careful," the man said, crowding Gustav so he had no choice but to climb the narrow, winding stairs. He tried to walk slowly, but the man prodding him wouldn't have any of that.

Gustav stepped out into the small area around the brass bell. The man with the rope had already secured one end to the hook supporting the bell.

"I checked it. Real secure. You're not gonna pull it loose when you fall."

"I heard of men's heads poppin' off if they fell too far," the vigilante with the pistol said. "You take that into account?"

"The boss warned me about that. He won't drop more'n ten feet. Reckon he can hang there till the crows peck his eyes out and the worms eat his flesh."

"Boss? What are you talking about?" Gustav asked. "Somebody told you to do this to me?"

"Amazin' how smart a man gets just before he dies."

"This one's got a ways to go before he's as smart as a sheep. Get him over here so I can drape the noose around his neck."

Gustav fell to his knees when the man behind him pushed hard. When the muffled shot sounded, he thought he was a goner, but no new pain shot through his body. He looked to his right, under the bell. His tormentor sprawled there, a bullet hole in his back.

"How'd you get up here?" the hangman asked, peeved.

"I decided to take a hand in this execution."

"Mrs. Murphy!" Gustav blurted.

"I told you to call me Lil."

"Nobody said anything about you bein' here. And why'd you gun down—" That was all the farther the hangman got. Skirts rustling, Lilith Murphy stepped over Gustav and swung her six-gun as hard as she could. She caught the hangman on the side of the head and forced him to his knees.

She wiggled around in the tight confines of the bell tower. The woman smiled wickedly and stroked Gustav's cheek.

"You are such a fine boy, and I'm sorry I misused you the way I did," she said. "Excuse me a minute. The crowd is expecting a show. If they don't get it now, they'll get curious."

She laid her six-shooter on the floor and secured the rope around the hangman's neck. He moaned and stirred, then struggled to stand. Dazed, it took him a second to realize his predicament.

"No!" he shrieked.

Lilith kicked the man's legs out from under him. He tumbled out into thin air.

Gustav flinched at the crack as the man's neck broke. Then the body slammed back into the side of the church.

"You saved me," he said, looking up at the woman. He saw an angel—an avenging angel. "Why'd you do that?"

"You're going to find out," she said. Her grin was devilish as she untied his hands, and they raced down the narrow staircase before someone figured out the hanged man wasn't Gustav Hammersmith.

CHAPTER 28

"Here's your gun." Lilith Murphy shoved the pistol into Gustav's hands. He stared at it, then looked up at her. "I picked it up when they knocked it out of your hands. Back where Thomas was killed. You remember that?"

"Of course I do," he said. The shock still froze him. The sounds of the cheering crowd below would die down soon when they realized the wrong man had been hanged—or not the one they expected.

"I saw Ben kill my husband," she said.

"That's why you saved me?" He ran his fingers around his collar. The feel of hemp crushing his windpipe and breaking his neck had been too close.

"Not entirely. I reckon I owe your father something." She grabbed his arm and pulled hard. Off-balance, he crashed into the bell, making it swing wildly. The raucous ringing forced him to clap his hands over his ears. This made matters worse. In his haste, he knocked himself in the head with the six-gun.

Lilith Murphy pulled on his arm again.

"If they come up here, they'll have a double hanging." She looked uneasy. "Maybe I'll end up dangling next to you. Petey was a hangman, you know. He took real pleasure in his former occupation."

"Before he became a judge?"

"Judge, jury, and executioner," she said. "Him and Ben have recruited quite a pack of wolves for their vigilantes." She turned, her skirts making a soft swishing sound. Hurrying down the spiral staircase proved harder than going up. She cursed a blue streak, again startling Gustav with her extensive vocabulary of swear words.

He followed as fast as he could without running over her. At the bottom, she held him back, then put her finger to her lips. Two men stood just inside the door, holding Reverend Dalton between them. The cleric saw Lilith and Gustav and started to speak. Lilith repeated her gesture. Dalton turned away suddenly and jerked free, plunging outside. Both his captors grabbed and missed, then went after him. He put up quite a fight.

"Don't just stand there. Come on. The reverend's buying us time." Lilith laughed. "He's such a sweetheart."

She slipped behind the altar and grabbed a ring set into a floorboard. Gustav wondered how she knew about the steps down into a cellar. Lilith jumped down. He dived after her and landed hard in the dark.

"Close the trapdoor. Don't let them see you."

He scrambled to his feet and obeyed. So far everything she'd said had paid off. He was there and with his neck still attached to his spine. The door clanged down.

"Wait a second. Don't blunder around."

He heard her skirts hissing as she did what she warned him against. The sudden flare of a lucifer was followed by dazzling light from a kerosene lamp. Gustav held up his hand to shield his eyes. He looked away and saw the cellar was outfitted with a bed, table, and chairs.

"What is this place?"

"The good reverend often spends time here when he doesn't want to go home," she said. Lilith sat on the edge of the bed and patted the spot next to her. "Sit down. You're shaking like a leaf."

"I almost got my neck stretched," Gustav said. He walked around the small hidey-hole and wondered at the woman's explanation. The reverend lived ten minutes away from the church.

Before Lilith could again invite him to sit beside her, footsteps in the church over their heads made Gustav jerk about and stare up. He slid his six-gun from its holster.

In a low voice, he told himself, "One round's been fired. Got five left. Five." He started to open the gate and replace the spent round. Heavy footfalls froze him. If the trapdoor opened, he had to shoot the instant a face appeared.

The footsteps faded away.

"They discovered they hanged the wrong man," Lilith said. "They can't find you, so they're getting the vigilance committee together to scour the town."

Gustav nodded. She was right. He slid the pistol back into his holster.

"We ought to wait them out." She patted the bed beside her again. The way the lamplight cast shadows across her face turned her into something devilish—or demonic.

Gustav began unbuckling his gun belt as he went to the bed.

"It's past midnight," Gustav said, checking his pocket watch. "I need to make an escape."

"Umm," Lilith said, stretching back on the hard bed. "I hate it when you're right." She sat up. "It's time to get out of town."

"Come with me," Gustav said. "There's nothing here for you now that your husband's dead."

"I can claim his half of the Double Cross," she said. "There's more to do. Not even Ben will oppose me." She fell silent for a moment, then pursed her lips as another thought came to her. "He'll try to remove me unless I stake out my territory where he can't do a thing."

"What do you mean?"

"Daniel wants to run the ranch. Thomas wanted to control the town. Ben wants both. I have to decide which I want. Town or ranch. Ben will find it hard to muscle in on both if I work to take whichever one I want."

"You don't like ranch life," Gustav said. "And here in town is too dangerous for you. Come with me."

Lilith ignored him. Gustav started to repeat his request, but she stepped up the ladder and opened the trapdoor. When she cursed loud enough for the dead out in the graveyard to hear, Gustav reached for his six-shooter.

"No, no," she said, impatiently motioning him to put away his smoke wagon. "Come along and don't make any noise. A footstep can sound like a drum beat. Echoes in the church will bring the vigilantes running."

He started to ask how she knew. The only times he had been in church before was for services. Dozens of people then made plenty of noise.

She scampered up the ladder and disappeared into the dark. He followed more cautiously. Head poking out, he looked around. Lilith stood at the back of the church, waving to him. He joined her after closing the trapdoor.

"I can get to the livery and get my horse—"

"Are you an idiot? Petey isn't. Ben certainly isn't. They'll have at least one vigilante guarding the stable. Probably more."

"I can't walk out of here. And where would I go?"

"Not to your uncle's ranch. The road between town and the Twin M will be watched."

"I'm caught here." Gustav tried to think it through. Nothing worked. He stepped out, stopped, stepped back.

The sanctuary of the church was safe and leaving was dangerous. His brain spun around and around.

"I'll help you get away. I owe you that much."

"You do?" Gustav turned wary. Lilith had been too good to him. She had saved his life and hidden him under the church floor and helped him pass the time as they waited to escape.

"You're a sweet kid, and you're a lot like your father. I never had a quarrel with the Hammersmith clan, as much as my husband hated you people."

"Why'd he hate us? That can't be right. He gave me a job!"

"How'd your uncle react to that?"

"He was furious."

"Thomas had a nasty streak. Hiring you was better than sticking a knife in Marshal's ribs."

"I'd have done that for him if he asked," Gustav said. "Me and my uncle don't see eye to eye."

She shrugged, then gripped his arm and whispered, "Be as quiet as a church mouse. Come on." Lilith pulled him behind until he saw her intentions.

They dashed across the alley behind the church to a ramshackle house that had seen better days. It had been abandoned by its owner, but Gustav doubted it was left too long ago. Lumber was at a premium in Osborne—Murphyville, he corrected himself—and most of the planking and walls were still intact. The roof had collapsed, but a little elbow grease and a claw hammer would pull the nails that were holding the boards in place.

"This is crazy," he said, "But I can use these planks over at the saloon. A customer shot holes in the ceiling. These would patch it up nice as you please."

"Gustav, sweet Gustav, you don't work there anymore." Lilith looked at him for a moment. "Is she worth getting your head blown off? This time Ben won't want you strung up."

"What are you talking about?"

Lilith threw up her hands. "Don't play coy with me. You and that little tart who tends bar can't keep your eyes off one another."

"Little Miss Molly is just giving me a place to stay until I can find a room of my own."

Lilith snorted and said, "Whatever you say. But if your horse has a couple guys watching for you to show up in the stable, Little Miss Molly's got a dozen men watching her, waiting for you to show up."

Gustav sagged. He had lied to himself about that. He wanted to see her and say goodbye. Lilith was a better companion. He'd ask again and convince her to come with him, wherever he went. It didn't matter she had used him to taunt her husband. Thomas Murphy was beyond caring now. That made Lilith a widow.

He sank down in a corner of the deserted building. Fort Davis wasn't too far away. Or maybe head southwest to Eagle Pass. He and Lilith would fade into the town and nobody'd ever find them. If Wanamaker and his vigilantes tracked them down, sneaking into Mexico guaranteed a secure hiding place. All he needed was some money.

"Little Miss Molly can give me money from the till," he said. "We're going to need a wad of cash to get away."

"There's no 'we' in the future, Gustav." Lilith stood on tiptoe and peered between two loose boards. "There's your ride out of town."

He stepped up behind her and put his hand around her slender waist. She wiggled just a little to remind him what he'd be missing if she refused to join him. Gustav saw a rider walking his horse slowly down the alley behind the church.

"I'll get his mind off tracking you down," she said. "Steal his horse and leave town."

"I can cut across country, avoid roads. There's no way

Wanamaker can ring the town with his vigilantes. There's got to be a way past them unless he's got hundreds of men."

"He doesn't need that many, but he has plenty. Maybe fifteen or twenty. He and Petey have been gathering their gunslicks for months."

"How does he expect to take over your ranch? Just steal it?" Gustav thought for a moment. "He's got to kill Daniel, too, doesn't he? But how's he get legal title with both owners dead?"

"Ben's nothing if not resourceful. I'm Thomas's heir."

Gustav put it all together, and it made him angry.

"He'll force you to marry him, so he gets ownership."

"Something like that. Now get ready. I don't know how long I can decoy that one. He's got a vicious streak."

"I can't let you . . ." Gustav's words trailed off. He spoke to empty air. Lilith had wiggled free of his hands and was already out in the alley, walking boldly toward the vigilante.

"Hayward! Mister Hayward! There you are." Lilith ran to the man and grabbed his gun hand. She spun the vigilante around. "I saw him. I know where he is."

"The Hammersmith kid? Where is he?"

Gustav's heart threatened to explode in his chest. Lilith was betraying him! And then he saw her ploy. She steered the gunman into a crossing street and pointed.

"He ducked into the grain and feed store. It has to be him."

"I'll fetch Petey and—"

"There's no time to get Mister Peterson. Besides, you're such a brave fellow you can handle him all by yourself. Come on. I'll show you."

Lilith kept pulling at the man until they were halfway down the street in front of the feed store. Gustav knew this was his only chance. He slipped from the abandoned building and walked to the vigilante's horse. The roan snorted and pawed at the dirt.

"There, there, nothing to get excited about," he said in a low, even voice. The horse calmed a mite. He walked around, took the pommel, and pulled himself into the saddle. A yank on the reins and the horse wheeled about.

And then everything went wrong. Gustav went flying through the air as the horse sunfished on him. All four hooves left the ground, and the horse arched its back like the worst bucking bronco ever in a rodeo.

He landed so hard it knocked the air from his lungs. Helpless, with pain stabbing through his chest as he fought for breath, all Gustav could do was weakly kick as he lay on his back in the street.

CHAPTER 29

Something moved in the house. Marshal Hammersmith rolled over in bed. His wife lay beside him, facing away. She wouldn't have heard the noise or be aroused by it. Her special hearing was always attuned to babies crying. That would bring her fully awake, no matter how soft the sound. Luckily, baby Joseph was fully recovered from his ailment and slept easily and well through the night.

But other sounds? Leonore slept like a log through them.

Marsh sat up and listened hard. His hearing sought out different threats. Anything to endanger his family woke him. On bare feet, he went to the window and looked out. A shadowy figure rode past the bunkhouse where the riders he'd hired snored away the night. All but one or two of them, he hoped, who ought to be out guarding the herd.

There hadn't been trouble with rustlers for some time now. The Comanches had moved on—or had been driven off by Caleb's friends. But not all the cattle thieves had been Indians. Ben Wanamaker could lie all he wanted, but Marsh was sure the Double Cross foreman had stolen his beeves and sold them to the railroad. In a way, that depressed him. He wanted the Union Pacific overseer to be guilty of the theft, not just knowingly buying stolen cattle to feed his crew.

Marsh rubbed his belly. Al Reed had plenty to answer for, just not rustling.

The distant rider didn't take the road into town as Marsh expected. Instead, he cut across Twin M land. That galvanized Marsh. He dressed hurriedly but carried his boots from the bedroom. The click of the heels against the floor was sure to wake even soundly sleeping Leonore.

Once downstairs, he pulled on his boots and settled his gun belt around his waist. He rummaged around in the gun cabinet and found a couple boxes of cartridges for his rifle. With all the thieving and stealing and assaults going on around him, he had learned his lesson.

Always be armed. Always carry plenty of ammunition.

He started to run to the barn, but his knees refused to work right. He had to satisfy himself with a stiff-legged walk. The cold night worked against him. When he got to the barn, more than this slowed him. Derby had no desire to let him saddle up or leave the warm barn. In the end, Marsh prevailed. His knees limbered up, and Derby let him gallop away into the night.

Marsh looked at the wheel of dazzling, bright stars overhead and judged it was past midnight. This wasn't a reasonable time for anyone to be prowling around his house, riding through his yard, or going toward his herd.

He was again surprised when the rider he trailed didn't go to the new pasture where the cattle had grazed for the past couple days. Instead, he cut past Bullet Butte and avoided the area where Marsh had discovered the Apache well.

For that, he heaved a sigh of relief. He wanted to keep his discovery secret until he figured out how to best use the water. The Apaches had kept it secret for their own reasons, ones he understood. Being able to water your horses and warriors gave them an edge in this desert at the edge of grasslands.

But the rider pressed on toward the Double Cross ranch. That meant the intruder was one of Murphy's men spying on Marsh and his family while he slept. That fueled his anger. He rode faster. Derby finally responded, feeling the cold night air and rejoicing in the wind whipping past them.

Marsh wanted to catch Murphy's man before he left land where he wasn't welcome. He cut down an arroyo and then popped up ahead of the man. He drew his six-gun and waited.

"I can shoot you out of the saddle, unless you put away that six-gun," came a voice he recognized. Marsh swung about in the saddle. He had been outflanked. In his rush to head off the rider, he had ignored the possibility that he had revealed himself.

"What are you doing out here, George? I thought you were one of Murphy's cutthroats."

"His vigilantes?" George Hammersmith snorted in contempt. "They're being paid by Murphy, but those are Wanamaker's hatchet men. He recruited them, and he tells them what to do. Murphy is too lost in grief over Gustav shooting down his brother."

"Do you think he did? Gustav has been sulking since his pa disappeared, but shooting Thomas Murphy in the back doesn't sound like him."

"My dear cousin's gone off the rails, as those railroaders say. He's plumb loco." George rode closer. He slid his pistol back into his holster.

"I can see him flying off the handle and punching Murphy. If Murphy made him mad enough, he might throw down on him and put a round into his head, like they claimed. But he wouldn't shoot him from behind."

"Maybe," George said, "maybe not. It doesn't matter. He got away from them. I'll give him credit for that. He out-smarted all of Wanamaker's vigilantes."

"Where are you going?" Marsh asked suddenly.

George half turned in the saddle and started to point, then settled down.

"Just for a ride. There's no reason for you to get your dander up over that."

"What are you going to do?"

"Not help my cousin, that's for sure," George said. "He's likely a hundred miles from here. How, I don't know. Don't much care. Gustav and I haven't been on good terms for quite a while."

"Nobody comes this way because he can't sleep. That's Murphy land ahead. What are you up to?"

"Nothing."

"You never could lie to me so I wouldn't know."

"Yeah, what about the time I—"

"George," he said sharply. "What's your business on Double Cross land?"

"Doing what you should have when they cut off our water. You took back the money we'd paid. We don't need the money as bad as we need the water."

Marsh almost told him about the artesian well. But that served his son's purpose of distracting him from the real reason he was on the edge of Murphy land.

"The windmill," Marsh said. "You're the one who pulled it down."

"Damn right I did!"

Marsh wished he could argue with George over this. He had smiled, just a little, when he'd heard that the well had been put out of business, at least until a new pump was installed.

"It's not our property."

"It was supposed to be used to give us water. I acted when you didn't, Pa. I never thought you'd get all weak-kneed about standing up to those crooks. I swear, Gramps would have come with me if I'd asked. I knew better than to tell you what I intended."

The gibe about Caleb helping when he wouldn't cut deep. It was too true. Somehow, he was feeling too old to stand up for his own rights and his own father wasn't. Caleb would have been the first one to tie a rope around the windmill's support.

"Are you going back to finish the job?"

"I know what you're gonna say, Pa. They'll be waiting. The vigilantes must have a guard on the wellhead. All I did before was pull down the windmill tower." George patted his horse's neck. "Then a friend stomped on the pump." He patted the horse again.

"Did the water come spurting out?"

"In a geyser?" George shook his head. "There wasn't any pressure. That's why the Murphys used a pump. There's no surface water."

"What do you intend to do tonight?"

"Finish what I started. There's a valve on the drill pipe. If that's broken off, they have one whale of a chore ahead of them to fix the well. It might take weeks. Longer."

"It won't bother the Murphy herd any," Marsh said. "They have their ponds full. All you'll do is shut off the water being sold to the railroad."

George nodded. His horse started whinnying and kicking up a small dust cloud. It was nervous just standing there. Marsh agreed with the horse. They were exposed, even if they were still on Hammersmith land.

"The track crew is moving farther south already," Marsh said. "The depot won't be done for another week or two, but that's not a big goal for Al Reed."

"Cut off the water for their engine, and the train comes to a halt."

"You're not thinking this through. If it comes down to a filled locomotive boiler every day or two, Murphy can use water he's already got in his pond. He won't drain even one pond before he can ship in new equipment."

"I want to make him work for every drop of that danged water. It was ours, Pa. We bought it fair and square. We paid good money, and Murphy stole it."

Marsh heard his son's anger mounting.

"Let's get back to the house," he said. "We can figure out what to do there."

"I know what needs to be done." George wheeled his horse around and trotted off in the direction of the Murphy well.

Marsh started to call out after him, then fell silent. It wouldn't do any good. He turned reluctantly to return home. He hadn't gone but a few yards when he tugged on the reins. Derby turned his head around and fastened a big brown eye on him.

"You, too?" Marsh shook himself, turned back, and galloped after his son. He thought George was riding into a world of trouble. The jibe about Caleb helping when he wouldn't still stung.

The worst part was that Marsh saw the truth in it. He had retreated into defending his ranch and his family. He had been too stubborn to see the truth. The time for defense was over. The fight had to be taken to the enemy.

To Daniel Murphy. And Ben Wanamaker. And the vigilantes.

He caught up with his son a quarter mile from where the windmill had once dominated the land. He stared at the point in the sky where blades had turned and un-oiled bearings had screeched. Now all that he saw was a patch of starry sky.

"I won't back down," George said as he drew rein beside him.

"If you want to destroy the valve you need at least two horses pulling on lariats," he said.

George looked at him for a moment. His face was hidden in shadow, then he said, "It might work better if we were at opposite sides. One of us pulls and then—"

"—then the other starts pulling while the other lets up. We rock it back and forth until it breaks off."

"That's one way. You have a better idea, Pa?"

"Nope." Marsh took his rope from the leather thong holding it. He played out a loop and swung it about. Countless times, he had roped a calf and yanked it off its feet. Now he was going to yank a hunk of iron out of the ground.

He rode toward the wellhead, every sense alert for trouble. Murphy wasn't a fool. He might be pining away for his lost brother, but he wasn't a fool. Even if he didn't post a guard, Wanamaker would. Marsh looked on the vigilante leader as the power that drove everything on the Double Cross.

For a full minute, they sat and waited for someone to notice the unexpected riders so close to the water valve. Straining as he might, he heard only the usual nighttime sounds. And the valve creaked and groaned as metal strained to hold itself upright. George's first assault on the windmill must have damaged the valve more than he thought.

He signaled his son, then cast the lariat. It fell with a soft hiss around the iron stub. A quick yank and a turn around the pommel told Derby what he wanted. The horse began backing away, as if Marsh had lassoed a cow.

A dark loop and a whir told him George had duplicated his roping on the far side. He leaned forward and Derby stopped pulling. The creak of hemp tightening told him George was applying as much pressure as he had. Then the rope went slack, and he urged Derby back.

He and his son kept up the seesaw pulling on the valve
for what seemed an eternity. He was ready to give up and
try something else when Derby jerked back and sat on his
haunches, as if the rope had broken. That didn't happen
often when roping cattle.

This time the rope had remained intact. But the valve had
pulled free and been dragged along a few feet. Water bubbled
around the open drill hole. Not much flowed out because
this wasn't an artesian well. The pump had to lift the water
from sixty feet below.

A quick spin released his rope from around the valve. As
Marsh drew it in, he heard the first sound that he and
George weren't alone.

"Whass goin' on? Who you people?"

Marsh saw a man staggering from behind a pile of
lumber intended to build a new windmill tower. In the
starlight, a six-shooter flashed in the drunken guard's hand.

"It's all right," Marsh called boldly. "Wanamaker sent
me to check on the well."

"Don't he truss me? I'm not drunk. Not much. Just a nip
to keep Jack Frost from . . ." The man stumbled forward a
few more paces.

"He thinks you're doing a fine job," Marsh said. He
coiled his rope and tied it with the rawhide thong on his
saddle. "You get on back to your post."

"Who're you? Ben's never said a good word 'bout me."

The guard's bleary eyes focused on the destroyed valve.

"Help! Help! We got raiders!" He began firing wildly.
With unsteady steps, he advanced on Marsh.

A whistling sound was quickly followed by the man
yelping as his feet sailed out from under him. George had
lassoed him.

"Leave the rope," Marsh ordered. "I hear men coming, plenty of them."

"After them, boys!" Ben Wanamaker's voice was unmistakable.

Marsh fingered the butt of his Peacemaker. Then Wanamaker's order was answered by a horde of men. This wasn't the time or place to shoot it out.

Marsh trotted over to George, who tried vainly to disentangle his rope. Marsh swatted it from his son's hand.

"Ride. There're too many of them."

"That's a good rope!"

"Ride!"

He galloped off, away from Wanamaker and his men. He was relieved when George paced him, heads down as they raced into the night. Their petty vandalism accomplished little, but he was surprised at how good it made him feel. George had been right. It was time to fight back and not let Daniel Murphy—and his vigilante foreman—have free rein.

CHAPTER 30

Gustav Hammersmith jumped at every sound. Shadows passed outside the burned-out building where he hid and sent his heart racing every time. He was sure the vigilantes had found him after searching every other business and house and shed in town.

He clutched his gun when the soft sound of a boot moving across the dirt floor startled him. Then glass crunched. Someone walked toward where he hid. Scattering broken glass on the floor had been a good idea. Nobody had a step light enough not to alert him. His gun hand trembled just a little as the figure moved closer.

"Gus? Where are you? I told you to stay here. If you've lit out and left . . ." Lilith Murphy sounded miffed.

"Over here. To your right." He slid his pistol back into his holster. He realized that appearing spooked at her arrival did nothing to elevate her opinion of him. Ever since she had saved him, she had acted like she was his guardian angel, his defender. He ought to be the one looking after the lovely woman.

After all, she had lost her husband.

Worse than that, she had seen Ben Wanamaker shoot Thomas Murphy in the back of the head. She had *seen* her husband murdered.

Without any law in town, other than Wanamaker and his vigilantes, she had no chance to bring the killer to justice. Gustav puffed up a little. He was her only chance of stopping Wanamaker from whatever evil he planned.

"Good," she said, gliding over. She bent and kissed his cheek. "I was afraid you'd hightailed it."

"I don't have a horse." He stretched and felt the twinges. He had hit the ground hard when he'd been thrown off the horse he'd tried to steal. Without her help finding a hideout, the band of vigilantes would have caught him for sure. Two fingers rolled under his collar. The death sentence was still on him, the verdict Petey Peterson had delivered.

Gustav remembered the mock trial with increasing anger. He tried not to show it, but the sudden flares of choler ran in the Hammersmith family. His uncle was the worst, but his cousin George showed it, too. Even his other cousin, Sarah, flared up. And his own pa? More than once, he had come home late at night with his knuckles all skinned up. He hadn't shown the flashes of rage around his ma, and Gustav knew he had never so much as touched her when the mood was on him.

That pent-up anger boiled over and scalded everyone else.

"It's just as well. I heard Petey sending out those thugs of his. They've got the entire town bottled up tight. You'd have to be an Indian to sneak past."

"It sounds as if they had planned for this a long time back. Osborne isn't an easy town to surround."

"Osborne," she said mockingly. "That is true of Osborne. It's not true of Murphyville. Ben has it locked up tighter than—"

Gustav clapped his hand over her mouth. Lilith tried to pull away, then heard what he already had. Horses outside. At least two. Then came the voices.

"We done searched this place, Ted. Ain't no reason to do it again."

"I saw somebody duck in here. You want to collect that reward or not?"

"A hunnerd dollars would do me real good."

"Petey's good for it. Ben, too. He's got that ranch all sewed up and tucked away in his hip pocket."

"It's a rich one. They ain't got as many head of cattle as the Hammersmith spread, though."

The two vigilantes entered the building. Gustav heard their boots crunching on the glass he'd scattered around. With most of the windows knocked out, they saw nothing out of the ordinary about broken glass strewn everywhere.

Gustav pulled Lilith back into the alcove he'd formed from a half dozen old crates. Kneeling down, he released her. She pushed him away and whispered hotly, "Don't ever grab me like that again." Her tone changing, "You know how I like to be grabbed. You can do that any old time."

Gustav slid his six-gun from its holster. This time, he rested his thumb on the hammer. If the two vigilantes got careless, they'd never find him. If they did spot him and Lilith, he was ready for them. The notion of killing a man hardened inside him. They accused him of a murder he hadn't done. Now he was ready to shoot without hesitation.

"Naw, ain't nuthin' in here. Let's go."

"You're right. I'm thirsty. That little girl at the saloon looks willing to do more than slake my thirst."

"Slake?"

"You know. When you're real dry and drink anything, your mouth stops tastin' like cotton. That's slakin' your thirst"

The voices faded. Gustav relaxed. He had been tense. He started to stand, but Lilith pulled him down.

"What's the matter?" he asked. And then he found out. The vigilantes had spotted him and only pretended to leave.

Shots rang out when he poked his head above the top of the crates. Splinters flew everywhere. One cut his cheek. He yelped and ducked back, colliding with Lilith. They went down in a pile.

By the time he got off her, he found himself staring down the barrels of two six-shooters.

"Lift that smoke wagon and we'll fill you full of lead," Ted declared.

"You know, partner, that might be better than gettin' his neck stretched. We'd do him a favor if we cut him down now and not have to cut him down from a noose," the other said.

"Reward's the same, dead or alive. I don't remember anyone sayin' we had to bring him in."

"That'd save Petey from havin' to hang him all over again, though he kinda likes bein' an executioner. He told me so."

"Go on," Gustav said. He glanced at Lilith, who wasn't too perturbed at being discovered. "Take me wherever you want."

"'Course we will," Ted said. "We caught you fair and square." He leered at Lilith. "We done got her, too. What do you think?"

"We got time," Ted said.

Their intent was obvious. Gustav almost went for his pistol, which was lying on the dirt floor.

"Me first," Ted said. He slid his six-gun into his holster and began unbuttoning his jeans.

"That's Thomas Murphy's widow. You can't—"

"Of course we can," Ted insisted.

"Ben. Ben Wanamaker is sweet on her," Gustav blurted. Lilith's reaction surprised him. She smiled and winked.

And then things got messy. Ted gasped as Lilith stepped

up and drove her knee into his groin. As he twisted about in pain, she grabbed for his gun. With surprising dexterity, she had it out and fired twice, point blank, into the other vigilante's chest. He took a step back and then toppled backward. In the same move, she whirled around and shoved the still-smoking gun into Ted's gut.

"You can't have what's not yours," she said. The report was muffled because she drove the gun barrel hard into his belly when she fired. His shirt caught on fire.

Ted was dying but wasn't aware. He made a feeble effort to put out the tiny fire eating away at his shirt. Somewhere in the middle of beating out the fire, he keeled over. Gustav picked up his fallen gun and trained it on the vigilante. He got no reaction. He poked Ted hard in the side. Nothing.

"Don't waste time, Gus. He's quite dead." Lilith took the man's gun from him, spun it around her index finger, then tossed it beside the other fallen vigilante. "Get his gun and fire it into the floor."

"It'll look like the two of them shot each other," Hammersmith said, figuring out her scheme. "Do you think Wanamaker will buy it?"

"Probably not, but what have we got to lose?"

Gustav discharged the gun and stepped over the bodies. It was time to get out of there. The gunshots had been muffled, but with the entire band of vigilantes prowling around town hunting for him, any gunfire would draw them like moths to a flame.

"Their horses are outside. We can take them and ride out."

"Gus, please. You're not thinking. If Ben or Petey can't find the horses, they'll wonder what really happened in here. They're not mental giants, but they are suspicious cusses."

"And they have the town bottled up," he said, more to himself than her. Lilith always seemed to be a lap ahead of him in this race.

"There's another way to get you away. It's so obvious they might not think about it. Come on." She took his hand and pulled him along behind her as if he were a small child being dragged by his mother.

As they moved from building to building, hiding in the dense shadows, he realized what she meant. Once she had pointed it out, it was obvious. Gustav hoped that it wasn't apparent to Wanamaker.

They reached the partially built railroad depot. The builders had long since turned in for the night. Momentarily hiding in what would be the depot lobby, Gustav looked out over Osborne. He had no choice but to leave. He had been there for the last ten years, ever since he was eleven. More than half of his life had to be discarded, put behind him, and if it wasn't, he was going to hang.

"Come with me," he said to Lilith. Gustav slid his arm around her slender waist and pulled her close. Their faces were inches apart.

He should have kissed her. He wanted to, but something held him back. Some small facial tic or the set to her lips or her eyes. Those deep, fathomless eyes warned him away. Or was it the ease with which she killed?

"Four men," he said softly.

"What's that?" She tensed in his arm and moved away a few inches. The distance might as well have been the same as rim to rim on Palo Duro Canyon.

"You've killed four men to save me."

"You don't owe me. I owe you. Or your papa."

"But you never hesitated. It was as if it meant nothing to you."

"Think of those men. They were nothing. Worthless."

"They weren't the first men you've killed, were they?"

"You stop worrying yourself into an early grave, Gus. Stay here and let me go dicker a while."

She slid lithely from his arm and glided away. She moved so lightly he wondered if her feet touched the floorboards. There wasn't even a whisper as Lilith went down the steps to the twin steel rails outside the depot.

He stood, feeling abandoned and more alone than he ever had. Gustav went to where a window had been roughed out in the wall and looked around outside. Wherever Lilith had gone, she was now swallowed up by the night. A few lanterns along the tracks sent bright streaks dancing along the steel rails, but no crew worked and no guard kept the piles of supplies safe.

The only crime in Osborne was pinned on him. Gustav rubbed his neck again. Lilith had said she was going to dicker, whatever that meant. He felt uneasy at the too real suspicion that she was buying herself safe passage out of town by turning him over to the vigilantes.

The sound of an engine nearby grew louder as the engineer shoveled coal into the boiler. When the steam whistle let out a long, loud blast, Gustav acted. The train had to be heading back north to El Paso for more supplies. An empty car or two would serve as his Pullman.

While the luxury would be lacking, getting away from this town was far more important. He took the steps down to the tracks two at a time. Crouching over, he made his way to the first of the cars. An empty flatcar. Stacks of railroad ties alongside the tracks gave him more cover as he worked along the line of cars until he saw the engine. The stoker and the engineer worked in the cab to prepare for the trip.

The iron monster shuddered and shook like a horse before a race. Only minutes before it left. Gustav cast a quick look behind. Empty. The entire distance to the half-finished depot was as quiet as a graveyard.

He slid under a freight car and came up on the far side to

further hide from any prying eyes in town. The freight car door refused to open. He dug in his toes and pushed as hard as he could. The balky door wouldn't budge. Desperation grew. His arms and shoulder muscles felt as if they would explode as panic fueled his renewed efforts.

Then the door slid an inch. The small victory drove him to throw his shoulder into the small gap. This moved the heavy door along its track enough to hop in. Gustav got his feet under himself and jumped up to sit in the open door.

He opened his mouth to cry out, but it was too late. Strong hands grabbed him by the shirt and lifted him upward and sent him sailing through the air. He landed hard enough in a pile of cinders to jar his senses.

Then hands worked all over him, taking his six-gun, punching him in the head, lifting and dropping him. Gustav twisted to get away from the punishment, instead turning toward a kick aimed squarely for his gut. Pain lanced through him as he doubled up. Through the roar in his ears, he heard a distant voice, "Got him, boss. What do you want to do with him?"

Gustav passed out before he heard the answer.

CHAPTER 31

"It was so kind of you to escort me home, Mister Peterson." Lilith Murphy tried not to spit. She had thought she could avoid the vigilantes, but they had proved too efficient for her to sneak past after she had talked with Al Reed. The railroad overseer had been surly and had left her with the feeling she needed to do more if Gustav was to get away.

She had barely gotten to the outskirts of Murphyville before Petey Peterson had ridden up beside her and demanded to know where she'd been. There had been only one destination she could name that made any sense and kept her from answering questions she wanted to avoid.

The Double Cross wrought iron arch with the Double-Cross on it passed overhead as dawn broke. The orange light of the new day cast on the black wrought iron turned it into a blood red that made her shiver. She wasn't returning home as much as she was riding to her death.

The entire way from town, she had remembered how Peterson boasted of being an executioner. She wondered how many men he had dropped through the gallows trapdoor. And how many more he had gunned down. He struck her as the kind of man who was more comfortable with a shot to the back than facing down his opponent.

"Is Mister Wanamaker already here?"

"Ben's out huntin' for that varmint what escaped the hangin'."

"And Daniel? Is he out looking, too, or is he here?"

Lilith recoiled at the evil laugh that escaped Peterson's lips. He quieted and smirked as he said, "You'll find out 'bout him soon enough."

"What's that mean?" She tried to fathom what Wanamaker's right-hand man skirted actually saying. He held his cards close to his vest. After the initial outburst, he fought to keep his face as neutral as possible.

"We had a dustup 'round midnight. Bullets were exchanged. But it's not my place to give you the news."

"News?" Lilith wanted to slap him. She put her heels to the horse's flanks and galloped to the house. She was out of the saddle and in the house in a flash. Room by room she hunted, calling Daniel's name. She pushed open the door to his bedroom. He lay on the bed, as pale as death.

"Reckon you found out, Miz Murphy. He's dead. He was killed defendin' the well from raiders. I—" Peterson cut off his words when Daniel Murphy stirred on the bed and moaned, his eyelids fluttering open.

"Lilith? You came back."

"Daniel, I was in town. What happened?" She sat beside him on the bed, then twisted around to stare hard at Peterson. She saw him mouth "But he's dead!"

"They came to destroy the wellhead. I heard hooves leaving, and I went to examine the damage. Shot. Got shot in the back." He rolled onto his side to show the bloodstained shirt. It had soaked not only the shirt but also the bedclothes where he'd lain all night.

"Why didn't you clean the wound?" She pinned Peterson with a cold look. He was still muttering to himself.

"Me and a couple of the boys brung him in. He was dead." He swallowed hard and said in a raspy voice, "I thought he was dead."

"That's a terrible mistake to make," Lilith snapped. "Get some boiling water. Are all the servants gone? What happened?"

"They all hightailed it after the gunfight." Peterson backed away out of the bedroom. "He *was* dead."

Lilith turned to her brother-in-law and laid a hand on his feverish forehead.

"I'll see that you're all patched up, Daniel. Don't fret."

"Lilith," he got out. "I was shot in the back."

She said nothing. She remembered what she had thought about Petey Peterson on the ride back from town. Peterson blocked the doorway. She shoved him away and went to get hot water and bandages. In the kitchen, she found a thin-bladed paring knife. The bullet was still lodged in Daniel's shoulder.

By the time she had hot water and returned, Peterson had left. Daniel had passed out, making it easier for her to dig around and find the small slug. She laid the bloody bullet in the palm of her hand.

It was a .36 caliber slug. Not many men on the Double-Cross carried such a small weapon. But Wanamaker did. Lilith wasn't sure what the odds were that someone attacking the ranch used the same type of six-gun. She wasn't much of a gambling type but guessed the answer to that was: not good.

A bit of sewing closed the small bullet hole that had been made larger by her knife digging around. Daniel breathed more easily, and some color returned to his face. Lilith stood and stared at him. If he died, she was the sole owner of the ranch. She had no love for Thomas's brother. She barely had any for Thomas. But keeping Daniel alive made life easier for her, at least for the immediate future.

Owning half the Double Cross made her rich. All the property Thomas had bought in Murphyville made her even wealthier. It also made her a target. Wanamaker was sweet on her. She imagined what fantasies grew inside his skull. Marry her, become the owner, and then see that she ended up like Thomas.

She closed her eyes and remembered how he had crept up on Thomas and shot him in the back of the head. Blaming Gustav Hammersmith gave him a convenient scapegoat. And he proved how ruthless he was. He'd use that to force her to marry him.

Unless she came up with a better plan.

Lilith made sure a pitcher of water and a full tumbler were on Daniel's beside table. Leaving him alone was risky, but she needed the help she had originally sought before being waylaid by Peterson. She stepped away and thought Daniel was safe enough from Peterson. For the time being.

She rummaged through the gun cabinet and selected two six-guns small enough for her to conceal in her skirts. Then she retrieved her horse and mounted it. It was a long ride to where she had to go.

Lilith pushed a vagrant lock of auburn hair from her eyes. She had sweated like a pig because of the heat and hated the way she looked. Then she told herself how pretty and well-dressed she was hardly mattered. If anything, the trail dust and harried look would work to her benefit.

If anyone would listen.

She drew rein outside the front door of the two-story ranch house, not sure what to do next. Call? Go and knock on the door?

Marsh Hammersmith came out, hand resting on the butt of his heavy Peacemaker.

"Miz Murphy," he said. "This is a surprise. I wasn't expecting a visit from anybody today, much less you after . . . well, after all the unpleasantness."

"There's more than you know, Mister Hammersmith." Lilith slid to the ground and smoothed her skirts. She nodded in George Hammersmith's direction when he came from the house. He whispered urgently in his father's ear. Lilith wished she was close enough to eavesdrop, but she caught only a word or two. Nothing that told her more than she already knew.

"You're not here to gloat about your husband cutting off our water," George said.

"That was Daniel's doing," she said. "But you haven't heard any of this. Daniel's been shot."

"What happened?" Marsh asked.

"Last night someone destroyed the pump and valve on our well and shot him in the back."

"We did no such thing!" George said, bristling. His father motioned him to quiet.

"Last night, you say? We didn't hear anything."

Lilith frowned. That was a silly thing to say. The Twin M ranch house was ten miles away from where Daniel was gunned down.

"Daniel is struggling, but he'll live," she said. Mentally, she added, *I hope.*

"Pa, whatever she wants can wait. We need to get to digging that new acequia you staked out."

"Son, don't be rude. Our quarrel's not with Miz Murphy." Marsh faced her squarely. "George had a good point, though. We're mighty busy. Why'd you come all the way out here? Not to tell us about your brother-in-law getting shot."

"It's Gustav," she said. "He's been framed for murdering my husband."

The entire world turned silent. For a moment, Lilith thought she had gone deaf. The two men were speechless. Even normal sounds disappeared. Then both Marsh and his son began yammering. Again Marsh silenced George.

"Tell us what's going on."

"Come inside," Leonore Hammersmith said. She wiped flour from her hands. She had been in the kitchen baking and came out to see about their visitor.

"There's no time. Everything is so confused," Lilith said. She stared at Marsh, marveling at how much he looked like Mason and how little he acted like his twin.

She shook off the comparisons running through her head and told them what had happened in Murphyville. She was out of breath when she told how she had convinced Al Reed to hide Gustav and keep him safe from the vigilantes.

"Why'd the railroader do a thing like that?" George asked. Then a disgusted look warped his face. "You threatened to cut off the railroad's water supply—the water you stole from us."

"It saved Gustav. You must fetch him and get him away from Wanamaker and his vigilantes. They've taken over town and have declared themselves the only law."

"It'll be better to get Gustav out of Brewster County," Marsh said, his lips pursed as he thought. He scratched his stubbled chin in a way that mimicked his twin. Lilith forced herself to ignore that.

"You can deal with Ben," she said. "I need to tend to Daniel. Whatever happened last night at the well drove off all my servants."

"You're alone? Did you leave Mister Murphy by himself?" Leonore looked angrily at her husband, as if it was his fault. George drew her back and again carried on a heated exchange that Lilith wished she was privy to.

"I had to. There wasn't any other way to let you know how much Gustav needs your help."

"He said he didn't want anything to do with the family," Marsh said.

"He's got a temper, no question," she said. "That's just

like his pa. Right now, he doesn't have a friend in the world."

"Except you, Miz Murphy," Marsh said. "You've gone out of your way to help him."

Before she could answer, Leonore cut in, "I'll go to the Double Cross and tend Mister Murphy. That's more than one person can handle by herself." She stripped off her apron and shoved the flour-covered garment into her son's hands. He reluctantly took it. "Hitch up the buggy, Marshal. I'll get some medical supplies." She cupped her mouth and shouted, "Sarah, fetch the box on the cupboard. The one with all the bandages."

"You'd do that? For Daniel? For me?" Lilith was surprised. All she had expected was for Marsh to rescue his nephew.

If he shot it out with Ben Wanamaker along the way, that was a bonus for her. Eventually, she had to eliminate her own foreman. While he rode at the head of the vigilance committee, firing him wasn't possible. He commanded too much firepower.

"You're sticking out your neck to help Gustav. The least we can do is help Daniel," Marsh said. "My wife's persuasive. She might convince him to give us our water."

Lilith's mind turned over the possibilities. The water was the key, but with the windmill and pump destroyed, what water that came from the well was needed for Double Cross cattle.

And the railroad. The crew had already laid track south of town. In a couple weeks, trains would steam through Murphyville on a regular schedule and need all the water that had been pledged to the Hammersmiths.

She doubted the Twin M had a chance of matching what the railroad paid for their boiler water. But that was something to be negotiated. If Daniel felt grateful enough, he might restore the other rancher's water rights.

Until then, she had to stay alive and in a position to deal with Wanamaker and his band of desperados.

With Leonore in the buggy rattling along and Marsh and his son trotting on either side of her, they returned to the Double Cross. She was almost disappointed when they didn't clash with Ben. That meant the fight for control of the ranch was going to be drawn out.

And deadlier.

CHAPTER 32

Al Reed balled his hands into bony fists. He wanted to whale the tar out of the kid who had tried to sneak a ride in the empty boxcar. A quick step and he towered over the freeloader, who was flat on his back in the dirt.

"Gerhardt!" Reed looked around for his assistant. "Bring a lantern. I want a better look at this one."

Gustav Hammersmith tried to sit up. Reed planted a boot squarely in the middle of his chest and kicked out hard. Gustav flopped onto his back and thrashed around like a fish pulled up on a stream bank.

"He the one, boss?" Gerhardt ambled over, a lantern swaying to and fro as he held it high. The light splashed over Gustav's face, showing how frightened he was.

"Who else could it be? He's all decked out like a cowboy. He's on the run. And any other cowboy on the run would be astride a horse. This one decided to hitch a ride on my train."

"That shows some gall, yes, sir," Gerhardt said. "But is he the *one*? The fellow she asked us to be on the lookout for."

"You feel a rope tightening around your scrawny neck?" Reed poked Gustav with the toe of his boot. "Answer me."

"You know who I am. Did Miz Murphy tell you all about my predicament?"

"I like that. *Pre-dick-uh-mint*," Gerhardt mocked. "This has got to be the one. Was there a decent reward offered?"

"The vigilantes weren't saying. But what we get is better than money."

Gustav sat up. He pushed Reed's boot aside when he tried to shove him back down.

"Water," he said. "That's what Lilith offered, isn't it? You don't want your only source of water turned off. That engine can't go dry, can it? What'll happen? Will it blow up or melt down?"

"Shut up," Gerhardt said.

Gustav ignored him. He got to his feet and faced Reed. This was the boss, not the man with the lantern.

"You need to listen to her. She gets cranky if you cross her." Gustav laughed. "That's why she's the new owner of the Double Cross ranch."

"It was her husband that got gunned down," Reed said. "She explained that you were framed."

"And that you should get me on a train out of town," Gustav finished. He was sweating buckets but tried not to show how nervous he was. Any hint of weakness and Reed was likely to belt him. From the look of his skinned, scarred knuckles, the railroad overseer used his fists first and talked later.

"Don't tell me what do to." Reed stepped up and cocked his right fist back, then froze. He turned his head around like a dog sniffing the air. Instead of hitting Gustav, he grabbed him by the front of his shirt and shoved him hard toward the empty freight car.

"What's up, boss?" Gerhardt swung the lantern around and pulled down a shutter to focus the light into a narrow beam.

"Somebody's coming. Horseback." Reed never turned to look back at Gustav, but his orders were obviously for the fugitive. "Into the car. Not a peep or it means your worthless life."

Reed turned and faced into the darkness. Gerhardt continued to shine the light around until it fixed on three riders walking slowly down the length of the train. They had started at the engine and were about finished with their scouting.

"Evening, gents," the lead rider said. "You out lookin' fer the killer, too?"

"I'm out here to make sure sneak thieves don't rob me blind. The Union Pacific Railroad takes a dim view of that."

"Reckon they take it out of your pay," the lead rider said. "Considerin' what you must get paid, that'd mean you'd be drivin' spikes for the next hunnerd years."

This caused the other two men to snicker. One nudged the lead rider and said, "You got a wit, Petey."

"And you got half a one," Petey snapped. He turned back to Reed. "You wouldn't be thinkin' on lettin' our condemned fugitive escape, would you?"

"I don't get mixed up in local lawbreaking," Reed said. "Just ride on and let me and my foreman get back to our work."

"Now isn't that interestin'," Petey said. "The two top men workin' this section of the railroad are out doin' the work of a regular railroad dick. Now why is that?"

"We got work to do, Gerhardt. You see that these fine gents clear out." Reed watched the open freight car door out of the corner of his eye. He wanted to shout at Gustav. More than that, he wanted to use his head to pound a railroad spike or two. The blasted fool had poked his head around the car door to watch what was going on. If any of the vigilantes saw him, there'd be lead flying all over.

Reed was aware that he wasn't packing. He had no call to when working with his own crew. If one of them got out of line, he'd use his fists. That left men bloody but not dead.

Teaching them a lesson was the important part. Finding skilled railroad crews was hard at the best of times. Out in the middle of the West Texas desert, it was nigh on impossible.

"We'll take a look around. Who knows?" Petey said. "You might have missed somethin' in your haste to do . . . railroad work."

"Gerhardt," Reed repeated. "Fetch Billy John and those reprobate brothers of his. Then escort these three off railroad property. No need to be gentle about it—if they put up a fuss, that is."

All three vigilantes reached for their six-guns. Reed never flinched. He had faced down an entire saloon filled with drunk Irishmen.

"Petey, let me."

The leader thrust out his arm to keep his hotheaded partner, who'd drawn his gun, from firing.

"Ben wouldn't like it if we shot up the railroad's bosses. He'd have to negotiate with a new bunch over in California."

"Wanamaker's only the foreman. Murphy owns the water," Reed said.

"Murphy caught an ounce of lead in the back of his head."

"That's Thomas. Daniel's an owner of the ranch," Reed said. He balled his hands again and rested them on his hips. With the lantern light behind him, he cast a long shadow. His silhouette showed a man with a trim waist, thick chest, and powerful shoulders.

"Ben tells what's left of the Murphy family to jump," Petey said. "And they ask how high on the way up. You could learn a lesson from that."

Reed took a step forward. The man with the drawn gun cocked it. Reed never showed the slightest hint of fear. He curled his fingers around Petey's bridle and began pulling.

Gently. Not enough to make the horse protest. It began walking.

"You leave my horse be," Petey snapped.

"You leave my railroad."

Reed watched the play of emotions on the vigilante's face. He looked bad in his men's eyes. All he had to do was give the word and both men would gun down Reed and Gerhardt. From the flash of anger and understanding on Petey's face, he knew where the real trouble lay. Wanamaker hadn't given the orders to shoot anyone but Gustav Hammersmith. Taking on the railroaders jeopardized the Union Pacific using Murphyville as a depot.

Without the railroad stopping there, the town might dry up and blow away. Wanamaker would be the king of . . . nothing.

The vigilantes cantered off, leaving a dust cloud behind. Reed watched until they disappeared into town. He spun and smashed his fist into the heavy freight car door. The boom sounded like a drum in the empty interior.

"What'd you do that for?" Gustav clapped his hands over his ears as he swung about and sat on the edge of the doorway, legs dangling down.

Reed judged distances, stepped up, and unloaded a straight punch to the man's solar plexus. Gustav gasped and flopped onto his back inside the car.

"I told you to stay out of sight. If any of those men chanced a look inside the car, they'd've killed you and never given it a second thought. You're more trouble than you're worth."

"You wouldn't say that to Miz Murphy." Gustav gasped and kicked about weakly, recovering from the punch.

"Getting water's always a chore for the railroad. It's nothing I haven't done before in a lot worse situations. That's why I'm in charge."

"You could have turned me over to Petey and his boys." Gustav rubbed his abdomen where Reed had punched him.

Reed considered hitting him again, just to vent some of his anger.

"Get out of the car."

"You *are* going to let the vigilantes string me up!" Gustav tried to scuttle away.

Reed grabbed a foot and yanked. It satisfied his need to hit something when he pulled his unwilling passenger from the freight car and dropped him several feet to the ground. He grabbed a handful of shirt and pulled Gustav to his feet.

"Come along and keep your mouth shut."

Reed was almost sorry when Gustav finally did as he was told. They walked to the locomotive, where the engineer in his tall, black-and-white striped hat fiddled with the steam valves. He pounded one with his fist and cursed.

"Got you a little help, Will." Reed put his hands around Gustav's waist and lifted him into the cab as if he were a small child. "You make him work for his passage."

"What're you tellin' me, Al? I gotta nursemaid him?"

"Your stoker can use the help."

"You mean I kin order him around, Mister Reed? I got me my very own assistant?" The stoker, already covered in coal dust, perked up. "I surely can use the help. He kin root around back in the coal bin and keep a steady supply fer me to stoke."

"If that's the way you want to use him, fine. You agree to that, Will?"

The engineer nodded. "Unless he knows how to fix valves, he's no use to me. Let him be Isaiah's trained coal monkey." The engineer snorted and shook his head. He pounded on a valve, then stepped back when its needle popped free and gave a new reading. "I'm ready to steam outta here." He looked over his shoulder and grimaced.

"Isaiah, I take that back. He's your untrained money. Keep him working or I'll toss you both off."

"Yes, sir." The stoker began barking orders to Gustav. The unwilling passenger climbed into the coal tender and began shoveling lumps of coal down a battered metal slide into the back of the cab.

"Feed the boiler, my boy, feed it!" Will yanked the steam whistle cord and let out three long hoots.

Reed stepped away as steam vented from the pistons. The powerful engine began driving the wheels. The train screeched as steel wheels tore into steel rails and the trip began. He was glad to see the train heading back to El Paso for another load of rails and ties. Those would let him extend the tracks twenty miles or more to the southwest and get him away from Murphyville and all its double-dealing.

He turned to see a solitary rider galloping up. He smiled. His current trouble was working for his passage to El Paso, and he was quit of him.

"He's on that train, isn't he?"

"Well, now, Wanamaker, you can catch up if you run that horse of yours until it dies under you. You can find out for yourself." Reed wasn't about to confess to the Double Cross foreman his part in getting Gustav Hammersmith out of town. There was considerable friction between Wanamaker and Lilith Murphy for control of their ranch. Reed wanted no part of it.

Wanamaker dismounted and dropped the reins to the ground. He strutted over to the railroad overseer and faced him squarely.

"I'm the head of the vigilance committee. We're about the only law in the area."

"Except for the soldiers out of Fort Davis. And the Texas Rangers."

"I don't see any of them here. Do you?" Wanamaker rested his hand on the butt of his six-gun.

Reed wasn't easily intimidated. He had seen blowhards like Ben Wanamaker too many times in too many places. He had dealt with rowdy railroad crews and come through with nothing more than a bloody nose and sore, skinned knuckles.

"How long'll it take for the home office to replace you?"

"Send a telegram and ask. My boss there's the railroad president. I do good work for him, so he's not overly inclined to replace me."

"He'll have to." Ben Wanamaker whipped out his pistol and fired until his six-gun came up empty. He kicked out the spent brass, reloaded, and looked down at Al Reed's body. He lowered the hammer and thrust his gun back into his holster. There wasn't any reason to waste more ammo.

The Double Cross foreman mounted and rode away slowly, heading back to town to call off the vigilantes' hunt for Gustav Hammersmith. Marsh Hammersmith's nephew might have slipped away, but there were other chores to do.

"Other trash to get rid of," Wanamaker said. He grinned at what he'd do—what he had done already. Heels raking the side of his horse, he galloped off into the bright dawn of a new day.

CHAPTER 33

"Not even Gustav would be dumb enough to stay here," George Hammersmith said.

Marsh looked around. Workers hammered and framers finished parts of the new railroad depot. More than a dozen men worked there, showing how urgent it was for the depot to be completed. The tracks farther south needed these men swinging sledgehammers and putting in spikes to hold the rails instead.

"She said she left him here," Marsh said. He slowly looked back into town. A deep breath did nothing to calm him. He rested his hand on the butt of his Peacemaker.

"Yeah, I spotted them as we rode in," George said. "There's no way Gustav got past them."

"Lilith said they hid out in a deserted building on the far side of town. That might be somewhere he thinks is safe."

"He never was too bright."

"George, he's your cousin."

"He's your brother's son. That makes him kin, but that doesn't make him smart."

"He never accepted his pa's disappearance," Marsh said. A knot formed in his gut. He never had, either. The difference lay in how they each dealt with it. Gustav left the rest of his family, came to town, and became a layabout, drinking up what little money he had. Marsh had a ranch to run and a family to support.

"I never got over it when Alamo got eaten by coyotes, but that . . ." George swallowed hard when he realized what he was saying. He muttered, "Sorry, Pa. He was your brother. I didn't mean anything by it, comparing my dog getting killed to Uncle Mason disappearing like he did."

"I'll find out what happened to him. First, we need to find Gustav."

"The vigilantes don't know where he is," George said. "They're too alert."

"And they'd have strung him up and gone to the saloon to celebrate."

"There's always somebody in the watering hole who thinks he knows everything going on in town. Shall we?" George turned from the construction. He hitched up his gun belt.

"Can't hurt." Marsh reluctantly followed his son to the saloon. The crowd inside surprised him. This early in the day, men ought to be hard at work. The hustle and bustle was so great that Little Miss Molly had trouble keeping up pulling beer and pouring shots.

"They need a faro table in here," George said. "They're not making any money off the drinks with the likes of her behind the bar."

"She and Gustav were . . . friendly," Marsh said. "She might know what happened to him."

"The two of them?" George shook his head.

"Not every woman can be like your ma or Consuela."

They worked their way to the end of the bar and waited. Little Miss Molly finally served the entire line of men and came to them. Her thin face was pale, and her eyes were sunk deep into dark pits.

"Looks like your boss has been working you hard," Marsh said. "Who is it now?"

"My boss? Mister Murphy got himself shot down. Heard rumors that the other Mister Murphy got shot, too, but he's not dead. Not yet."

"My wife is out at the Double Cross to help tend him."

"Help? You mean that bi—" Little Miss Molly sniffed in disdain. "You mean his sweet l'il wife's helpin' them? Daniel had better sleep with one eye open to keep her from cuttin' his throat. She wants that ranch bad."

"Have you seen Gustav?" Marsh asked in a low voice. Little Miss Molly leaned closer. He repeated the question. She recoiled.

"I thought I seen him get his neck stretched. Turned out to be Harvey Lincoln. Harve was a no account and followed Ben around like a puppy dog. He even tried to be as mean as Petey. If you ask me, he deserved what he got." She pointed to Petey Peterson at the far end of the bar. "Him and his vigilantes might as well own this place. Petey told me all his boys get free drinks."

"That explains the crowd," George said sourly. "Even in a one saloon town, you don't get this many customers outside of Saturday night."

"I'd rather serve them rowdy cowboys when they get drunk. These fellows are plain mean—and that's before they start drinkin'."

"Whose tune are they dancing to? Peterson's or Wanamaker's?" George shifted uneasily as he waited for the answer. Marsh put his hand on his son's shoulder.

"What's it matter?" Little Miss Molly went on. "There's gonna be a tussle if you don't order something. Them's the new rules."

"We're leaving," Marsh said. Before he pushed back

from the bar, he looked hard at her. The question hung between them.

"Can't help you," she said. Little Miss Molly worked her way back down the bar, filling beer mugs and emptying another bottle of rye. At this rate, the entire vigilance committee would be drunk by noon.

Father and son started out, but Peterson blocked their way.

"What's the matter? Our whiskey's not good enough for the likes of you?"

"It costs too much. We're flat broke," Marsh said.

"Don't know why that's true. You got plenty of money in your pocket from not havin' to pay for water anymore."

Marsh stepped between the vigilante and his son. George's temper reached the boiling point too quickly. He didn't want him blurting out anything about the destroyed windmill and water pump at the well. If Gustav had set the town against him, such a confession on George's part would set off a battle to make Antietam look like a Sunday picnic.

"We're just fussy about who we drink with," Marsh said. He watched Peterson bristle. Then the gunman settled down.

"Be sure to talk to Wanamaker. I'm sure he wants to talk to you, too, like he does other folks."

Marsh had no idea what Peterson meant. That he stepped aside and let them leave was good enough. Outside, George growled deep in his throat like an angry dog.

"He was asking for it. We should have—"

"We're hunting for Gustav," Marsh cut in. He looked over his shoulder. Peterson and two of his men huddled together, watching him. They knew something. Marsh figured he had to find out what it was.

"Do you think they've already caught him?"

"They're not acting that way. He would have lorded it

over us if they had caught Gustav." He swallowed hard at the idea of the vigilantes doing more than that. Peterson would have demanded they take Gustav's body back with them if they had caught him.

This built up his optimism.

"Poke around and see what you can find. Reverend Dalton might have some idea."

"He didn't do much to stop them from hanging Gustav," George said. "If we can believe Lilith Murphy."

Marsh pointed toward the church. George walked away, grumbling to himself. For a moment, Marsh considered going with him. Keeping his son out of trouble meant more than finding his wayward nephew. Then he headed back to the half-built railroad depot. From everything Lilith had said about leaving Gustav there, he might be hiding out nearby.

He had barely stepped onto the completed platform when Al Reed's assistant accosted him.

"You can't be here. The boss wants this place done by sundown. You're gettin' in the way." Gerhardt blocked him from searching the depot.

Marsh doubted Gustav was still there with so many workmen coming and going. Even if Reed had agreed to hide Gustav, as Lilith said she had negotiated with the railroad overseer, the chance one of the workmen would turn him over to the vigilantes was too great to ignore.

"When did the train leave?"

"Before dawn. It'll be back by late tomorrow. We got a schedule to keep."

Marsh backed off and let Gerhardt shout at the crew to work faster. He went around to the tracks and looked north. Track was being laid miles to the south of town. That was the obvious place for Reed to be if his assistant remained there in town. But Marsh had a feeling in the gut about finding Reed.

His fingers brushed the butt of his Peacemaker. He had a score to settle with Reed, even if he had spirited Gustav away from the vigilantes.

"First, Gustav, then take care of Reed," he told himself.

Mounting Derby, he rode slowly along the tracks. The steel rails were scratched where the heavy locomotive had parked for several days. When he got to the water tower, he looked at it and considered all that George had done to the Murphys' well. Dragging down the windmill hadn't been enough to stop the flow of water. Blowing up the water tower would only put the railroad out of business until they hauled in enough water to keep the engine's boiler from running dry.

He started to ride on, then saw a box left under the tower. Marsh rode closer, dismounted, and pried the lid off the crate. A dozen sticks of dynamite rested inside on a bed of sawdust. Tucked into the side were three blasting caps and five feet of waxy, black miner's fuse. Why it had been left there was a mystery.

"Maybe it's nothing more than carelessness. Reed was in a powerful hurry to build through town."

Using the butt of his six-shooter, he pounded the nails back into the crate lid, then lashed the box over his saddlebags. Nobody was likely to accuse him of stealing railroad property if he avoided Gerhardt and the depot.

Unless he found Al Reed.

He swung into the saddle and rode another hundred yards. The crate of explosives bobbing and bouncing around made him increasingly uneasy. He knew how to use dynamite. And he knew how cantankerous it was. The nitroglycerin in each stick was sensitive to heat and getting more unstable minute by minute. A single jolt might set it off.

Marsh wheeled about to fetch his son and clear out when some shiny brass caught his eye. He walked Derby over to the far side of the tracks and counted. Six spent shells. He looked up from the cartridges and saw Reed's body at the bottom of an incline.

What had happened looked clear. He still hopped down and examined Reed. Six shots in the chest. All the holes were closely spaced. Burn marks on two of the holes told how close the shooter had been when he plugged the railroad overseer.

Marsh backed away and picked up a couple of the empty cartridges. They were all shiny, so they hadn't been on the ground very long. He tried to stick his little finger in. The cartridge was too small.

"This looks to be a .36 caliber," he said softly. Only one man he knew in town carried such a small caliber pistol. He tucked the brass into a pocket and cursed Ben Wanamaker for finishing off Al Reed. After the beating the railroader had given him, Marsh wanted to settle affairs himself.

Wanamaker had saved him the trouble. And that made him mad.

He now had a new score to settle with the Double Cross foreman and leader of the vigilantes.

CHAPTER 34

"I want to see it for myself," George Hammersmith said.

Marsh stared at Bullet Butte. He had returned to map out the flow of water inside the rocky spire several times, but always at night, always alone. The threat of the Lipan Apaches finding out he shared their secret was great. The water gave the Apaches their only trump card over their traditional enemies, the Comanches. In this part of West Texas, water meant the difference between survival and death.

He felt a pang of guilt in not sharing the knowledge of the underground water with the soldiers at Fort Davis. They fought and all too often died because of water. The Apaches had run them ragged for years because one side knew where the water was and the other didn't.

It got mighty hot in those blue wool federal uniforms. Hot and thirsty.

Marsh pushed aside the tinge of guilt he felt. He was in a fight for survival himself. Not with the Apaches or even the herd-raiding Comanches now, but with the adjoining ranch. The Double Cross was well named. Too well named, from everything he had learned over the past couple months.

Leonore and Consuela had helped Lilith nurse Daniel

Murphy back to health, and he had shown his gratitude by threatening to have them horsewhipped if they didn't leave his spread immediately. The loss of his brother weighed heavily on Daniel Murphy, too heavily for Marsh's taste. He had lost his own brother. Having a twin simply vanish was worse than a brother being killed.

Marsh had no body to bury, no funeral service to attend. Mason might be alive out there somewhere, but deep down, Marsh doubted it. Mase Hammersmith was many things, but vanishing without so much as a fare-thee-well wasn't like him. His horse and tack were missing, but all his other possessions remained at the Twin M ranch house.

"Pa. Pa! Stop daydreaming. I want to see the well." George edged his horse closer to his father.

"Not yet," he said. "The Apaches are watching the butte too closely. It takes me a long time to sneak up there and only after they have taken all the water they can carry."

"I'll go with you."

Marsh looked hard at his son. He understood George's urgency in seeing the water that promised salvation for the ranch, but too much activity before they were ready meant increasing danger, not only to whomever climbed up Bullet Butte but also to the cowboys working the herd. And the entire Hammersmith family.

He was sorry he had mentioned it to his son, but soon enough everyone would know.

"The Apaches won't stop at killing anyone scaling the rock. To scare us off, they'd burn down the house and barn and bunkhouse. They'd kill our family if they thought it would keep us away from the well."

"They'll catch on eventually." George patted the survey equipment strapped onto his horse. "We can only decoy them so long." He cleared his throat, stared at Bullet Butte, then asked, "Can your Lipan friend help us any?"

"Night Wolf?" Marsh shook his head. He had saved the Apache's life but long since had used up any credit he earned with the warrior. "I can't figure out how he thought showing me the water wouldn't end up with us using it for the entire herd."

"Maybe that's not the way Indians think. They are hunters and nomads. They use the water and move on. It's possible running the water into acequias isn't something he'd ever think of."

Marsh snapped the reins and got Derby walking slowly toward Bullet Butte. What George said was right. Night Wolf was a fighter, not a settler. That was part of the problem with trying to force the tribes onto a reservation. It went against their way of life if they weren't out raiding and killing their enemies.

"We can start laying out where to dig the new irrigation ditches from the big pond rather than going to Bullet Butte and beginning there."

George followed, struggling to keep the survey equipment tied down. Marsh looked at the looming Bullet Butte and knew that they'd have to move closer soon. That would either spook the Apaches or make them move on. For all he knew, they had other watering holes that didn't require them to scale a mountain and carry their water down on their backs.

The large stock pond was down to a quarter of its capacity. He shook his head in wonder at how quickly the cattle drained the water. It was hot, they were thirsty. If water didn't flow soon, those cattle would be dead from dehydration.

Even as that worry crossed his mind, Marsh looked at the sky. As always, his hopes for rain clouds were dashed. The few clouds moving quickly across the sky were thin, lacy, and high. He needed the heavy-bottomed puffy clouds from the Gulf to believe rain was coming.

"Let's get to it," he said. He dismounted and set up the survey equipment.

For the rest of the day, he and his son laid out a new set of irrigation ditches that didn't connect with the one running onto the Murphy ranch. Anyone seeing where they drove stakes with tatters of white muslin bedsheet attached had to believe they'd lost their heads. Loco weed grew all around, but Marsh ignored it and hoped his cattle did, too.

He was crazy enough without chewing on the jimson weed.

"We can finish laying out the main channel before sundown," George said. "That'll take us real close to Bullet Butte, though."

Marsh ran through all the reasons not to appear too interested in the rock spire until they were ready to tap the water. But he hadn't seen another rider all day long. The closer they got to Bullet Butte, the more deserted it seemed. He felt the cold loneliness of sundown approaching and considered that if they quit now, they'd have to return at dawn tomorrow.

Other business mattered, too, if he wanted to get the water flowing.

"Let's finish it off," he decided.

They worked closer, mile by mile until it was twilight. He peered through the lens and waved his arms around to move George over. This part of the acequia had to end immediately under the spot where he thought water was easiest to extract from the butte. The case of dynamite he had taken from the railroad construction camp would blast open the side of the rocky spire.

He straightened, the last of the stakes driven to guide the workmen. He waved to George. Then waved again. His son was nowhere to be seen. Marsh peered through the surveyor's lens again and slowly panned around, hunting for any movement.

Marsh whistled and Derby trotted over. He swung into the saddle and galloped to the last stake George had driven.

As he neared, he called out. When George failed to reply, he drew his six-shooter. Slowing, he looked around. His son was nowhere to be seen. He went to the last stake driven and stood in the stirrups. The twilight deepened and impenetrable shadows grew. The huge pile of rock that was Bullet Butte blotted out what little light was left from the setting sun.

He settled down in the saddle and listened hard. A coyote howled in the distance. Winds whispered through the creosote bush and mesquite. A sudden rustling caused him to twist about, his pistol cocked and aimed. All he saw was the hind end of a cotton-tailed rabbit scurrying away.

He dropped to the ground, holstered his pistol, and pulled his Winchester from the saddle sheath. Whatever had happened required more firepower than the six-shooter was likely to give. Marsh studied the sunbaked ground and found only small scuff marks. In the dim light, he wasn't able to decide where they had gone or even if anyone had sneaked up on George.

An Apache had the skill to creep silently. George had been concentrating on aligning the stakes with his transit. But why had an Apache not slit the white intruder's throat? There wasn't any reason to kidnap him. Or if he had been killed, why spirit away the body?

Marsh slid down an embankment of an arroyo and walked as quietly as he could on the gravelly bottom. They had to avoid putting their acequias near to these torrentially cut channels. It'd rain again someday, and floods washed out banks with surprising speed.

He stopped when he heard guarded whispers. Moving toward that side of the arroyo, he peeked over the rim. Two dark figures knelt beside a third. From the position of the man stretched on the ground, he'd been hog-tied. As he moved about, Marsh saw the gag in George's mouth.

His son had been captured. And the whispers came to him more clearly now as the two desperados argued.

"He's close enough," the first said. "Goose him. Get him to cry out so we can lure his old man in." He held up a gun. The dark metal was outlined against the remnants of the sunset.

"He'll call out a warning. We want to get both of them. If this one—"

Marsh rested the rifle on the arroyo bank. He drew back the hammer. The metallic click caused both the kidnappers to freeze.

"What was that?"

"Trouble," his partner cried. They jumped to their feet. Both lifted their six-shooters and aimed into the twilight.

Marsh squeezed back on his rifle trigger. The Winchester bucked. One of the kidnappers spun around, yelping. In the twilight, Marsh had missed a clean kill but had winged the man.

Before his partner could turn his gun on George, he found himself flailing about. George wiggled and kicked like a worm. His tied feet crashed into the standing man's knees, upending him. Marsh no longer had a shot at either of the men as long as they stayed low on the ground. If he fired at them, he was more likely to hit his own son.

He scrambled out of the arroyo and tried to remain low as he rushed forward. Seeing one man lift his gun, Marsh screeched like a banshee. The sudden cry of pure death momentarily confused the man. Marsh reached him and reared up. He let gravity do all the work. He relaxed and fell straight down, his rifle butt crashing into the man's head. The sick crunch of bone told him the man was out of this fight.

"George, where's the other one?"

His son's answer came out muffled by the gag in his mouth. Marsh plucked it out. George gasped for air, then said, "Down that way. Toward the butte. Be careful, Pa. I think there're a couple more of them."

Marsh reached behind for the sheath in the middle of his back to grab his knife. But he realized he had no reason to be wearing the sheath because Night Wolf had stolen his knife. Cursing, he clawed at George's bonds. The knots finally came free.

George rubbed circulation back into his hands, then reached over and plucked the six-gun from the hands of the man his father had knocked out cold with the rifle butt.

"Three of them left?"

"Can't say for sure. They never showed themselves, but the way these two talked, they weren't alone."

Marsh silently pushed George toward the arroyo. This time he took the high ground because he had superior firepower with his Winchester. When George's head dipped under the bank, Marsh set out. With long strides and bent over, he made his way in the direction taken by the man he'd winged.

Foot-long tongues of flame leaped from ahead. Lead whined past him, but he kept moving, dodging now that he knew where his attackers had taken refuge. Their ambush failed. The darkness behind him kept him from showing a silhouette. The last light of dusk gave him an occasional glimpse of the men firing at him.

Marsh got off another shot. The firing from that direction ceased. He kept moving that way and jumped over a low rock, expecting to find either a wounded or dead ambusher behind it.

Nothing. He dropped so his nose was only inches from the rock. He hunted for a drop of blood to show he had at least hit one of the man so intent on gunning him down. Nothing.

Gunfire from the direction of the arroyo warned him that George was in the fight. They had the gunmen trapped between them. Marsh levered a fresh round into the chamber and headed for the fight.

A hat popped up from the arroyo. He fired. The hat went sailing through the air. Marsh rushed forward and came to the edge of the deep arroyo. He aimed his rifle down, only to find himself looking down the muzzle of a six-shooter pointed up at him.

George wasn't wearing his hat. Marsh's bullet had sent it flying across the arroyo.

"I almost killed you," Marsh said, horrified. He looked around, but he and his son were alone in the dark.

"It's a good thing I have good reflexes," George said. "I was ready to shoot anyone poking his mug over the rim."

"Where'd they go?"

George climbed from the arroyo and looked around. He finally pointed back toward the spot where the last stake had been driven.

The pair of them returned as quietly as they could. One ambush was enough.

"Here's the stake. Where's the desperado I knocked out?" Marsh began hunting for the man he'd slugged with his rifle butt.

"He should be about here," George dropped to his knees and put his face close to the ground. "The dirt's all scuffed up, but he's gone."

Marsh wasn't sure his son had found the right place, but he wasn't able to find anywhere else as good.

"They came back and took the body so we couldn't identify them."

"One of them might have been Petey. Petey Peterson," George said.

"Can you swear to that?"

George shook his head.

It had been dark, and no proof remained that the vigilantes had attacked them on their own land. Marsh rested the rifle on his shoulder. He had worried about a range war starting. This looked like the first skirmish in what could turn bloody real fast.

CHAPTER 35

"I'm going," Marsh Hammersmith said. "There's no reason to stop me."

"You'll get yourself killed, dear. That's enough for me to stop you." Leonore Hammersmith stood with her arms crossed. She glared at him. This only hardened his resolve.

"That bullet broke the upstairs window. What if Consuela or the baby had been in there. You can't want them hurt."

"I can't want *you* hurt. Do something else."

"What is there? The only law in Osborne—I refuse to call it Murphyville—are the vigilantes. George is sure that Petey Peterson was one of the men who tried to kill us three nights ago."

"You can go to the Texas Rangers," she said. Her voice carried just a hint of uncertainty now. She knew what he was going to say before the words came from his mouth.

"I'm sure the Texas Rangers will rush right on over when they hear a window's been shot out."

"It was past midnight. That wasn't any accident."

He took her in his arms. Leonore tried to pull away, but he held her until she stopped resisting.

"We need a lawman in Osborne . . . in the county. But as

long as Daniel Murphy is running the town, that's not going to happen."

"I'll see if I can't convince Mayor Galveston to hire a marshal. He's a venal, crooked little man, but he has to see what's going on."

"You know he's being paid off by Murphy," Marsh said. "Worse than that, he doesn't have clout, not with the town council anymore when they all voted to build the depot he argued against. Nobody'll vote for him when the next election rolls around."

"He shouldn't have opposed the railroad depot being built. Why'd he do a silly thing like that?" Leonore extricated herself from his arms. "The first train to come brought all kinds of goods from El Paso that had to be freighted in by wagon before. Luxury goods and so much cheaper than we've ever seen," she said wistfully.

Marsh eased toward the door. She was thinking of things other than him confronting Daniel Murphy about the vigilantes taking potshots at the house. A range war meant less to her than it did to him. She'd never seen the carnage caused when all the hands on one ranch declared open season on cowboys from another. When he was hardly ten over in the piney woods of East Texas, three different ranches had all declared war on one another.

Forty men had died over the eight months of vicious hostilities. And he had heard about the Lincoln County War still raging to the north in New Mexico. Not even the governor of that territory could put a stop to it. The ranchers' war had attracted some of the most famous—infamous—gunfighters, making it even more deadly and vicious.

Marsh wanted to keep all of West Texas from exploding in a similar carnage. And it would. He'd never give in to Daniel Murphy and his vigilantes. While he had almost no chance to convince Murphy to call off the blood feud, he had a small chance. A very small one. That was enough for him to try to reason.

He stepped up into the saddle and gave Derby his head. The stallion flew like the wind, as if he knew exactly where Marsh wanted to go and why. After a mile, the horse slowed. Marsh varied the gait to reach the Murphy spread without killing his mount. When he knew he was on Double Cross property, he kept a close watch for any sign of Wanamaker's men. They were as likely to shoot him as listen to why he needed to talk to Murphy.

Wherever the vigilantes were, Marsh saw nothing of them and rode unchallenged to the ranch house. He cast a quick look at the well he and George had damaged. The valve had been replaced, and a new pump stood nearby. The windmill tower was constructed, and the blades were laid out on the ground. Putting them into place on the wheel was the work of a day. Two at the most. The Murphy well was close to bringing water to the surface again.

He stopped and waited when Lilith Murphy stepped out of the house. She had a rifle laid in the crook of her left arm. If any woman looked capable of shooting the pip off an ace at fifty feet, she was the one.

"You've got more stones than I expected, Marshal," she said. "You came by your lonesome? No posse backing your play?"

"Nope, just me."

"That brings me to another question. What *is* your play?" She sounded more amused than vindictive.

"I need to talk to your brother-in-law about the feud between our families."

"So you think you're a peacemaker? Save your breath. Daniel's not inclined to say a single neighborly word to you or your kin."

"Got to try."

"Dickering with Ben might get you farther." She saw his expression. Lilith shrugged her shapely shoulders. "You figured out he was the one that shot out your window. You're not steaming mad, so that must mean nobody was hit."

"That was the baby's room. He happened to be sleeping with his ma and pa. Otherwise glass would have showered down on him. Or worse. He might have been hit."

"Your clan's always been lucky, Marshal. Ben was talking about burning your house down but decided just to have a little fun before doing it. That's his way. He wants to scare you so he'll feel all puffed up and ready to kill."

"Daniel," he said. "I need to talk to him."

"No, Marshal, you want to talk with him. There's a difference." Lilith walked over to where he sat on his horse. She looked up, her gray eyes sparkling. "I could get used to a man like you around here."

"I'm married."

"So was Mason," she said. Lilith shrugged again. "I'll ask Daniel if he wants to talk. The answer's likely to be 'no.'"

"I'll wait."

She spun around, her skirts swirling out. She gathered them to step over the threshold into the house. Marsh wondered if she would bother asking. Within seconds came loud, angry shouts. He wasn't able to make out the exact words, but the tone told the story. Lilith returned before he had a chance to let out the breath he had been holding in anticipation.

"You heard what he had to say. I never realized Daniel had such a vocabulary. Some of those words, well, even I don't have any idea what they mean."

"I'll—" He started to dismount.

"You'll do nothing of the sort." Lilith raised the rifle from the crook of her arm and covered him. "Daniel is a sick man. Maybe a little bit in the body but a whole lot in the soul. He's had his world about destroyed by Thomas's death."

"Things aren't falling apart. He's able to rebuild the windmill."

Lilith laughed without humor. "I'm responsible for that. Ben wanted to take over, but I knew if I let him start giving orders, he'd steal the whole ranch from me. As long as it looks as if I control the water, I keep a handle on the ranch."

"Where is he?"

"Ben's with the rest of his gang in town. About all they do is get drunk and raise Cain. If they tried to stop the criminal element, they'd throw each other into jail. If the town had a jail."

"Murphyville," Marsh said. He failed to keep the mockery from his voice.

"That's right, Murphyville. It's a fitting tribute to a great man gunned down in the prime of life. Thomas had grand plans for the town. Some of them are happening because he courted the Union Pacific Railroad. The train's only able to shuttle between here and El Paso right now, but a car or two filled with goods is bringing new prosperity to town. It continues down south to the end of the tracks, then heads back. Some folks are actually buying tickets to go to El Paso."

"Osborne is going to become a real city," Marsh said.

"It is. And the name's Murphyville."

"If you ever hire a law dog for the town, whatever you want to call it, you might hand these over to him." Marsh fished around in his pocket and tossed a couple of the .36 caliber brasses to the ground in front of her."

Lilith used the toe of her shoe to move them around in the dust. She looked up at him questioningly.

"I found those next to Reed's body. The only one who uses that small a caliber is—"

"The same man who killed Thomas," she cut in unexpectedly. "I know Gustav wasn't responsible. Truth is, I saw Ben shoot Thomas."

"That's why you helped the boy escape."

"I'm not such an ogre, Marshal. Really."

"Do what you can to head off a feud between our families." He started to wheel Derby around, then stopped. "Over yonder. Back of your barn."

"What? Oh, the pipe. What of it?"

"Are you using it to repair your well?"

"No need. The borehole's all drilled, and the only part being replaced is aboveground." She walked toward the barn. Marsh paced her. "Do you have a hankering for some pipe like that?"

"Is it for sale?"

"Everything is, for the right price."

"You have any valves that fit the pipe?"

"Several. I don't need them, either, for the repair. What're you asking for?"

"How much?"

"To buy it or how much pipe do I have? There's only about forty feet."

Marsh closed his eyes for a moment and pictured Bullet Butte.

"All forty feet and two valves," he said. "What'll you charge for that?"

They dickered a while. Lilith agreed to ten head of cattle. Marsh hated to give up that many valuable cows for the hardware, but he got a real sense of what payment might be extracted by the woman if he bartered much longer.

"Take it into town and leave it at the feed store. Josiah will store it for me until I pick it up. It'll take a day or two to drive my wagon in."

"It'll take that long for me to arrange transport. All the hardware was freighted out by the driller. He's long since moved on over to Marfa. Gossip is that the railroad wants a watering station there, too. He wants to get a jump on everyone else while it's still a tiny little town."

"So he can do like Thomas did here?"

Lilith looked bored with the subject.

"What they do down the line is of no concern. I have a ranch to run," she said.

"Three days," Marsh said. "In three days, I'll pick up the pipe in . . . Murphyville."

This brought a broad smile to her lips. The way her lips pulled back was more feral than human. Marsh saw that the woman considered this small capitulation on his part a major victory for her. He didn't care as long as he got the pipe.

"Come on back any time, Marshal," she said. "You'll always be welcome." Her smile softened a little as she added, "By some folks on this ranch."

He pinched the brim of his Stetson and urged Derby into a gallop to get away from the Double Cross. Marsh didn't feel secure until he reached the boundaries of his own spread.

CHAPTER 36

"I'll go," Marsh Hammersmith told his son. "You stay here and watch over the others."

More gunfire in the distance disturbed the still night. Even the coyotes had stopped howling when the moon set, but the gunshots continued. It sounded as if a war was being fought.

"Take some of the men with you," George said.

"Keep them here, in case you need them. From the sounds, there must be a small army out there."

"Getting a window shot out is nothing compared to you getting filled with lead." George checked his six-shooter to be sure it was fully loaded. He looked up at his father. "You can't take them all on by yourself."

Marsh shook his head. "I don't intend to. I want to sneak up on them and find what they're up to. If they were here to do damage, they wouldn't make such a racket."

"It's a trap, Pa. They want to split us up. Let me come with you."

"Your ma, your wife and son," Marsh said, "matter more. Keep them safe. I promise I won't tangle with them. I only want to find what they're intending to do."

George protested some more, but Marsh brushed off the argument. The fusillade had faded into the distance. No new gunshots replaced the original volley. If the roar hadn't been so overwhelming, he would have thought hunters were poaching on his land.

Or Murphy's vigilantes were shooting cattle out of spite. This seemed different, and try as he might, he couldn't put his finger on what was going on. Seeing it firsthand was his only chance to satisfy his curiosity.

What he'd told his son was true, but he doubted there'd be any trouble at the house. It was a gut feeling and nothing more.

Astride Derby, he rode due east. If the commotion had centered around Bullet Butte, he would have been more cautious. But this came from the direction of his stock pond. As he neared, he saw several fires burning. His heart leaped in his chest. Murphy—Wanamaker!—intended to set fire to the dry prairie grass.

He calmed down when he smelled the aroma of cooking beef. Dealing with rustlers was almost a relief. They stole his cattle to eat them. That cattle theft was better than torching the entire prairie told of the dire straits this part of West Texas endured.

With a quick hop, he hit the ground. A rock dropped on Derby's trailing reins held the horse in place behind a hummock. Rifle in hand, he crept up the slope and flopped on his belly. He peered over at the stock pond. Ripples on its surface reflected four fires. Slowly studying every detail made him frown.

A celebration went on. The steaks were passed out on tin plates, amid loud laughter and joshing. The men, five from his count, hardly looked dangerous. This might be a friendly dinner rather than something to fret over.

He watched the dark shapes eating. He expected them to pass around a bottle of whiskey as part of the celebration, but no one had any liquor. They drank from tin cups occasionally filled from his stock pond.

"You don't have to lie there on the ground like some danged sidewinder. Come on down and join the party."

Marsh rolled over. His finger brushed across the rifle trigger, but he didn't fire. The silhouette behind him was well known.

"What are you doing out here, Pa?"

"Now, Marshal, that's a question I ought to ask you. Me, I was huntin' for a tree to relieve myself on. This old body's wearin' out." Caleb Hammersmith stretched. "Ever'thing either dries up or leaks when you get to be my age."

"Those are your . . . friends?" Marsh sat up and jerked his thumb over his shoulder in the direction of the revelers.

"Proud to say they are. I reckon it was them whoopin' and hollerin' that brought you out of your nice, warm bed."

"I'd rather be there with Leonore than worrying about yahoos shooting up the house."

Caleb nodded slowly. "I heard about that in town. Seems Wanamaker's braggin' on it. Damn fool don't realize he's sayin' all he can do is hit the broad side of a house with his lousy marksmanship." Caleb reached down with a callused, leathery hand. "Come on, boy. Join the festivities."

Marsh let his father help him up. He trailed Caleb over the hill and slipped and slid to the bottom, where he hesitated. What reception he received was likely to determine how much lead he'd have to expend.

"Men, my boy's come out to join in," Caleb called from the nearest fire. "Come on over, Marshal. We got plenty of steaks to go around."

"There's plenty because you've got quite a herd," Kingston said. He held up a knife. A hunk of rare meat was impaled on the tip. "The cattle that're left will fetch you a tidy sum."

Kingston popped the morsel into his mouth and pointed to a rock next to him with his knife. Marsh settled down there, still clutching his rifle.

"Glad you feel enough at home to take down a heifer for your own meal," Marsh said sarcastically.

"Your pa there's a real generous man. He gave us whatever we wanted." Kingston half closed one eye as he peered at Marsh. "You don't think we *stole* one of your beeves, do you? He gave us one for our trouble. Our choice."

Marsh glared at Caleb. "I'm not sure they were his to give away."

Caleb laughed, picked up a plate, and began cutting at the sizzling steak with his knife.

"Over the years, I shed my sweat and blood for the Twin M. This is small enough pay."

"You should have told me." Marsh wasn't sure what he objected to most. Caleb had spent long hours with the cowboys driving the herds over prior years and had not taken any pay other than room and board for his work. His advice had even been useful. The old man had seen things and done things over the years most men never even dreamed about.

Marsh just wasn't sure which were true and which were woven from whole cloth by an overactive imagination.

"You hang onto that rifle like baby Joe does that blanket of his. At least you don't suck your thumb."

This produced a round of laughter from the men. Marsh bristled at being the butt of the joke.

"Don't be so nervy, son. You're among the best friends any man could have in Texas or anywhere else."

Marsh rested his rifle against a rock and found his hands full of a tin plate with a hunk of steak on it. He looked at it. He'd eaten dinner hours earlier, but the aroma made his nostrils expand and his stomach growl.

"Go on, son. Eat it." Caleb pointed at the plate with his knife.

"Why not? It's my cow." Marsh piled into the meat.

Wherever his herd ended up, people there were in for good eating. He was half finished before he found his voice again.

"You're celebrating. What's the occasion?" He looked around. The men turned their eyes to his father, then Kingston.

"We finally run 'em off," Kingston said. He dropped his cleaned plate beside him and picked his teeth with the tip of his knife. "The Comanches. Chased the lot of them north. They'll likely hide out in Palo Duro, and finding them there's not a chore I want to take on."

"Dangerous country," Caleb cut in. "I don't blame you and the boys for not goin' after 'em."

"Colonel Mackenzie flushed most of 'em out years back, but those devils know the land and can hide better'n a lizard in the sand. Smitty's right. There's no way we can catch 'em now."

"Be content, son, the boys shooed them away." Caleb looked self-satisfied, beaming at the men around the cooking fires.

"I wish they were the only rustlers to worry about," Marsh said. He polished off his meat in short order and dropped the plate to the ground beside him as the others had done. What scraps remained were swarmed on by ants. If the men left the camp, bigger scavengers would clean the plates completely.

"The Double Cross wranglers still botherin' you?"

"Them, Wanamaker's vigilantes."

Kingston exchanged looks with his other men, as if warning them to remain silent. Not for the first time, Marsh wondered about them. Why would bounty hunters be happy to only shoo off the Comanche raiders? There wasn't any money in that for them.

"We heard rumors of the killings. The railroad overseer and Thomas Murphy. But they're only rumors, aren't they?"

Kingston's question was pointed and asked in such a way that he wanted Marsh to deny them.

"They are, yes, sir, King. That they are. You know how townsfolk love to make chin music about the smallest things." Caleb shook his head to keep his son quiet.

Marsh understood. The small band of Caleb's friends weren't inclined to chase down Gustav. They owed the old man something, and capturing his grandson and turning him in for whatever reward there might be paled in comparison to their debt. Marsh wondered about his pa's connection with these men. They were older, but nowhere near as old as Caleb Hammersmith. The youngest, Clay, was hardly older than Gustav or George.

If Gustav had escaped on the train, he'd be smart if he reached El Paso, then looked north to Santa Fe or west to California. Getting as far from Murphyville as possible was the smart thing, but Marsh knew his nephew wasn't able to think things through like that. He wasn't dumb, but his impulsive behavior got him into trouble he wasn't able to get away from. He had only gotten worse since his father disappeared.

"You headin' back to Fort Worth now?" Caleb sipped at his tin cup of water and eyed his friends over the rim.

Marsh had seen gamblers do the same thing when they wanted to hide their faces and keep their reactions from being read. All the others stared at Caleb like they were hungry wolves and he was their prey. This was a pack of dangerous men, yet Caleb fit in. Not their leader, not exactly, but someone they looked up to as if he had ridden with them and gained their respect.

Worming the facts of his history from the old man was futile. Marsh had tried for years and finally gave up. It looked now that he had been wrong in writing off Caleb's stories of riding with outlaws and being present at fabulous events. They carried a grain of truth. Just a grain, perhaps, but he wasn't spinning a tale made of whole cloth.

"That's the way it looks. We got that new Ranger captain snappin' at our heels. Avoidin' him is foremost on our minds at the moment," Kingston said. He glanced at Clay, then at the plates.

That was all the goad the youngest of the gang needed to begin collecting plates to take for cleaning.

As Clay bent over next to Marsh, his vest flopped open. Marsh reached out and held the cloth back to get a better view. A Texas Ranger's badge gleamed in the firelight.

Clay pulled away and snorted.

"That was my pa's badge. I took it off his dead body."

"The only reason Clay took it is 'cuz it's hammered out of a silver Mexican ten peso coin. If he ever crosses the Rio Grande, he thinks it'll buy him a shot of tequila and the night with a purty señorita." Caleb laughed uproariously. The others joined in and began swapping increasingly improbable stories of their own amorous adventures.

Marsh listened for a spell, noting how Caleb skirted around, not adding to the stories, possibly out of not wanting his son to think poorly of his dead ma. He finally stood and said, "I've got to get up early."

"Your cattle, rustlers, vigilantes," Kingston said. "Glad you could join us for our little jamboree."

"Thanks for running the Indians off." Marsh hesitated to ask about any Lipan that the gang had also chased away. Night Wolf and his tribe had to fend for themselves.

"Why don't you take Smitty with you? That way we can all tell our stories about him behind his back." Kingston slapped Marsh on the back in a comradely way, as if he was an accepted member of their gang.

"That'd liven up your pathetic stories, King. That's for certain sure." Caleb stepped between the men and herded

Marsh away. "It's time to hit the hay. My son's not as young as he used to be, and such frolickin' wears him out."

Marsh and his father left the others around their small campfires, joking and starting into another round of story-telling. Somehow, he felt a loss as they mounted and rode back to the house. Even if these men wouldn't be on Gustav's trail, he still felt as if friends were leaving.

CHAPTER 37

"A big day for the town, son. I heard tell that Murphy's gonna open the saloon after the ceremony with all the drinks for free." Caleb Hammersmith poked his son in the ribs. "There ain't no reason for Leonore to ever find out you imbibed just a nip or two."

"She'd know," Marsh said absently. He was less interested in what his father said than in watching the crowd gathering to hear boring speeches about how the railroad had come to Murphyville and that Mayor Galveston was pleased as punch about it.

"Only if you told her. Though I have to admit, Leonore's got an extra sense about these things. It's a good thing we don't live anywhere that there's a temperance movement. I've heard tell those places turn into dried up and ready to blow away cities when the womenfolk start marching with banners and sayin' bad things about demon rum."

"There's George. I wasn't sure if he intended to come into town."

"You got him and that crew from over in Mexico workin' double shifts to dig a new acequia. You both have been out in the sun too long. Sunstroke. That new ditch don't go anywhere."

"I'm fixing to steal Murphy's water."

"You're off by miles. Now, in my day . . ."

Marsh no longer heard a word his pa said. In the days since Caleb's friends had left, the old man had been rambling on about this and that, distracting everyone. Not a whit of it was worth listening to. Caleb spun his stories more to hear himself talk than to make much sense.

Marsh suspected Caleb missed his band of bounty hunters, if that's what they were. It might have been more sensible if he'd ridden off with them. They all seemed to look up to him for some reason.

"They're starting," Marsh said, moving closer to the stage. Red, white, and blue bunting dangled down. One corner had blown free in the wind, but no one rushed to refasten it. The entire platform wobbled a bit as Daniel Murphy, Lilith Murphy, Mayor Galveston, and Ben Wanamaker climbed up.

If there'd been even one more person on the platform, it would have come crashing down. Marsh took this as a sign of where the town was headed. He knew why the railroad had agreed to change the name from Osborne. They needed Murphy water for their steam engines. But everything else happening in town bothered him even more.

Daniel Murphy stood to one side, arms folded on his chest and looking fierce. His dark mood seemed to make Lilith jumpy. Mayor Galveston hardly noticed, and Ben Wanamaker's expression showed smug satisfaction.

"Ladies and gents, fellow citizens of this great and wonderful town, formerly known as Osborne and now carrying the proud name of Murphyville, I welcome you." Galveston threw both hands into the air, signaling a volley fired into the air by a half dozen men near the saloon.

Marsh saw that the honor guard was composed of only vigilantes. Petey Peterson commanded them from inside the saloon.

"Long-winded cuss, ain't he?" said Caleb, not trying to

keep his voice down. He cupped his hands and used them as a megaphone to call out, "Get on with it, Gally. If we don't die of thirst first, you'll bore us all to death." He began hooting and hollering derisively.

"Settle down," Galveston said. He was obviously peeved at Caleb's catcalls. "We got a lot of speechifying to do. I want to—"

"We got to let Daniel Murphy have his say." Ben Wanamaker stepped in front of the mayor and shouldered him away. Galveston started to protest, then turned white. His mouth flopped open and he stepped away.

Marsh followed the mayor's line of sight and saw what had shut up the politician so completely. Petey Peterson had drawn a bead on him. Marsh wasn't sure the vigilante would pull the rifle trigger, not in public, but Galveston was convinced.

Daniel Murphy stepped up. He thrust his hands into his pockets, and he stared at his feet. This wasn't a man preparing to launch into a long-winded talk. This was a defeated man surrendering. Marsh stepped forward to better hear the rancher's mumbled words.

". . . no call to stay in town after my brother was killed. Just want to run the ranch." Murphy wobbled a little. Lilith came to steady him. She whispered in his ear. He pulled away and looked at her, fire in his eyes. This was the most emotion he'd shown from the podium.

He whirled around and stumbled off. Lilith hurried after him.

Mayor Galveston tried to take over again, but Wanamaker again stopped him.

"Our next order of business, now that the depot's ready for opening, is choosing our next mayor."

"What? I'm mayor. What are you saying?" Galveston edged around to put Wanamaker between him and Petey with his rifle. That no longer worked. Other vigilantes had spread out and taken posts where any one of them had a decent shot at the politician.

"I'm saying the entire town council has voted you out because of incompetence."

"I did my job!"

"They voted you out because you were the only one in the town to oppose the railroad building the depot."

"He paid me to vote against it," Galveston protested. "Thomas Murphy paid me to bribe the councilors to vote for it, and he told me to vote against . . ." His voice trailed off.

"Another count against the mayor," Wanamaker said. "Make that *former* mayor who just confessed to being bribed."

"Thomas was killed! He was gunned down and—"

"You confessin' to that, as well, Gally?" Wanamaker used the mayor's nickname as an insult.

"No, no, it was Gustav Hammersmith. He was convicted. He—"

Caleb began shouting then. Marsh tried to hush his pa and failed. Responding was exactly what Wanamaker wanted. This nailed Gustav's guilt in the minds of everyone gathered for the railroad depot dedication.

Marsh saw how the crowd pulled away from him and Caleb until they were in the middle of an empty circle. Caleb calmed down and stewed as Galveston was silenced, then stalked off muttering to himself.

"It's my proud duty to introduce you to the man selected by the town council to be your new mayor. Me!" Ben Wanamaker stepped forward and held his hands up in triumph. The crowd fell silent. Only when the vigilantes began cheering did any of the others in the crowd start applauding. Their response was weak until Wanamaker got to the point most of them had shown up to share.

"Free drinks! Mayor Wanamaker is givin' you free drinks the rest of the day!"

This caused a cheer, but it was as much relief as it was enthusiasm for the newly appointed mayor. Marsh turned to the side so that he could shoulder away men pushing past to get to the saloon. For an instant, he pitied Little Miss Molly. She would be worked to a nubbin. Then he knew she had a choice. With the train coming into Murphyville now, she had an easy way to leave.

Everyone in town did. Marsh suspected that life would get mighty tough for the ordinary citizen with Wanamaker running things. Not only was he mayor, he also held the entire town council under his thumb and enforced his own rule with the vigilantes.

Marsh wanted to get out of town before Wanamaker decided he was guilty of some minor infraction and decided to string him up in place of Gustav.

He went hunting for his pa. Caleb had stormed off as if getting into trouble was in the cards. Marsh worried that Wanamaker might take out his ire on the old man. Hunting for ten minutes got him nowhere. He decided the only place to look now was the livery stables. As he turned down the street leading to the corral behind the stable, he spotted Lilith Murphy's buggy. It had been hitched up and the horse stood patiently, munching away at grain in a nosebag.

Voices carried to him. Caleb spoke too loudly and whoever was with him too softly. Marsh reached the corner of the stable and immediately swung back around to stay out of sight. His father stood inches away from Lilith Murphy. The two had their heads together and were arguing about something.

"I tell you, it's the only way," Caleb said.

"It's dangerous. You know how many men he has riding with him now?"

"Eighteen," Caleb said. "Don't look so surprised. I know

what I'm gettin' into. I can even name most of 'em, the ones with rewards on their heads."

"I wondered about that. Ben's always walked a narrow line, but the men with him all came, well, they came from the other side."

"He's got a wanted poster out on him somewhere. He has to. No varmint that mean's not left a trail of blood behind him."

The two lowered their voices and continued whispering. Marsh caught only a word or two. They weren't going to show their hand, so he had no reason to keep eavesdropping on them.

He rounded the corner and waved when Caleb caught sight of him. Marsh blinked. His pa had gone for his six-gun with more speed than he expected from such an old man. The glint in Caleb's eyes showed he would have hit his target if he'd pulled out that smoke wagon and got it rolling.

"There you are, son. You all likkered up?" Caleb sniffed and shook his head sadly. "I don't smell a drop of Wanamaker's free booze on you. I don't know where I went wrong raisin' you. Never pass up a free drink."

"Even if Wanamaker and his vigilantes are the ones offering it? I won't be beholden to them, even for the price of a single drink." He looked at Lilith. She met his gaze boldly.

"Thomas never intended for the saloon to make money. He wanted to use it like Wanamaker is—for bribery."

"It sounds like he worked Galveston and the town council to perfection," Marsh said. "He snared them both."

"He spent a thousand dollars for that bribe," she said. "Don't look surprised. Of course I know all about it." She sucked in a breath and released it slowly. "Gustav saw the money changing hands. That's why Wanamaker wants him dead."

"He can always blame your husband," Marsh pointed out.

"It makes more sense to Ben if he wraps up your family in the corruption. Gustav might convince someone that never happened." She smiled just a little. "The boy is both rebellious and naive. That quality convinces people he's not telling the truth."

Marsh wondered at Lilith's part in Gustav escaping. Why should she care?

As if she read his mind, she looked him squarely in the eye and said, "I owe it to his father."

"What's Mase got to do with this?" Marsh found himself talking to the woman's back. She'd whirled around and hurried for the buggy. He started to stop her but found Caleb's hand gripping his arm, holding him back.

"She's got work to do, son. Don't bother her none. Not right now."

"What's going on? The two of you looked to be thicker than thieves."

"Thicker than thieves, eh? I like that. It fits me. I never tole you 'bout the time I was in Houston and got caught up in the middle of a bank robbery, did I? There I was, surrounded by four bandits, all wearing masks and shootin' anyone who stirred."

"Pa." Marsh was in no mood to listen to another tall tale better told around a campfire.

"What was I to do?" Caleb ignored his son's disgusted tone. "I didn't want to get ventilated, so I pulled up my bandanna and pretended to be one of the gang so they wouldn't shoot me." He chuckled. "It worked. I rode with them for almost a month. They were a dumb bunch of road agents, never catchin' on I wasn't one of them."

Marsh watched as Lilith snapped the whip and drove her buggy down the street. At the intersection, she turned toward the Double Cross ranch. She got out of town. That was something for him to do, too.

"Come on, Pa. Let's go back home."

"Without even dippin' my snout in a free drink? What kind of boy have I raised? What kind?" Caleb shook his head sadly.

Marsh had to listen to his own father deriding him for not being a freeloading drunk all the way to the ranch house.

CHAPTER 38

"We ride in, bold as brass, get the load, then hightail it. We can finish in less than ten minutes," Marsh Hammersmith said. His own words rang hollow. Nothing was ever that easy.

"That's only if she hasn't double-crossed you," his son said. George shared Marsh's worries about what could go wrong.

"George, you need to show some confidence in your fellow man," said Caleb. "In this case, I reckon that's your fellow woman."

"Lilith Murphy is as undependable as a sidewinder," George said.

Caleb sighed and got a dreamy look.

"She's got the same curves as a sidewinder, too. You see how she moves? There's always this little wiggle just like—"

"Pa. Are you going to help or are you going to daydream?" Marsh looked around nervously. He was driving their wagon across Double Cross land and expected Ben Wanamaker and his gang of vigilantes to pop up from behind every creosote bush and mesquite tree.

"No reason a fellow can't do both," Caleb said. "You

take life too serious, son. You, too, grandson. There's more to life than . . . whatever the hell it is we're doin'."

"We're picking up equipment I paid for," Marsh said. It still rankled that he had bartered ten head of cattle, but he had the feeling that any further negotiation with Lilith would have gone against him. The cows were nothing compared with water. That meant the difference between slaughtering their entire herd and giving the wily woman what she had asked for.

"There's the road leading up to the Double Cross ranch house," George said. He touched the butt of his six-shooter. "Do you want me to ride ahead and be sure it's safe?"

"It won't matter. I'm not outrunning any vigilante on horseback driving this rig." Marsh wished he had Derby, but his stallion didn't tolerate being hitched up as a team animal. The two mules he used were slow but powerful. He wished he knew how heavy the equipment he'd traded for was.

"He's got a point, George," said Caleb. "This reminds me of the time me and some friends were holding up trains outside of San Antone. We—"

"Pa," Marsh snapped. He was nervous about this entire deal. He wasn't in the mood to hear fanciful tales. Lilith had told him she hadn't been able to move the pipe into town because Wanamaker blocked her at every turn. If he wanted the pipe, he had to pick it up from behind the Double Cross barn. Marsh was on pins and needles that she had set them up for an ambush, no matter that Caleb claimed it was safe enough to trust her.

"I'll stand guard," the elder Hammersmith said. "You'd only accuse me of gettin' in your way."

Marsh pulled the wagon around behind the barn. Fifty yards away, the newly constructed windmill tower rose higher than thirty feet. The blades whipped around in the stiff breeze, flashing silver with every turn. The pump worked up and down, and a steady rush of water was lifted from the well sixty feet underground.

"For two cents, I'll pull it down again," George said sourly.

"There's the pipe," Marsh said. He edged the mules closer and finally halted. They weren't inclined to get too near to the shed where the lengths of pipe were stored.

"Them's the shutoff valves?" Caleb pointed to crates beside the pipe.

"Lilith said it'd all be in one pile," Marsh said. "Come on, George. Let's load it and get out of here." He looked around again to be sure Wanamaker or one of his henchmen wasn't training a rifle on them. It'd be an easy enough story to tell in town that he'd caught the Hammersmiths stealing and had brought them to justice on the spot.

"I'll scout around," Caleb said.

Before Marsh could stop him, his father trotted toward the house. Marsh caught his breath. Lilith came out and waited for Caleb. The two of them began a heated palaver, just as they had before in town. Marsh was too far away to hear. What they had to discuss was of no matter. Getting the pipe loaded was.

He and George worked to get the ten-foot lengths of pipe secured in the wagon.

"Will four be enough?" George asked.

"It's all there is. It has to be. Help me load this crate. The valve's heavier than I thought."

"You're just getting old and feeble, Pa." George grinned when he said that. But the two of them were barely able to hoist the crate into the wagon bed.

"That's heavier than I thought."

"One's all that is here." George poked around in the shed. "There's some tools. I'm not sure what they are."

Marsh decided to load the devices into the wagon, too. One looked suitable for cutting a thread on pipe. Another was a large iron plate with a hole the size of the pipe bored through it.

"All done," George said, dusting off his hands. "Let's ride."

"Getting your grandpa to stop socializing might be harder than loading the pipe."

Caleb and Lilith still talked, now looking like old friends. She stepped back and waved to Marsh. He touched the brim of his Stetson.

Caleb returned and said, "It's all square with her. She's a real purty gal, that Lilith Murphy."

"And not ten minutes ago you were comparing her to a venomous snake." George glared at Lilith. She blew him a kiss, laughed, and returned to the house.

"She's teasing you, boy."

"I'm a married man," George said.

"But that don't mean you can't think about her, just a little," Caleb said. "Why, 'fore I met your pa's mother, I—"

Marsh convinced the mules to start pulling. They hadn't liked being near the shed. Now they refused to leave. Applying the reins judiciously, he made the mules take first one step, then two. When the loaded wagon creaked and began rolling, the pulling was easier. The mules relented, found the road away from the Double Cross, and were soon on the trail to Bullet Butte.

"Another half hour," Marsh said, as much to himself as to the others. "Then the work begins."

"But not the gunplay," George said. "Look out north."

A dust cloud swirled about and moved slowly in their direction. The calm wind warned that something else had kicked up so much dust. Marsh guessed at least five riders galloped in their direction.

"We're on our own property," Caleb said. "For the past few minutes."

"But not by much," he said. If Wanamaker wanted to kill

them, he always had the excuse they were on Double Cross land. He wouldn't even need to drag their bodies back a mile or two and make that a fact.

"It's Wanamaker," George said, pulling out his rifle. "I can take one of them out before they get too close." He lifted the rifle to his shoulder and sighted.

"Wait. Don't shoot. That'll start a fight for sure," Marsh said.

"How'd I ever raise such a lily-livered coward as a son?" Caleb said in disgust. "Your boy's got the right idea. Reduce their numbers. Shoot first. That's how you stay alive." He pulled out his own six-gun and cocked it.

"Hold on," Marsh said more sternly.

And then Wanamaker and eight vigilantes circled them. It was too late to fight it out and hope to win. The best the Hammersmiths could do now was take a few with them if it turned bloody.

"Well, now, what are you haulin' around, Hammersmith? Is that the water pipe I had out in the shed? The pipe left over from drilling the well?"

"This is Twin M land," Marsh said. He rested his hand on his Peacemaker. None of the vigilantes moved for their weapons. That gave him some confidence they'd ride away without swapping lead.

"I'm entrusted with keeping the peace 'bout everywhere outside Murphyville," Wanamaker said. "Me and the boys, that is. The official Murphyville Vigilance Committee, duly authorized by the mayor."

"You're the mayor."

"Why, yes, I am," Wanamaker said. His grin was wide and evil. "It's a good thing for you to remember it since I run Murphyville and all the land ten miles from it."

"And the railroad," Petey Peterson cut in. "Don't forget you tell those railroaders what to do."

"The Union Pacific Railroad is beholden to me. The Double Cross gets special shipping rates for our cattle."

"The reduction for them," Petey went on, "means the rest of you gotta pay more. The railroad's not about to lose money."

"Nope," said Wanamaker. "It's not good for the railroad to lose money. They might bypass us now that there's rumors of Marfa becomin' a water stop, too."

Marsh said nothing as the vigilante leader rode closer and peered at the freight.

"Speakin' of water, it looks like you're takin' my pipe somewhere other than my wellhead."

"The ranch belongs to the Murphys," Marsh said. "Daniel and Lilith. And she sold us the pipe."

"Did she now? I'll bet you had a fine time negotiatin' with that purty li'l filly."

"She has a way of makin' it hard," Caleb said. "We all came away satisfied after the small talk."

"Don't push me, old man." Wanamaker glared at Caleb. All he got in return was a mocking laugh.

"Unlike some folks who ride around all day, we've got work to do." Marsh distracted Wanamaker from pushing the matter with Caleb. "Clear the road, and we'll be on our way."

"You think to drill a well and use that pipe?" Wanamaker's lips moved as he counted. "You got forty feet of pipe. We had to drill down sixty 'fore we hit water."

"I'm counting on being luckier."

"The driller's moved on. Him and his crew are—"

"—in Marfa, getting that town ready to snake away your exclusive with the railroad," George said.

"In Marfa," Wanamaker said, pretending not to have heard. "It won't be for weeks, maybe months, 'fore him and his crew return. By then your scrawny old cows will be all dried up."

"There's always a market for jerky, Ben." Petey laughed

at his own joke. "Only it'll cost them a fortune to ship it on your railroad."

"I see you got at least one rider with you what's been kicked in the head by a horse;" Caleb said. "You'd better get on back to town and see if a shot or two of whiskey won't fix such crazy talk."

Marsh snapped the reins. The mules showed enthusiasm for being somewhere else and pulled strongly. The wagon rattled along the road. George and Caleb rode on either side. Marsh tried not to let the vigilantes' catcalls get under his skin.

He succeeded by staring ahead at Bullet Butte and the promise there.

The mules were cranky from being pushed so hard, but he reached the spot at the base of the butte with more than half a day of light ahead. The workmen he'd hired away from the Double Cross had finished the last few yards of acequia, so it came right up to the rocky spire.

Marsh looked up and got a kink in his neck. This close up to the butte made it look as if it held up the bright blue sky. More than this, he wanted to be sure there weren't Apaches hiding above him. The Lipan band traveled widely. They might not be anywhere near. He hoped that was so because he knew they'd fight to the death to save their secret watering hole.

"Unload the pipe and valve and get the wagon out of here." He sent two of the workmen to fetch the crate with the dynamite and then studied the solid stone face.

Marsh pressed his hand into the stone. He closed his eyes. While it was his imagination working hard, he heard the rush of cool, clear water only inches away.

"How're you going to get everything set up, Pa? If you blast and the water rushes out, there won't be any way to put in the pipe and valve."

"I've scouted this the best I can. A blast hole right about

here"—he tapped the rock—"won't breach the water. We put in the pipe, secure it with the flat plate with that hole drilled through it, then install the valve." He took a deep breath. "Then I blast again above the pipes and valve and hope it all comes together right."

"There's a crevice," George said. "Why not lay the pipe in there? It'll save having to blast a hole."

Marsh worked around and saw the crevice his son had spotted with his sharper eyes. He worked his way back a few feet until he feared being wedged in too tight to get free. From what he saw, this was about perfect. The plate at the back of the crevice would be driven forward by the water and held in place by the pressure. A little work with the cement he'd brought would hold the pipe in place and seal the passage.

"Your plan's better'n mine, George. Let's get to work."

Between the two of them and the workers, they had everything in place as the sun set.

"Will the concrete hold if it's not properly dried?" George scraped at it with his thumbnail.

"I'm not waiting a week for it to set. Now. We blow the well now," he said, having decided.

"I've got the valve open. The pipe runs straight for the end of the acequia." George took a deep breath. "The really dry acequia."

"Let's change that," Marsh said. "Clear the area. I've done a little blasting, but it was mostly stumps. I don't want to get this wrong."

"Then let an expert set the charge, son." Caleb pushed him away from the crate of dynamite. "I looked that hole over and know perzactly what you need. Cut me five feet of miner's fuse."

"Five minutes' worth?"

"I don't run as fast as I used to, but I can get clear in five minutes." Caleb took a bundle of dynamite, bounced it up and down in his hand, then added two more sticks. "This'll be just right. Now give me the blasting cap."

Marsh winced when his father bit down hard on the mercury fulminate cap and attached it to the fuse. The cap-fuse combination was worked into the middle of the dynamite bundle.

Caleb sauntered to the crevice with the pipe and its attached valve sticking out of the mountainside and wormed his way in. Marsh heard cursing and the scrape of rock minutes before Caleb extricated himself.

"I fixed it good. The blast'll close off what space there is along the pipe." He held the end of the fuse. "Gimme a lucifer and I'll light 'er up."

"This is my honor," Marsh said, pulling the end of the fuse out of his pa's hand.

"Honor or folly," George said. He took Caleb's arm and pulled him away. "Come on, Gramps. He won't light the fuse until we get far enough away."

"What fun's that? It'll be another five minutes 'fore it blows. When you're as old as I am, you want things to happen *now*."

"Tell me, Gramps, where you learned to blow up things." George led him away. Caleb rambled on about the first bank vault he'd blown up. When Marsh no longer heard him, he held up the fuse and uttered a quick prayer.

He had everything riding on this. If it didn't work, the Twin M was headed for bankruptcy. Water was everything in West Texas, and he was all in.

The lucifer flared. He applied the flame to the fuse. It sputtered and then began its inexorable march into the mountain. He wanted to stay and watch, which was crazy. Marsh made certain the valve was wide open, then walked a few feet and jumped into the dry irrigation ditch.

For what seemed an eternity, he walked. Then the ground shook beneath his feet. He stumbled and went to one knee. He regained his balance and turned toward Bullet Butte.

The wall of water bowled him over and carried him along. Success!

CHAPTER 39

"Are you ready?" Marsh Hammersmith licked his lips nervously and tasted dust. If anything went wrong, not only would he be eating dirt from six feet under for all eternity, so would his son.

"Yeah, Pa. I want to get this over." George looked around, as nervous as his father.

Marsh pressed against the wall of the Double Cross ranch house. The window was wide open, so he could see and hear everything happening in the sitting room. He'd have to be careful not to give in to the urge to watch. Ben Wanamaker might spot him, and their scheme to make him confess everything would fall through.

He slapped George on the back. His son slid the leather thong off the hammer of his six-gun, adjusted the holster on his hip, and climbed through the window. He walked slowly to the middle of the room and looked around.

His growing nerves were contagious. Marsh began to fidget, too. He dropped to his knees outside the window and pressed his ear against the wall, trying to hear everything better. It looked as if George was alone in the room. Marsh worried that he was. Caleb's friends were supposed to position themselves throughout the house to become witnesses to whatever Wanamaker said. If he couldn't see them, were they even there?

Marsh felt a hollow feeling in his gut for trusting Kingston and the others. His father vouched for them, but they were ruffians. Worse. They were bounty hunters and had no loyalty to anyone except making a few dollars off the fugitives they caught.

"What're you doin' here?"

The demand froze Marsh. Wanamaker had come into the room and found George.

"I was hunting for you," George said.

"Now ain't that rich? Why'd you bother?"

"I pulled down your windmill," George said. "Then I tried to destroy the valve and make the well useless."

"I don't understand why you're tellin' me this. Unless you're also confessin' to shootin' Daniel."

"That wasn't my doing. My gun never left its holster. What I think is that you tried to kill him just like you killed his brother."

Wanamaker laughed. Marsh chanced a quick glance into the room. Wanamaker stood with his hand on his pistol, ready to throw down.

"You'll never prove that. Either of the shootings."

"There're two witnesses to you gunning down Thomas. Lilith saw you. And Gustav can testify, too."

"He's on the run because he's the one convicted of killing my boss. My former boss. And who'd ever believe Lil? She had too much to gain by her husband getting murdered like he did. She's half owner of the ranch. Maybe she and your cousin conspired? That's more believable than me killing Thomas and tryin' to shoot Daniel."

Marsh cursed. Wanamaker wasn't fessing up the way he'd hoped. George would have to be cleverer.

"Next thing I know, you'll deny gunning down Al Reed."

"Who cares about him? He was only passin' through."

"He wasn't going to pay you the extortion money for the water, was he?"

"He said he dealt with crooks like me all the time. I had the contract he signed with Thomas. There wasn't any reason to let him get in the way of everything else I was doin' in town."

"So you shot him."

"Six times," snapped Wanamaker. "That was a mercy killin'."

"He wasn't armed."

"Neither was Thomas. That shouldn't stop a man with higher ambitions."

"Like you," George said, goading him.

"Like me. I got it all now. I run Murphyville, and the railroad jumps to my tune. It won't be long before I get rid of Daniel and force Lil out."

"She's smarter than you."

"Is she?" Wanamaker sneered. "She has every man wrapped around her little finger. That's all the sway she has. I have this."

Marsh peeked in again. Wanamaker had whipped out his six-gun and had it trained on George. George's fingers had tightened around the butt of his six-gun, but he was too slow.

"You can't get away with shooting me," George said.

"You won't be the first Hammersmith to meet his end at my hand," Wanamaker said.

Marsh swung about on his knees and rested his Peacemaker on the window sill. He drew a bead on the Double Cross foreman.

"So you brung your pa to back you up. That figures," Wanamaker said. "In fact, I counted on it. I saw the pair of you riding onto the ranch. What a pair of idiots. First you dig ditches to nowhere, and then you think you can outwit me."

"Drop the iron, Wanamaker," Marsh called.

"You drop yours, Hammersmith."

Marsh tensed when cold steel pressed into the back of his neck. He looked over his shoulder. Petey Peterson had crept up on him. He had been too intent on Wanamaker facing down George to notice.

"What are we gonna do with them, Ben?"

"Don't shoot 'em here. Murphy is in the house, and he's on a tear. The last I saw he was wavin' a shotgun around."

"I heard these two boastin' on how they was gonna kill Murphy, just like Gustav gunned down Thomas. We came across them after they killed Murphy, shot it out, and killed the pair of them. All that sounds real likely, don't it, Ben?"

"I'd like to see them swing," Wanamaker said. "I was robbed when Gustav slipped out of town."

"Don't get too fancy, Ben. Puttin' a slug in each of 'em is sure. As much as I'd like to practice bein' a hangman again, lead's a quicker way to hell for these owlhoots."

"You're right, Petey. Sometimes I get too tricky. It's better when I just shoot 'em like I did Thomas and that railroader." Wanamaker made a satisfied sound, a smacking noise with his lips like he'd just tasted the best peach cobbler in all of West Texas. "It felt good puttin' that lead into Reed. One shot after another until all six rounds were fired."

"Let's cut 'em down in the barn. Nobody'll disturb us there," Petey said. He stepped back and motioned with his six-gun for Marsh to precede him.

As his muzzle pointed off target, a dark shape blotted out the sun. Then it crashed into Peterson, knocking him backward.

"Clay, look out!" Marsh cried. He grabbed for his fallen gun and fired. Clay twitched as Marsh's bullet tore a hunk of denim from his jeans.

But the shot was about the most accurate Marsh had ever fired. The slug drove past Clay without so much as grazing him and buried itself in Petey Peterson's chest. The vigilante gave a gasp, then a gurgle, and his legs folded under him. He sprawled on the ground, sightless eyes staring up at the cloudless Texas sky.

Marsh wasted no time congratulating himself for his skill—and luck. He whipped around and scanned the room. Wanamaker had taken refuge behind a chair.

"George, are you all right?"

"My gun's out in the middle of the floor, Pa. I can't get to it."

Marsh began blasting away at the chair. Splinters flew and padding filled the air. George dived, scooped up his six-shooter, and fired a few more times to turn the chair into wormwood.

"He's not there," both of them called at the same instant.

"King's got him," Clay said confidently. "He was out in the hall."

Marsh wasn't so sure. Wanamaker was a slippery cuss. He backed away and looked around the yard.

"We have trouble," he told Clay. "The vigilantes!"

The words had barely escaped his lips when a hail of bullets ripped past him and cut holes through the wall. Marsh dived through the window, then swung back and fired at the attacking vigilantes to cover Clay. The young gunman was gone like smoke in wind. All that remained was Peterson's body on the ground.

Marsh emptied his Peacemaker, reloaded, and fired some more. He tried to count the opposition. He quit after four. George crowded beside him and added his gun to their attempt to force the vigilantes back.

"We need to get out of here," Marsh said. A bullet emphasized their dangerous position as it drilled through the wall between them. "There's an army of Wanamaker's men out there, and they're all aiming to lift our scalps."

"Wanamaker escaped into the hall, but where'd he go

after that? We might walk right into his line of fire," George said.

"Go," Marsh said. "We're not going to make it much longer here."

He fired as his son duckwalked to the door leading into a long hallway. Marsh emptied his Peacemaker once more, reloaded, and followed.

"Where're Gramps's friends?" George began edging along the hall. He kicked open each door as he came to it. Marsh covered him.

"We should never have depended on them. A better question's where's your grandpa?" Marsh worried that Caleb, reliving his salad days, would enter the fight with no sense of the danger.

"Haven't seen him." George threw open a bedroom door and almost got his head blown off by a shotgun blast. He staggered back and pressed hard against the wall, panting harshly.

Marsh never hesitated. The instant a second barrel was discharged, he stepped into the door and found the vigilante working to reload. His first shot hit the man in the arm. Nothing serious. His second in the same arm caused the vigilante to drop his shotgun. The third round was exactly placed and hit the man in the temple as he spun around, fumbling for the six-shooter holstered at his side.

Behind him, George opened fire down the corridor.

"It's Wanamaker. He's got Miz Murphy."

Marsh pushed George back and took the lead. As he advanced, he reloaded. Facing Wanamaker without a full cylinder was a quick way to die. He chanced a quick look around a corner. He barely ducked back before Wanamaker opened fire. Bits of plaster flew into his face.

"Come on out, Hammersmith. Just me and you."

"Let her go."

"You'd like that, wouldn't you? She's almost a part of your family."

Marsh ignored the taunt. He started to step out when George opened fire past him, toward the far end of the hallway. A quick look showed that Daniel Murphy had stepped out and waved around a six-gun. George's rounds drove him back into the room.

"You don't need her as a shield, Wanamaker. She's no good to you."

"She wouldn't have anything to do with me. Not even when I shot her husband. That's ingratitude if I ever saw it."

"You go out there, Pa, and he'll kill you and then her." George reloaded. "If we both pop out, one of us can nail him."

"We'd get him and probably Lilith, too."

"No loss. She went along with the scheme to cut off our water. She's as guilty as any of them."

Marsh held his son back.

"Outside, Wanamaker. The two of us face off outside."

"You finally came up with a decent idea. That's the way I want it, too, Hammersmith."

Another quick peek. Wanamaker dragged Lilith Murphy through a door out back of the house. For a moment, all Marsh saw was the woman held hostage and the new windmill behind her. That image burned in his head as to all that had plagued him. Water and rustlers and being in a position where he lost, no matter what he did.

He took a breath, then darted across the room and stood beside the open door.

"Let her go and I'll come out, Wanamaker. See?" Marsh holstered his pistol and momentarily showed it.

"Come on out and meet your maker," Wanamaker called.

"It's a trap, Marshal. His men!" Lilith fell to her knees when Wanamaker shoved her away. Then he backhanded her across the mouth, silencing her.

Marsh stepped into the doorway, expecting a deadly rain of lead to come his way. The expression on Wanamaker's face told him the vigilante's trap hadn't worked the way he expected. Both men went for their guns at the same instant.

Marsh was a split second faster. He fired and spun Wanamaker around. The man fell to his knees, clutching at his side. Before Marsh got off a second round, a hand reached out and grabbed his wrist, forcing his hand down.

"It's over, son."

Marsh's eyes widened in surprise. His father kept him from finishing the job he'd started. He tried to jerk free, but the old man's grip was surprisingly strong.

"They've got him." Caleb pulled Marsh outside but kept his grip. "That's how you do it. They've got him and all the rest of his filthy bunch."

Kingston and Clay moved in on either side of Wanamaker and yanked him to his feet. Clay plucked the vigilante's gun from his hand and shoved it into his own waistband. For an instant, Marsh was blinded by the silver flash as sunlight caught the badge Clay had pinned to his chest. Then he and Kingston half dragged Wanamaker off.

"Where are the rest of the vigilantes?" Marsh looked around. The Double Cross yard was empty of the small army he expected to see.

"King and the boys took care of 'em. Not much of a chore since Wanamaker's gang were braggarts and not fighters."

"All of them?" Marsh felt shock setting in, numbing him. "There were a dozen or more. Kingston and his gang. Four men? They took care of all of Wanamaker's men?"

"Reckon so. The ones that didn't get themselves kilt lit a shuck. They won't stop running until they're all the way to Indian Territory. Maybe Mexico, if they got a lick of sense, and not many of them did. That's where I'd go to hide. Mexico. There's a fine little cantina down around

Veracruz you wouldn't believe. Best pulque anywhere. One night there I—"

Marsh shook off his daze and turned away from his pa. The story might be thrilling, but it was also probably a lie. He helped Lilith to her feet. Her lip had been split, and a nasty welt on her cheek showed how powerfully Wanamaker had slapped her.

"You saved me. I owe you." Lilith tried to brush the dirt off her dress and only smeared it.

"We're even. You kept Gustav from getting his neck stretched."

"He's in El Paso. Or that's where I told him to go."

"Pa." George came up and shook his shoulder. He pointed.

All of Caleb's friends rode in a circle around a bound Ben Wanamaker.

"Where're you taking him?" Marsh called out.

Kingston replied, "To justice." He touched the brim of his hat and heeled his horse. The others herded Wanamaker along, but Marsh heard their prisoner shout, "You ain't seen the last of me, Hammersmith. Not like Mason. You'll never see him again!"

The tight knot of riders turned onto the lane leading to the main road and in seconds vanished in a dust cloud.

CHAPTER 40

"I tried to convince him, Marshal, but he won't listen to me," Lilith Murphy said. She reached out and laid her hand on his.

Marsh felt like pulling away but left his hand under hers, resting on the tower support. The windmill turned sluggishly and sent vibrations throughout the tower. The bearings needed lubrication, but Marsh knew mentioning that was only a distraction. The woman was lovely. Lovely and seductive. Like a coral snake.

"You need to hire a new foreman," he said, trying to sidetrack her wiles.

"I know, but there's so much falling apart around here, it's as if that is minor. Yet it isn't, is it? A good foreman takes care of repairs and chores and watches over the herd and . . ."

"Lilith," he said, perhaps too harshly. "It's all right if you won't fill my acequia again."

"But your herd'll get thirsty, Marshal. You need that water."

"Sell it to the railroad. I'll find a way to replace the water."

"There's no replacement unless it rains." She held up

both hands to the sky, as if imploring some rain god to open the heavens and send a downpour.

Marsh used the woman's movement to draw his hand back away from her.

"You've done plenty to help, turning the tables on Wanamaker and his vigilantes. The town council has decided to hire a marshal now. The county might even spend the money to hire a sheriff, now that the railroad money is beginning to flow into Osborne."

"Murphyville," she said with some satisfaction. "Get used to calling it that. It's the only tribute to Thomas's memory there'll be."

"Murphyville," he conceded. "You'll have to tell the new law dog that Gustav wasn't responsible for your husband's death."

"Gus," she said softly, a distant look in her eyes. "I'll go to El Paso and bring him back."

"There's no call to do that," Marsh said. "Let him work out his problems." He sighed. "Too many of them are with me, with his ma and the rest of the family." Before he said another word, the roar from a shotgun rolled across the yard from the direction of the house.

"Get off my land. I'll kill you, Hammersmith. I'll see you in a grave. You're responsible for all my trouble." Daniel Murphy rushed from the house, his shotgun aimed at the sky. He loosed another blast, then worked to reload both barrels.

"He's likely to aim at you, Marshal," she said. "I can't reason with him at all."

"Don't bother. And Gustav—"

"I'll do right by him. I promise," she said.

Marsh stepped back to keep her from giving him a kiss.

"You won't steal my water!" Daniel Murphy stalked toward the windmill tower, shotgun levelled.

"Get out of his way," Marsh warned her. "He'll shoot you to get me." With that, he turned and vaulted into the saddle. Derby reared, pawed the air, then showed how apt his name was. The stallion galloped so fast Marsh was certain they outran the load of buckshot Daniel Murphy sent their way.

Marsh stood on the lip of his stock pond. Only a week earlier, the water level had been low and threatened to show muddy bottom. Now it was half filled with sweet water. The cattle no longer had to be herded to keep them from wandering off in search of small springs or other ponds. This drew them like flies to flop.

"It won't be long before we have to see if that valve works," George said, coming up beside him.

"We wouldn't want to overflow the pond's banks, would we?" Marsh beamed at the idea the Twin M had more water than they could use.

"If we can find them, putting some catfish into the pond would make for good eating."

"I always enjoyed it when your grandpa and I went fishing. He's as good an angler as he is a storyteller."

"You mean his fish stories are as outrageous?" George laughed. It was the first genuine laughter he'd uttered since Marsh couldn't remember when.

"When we lived in the piney woods, we went fishing and the first one I pulled out was—"

"Don't you start, Pa. Your stories'll never be as outrageous."

"Not even if I told you I caught a big white whale?"

"Not even if you named it Jonah," George said. "What's that pen for over on the far side of the pond?"

"Cattle. I intend to keep two or three head in it all the time."

"Why?"

"Payment," Marsh said. His son looked at him as if he'd been out in the sun too long without a hat. But explaining wouldn't help George understand the debt he felt.

Night Wolf could raid and "steal" the cattle without too much problem. The "theft" would raise him in the esteem of the rest of his Lipan band. He was sure they'd continue to sample the water pouring from Bullet Butte but no longer had to make the perilous climb to the top. He owed the Apache brave for saving the Twin M ranch.

Marsh just wished Night Wolf hadn't stolen his knife. It had been his favorite.

It was supposed to be a simple robbery. A fortune in gold for the taking. What Hack Long and his outlaws hadn't figured on was the Texas Rangers pouncing on them like a pack of rabid wolves. Desperate to escape, Long led his men south of the Rio Grande, where they ran afoul of Mexican Rurales and were imprisoned.

Unwilling to die behind the bars of the hellish prison where life is worth less than a peso, Long's band of desperados break out of jail and split up to escape. Now, Two-Horses, Luke Fischer, Gabriel Santana, Billy Lightning, and Long are scrabbling along a desolate landscape, heading for Texas to reclaim their ill-gotten gains and while being hunted by dogged lawmen, merciless Comanches, and a violent gang of bandits who also want the stolen gold.

Though they be thieves and outlaws, Long and his men aren't nearly as deadly as their pursuers. They may not deserve forgiveness for their sins, but only death passes judgment on both the good and the bad . . .

National Bestselling Authors
William W. Johnstone
and J. A. Johnstone

THE WICKED AND THE DEAD

The Hair-Raising Tale
of Hack Long and His Outlaw Gang

On sale now, wherever Pinnacle Books are sold

Live Free. Read Hard.

www.williamjohnstone.net

CHAPTER 1

The bare prison courtyard deep in Coahuila, Mexico, was hot as hell's foyer, and Hack Long would have given anything to be somewhere cooler. Dirt and rocks packed by decades of hooves and human feet reflected the desert sun's rays back against the brick, rock, and adobe buildings, making the enclosure feel like a massive oven.

He sat on the ground in a sliver of shade with his back to the rough exterior wall, chewing at a tough piece of meat that could have come from a cow, bear, horse, donkey, or wolf. Dog, for all he and the others knew. He'd eaten plenty of dog in Two-Horses's village over the past few years, when they were in the Indian Nations.

It didn't matter. The plain, familiar stew was nourishment, and they all needed to keep up their strength for the next struggle to survive that was sure to come. Bland food was strange down in Mexico, because the smell of onions, peppers, and spices wafting from the *comandante*'s office and the adjoining guards' barracks made their stomachs rumble several times a day.

He and the boys figured the grub they brought to them was boiled up well before anything else was added, other than the salt needed for the prisoners to survive, providing another form of punishment for all those locked up in that hellhole. Only on Sundays were their tortillas and beans flavored with *nopales* and chilis so hot they seemed to be an added punishment instead of a treat.

Hack and the hard-eyed boys with him ate every bite of whatever the Mexicans dished and were proud to get it. They had to stay strong, because only the fit could survive in a world of bandits, murderers, and thieves.

There were two kinds of men in Purgatorio. Predators and prey. Sometimes Hack was of the mind that only the wicked survived, while the dead were finally released from the tribulations that delivered them to dry graves outside the penitentiary with startling regularity.

The Long gang, as they were known both inside and outside of the prison, long ago proved capable of protecting themselves, but it was essential they continued to project a sense of menace worse than what they'd been dragged into.

That made them harder men than when they had stumbled through the gates of the Mexican prison in chains. None of them were without scars, and over half of those they had were earned in attacks and fights that usually resulted in the deaths of the instigators.

With only fifteen minutes to eat before going back to the copper mines, though it always seemed much shorter, Luke Fischer lowered himself to the hard ground beside the gang leader and adjusted his position to keep an eye on the other prisoners. "You feel it?"

"I do." Jaws aching, Hack shifted the tough piece of meat to the other cheek and chewed some more.

One of the newer inmates, a guy with a wispy mustache, passed the American prisoners, looking with dead eyes for a safe place to eat away from those wolves who stole food. Swift attacks to take the weaker men's twice-a-day allotment usually spilled more than they gained. The slender young man named Escobedo had only been there for a week, and in those few days, he'd lost half of his portions as well as his shoes.

Eyes glassy with hunger, work, and fear, he sat only a dozen feet from the Norte Americanos and wolfed down his meal. Two fresh cuts from an altercation the night before marred the smooth skin over one eyebrow and the opposite cheekbone.

Andelacio Morales rose from where he squatted with a clot of other prisoners near the long row of cells and swaggered across the bare yard. Hack couldn't *stand* that man because he stunk so bad. That's part of why he and the boys steered clear of him whenever possible.

He was also the worst, most black-hearted human being Hack had ever seen. Morales's worn-out shoes crunched on the gravel and yard packed hard by decades of footsteps. Even the hot air stilled as the man towered over Escobedo, who kept his eyes lowered to the tin plate between his knees. Escobedo seemed to collapse inward as his spirit vanished. Hack sensed that he wished to sink into the ground.

Morales towered over Escobedo and spoke to him in Spanish. "Your portion."

The younger man quickly tilted the bowl and swallowed without chewing. His Adam's apple bobbed as he swallowed, and Hack wondered how he got any of that gristle down without chewing.

Morales's face twisted. "The rest of that's mine."

Like a child, Escobedo twisted sideways to protect the bowl until he could get the last mouthful.

For the past several months, the Long gang had stayed out of the trouble that swirled around them like a *chiindii*, the Navajo word for a dust devil. That's what those little fights in the yard reminded him of, the skinny twisters of sand that walked across the desert floor. Those kinds of fights were as common in Purgatorio as breathing.

Knowing what was coming next, he put down his empty bowl and rose, using only the muscles in his stout legs. The corners of his eyes tightened, and Hack wondered why he was getting involved in someone else's business.

It didn't matter, that familiar tingle in his head rose with a hum. There are some things in this world that the wanted outlaw won't tolerate, and one of them was people who preyed on other, weaker men. The red tinge at the edges of his vision would soon narrow down to a tunnel with only Morales at the end. It had happened more times than Hack or his best friend Luke cared to admit.

He shifted over to make Morales see a fresh target rather than his young victim. "Go away and leave him alone."

The hulk of a man didn't take his eyes off Escobedo and the tiny bit of food left in the wooden bowl. "I'm not talking to you, *gringo*."

Across the yard, Juan Perez perked up. From the corner of his eye, Hack saw the head guard grin at the incident boiling to life in the hot sun. That evil man liked nothing better than watching a good beating, and he didn't give a whit about who was on the wrong end.

When he was a young man, Hack's old daddy always said to get the first lick in on a fight and to use anything that came to hand. The only things he had nearby were his fists, and Morales was hard as the packed ground under their worn-out old boots.

"But I'm talking to you, *estupido*." Hack's right fist shot out in a blur and landed squarely against Morales's jaw, spinning him to the side. A hard left landed on the point of his nose, which exploded in a gout of blood that gushed from both nostrils. The cartilage crunched under Hack's large knuckles, and the man's expression went dull.

Morales staggered backward before regaining his balance. Pursuing his advantage, Hack followed up with two more swings that immediately split the skin over Morales's eyebrow and split his cheek. The stunned man blinked several times to clear his watering eyes. Half a dozen of his *compadres* gathered behind him like regimental troops, as if preparing for a charge, shouting and urging him on.

Still behind Hack, Luke Fischer barked a laugh and rose to square off with the others. Using his fingers to comb back a tuft of brown hair from his forehead, he set his feet in case somebody charged. "Damn, son. I think I just saw water shoot out of six holes in his head."

The other members of the incarcerated Long gang heard Luke chuckle. Two-Horses, Gabriel Santana, and Billy Lightning put their bowls on the ground and stood as one. The boys drifted behind Hack and scattered out. Had the members of the Long gang been armed, it would have had the makings of a shootout with deadly results. They were all experienced gunmen and had done their share of killing both good and bad men.

Instead, they faced Morales's lackeys and prepared to fight.

Morales was an experienced prison brawler, and a couple of hard licks and a little blood didn't faze him all that much. A large man, he'd survived innumerable fights by using his weight and power. He shouted and rushed in to get his hands on Hack, where he could use his considerable prison experience gained from years of preying on weaker men.

Hack was far from weak and had no intention of letting that happen. Planting his right boot, he cocked his arm as if ready to swing. The instant Morales ducked his head to plow a shoulder into his chest, Hack settled back to use his own motion against him.

As a former town marshal, train and bank robber, and range rider who'd fought his way across most of Texas, bustin' knuckles with someone else was nothing new to the gang leader. He'd learned long ago to let a man use his own leverage against him and almost felt comfortable with what was about to happen.

When Morales charged, Hack swiveled and dodged, at the same time grabbing the inmate's arm, and used the man's momentum to swing him headfirst into the prison wall. The convict's skull and shoulder hit the solid rock and brick with a crack. The impact stopped the man's charge, and his knees buckled.

Morales went down for a second, but using the wall to steady himself, he regained his feet and pushed off with both hands, addled for a second time in fifteen seconds. He shook his head to clear it, and blood flew. Gritting his teeth, he growled like a furious coyote and rushed at Hack.

Those friends of his were moving in, and Hack had to finish up fast. Only men who lost their tempers wanted to continue a fight just to maim and hurt. He wanted that mad dog down for good in the eyes of those who saw him as their leader, so he wouldn't have to look over his shoulder every day for the rest of the time they were there.

Morales shook his head a second time to clear the cobwebs, and droplets of blood flew like rain once again, splashing on those nearby. His face was a mask of blood that poured from his nose and a gaping split in his forehead wide enough to look like a second mouth. The edges separated enough to show his white skull, which was soon covered in red.

Hack reluctantly gave him one thing, the Mexican prisoner was tough as a horseshoe nail and had no intention of stopping. He came in again, and Hack swung a soft left that the inmate easily blocked, but it left him open, and an uppercut that started at Hack's rope belt and aimed at the top of Morales's head finished the fight. His teeth clacked from the impact that shattered his jaw, and he dropped in his tracks like a puppet with the strings cut. He hit the ground blowing bloody bubbles mixed with broken teeth.

Breathing hard, Hack faced Morales's friends and squared off with them. "This'll be the rest of you if y'all take one more step. This is over." He pointed at Escobedo. "And you leave this man alone."

Still making eye contact to maintain their machismo facade, they drifted off like leaves in the wind, leaving Morales unconscious in the dust. Hack's boys stayed planted where they were, in case someone whirled to charge. When all the other inmates were back to their places in the shade, they relaxed and went back to their own small pieces of ground.

Escobedo nodded his thanks and pushed his back closer to the rock and mortar wall, as if ensuring no one could get in behind him. He tipped the bowl into his mouth and finished the food Hack had fought for.

Hack licked his thumb and rubbed at the now raw knuckles on his left hand. All the roosterin' over with for the time being between them, he picked up his own wooden bowl and returned to his previous spot in the shade to suck in another mouthful of now cold stew.

The shirt hanging on his thick shoulders wasn't much more'n a thin rag, but a new rip in the back that ran from shoulder to waist parted when he sat. "It's a good thing this storm is coming." He picked up the conversation as if they'd never been interrupted. "They won't make us work for a day or two while it passes through, and Escobedo there can rest up."

Luke scratched at his brown whiskers. "I'm surprised you stood up for that feller."

Hack chewed for a moment longer and nodded at Escobedo, who watched his tormentor's lackeys haul the unconscious man off. "He'll make it now, maybe. Did you hear what happened in his cell last night?"

Luke swallowed the last of his meal. "Escobedo's tougher'n you think. He whipped Torres one-on-one."

Two-Horses stood in the sun, picking at a callus on his thumb. His face was wide, jaw solid, with prominent, protruding cheekbones. It was his white man's blue eyes that set him apart from his Comanche roots. Round in shape and always narrowed against the light, they spoke of mixed blood that almost no one, white or red, could abide.

He seldom spoke, but he seemed surprised Hack had waded into a fight that didn't have anything do with any of them. "So why'd you help him?"

"Because what they did wasn't right. Torres paid one of the guards, and I figure it was Perez, to open Escobedo's cell after lockup. Torres slipped in, and about five minutes later they had to carry what was left of him out. They locked the cell again, and nobody said a word. That's why I think Escobedo can handle himself, but two fights so close together can drain a man down to nothing.

"The truth is, I don't like it that Perez is playing games with everyone in here. Next time it could be me, or you, or any one of us who's not up to snuff at the moment and can't defend themselves."

"Why did he let Torres into Escobedo's cell in the first place?" Gabe Santana wanted to know. Besides Luke, Gabe had been with Hack longer than the others. A lithe, slender man with black hair, olive complexion, and somber eyes, he'd been a man to ride the river with from the first time Hack laid eyes on him up in Llano County.

"Because I heard there was a bet over who would win."

The youngest of their group, Billy Lightning, scratched at a red spot on his forearm where a scorpion had stung him a week earlier. Looking more like a schoolboy, Billy had only a few light whiskers along his jawline and a dusting of blond strands on his upper lip. "Torres woke up in the hotbox this morning. He's still in there as far as I know.

"I knew a guy who spent three days in the Yuma hotbox," Luke interjected. "Killed him deader'n Dick's hat-band. Fell out about five minutes after they let open the door. It was a crying shame for a tough man like that."

"I bet Torres wishes he'd never tangled with Escobedo." Santana stretched his legs into the dry sunshine, studying what was left of his worn-out boots.

Billy used his thumb to rub at the knot left by what he'd grown up calling a stinging lizard, which was a local description of scorpions. "You could have let Escobedo handle himself. Now you'll have Perez thinking about you and what he can do to us."

"Don't matter. I dislike Morales, and now that's settled," Hack answered. "Sometimes you have to refresh folks' memories, too."

Taking advantage of the time out of their cells and the mine, Hack adjusted himself in the narrow shade thrown by the twelve-foot wall to keep the sun off his head. The guards allowed each man a cap, of sorts, but it fit so snug, the hot material against Hack's skull felt like it was baking all day. He'd often thought he'd give anything for one of the tall sombreros worn by the locals that provided a cushion of air on top and wide brims to shade a man's face and shoulders.

Shoot, he'd even settle for one of the military-style caps with the leather bills the guards wore. They were a by-product of the French influence there in Mexico, but Hack really wanted a good, soft felt Stetson like he'd worn across the river. All Texans love their hats, horses, and depending on the man, their dogs or women.

Only one prisoner had a hat of any sort, and that was Torres, but it would go into the grave with him if the hotbox took his life. The guards took what they wanted when a man died, and the rest was either distributed to the peasants in the nearby community or buried.

As the boys finished their thin stew, the Long Gang sat quietly for the last few minutes allotted for dinner until an old man with sunken cheeks stopped beside them and spoke in Spanish.

"Ah, *los terribles cinco*. Do you feel it, the air?"

"The five of us aren't so terrible, unless these boys get riled, but it seems a little hotter out here than usual," Hack said. "Of course, this place is only a couple of notches below the boiling point in hell anyway."

The man smiled, revealing only two bottom teeth left in his head. "The wind, it comes from the south. There is a storm on the way. *Muy malo*. This time of the year, they blow off the *baja* and bring rain and life to the desert."

The last to finish his stew was Billy Lightning. He paused with the bowl still against his mouth and swallowed. "I *thought* I felt something in my bones."

"I am an old man and have seen it once for each decade of my miserable life. If I was much younger, I would ready myself to escape from this hellhole when the storm hits."

As was his habit in the Mexican prison, Hack glanced across to the guards huddled around a water bucket in the shade of a stick-and-timber portico leading into the *comandante*'s office. They were laughing and paying more attention to a dice game than their prisoners, knowing the noonday heat would dampen any ideas of trouble.

"Have you ever seen it done, an escape from this place?"

"No, but I've heard about it. No one has broken out of here in nearly twenty years. The last time was the dark of the moon, but the one before my time was when fifteen men climbed the wall. Only five got away. The others were killed by the Apaches they used to track them. For every man killed, the one who did it received two pieces of gold."

"Apaches working with Mexicans?"

"Civilized Apaches who live that way, in the Chisos Mountains."

A tingle ran up Hack's spine and an idea formed, making

him feel more alive than he had for months. "How long does it take them to get a tracker from out there?"

"It would be at least a day, unless a couple were in the village for supplies or mescal."

"There's no way to get out of the cells, though, once it starts storming."

"You can be like Torres. Bribe Perez there to let you out for a midnight fight. If it was me, I would tell him you knew Escobedo outside and needed to settle with him. Perez loves to gamble like he's doing over there right now, shooting dice, and would welcome to see a match with you and Escobedo, and he'd bet on you to win."

"Well, I've already stood up for him."

"So you could kill him yourself."

Hack forced a grin off the corners of his mouth. He'd been there for so long his mind didn't seem to work, and that idea had never occurred to him. And there it was, an old man giving them all a way out, served on a platter. "Then I could take Perez, get his keys, and let the others out."

"That is a good plan."

"Why're you telling me this? This is your plan, not mine."

"Because I am too used up to fight and run. I will die here, but the other reason is that I don't like Perez and would like to see his dead eyes open and collecting dust."

Luke drew in the dust with a forefinger. "Mighty hard talk, just because you don't like the man."

"He cheated me in a dice game when I first came here and took my shoes." The old man looked down at the worn-out *huaraches* on his feet. The pitiful sandals had been repaired so many times with strips of leather they almost looked like small mops. "My good shoes would not fit him, but he sold them in the village and used the money to entertain one of his sporting ladies.

Close enough to hear, the rest of the guys remained

silent, but they were working things out in their own minds. They'd learned not long after arriving at the prison that groups involved in too much discussion brought suspicious guards. They were Hack's men, but they had their own minds and did what they wanted. They came and went when the Long Gang was working north of the river. Though these were his core group, there were others from time to time.

Instead of gathering to hear, Two-Horses and Gabriel Santana were stretched out along the wall, pretending to sleep. Billy Lightning sat four feet away, sanding a callus off his hand with a rock. They were all listening, and if someone was close enough to feel the rising tension and elation, it would easy to tell that the men who'd resigned themselves to incarceration were once again ready to ride.

CHAPTER 2

The chief guard, Juan Perez, rose from an arbor shade reserved only for him and his men, and he sniffed the air like a dog, filtering much of the scorching air through a mustache that sprouted thick and heavy against his nostrils. In addition to the dust and manure coming from a corral outside the walls, there was a hint of dampness.

He kicked a resting guard's foot and poked another's shoulder, prodding them from the raw wooden benches against their quarters' wall. "Get up. These men need to work and a storm is coming. The *comandante* will want one last shift back to the mine before the rain falls."

Though he and the *comandante*, Raul Mendoza, would have preferred for their prisoners to work from morning to night, they had long ago discovered that a full day in the mine would kill them, and a dead prisoner couldn't make money for the *jefe*'s pockets. Instead, they dug for half a day, then returned to the prison as the second shift took up shovels and picks to worry copper from the mine, then they'd switch again.

Although he acted as if he was irritated, Perez was pleased with the changing weather. He heard the day before that his favorite cantina server was back at work. Juana had been taken to Mexico City by a soldier loyal to Porfirio

Días, the country's president, but for some unknown reason, he'd sent her packing, and that was fortunate for Perez. A rainy day meant he could leave the prisoners in their cells and visit with her to spend his money.

It wasn't that they couldn't work in the mines while it rained, but Comandante Mendoza was afraid the inmates would use the weather in an attempt to escape as they were moved back and forth between the mine and the prison. Better to let them remain behind bars, and besides, everyone wanted some time off, and that went for him and his men, too.

He paused to stare in the direction of the little mining village that lay between the ancient structure that was once a mission run by friars and the entrance into the low, barren mountain that looked like an animal's burrow.

Against a backdrop of gathering storm clouds and lit by the sun that was not yet covered, two spirals of buzzards turned lazy circles over areas of interest. Perez studied the scavengers, wondering if it was human or animal bodies that lured them to those particular portions of the sky. He loved the scavengers, and once even had the opportunity to share a *trabajador*'s pleasures while letting her do all the work as he laid on his back and stared out of an open window to watch the carrion birds float overhead.

Maybe it would happen again sometime soon. With that pleasant thought in mind, Perez remained where he was in the shade as the guards kicked the afternoon shift upright and those who'd been in the mines that morning went to their hot cells. Spending time in those hot, airless cubicles was a different kind of punishment and wasn't considered as a pleasant gift.

Finally bestirring himself, Perez used a fingernail to pick at the dirt crusted in the corners of his eyes and followed the men past the hotbox. He paused beside the sunbaked door in the windowless structure made from hand-packed adobe. "Torres, are you still alive in there?"

The man who'd been beaten within an inch of his life by the newest inmate groaned an answer, and Perez chuckled. "It seems that you are. Feel better, my friend. We need another match between you and the boy who put you in there." He gave the hotbox a slight kick, doing nothing but dislodging crumbling sand and rocks. "You cost me a lot of money, *amigo*. That's why you're in there. You need to earn it back, and possibly, your life."

It was a blistering afternoon with not a cloud in the sky. He watched the prisoners march out of the front gate and went inside *la oficina del alcaide* to cool off a little and visit with the *comandante*. Raul Mendoza always had interesting stories to tell.

Visit our website at
KensingtonBooks.com
to sign up for our newsletters, read
more from your favorite authors, see
books by series, view reading group
guides, and more!

BOOK **CLUB**

BETWEEN THE CHAPTERS

Become a Part of Our
Between the Chapters Book Club
Community and Join the Conversation

Betweenthechapters.net